MW01205481

To *Whom* *It* *May* *Concern:*

A Struggle to Survive

by

Joseph A. Klingman

DORRANCE PUBLISHING CO., INC.
PITTSBURGH, PENNSYLVANIA 15222

Due to some graphic scenes, this book may
not be suitable for all readers.

ISBN #0-8059-5487-5464-3
Printed in the United States of America

First Printing

For information or to order additional books, please write:
Dorrance Publishing Co., Inc.
643 Smithfield Street
Pittsburgh, Pennsylvania 15222
U.S.A.
1-800-788-7654
Or visit our web site and on-line catalog at *www.dorrancepublishing.com*

This book is dedicated to
everyone who has
helped make me
who I am today.

Chapter One
My Name Is

My name is Cynthia Thomas. It's not an unusual name, nor is it spelled in an unusual way. In fact, it's rather common. I'm just plain old Cynthia Thomas. No one ever cared enough to even call me Cindy, which I would have hated anyway, and I would have asked he or she to stop it immediately. I come from an ordinary town. It's not too big. It's not too small. Nothing extraordinary ever happened there, except that I was born there. No one ever thought that was extraordinary. I was just another child, born to just another family, in just another city. There is nothing out of the ordinary or fancy about it. I just was. I always wanted to be more. I always knew that I was.

From the time that I was a little child, I knew there had to be more, something else, something better, bigger, more exciting to do, to be. I also knew that I was being held back from getting there. I guess the part of that emptiness was always wanting to be wanted just a little more, not more than anyone else, just a little more for me. I was never wanted enough. I always saw others being wanted and fussed about, but not me. My earliest recollection of the English language was, "You know, girl, children are to be seen and not heard." Oh, how I hated that. Nevertheless, I wasn't permitted to speak very often. My expression wasn't wanted or needed as everyone around me constantly reminded me, which was mostly my family. So, I was forced into submission at an early age. It was just too bad that girls at that time couldn't enlist in the military. I would have followed every order, any order from anybody just to be noticed, just to be told, "Good job, soldier." Any old bone thrown my way and I would have gobbled it up.

I don't remember ever being praised for anything good that I did. And I know that I did good things, because as a child my brothers and sisters and I were beaten with a leather belt if we ever did anything wrong or ever made a mistake, which, of course, was often. After all, we were just children. We were always supposed to know more than we possibly ever could, and do more than we ever could. We lived in fear.

As a result, we were like little soldiers, scrubbed clean from head to toe in starched and ironed clothes and marched out to school or church or wherever to show the world how well behaved we were, all the while wild with fear that if we ever did anything wrong, even innocently wrong, we would receive the hard side of a back hand across the mouth, or a naked butt-belting in public, which did happen. The best of all was expected and demanded from me, because I was the oldest and a girl. I had to set a good example for my little brother and sisters. Being a girl only made it harder.

I remember a time during first grade when I was enjoying a moment of euphoria. I don't know why I was so happy at that moment; maybe, because I had brought home straight A's in school, had done all my homework, helped my little siblings with their homework, helped with the supper, helped clean the kitchen, and had bathed and dressed myself in warm pajamas. I just knew that I was safe. I had done everything so perfectly. Maybe if I slipped up on the couch next to Mother, she might let me lay my head on her lap for just a moment and she might pat my head just a little. It was not to be.

As soon as I showed myself all scrubbed and clean and ready to nestle down close to her, my hand was jerked up by my father and forced to endure a bare butt beating. It caught me off guard. It was as if they had been laying in wait for me so that they could spring their attack. It seems that the straight A in penmanship wasn't good enough for my father. The teacher had written a little note that said, "COULD DO BETTER." All I had seen was the A. It wasn't an A-plus.

There was nothing worse in my house than "COULD DO BETTER." If a professional teacher could say "COULD DO BETTER" then I must be a loafer, not doing enough, just getting by, a liar, and a cheat. I was called all sorts of things at times like this. This time I was totally unprepared and caught off guard. I felt attacked. It was an attack. I was attacked. I was pulled to the kitchen table and told to write my name one hundred times on my red Cherokee tablet with my number two pencil, and every letter better be perfect. My father shouted, "And, I don't care how long it takes you."

I cried and cried uncontrollably. I was told to stop that crying and get busy writing. I had never felt so hurt. I was reminded that the teacher was a friend of the family. She was now a Notre Dame nun but had previously been a playmate of my father and they had grown up in the same neighborhood. I knew that for no good reason he was more embarrassed for himself. It had nothing to do with the stupid penmanship and me. I was forced to suffer for him and for nothing.

I finally was allowed to go to bed that night. I think that I reached fifty times writing my name. "That's enough for now. We're all tired of hearing you cry. Now, tear all that writing up and throw it in the garbage, and go to bed," said my father, still with anger in his voice.

As I walked down that long hallway to my room, I can still remember the stillness in that house. My siblings looked on as I tried to stifle my crying. I could feel that they wanted to say something. "Don't anybody say a word to her," said my father. As I crawled into bed I heard my door slam shut. I knew that this was a form of torture and that I didn't deserve it. I knew then that this was abuse. I had been physically and verbally abused. I had been cut off from my comrades. I suffered. All I had wanted was a little pat on the head. I wanted to be loved for just a special second of time, not for anything special, just because I was worth the effort. Instead, I was a prisoner of war. I went to sleep that night knowing how to love a little less. But, in my heart, I knew that I would continue to seek love and acceptance, and I prayed and prayed that someday it would come along.

Another Time Another Beating

I have other recollections of beatings, but the other one that stands out most in my memory is when I was about nine years old. It seems that my father had decided that I was old enough to learn how to help him in the yard. I would call it our yard, but in reality, it wasn't. It was his. It was his playground. He loved his yard and it was his own private sanctuary. It was a place for him to experiment with his creative juices. He planted all sorts of trees, large flowerbeds, shrubbery that would grow as tall as the house, and, of course, the lawn always had to be perfect. There was little room for us to play. We usually played on the old concrete driveway, which was hot during the summer.

One afternoon my dad came home from work, and decided that the yard had to be cut just exactly at that moment. He had a bad day at work and was in the worst of moods. Tonight supper could wait.

"Here, girlie, take this butcher knife. I want you to trim all these weeds from around the trees and shrubs and edge the driveway with it too," he said. "And, whatever you do, don't leave this knife outside or it will rust. Now, remember, you must bring the knife inside to your mother when you are finished."

I had never been permitted to handle anything sharp, and my father always kept the knives very sharp. He would take great pleasure in sharpening them in front of us, almost threateningly. I was scared to death. I took the knife and went to the first tree. I cut as best as I could, but I wasn't good or fast enough. He finished mowing the lawn just as the sun was about to set and it was already getting dark.

"You mean to tell me, girlie, that you're not finished yet," my father said disgustedly. "Well, you're so slow, you'll never finish tonight. Just leave everything. You will have to finish it tomorrow."

So I did. I put the knife in the ground next to the tree where I was working. He saw me do it. Everything seemed okay. I don't remember why I didn't continue the next day. I must have forgotten. It was late in the day and I was taking my bath before supper. It had been a very hot day. It must have been August, and August in south Louisiana is almost unbearable because of the heat and the humidity. We didn't have air conditioning then, and I was getting to that age where I wanted to look pretty all the time and good hygiene was a must. I remember that I wanted to be very pretty for my father when he came home from work. Maybe it would make him feel better if I was looking pretty and helping mother in the kitchen like a good girl should. It didn't.

I was still sitting in the cool bath waster just rinsing my hair, when I heard his car door slam. He was home early. Suddenly, a cold chill ran down my spine. I remembered that I had left the knife in the yard, and that I hadn't finished cutting of the weeds or trimming along the long driveway. I was naked and wet. How could I possibly get out of here and get that knife before he found out? I didn't make it.

The door to the bathroom suddenly burst open. My father was in a lathered rage. His face was as red as burning coal, and he had his shoulders hunched so forward that he looked a little hunch back. To my horror, the knife was in his hand. Naturally, it had a little rust on it from the morning dew. It was nothing that couldn't be remedied.

"Daddy," I said. "I'm in the tub."

"I don't give a good goddamn if you're swimming the mighty Mississippi River," he screamed at me for all the family and the entire neighborhood to hear. He grabbed me by my wet hair and pulled me out of the tub, naked and wet. He pulled his black leather belt out of his khaki pants and proceeded to beat the living tar out of me from the top of my shoulders and all the way down to my ankles, all the while ignoring my screams of pain. I didn't scream for help. I knew no one would come to my rescue, especially my mother. And, all the while I had to listen to him say, "This hurts me more than it hurts you, but, it is for your own good. You have to learn to obey. You better put on your dirty old clothes there on the bathroom floor and go outside and finish your work. Here is the knife. Don't come back inside until your finished."

I started to dry myself, but he screamed, "No, you don't have time for that. Just get dressed wet and hurry up." I put on my old, dirty clothes and picked up the knife. He watched me as I did so. I was hurt, physically hurt. I was in emotional turmoil and pain. I was suffering horrible embarrassment as the whole neighborhood and family was hearing everything and would be watching me come outside. As I turned around, I thought about stabbing him. It would be so easy. That was the first time that I ever thought about murder. It didn't happen. Before I could have reacted he screamed, "Just get out of my sight."

I ran down the hall dripping water with every step, and through the tiny kitchen and let the screen door slam shut. I hear my mother sing out, "Don't run with a knife, dear, you might cut yourself." What was she thinking? I had just had the most horrible, torturous experience of my life. She didn't make him stop. Why was she was pretending to be so motherly and worried about the knife? Where was her mind? I had these thoughts then, and I still have them today.

It had been dark a long time before my father yelled for me to come inside. As I did so, he said, "So, bring the knife over here for me to see. Well, you've ruined it, now. See here, you dented it all along the edge. Go throw it in the garbage and then go to bed." I was starving. The family had already had supper; nothing had been saved for me. I knew better than to even say one word. I knew that I couldn't even get cleaned up. I didn't feel safe. I would have to lock the bathroom door from now on.

I didn't cry myself to sleep that night. I had cried all my tears during those long hot hours in the dark cutting those damn weeds. It was the first time I started feeling numb, a sort of nothingness inside. If I had let my brain fully realize what had happened, I surely would have gone mad. I did pray that night. I prayed a lot as a child. It was my only lifeline to the future. Hope was all I had. I prayed that I wouldn't be so stupid anymore, that I would learn to obey, and to learn to be a good little girl. Maybe then the beatings would stop.

Chapter Two

Answered Prayers

By the time that my tenth birthday occurred, I surely was beginning to be a big girl, that is, I was physically overdeveloped for my age. I was the tallest girl in my class. My dark brown hair waved naturally around my shoulders, and I was already wearing a little brassiere. My mother had come home from shopping one day, something she hated to do, and simply tossed it to me.

"Here," she said. "Put this on. There are two in there, so you will have to wash one in the sink every night and hang it on the line to dry." She and I had never talked of these types of things before. But I knew what to do. I had been doing most of the family washing since I was eight years old. It was just the coldness of the way in which she presented it to me. There was no loving, confidential mother-daughter talk. I felt cheated and I felt cheap, like I just didn't matter.

But something good did happen. Shortly thereafter, my father and I had a little talk. I say my father and I not because my mother wasn't present. She was. She just didn't talk. As I recall, she just sat there by my father, dutifully, with her hands folded neatly together on her lap, just resting on her skirt. She wasn't allowed to wear shorts or pants, or peddle pushers, as they were called back in the 1950s. My father always insisted that she wear a housedress when at home. I remember her washing and ironing those dresses everyday. It was such a painful chore for her. She complained about it under her breath just enough for us to hear, but only when father was away at work.

6

One afternoon my father and mother were sitting in their room. They called for me to come in. I will always remember that it was my father that called for me, not my mother.

"Cynthia, come in here for a minute, please," called my father. I was shocked. I had never heard him use a pleasant tone such as this with me. I was cautious and a little afraid. As I approached them my father said with a little smile, "Pull up that chair, and sit in front of us. Your mother and I have to talk to you."

Oh, my God, I thought. *Someone is dying and I have been such an ungrateful brat. I am so sorry, God. Please, please don't let this be what this is about.* It wasn't.

"Now, Cynthia," started my father, "You are growing up so fast. You are maturing into a young lady right before our eyes." Somehow, this was beginning to sound like it was my fault. I felt that shallow, hollow feeling starting to mount inside of me.

"It is time for you to know the facts of life," he continued, as if he was an authority on the subject in the tone of a college professor. I had heard that term before, *the facts of life.* I didn't exactly know what it meant, but every time that I had heard that term whispered, a dreaded fear filled my soul, and I felt a little ashamed and embarrassed. I didn't know why; I just did.

He continued, "Cynthia, do you know where babies come from?"

I was relieved. *He's talking about birth,* I thought. *Maybe no one is going to die after all.*

"Yes, sir, I sure do," I answered proudly. The expression on his face suddenly changed. I knew this look. Surely, a slap was coming soon.

"Well, where do you think they come from?" he asked, suspiciously.

"Why, from right here in the woman's stomach," I answered innocently.

"You little slut," he yelled. "Who have you been talking to? Some dirty little boys in the playground at recess?" He grabbed my wrist. "Tell me who has been teaching you about sex," he said with clenched teeth.

I begged, "Nobody. Nobody. I just know that the baby comes from the woman's body."

"How do you know that, young lady?" he continued.

"Well, every time Miss Rosalie gets fat, you and Mom always say, 'She's going to have another one.' I just figured that part out on my own." Miss Rosalie was our next-door neighbor and she was always having a baby.

He calmed himself a bit. "Oh, I see," he said. "Well, Cynthia, there is a little more to it than that. In nature there are males and females. You know that, I know. The males carry the seed, and the females carry the egg. When the seed of the male and the egg of the female come together, then that makes a baby. That's called mating. It's all about nature. Do you know that birds do it while they are flying?"

"No, sir. I didn't," I said, shyly. I didn't know what he meant about "doing it." I was fairly sure that I had better not ask.

"Cynthia, pretty soon, now, boys, males you know, are going to start noticing you," he said. "You know, honey, because you're so pretty." He had never called me honey before. I could only presume that he was trying to be nice and was stumbling all over the place. "You know, every boy wants a pretty young girl on his arm," he said gaily with a smile. "But you mustn't let him go too far. If you let a boy go to far, then your reputation will be ruined forever. Boys tell other boys. If you have known a boy for a while and you really like him and he shows you the proper respect, then maybe, you might let him hold your hand, but never let him put his arm around your shoulder. You know one thing leads to another. What I am saying, and it is a law of the church, is don't let him do it to you until after you are married. Do you understand me?" he finished.

Naturally, I said, "Yes, sir."

"Well, good," he said. "Now your mother wants to say something to you. Mother, go right ahead and say what you want," he instructed her.

"Cynthia," she said sternly. "Just remember to always keep your knees together."

"Yes, ma'am," is all I could manage to say.

"And, Cynthia, there is one other thing that I want to tell you," Father said. "You are too mature, too old, to get any more spankings. If I was to spank you, you might manage to actually permanently hurt something. I am not going to spank you any more. You are old enough to use your head and not do any stupid things for which I would have to spank you. I am sure that you will still need to be punished for something, but I will not take my hand or my belt to you ever again. After all, I want to be a grandfather, someday."

My mother suddenly cleared her throat saying, "That's all for now, Cynthia, you can go."

"Thank you," is all I could think of saying as I left the room. I was a wreck. I was so confused that I didn't know what to do or not to do. *Just do nothing. That's the best thing that I can do*, I thought sadly.

The next weekend, my family drove to the country to visit my mother's parents, my grandparents. I always looked forward to these trips. They were usually stress free, and I loved being in the kitchen with my grandmother. She taught me all I know about cooking, especially baking. I wore my prettiest and newest shirt and short outfit. I remember the shorts were red and the shirt was white with short sleeves. The collar had little red roses with green leaves embroidered at the tips. I had my hair up in a ponytail with a blue ribbon. I thought that I looked so cute, and I was proud of myself for looking so good.

As soon as the family was assembled on my grandfather's big outside porch and my grandmother was serving the coffee, my father announced to everyone with great pride, "Well, everyone, now Cynthia is a young lady. Her mother and I told her the 'facts of life' last week." Everything suddenly went into slow motion for me, except the rattle of the cup and saucer into which my grandmother was just pouring the coffee. That sounded like an explosion to me. I was absolutely mortified that he would say that. I was so embarrassed that I blushed. I felt hurt and betrayed. How could he tell such a personal thing as that? I ran off the big porch as soon as I could. I found myself sitting in my grandmother's room. I could hear the men joking on the porch. One of my uncle's was saying that my father better be careful. He could be a grandfather himself pretty soon, now. I was only ten years old. How could they be making me into a joke, especially about that?

After a while, my grandmother came in and sat beside me. She took my hand in hers. I broke down crying. She cradled me in her big-bosomed chest, and just let me cry and cry. Finally, she gave me her dainty lace handkerchief saying, "Here, child. Dry those pretty blue eyes. Don't you listen to all that man talk. You'll understand one day when you are a little older. But, I will tell you this. You know the story of Adam and Eve. I know you do. I have read it to you since you were just a little girl. Well, when Eve gave in to the temptation of the serpent and ate the forbidden fruit, and then enticed Adam to do the same, she took on the burden of bearing children for the rest of womankind until the end of time. Child, it is time that you knew that as a woman you will also have to bear that burden, and your time will come. It's just being a woman; meanwhile, just remember to keep you knees together. Now, come and help me serve the pie. It's fresh apple, and I know it's your favorite."

For some reason she comforted me in a small way. I guess by being a little sympathetic to me, but I was more confused than ever. As I lay in that big, old country house that night, I could hear those lonely sounds that you only hear in the country, the low mooing of the cows in the meadow, the hoot of the owl in the old Magnolia tree out front. I could smell the mist from the river bottom. I could fairly taste the night. I wondered what it all meant, and I wondered sadly what was happening to me.

Chapter Three

I Wanted a Boyfriend

By the time I was fifteen, I was being called a raving beauty by every-one. Even my mom's beautician said that I was a real beauty and that I would be a lucky catch for some handsome boy. My mother smoldered silently giving me that look of "you better not let me catch you with some boy." She made me feel that I was a bad girl and was sure to get into trouble. I had made the cheerleader team and had been asked to the homecoming dance by a senior. I was only a sophomore. I had to say no. My father said that I was too young to date. Naturally, my father had me in a Catholic school located within walking distance of our house. My father's attitude towards me had entirely changed. He took me everywhere with him. He was proud and showing me off. For some reason, he started calling me his little cutie. He was still very strict with me. However, he was trying to be nicer. He would know one day that I still remembered the first ten years of my life, and how I had lived in fear, and that I still remembered the beatings. I would show him the scar on the calf of my leg. I hadn't forgotten. Someday I would remind him. I would make him cry. I would make him sorry. I would wait until he was old and sick.

Meanwhile, even though I wasn't allowed to date, I still knew how to meet boys. It was my father's idea that I should learn the value of money, and that would be earning it myself, no handouts. I got an after-school job as a cashier in the large grocery store just around the corner. I walked home everyday from school in my little red, white, and blue jumper. I had a snack, said very little. I would change into my white cashier's outfit. It had a skirt and a blouse and a little blue vest with my name on it. My mom would always say, "You better hurry, or you'll be late. You know there are a hundred other girls just waiting to take your place." This always made me feel dumb and scared, and that I should always be in a hurry, afraid that I wasn't good enough. I think it was just her way of putting me down. I know she enjoyed it and she resented the attention my father was giving me.

At my job, I had an instant crush on the most handsome boy. His name was Eddie Morgan. He was a junior at the public high school. He was so cute. He had strawberry blond hair, combed back in the fashion of the day with a little curl in front. And he had a brand new car, a convertible sports car. I was just dying for him to ask me out for a ride. As soon as I would get to the store, I would rush to the ladies room and make the skirt shorter by rolling the waistband over and over, then pulling the vest over that to hide it.

Eddie didn't notice me at first. At least, I didn't think so. After about a month, we were closing the store one night and he asked me if I needed a ride home. It was only three blocks, but I said with a smack of my gum and a little smile, "Sure." I thought I was so cute.

Almost every evening after that Eddie would give me a ride home. He never tried to kiss me or touch me or make any moves on me. I knew he had a real girlfriend, a girl that had already graduated from his high school. She was two years older than he was. I had overheard him talking to the stock boys, some of whom were from my own high school. She had taught him all about sex the year before. I, also, had been taught all about sex, except that my teaching came at my school. This was during a time when schools didn't have to ask permission from parents to teach sex education in the school. Our courses started in eighth grade. They were extremely comprehensive and continued through my senior year in high school. It was all extremely clinical, of course. But we also had different guest speakers. We had a priest speak, a single woman, a single man, a married couple, a marriage counselor, and a clinical psychologist. They really covered all the bases. After I saw the medical film on reproduction, there was little doubt in my mind that I knew more about the subject that my parents. That little talk that they gave me when I was ten still didn't make much sense.

That entire summer of 1966 flew by. It was my first summer to work full time at the grocery store, and Eddie was there everyday. We started taking our breaks together. We would stand around in the back of the store and have a Coke. Eddie didn't smoke, so I quit. Actually, I had only smoked about two packs since I had started the year before. That's one thing my parents didn't know about me, and I was proud of it.

Later on we started taking our lunch breaks together, too. Everyone at the store was calling us the "love birds." The head cashier was so jealous. She was extra hard on me, telling me to lower that skirt, not to wear so much makeup, and not to tease that hair so high. I would comply for a while, then, just start all over again. I would have to transform myself, anyway, before I went home.

I remember one particular evening that summer when Eddie drove me home. He stopped the car in front of the house. He never did that. He always kept the motor running, expecting me to jump out. So we just sat there for a while and talked. Finally, he threw his arm around the back of the seat and turned to me. He had the most admiring look on his face. His eyes were sparkling and his smile spread from ear to ear. He said, "Cynthia, I have never known a girl like you. I just want you to know how much I appreciate our friendship. I hope that I will always know you, no matter what happens in our lives." And, with that he moved closer and kissed me on the cheek. It was the dearest and most tender moment in my young life so far. I started to get all flustered, but managed to maintain my composure, but trying not to be to casual. I said that I felt the same. He just looked at me and smiled. I got out of the car, and as usual, he sang out, "Bye, Cynthia, see you tomorrow at the store." I would always turn around and give him a little wave.

As soon as my foot hit the first step on the front porch, the light there came on. The door swung open and my father reached out and pulled me into the house by my ponytail.

"What the hell do you think you are doing out there in the car with that boy," he raged at me.

"We were just sitting and talking," I said. "He always gives me a ride home."

"I thought I told you that you were not to start dating boys until you were eighteen," he said. I remembered that. The gist of that conversation was that at that age, if I were to get knocked up, as he put it, I would be out of the house, me and the baby, his own daughter and grandchild. I had realized then that he was threatening abandonment. It would not be the last time that threat was made to me.

"We weren't on a date. He was just giving me a ride home as usual. Anyway, he already had a girlfriend." I turned around to go to my room as if to dismiss the situation.

"So, what was all that smooching going on out there," he yelled as he yanked me around.

"He was just giving me a little kiss of friendship. How was I supposed to know? I didn't ask him to do it," I said sarcastically. That was too much for my father. He was working himself into a lather. I hadn't seen him this mad in years, and with that I got my first slap from a man as a teenager. I reeled across the room hitting my head on the door jam as I fell to the floor. My mother screamed and caught my father's hand, as he was about to give me another slap. My lip was bleeding and my head was pounding. I was so surprised that I could only lie there crying. He pushed my mother back and she fell across the coffee table onto the couch. He reached for me and pulled me up by my blouse. It tore at the sleeve and the top buttons popped off. I didn't know what he was going to do next, maybe strip me and give me a bare-butt spanking. I was fearful for my life. But he just held me there, showing me his power.

"Where did we go wrong with you, Cynthia?" he asked. He looked wildly around at my mother, as if she was going to somehow answer him. He pulled me closer and my blouse tore a little more. Blood was now running down my throat and onto everything, my blouse, my slip, and my brassiere. It was everywhere.

"We tried to bring you up right. We gave you everything," he yelled. "What do you think your little brother and sisters think when they see you out there in a car having sex? Do you think that is a good example to set for them? And, don't you have any shame doing something like that in public? What do you think the neighbors will say?"

I got it then. He was still more concerned about our family image than the reality of the situation. He almost always thought the worse. "We weren't having sex. He just gave me a friendly little kiss on the cheek to tell me how much he appreciated our friendship," I whimpered.

"I'm the only one who can give you a kiss on the cheek, and your mother, if she wants, and your family. You are too young for this sort of thing, Cynthia. From now on you will walk home. No more rides from Eddie. Do you understand me, girlie?" he said with a grimace. It really hit me then. He was in the middle of a father's jealous rage. Again, it really had nothing to do with me or the reality of the situation. It was just he and his suspicions and his own limitations to think further than his own nose.

I was silent. He let me go. I turned and ran to my room and screamed at him, "At least I kept my knees together."

He knew I was mocking him and mother. He kicked in the door. "You little slut," he growled. "Who do you think you are talking to? How could you let him kiss you, especially knowing that he already has a girlfriend? Do you want to be known as a man chaser?" With that, he grabbed me by the wrist and with his fist knocked me in my right eye.

"Help, help," I screamed. "He's killing me." I knew no one would come, but my mother was running down the hall. He was hauling me backwards and ran right into her knocking her down. That didn't stop him.

"I'll teach you a thing or two about men, girlie," he screamed. "But first you're gonna cool off a little." He pulled me to the kitchen and threw open the refrigerator door. He pulled out the large pitcher of ice water that mother always kept there. He poured it all over me.

I screamed and screamed, "What are you doing to me? Are you trying to kill me?"

"If I have to," he said under his breath. He hauled me down the narrow hall and into the little bathroom, shoved me into the shower, and turned on the cold water holding me there for ten minutes. I was sure that he was trying to drown me. I knew that I would have to submit, or, surely, he would have.

"I'm sorry, Daddy. I won't do it again. I promise. It was my entire fault. You're right," I said miserably.

"You're damn right I'm right. Now, get yourself cleaned up and go to bed. Don't say a word to anyone in this house tonight, and, by the way, you are grounded for a month," he said as he calmed himself a bit. He stormed out of the bathroom, slamming the door on his way out. I just crumbled into the tub of cold water, not caring anymore. I cried for I don't know how long. Finally, my mother came in.

"Cynthia," she said. "Get up from that cold water. Are you trying to catch pneumonia? You know we can't afford any more doctor's bills now." I never looked up at her. I knew then that I hated her. She knew by my silence that she had said the wrong thing. "Well, are you all right?" she asked.

I was dazed and amazed. Was I all right? Was she so blind, or just plain stupid? She had just witnessed her oldest daughter get beaten by her own husband. She had been knocked down twice herself. I started to get out of my bloodied clothes. As she reached to help I said, "Don't. Don't touch me. Don't touch me ever again." She drew back.

"Okay, dear," she said.

She ran a hot bath for me and poured in some of her cheap bath beads. She always thought herself so elegant for taking baths with bath beads. She said, "I understand that you are upset right now. But you'll see. Some day you'll understand. Your father is only trying to protect you. He loves you so much. Why you are the twinkle in his eyes."

"I thought that was your job," I said sarcastically. I looked up at her and just glared, daring her to speak. She was speechless. She spread her hands on her starched skirt, a habit she always had when she didn't know what to do.

"Well, I'll leave you, now," she said slowly. She walked out and closed the door silently. I jumped out of the tub and locked the door. I had no idea what might happen.

I went to school and to work the next day with a cut lip and a black eye. I told everyone that I had slipped on the concrete front porch. So I had learned lying from my father along with the violence. I'm not sure anyone believed me, but no one challenged my explanation, not even one of my teachers. They didn't want to know. They didn't want to get involved. I knew that they just didn't care. Only Eddie asked me for the truth. I stayed with my story. I told him that he couldn't give me a ride home anymore. He told me that he didn't believe me. He had figured it out for himself. He even offered to come over to the house and try to explain everything to my father. I begged him not too. I turned comical, telling him that he was playing too much drama into the situation, that maybe he should become a writer or an actor, that his imagination was too active. I also told him that if he were really my friend he wouldn't ask me any more questions. He agreed. I also told him that I would always be his friend. He told me the same. We would keep our pact.

There was silence in that house for many days to come. Silent days turned into silent weeks. No one was talking to anyone. Eddie and I remained friends at work. I still adored him. Secretly, I wanted to be his girl.

The summer wore on and school finally started. I was still grounded. I was going to miss the Jamboree Dance. But when I came home from school that first day I found the most beautiful dress laid out on my bed. It was a light blue organdy with little blue sequins and rhinestones sown onto the bodice. The skirt was made of ice-blue taffeta. It had a little can-can under-skirt to make it stand out. But my biggest surprise of all was that it had spaghetti straps; it didn't have a full top. Over a chair was a matching evening wrap. It was the most beautiful thing that I had ever seen. I was so excited. But what did it mean? As I sat there admiring it, my dad walked in all happy and warm-acting. He hadn't spoken to me for three weeks.

"Hello, my little cutie. Do you like the dress? I went to the store and picked it out myself. Why don't you try it on and come on out and model it for us? In that box over there are the matching shoes and purse. The saleslady said that it made the outfit. That it just wouldn't be complete with out them." I was in a dream. This couldn't be happening, and, what was the dress for? I knew that it had cost a bundle. Where was I supposed to wear it? I was still grounded.

I put on the dress, and I found stockings with the shoes and the little evening bag. I felt so proud to be wearing it. I walked very slowly down that narrow hall and into the living room not knowing what to expect. My father had assembled the whole family to watch the charade.

"Cynthia, you look beautiful," said my father. "Doesn't she dear?" he asked my mother.

She poked her head around the corner of the kitchen. She gave me the once over and said, "Yes, she looks lovely." I could tell that she had said what she had been expected to say, that even she didn't dare disagree with father. I wished that she had looked at me and had really meant it. I was starting to feel a little self-conscious. My little brother and sisters told me how beautiful I looked in that dress. He had told them what to say. He was really calling a truce in the house, trying to look like the benevolent father and the hero and the one who won and got his way.

"But what is it for?" I asked.

"Well, cutie, you know, it's for the Jamboree Dance next Saturday," answered my father with surprise in his voice. He looked at the children, smiled, and winked at them.

"But, you said I was grounded for a month, and so I didn't get a date," I said a little hesitantly.

15

"Oh, you're still grounded, Cynthia," answered my father. "But I don't see why you can't go to the dance."

"I can't go alone," I said imploringly.

"Oh, you won't be alone, cutie. You'll be with me. I've been asked to chaperone. And, since I'm going, I saw no reason why you should have to miss it."

"But Mother should go with you, not me," I said.

"Oh, your mother doesn't want to go. Anyway, she wouldn't look half as good as you in that rig you're wearing." I was shocked. He wanted me to be his date to the dance.

"But, I can't go to a dance with my father," I begged.

"And, why not?" he asked strongly. "You can smooch all night long in a car with a strange boy in front of your house for the whole neighborhood to witness, but you're too good to keep your old dad company at your own dance. You don't even have a fellow to go with. Why, you should be grateful that you are going at all. Don't be an ungrateful bitch, Cynthia. Men don't like it."

I was absolutely mortified. I just stood their feeling stupid, and I knew that I was going to look stupid walking into that dance with my father. I was trapped. I didn't know what to do. I was smart. I could think of something. Maybe I could throw myself down the front steps and break a leg, break an arm, anything, something. Maybe I would catch the flu; I would be too sick to go. I had to have time—time to think, time to plan.

I went to work after school the next day. I casually mentioned to Eddie that I was going to my first dance that Saturday at the gym, the Jamboree Dance, and that my father had bought me the most beautiful dress to wear. He instantly wanted to know how I suddenly got ungrounded. I lied. "Oh, you know, Eddie. Some girls just have a way with their fathers. They usually give in eventually," I said a little too smugly.

"Look here, Cynthia, who is he letting take you to that dance?" he asked strongly.

I turned on him and said, "What business is it of yours anyway, Eddie Morgan. You have your own girlfriend to screw around with."

"Because I don't want you going out with some trashy boy that you don't really know. You have to be careful with boys, Cynthia. They will take advantage of you in a moment, or, at least, they will try," he said loudly, but trying to be oh-so-brotherly.

"Well, Eddie, you ought to know. You're a boy. Right?" I asked.

I was so mad that it wasn't him that was taking me to that dance. It should have been him. I knew that I would be so safe and have such a good time with him. As I walked home that night, he pulled up along side of me and rolled down his window of the car and said, "This is not over, Cynthia. I'm gonna find out who it is if it is the last thing I do."

"Like I said, Eddie. Why should you care? I thought you had a full plate to handle with your own older girlfriend," I snatched back at him.

"I am. That's all. I m gonna find out," he said as he rolled on down the street.

I didn't go to work the next day. I called in sick. I didn't want to see him. I just wanted him to have a little more time. But by the second day, I had to go in. As I entered the store, I noticed that it was unusually slow. I didn't see Eddie. I dutifully went to my cashiers station, and, of course, I had an immediate customer, and then another. Other customers started coming in and we all got busy. Finally, I heard a voice over my shoulder saying, "I know your secret. Don't worry. I have a plan." I just had time to turn around to see Eddie heading in the other direction. How could he have possibly found out? He must be faking. I found out on my break.

Eddie was already waiting in the back having already finished his Coke. He had a fresh one for me. "Thanks," I said as I lit a cigarette. I had started smoking again.

"Now, Cynthia, you know smoking is bad for you health," he said as he took the cigarette out of my mouth. I lit another one. He did the same. I was furious.

"Stop it," I said, "or I tell the manager."

"Okay, little cutie," he said.

"What did you call me?" I asked with great indignation.

"Nothing," he said with his eyes to the floor, but I could see that little Eddie smile coming to his face.

"Oh yes you most certainly did," I said. "You called me little cutie. No one calls me that. My name is Cynthia, and that is what people call me. I abhor pet names." I was trying to be so theatrical and righteous.

"Well, I happen to know that somebody calls you little cutie all the time," he said with a little knowing laugh. I challenged him.

"Who?" I asked. "Just who do you think calls me that?"

"Well, you father for one," he said. I was horrified. I just snapped. I slapped him across the face as hard as I could. It left a red handprint. I had been taught the practice from a professional, my father.

"Wow," he said good-naturedly. "You must be really upset about him taking you to the dance."

"He most certainly is not taking me to the dance. As a matter of fact I am not going at all. Anyway, how did you found out?" I asked defeated.

"I skipped last period today and gave your little brother a ride home. He spilled his guts in no time," he said calmly.

"That little stinker," I said. "Just wait till I get home. I'll give him something to snitch about." I already had violence growing in my veins, even at sixteen years of age.

"No. No. You won't do that," said Eddie.

"And, why not? Who's to stop me? I'll do as I please," I replied, trying to be as huffy as possible.

"Undoubtedly, you don't do as you please, or else you would be riding home with me, and you wouldn't be going to the dance with your father," he continued.

"It's a lie. It's a lie. I am not going to the dance with my father. I am not going at all. I am going to be sick. I am sure of it," I said, desperately trying to convince him.

"Now listen, Cynthia," Eddie said. "I know all about it. Your father is a chaperone. He has even bought a dress for you to wear. And he expects you to wear it. And you don't have a date. And if you don't want it to appear that your father is your date, you will stop this stubborn charade and listen to me."

"Well, what is it that you have to say that is going to make such a big difference?" I said with as much dignity as I could muster.

Eddie said, "I have a plan. Now, listen to me. This is how it is going to work."

Eddie told me all about his plan. His girlfriend was going to be out of town, so he was going to be available to help. I fairly skipped home that night. I even let Eddie drive me the first two blocks. I was in heaven. It was all going to work out perfectly. I was going to the dance, and it would be wonderful.

Saturday night came. My mom took me to her beautician, and had my hair pulled up high on my head with little ringlets streaming down. She even put in little sparkling rhinestones here and there. Then she talked my mom into letting her experiment with a little makeup on me. My mother couldn't refuse. She would have looked like the prude that she was, or, at the very least, rude.

When we arrived home, my dad was a little surprised, but he didn't say anything about the makeup. He just said how pretty and grownup I looked. I guess unconsciously, he thought that I was his date.

I hurried and slipped into my new dress, stockings, and shoes. My mother came in to make sure everything was right. "Now, dear, you must keep this wrap around your shoulders. I think you are showing just a little too much for a young girl of sixteen."

"Yes, Mother," I said. "But I'll be seventeen in a few months."

"Cynthia," she said. "Just keep it around your shoulders. I don't want anyone getting the wrong idea."

How could the idea be any crazier, I thought? *My dad is supposed to be my date.*

My dad had my mother take all our pictures. First I took one with him, then one with my little brother and sisters, and finally, he took one with just her and me. She looked so despondent and disappointed and sad. I couldn't think about it then. I would just have to think about it later. Tonight was too important.

My dad and I walked down the sidewalk arm and arm. He even opened the car door for me, just like a date would do. He slipped in the other side, and off we rode to the gym for the dance. As my dad parked the car, I let my evening bag slip down into the floor of the backseat. We had walked about half way up the walk to the gym when I said, "Oh, Dad, I must have left my bag in the car. I'll just run and get it."

"Oh, no," he said. "I'll get it for you, my little cutie."

I cringed, but I was already back at the car. As I supposedly searched for my bag, other men that my dad knew who were also chaperones came over to greet him, and to my relief, they all walked in together. He had sort of gotten wrapped in the crowd and was in the gym before he knew it. Our plan was working so far. But I couldn't walk in alone. I kept waiting. First five minutes, then ten minutes went by. If something didn't happen soon, I knew that my father would come looking for me.

Suddenly, I saw Eddie running down the street. "Sorry, I had to work a little late. They missed you at the store today."

"Oh, I don't care. I'm ready. Are you?" I asked.

"Yep," is all he said.

I walked a few steps ahead with Eddie following almost, but not quite, behind me. As I opened the door to the gym, Eddie made a little jump for the door, and we sort of walked in together. All the other boys and girls there just presumed he was my date. I walked over to my father and told him that I was sorry for taking so long.

"It is not important now, dear. You are here and that is what is important," he said. Eddie had made his way to the men's room in order to stall for a little time.

My father, with me on his arm, walked me around and introduced me to all his friends. They were all very cordial. They all wanted to dance with me. "Oh, no," my father said. "Fathers first." They all had a big laugh over this. And, so, I had to have the first dance with him, but before it was over, all the other dads were cutting in, and that was the end of that. I excused myself to freshen up a bit. I found Eddie over in the corner. "Wait for me here," I said. "Everything is working out wonderfully."

When, I came out of the ladies room I said, "Give me two minutes. Then, come over and ask me to dance."

"Okay," Eddie said. "But don't forget to introduce me by my middle name, David."

"I won't. I know the plan. Now, stay cool," I said.

I walked across the gym floor taking my time and saying hello to friends that I knew, and I enjoyed all the compliments on how I looked. All the boys wanted to dance with me, but their girlfriends insisted that it was time for a Coke. So I slowly strolled over to where my dad was standing just as a dutiful daughter was supposed to do. We had only exchanged a few words when Eddie appeared.

"Oh, Dad, I would like for you to meet David," I said proudly. "David, this is my father."

"It certainly is a pleasure to meet you, sir. Cynthia has told me so many good things about you. I wish my dad was around more, but he has to travel a lot for his job."

My father had never gotten a good look at Eddie that infamous night in the car in front of out house. He took a very close look at Eddie "David." He didn't recognize him from Adam. And he didn't want to look stupid in front of the other chaperones. Eddie continued, "Do you mind if I steal your daughter away from you for awhile for a dance or two." My father was completely caught off guard.

"Why, you're not stealing her away from me. She's just here...that is, she's supposed to be helping with the refreshments," he said. But before he could say any more, Eddie-David had swept me onto the dance floor and over to the other side of the gym, where I had made sure my table would be. We danced there the remainder of the night.

I know my dad made several inquiries that night as to just who David was. Some old man got him confused with some other kid that went to my school, and went on and on about what a good fellow he was, and from what a fine family he came. The chaperones had spiked their own punch. He went on and one. It seems that he liked to have a little more that Coke in his cup and had brought his own flask. He shared it with all the men, and my dad had one or two. He seemed to relax a little.

About 10:30 P.M. he did find us over in a corner with some other kids just hanging out and talking and the dancing was still going on. He approached me and said that it was time to go. I just pulled him out onto the dance floor and danced and danced and did my best to charm him. The other kids thought it was so cool. Finally, he said that he was tired and that it was almost 11:00 P.M., and that it was time to go. I looked so sad. Just then Eddie-David jumped in and said that if it were all right with him, he would be glad to take me home. It was just a few blocks, and it wouldn't be out of his way at all.

My father gave both of us a strange look, but, finally, said okay, but that I better be home no later than five minutes after twelve o'clock. That would have been five minutes after the dance was over and the amount of time to drive me home. He would be waiting up for me. I was thrilled and delighted to see him disappear through the double doors of that old gym.

Eddie and I spent the next hour in each other's arms, dancing and dancing. I felt like Cinderella at the Ball and that Eddie was my Prince Charming. I also felt like a little champion, since we had put one over on my father.

My father saw me in a different light after that night. He saw how beautiful and smart I was, and how the other kids really liked me. As a man, I think he admired me because other men desired me. He certainly treated me differently after that dance, more like an adult. I turned seventeen years old that spring, and I think it made my dad feel a little older. His own mother had died that cold winter. At the funeral, he mostly sat by me. Mother sat in a corner away from the casket. She was little comfort to him. They were drifting apart; I could feel it. He held my hand and cried. He cried for his loss. He cried in the face of his own mortality. I cried because I was trying to find the courage to really love him again. I felt a little sorry for him.

Chapter Four

I Become a Woman

I was skipped ahead a year in school because of my grades. I took all the required tests that next summer and passed every one. I was a senior now. I was looking forward to college. I was secretly and frantically applying for scholarships all over the country. If I didn't get a scholarship, then I would have to use my father's meager savings and attend the local university. It wasn't a bad university, I just wanted to get away from home. Mother and Father were not getting along any better. They were further apart than ever. It was very difficult living with them, and I always tried to nurture my younger brother and sisters who were coming up right behind me. But I wasn't going to get stuck staying home to raise them and miss my chance at college. Mother and Father would have to make their own lives work for themselves. It was their job to keep their marriage intact. The sooner I was out of there, the better off I would be. After college, when I was out on my own, then, maybe, I could help my little siblings escape too.

During this last year of school, I continued to work at the grocery store after school. My dad tried to convince me to come straight home after school, that I didn't need to work there anymore. But I wasn't going to be his surrogate wife, and I wasn't going to referee for them. Every weekend I stayed over at a girlfriend's house. I think most of my friends must have known about my parents' problems at home, and were generally glad to have me. Eddie and I started to hang out more together; although I felt that I was going in a much different direction. Father didn't seem to notice. He still called him David, although he must have known that his first name was Eddie. He never admitted that he was the boy about which he had given me a beating. But he must have known and was too much a coward to admit it.

I do know that he needed me more during this time. Mother was letting him down so much. She was missing much of the day. We never knew exactly where she would go. She let the house go. Stopped doing the housework. Stopped cooking. She barely managed to get the little ones ready for school, and she was never there when they came home. Even Eddie pitched in to help. Neither Mother nor Father seemed to care if he was there or not. I guess they were just glad to have some help. I always had to rush home after school during that last year in order to bring some semblance of order to the house and organize dinner and get ready for work myself.

Father was coming home later and later himself. That was some relief, anyway. I could work better with them both out of the house. It was at this time that my oldest brother, Jonathan, and I got very close. One day I sat down and had a long heart to heart talk to him.

"Jonathan, I know that you are only fifteen years old, but, there are some things that you need to know," I began.

"You mean about Mom and Dad," he said.

"Yes," I answered.

"Are they getting a divorce?" he asked.

"I hope not. Not soon anyway," I said, unsure where to go from here. "Look, Johnny (as we called him), next fall I will have to go away to college if I want a really good education in business. I can't get it here. You're going to have to hold things together around here for a while. Do you understand? Can you do it?"

"Like what?" he asked.

"Well," I said, "anything that Mother isn't doing for one thing, like getting the others up for school, help keep the house clean, and learn to do some simple cooking. Look, I know this comes as a big surprise, and your just fifteen years old now, almost sixteen. You have just got to keep things going around here until I can come back and help. And I will be in from college now and then, and on the holidays."

"How about the summers?" he asked solemnly.

"No, once I get in, I am going to have to go all the way through to graduation to get that degree as soon as possible," I answered him as honestly as I could. He started to cry. I had never seen him cry before, not since he was a little child.

"You will come back and get me, won't you, sis? You won't leave me here forever," he sobbed.

"Of course, not," I said. "I am going to get us all out of here, but it is going to take you and me and all the help we can get. I know we can do it. I believe in me and I believe in you. Are you with me?"

His only answer was, "What choice do I have?"

"Not many, now, I know," I said. "But, I am going to make sure that you have many choices some day. Just wait and pray, and you'll see. I keep my promises." He gave me a big hug, the first as big sister and little brother, little adults trying to figure out the rest of their lives together.

That last year at home, so many things happened to change my life. I was just thankful for the times that Mother and Father were home and things, at least, seemed somewhat normal. It gave me some breathing time. During spring break, our class was going to the beach. To my surprise, there was no objection from the home front for me to go. I had my own money, so it wouldn't cost father anything. I was so excited. Eddie was to meet me there. We had been seeing more and more of each other. His girlfriend had outgrown her high school sex partner and moved on to older men, mostly older college men, and he just got left behind. I was glad; maybe, he would be mine after all.

As the day approached for me to leave for a trip to the beach, both my father and mother grew more apprehensive about it. I was asked all sorts of questions. It was interrogated over and over. Naturally, I never mentioned Eddie. As we planned it, he was to come a day late. On the afternoon that I left, he came over as usual, and my father had to tell him that I had gone on a little vacation.

"Of course," he said. "I forgot all about it. Well, see you later."

"Oh, Eddie, wouldn't you like to stay for supper. It would do us good to have a nice long talk."

This caught Eddie off guard, but he said okay. I guess my father had started to think too much ahead, that maybe Eddie and I were going to get married someday and he started asking Eddie about his intentions towards me, and what his plans were for the future, what college he was going to attend, what was his major going to be, and all sorts of things like that. The next day Eddie and I had a good laugh about the "old folks," as we now called them.

I had a room with four other girls. Eddie had a room all to himself across the street. Naturally, I stayed with him. As soon as he drove up, I just threw my suitcase in the back of his car and across the street we went. We never planned it; we never talked about it. We just knew the time was right. That night I became a woman. It was my first time with a man. I guess women never really ever forget their first time. I never did.

As we entered the motel room, I didn't even feel cheap or guilty, or anything like that. I knew exactly what I was doing, and I didn't care that we weren't even married. I don't think that I even thought about that. I just knew that I loved him dearly, and he was so damn handsome. He really turned me on just to look at him. I was excited.

I knew that Eddie had been here before and was acting very casual, kicking off his shoes and flopping down on the bed with that little Eddie grin. "So, here we are," he said teasingly. That smile drove me crazy.

"That's right," I said. "Here we are." I took a quick look around the room not knowing exactly what to do. I wasn't cheap, but the room was a little shabby, which didn't help. "Ugh, Eddie, you'll have to excuse me. I need to get ready."

"Oh, sure, take all the time in the world. I know you women have to get things right first," he said with a shrug. "After all, we have all night."

I took a quick shower and tied up my hair with a red ribbon. I applied just a hint of makeup including the reddest lipstick I had. I just couldn't step out in my baby-doll pajamas. So I just wrapped the towel around me and slipped out of the bathroom. To my surprise, Eddie had made a little toga out of the bedspread, being naked underneath. He looked at me and I looked at him, and we both fell on the bed laughing hysterically.

After we recovered, Eddie said, "Wait, just a moment. I have to set the mood." With this he lowered the lights. The drapes were already drawn shut, of course. He opened his bag and brought what must have been a dozen little candles and he lit the room with them. He had also tucked away a bouquet of flowers. He had brought a bottle of red wine and two plastic wine glasses. He presented me with the flowers in one hand and the glass of wine with the other. He was trying to make it so romantic and not look so cheap. It was the sweetest thing anyone had ever done for me before. It was so thoughtful. He knew that it was my first time. I have always remembered this kindness.

I had never consumed alcohol before, so one glass went straight to my head. I slipped under the sheets and lay there just being in a state of happiness and great anticipation. I looked over at Eddie. He set his wine glass down on the table. He let the toga-spread slip to the floor, showing me all his male nakedness. He made a little turn around just to show me everything. My eyes took in everything. He was already fully erect.

My heart was racing and my anticipation was turning into fear and a little dread. Still, I said nothing. He just gave me that little Eddie smile. He came around to my side of the bed. Very slowly he pulled the sheet all the way off the bed, all the while enjoying my nakedness. He lay down next to me and pulled me close. He was very tender and kissed me very slowly on the lips. His hands and arms wrapped around me. I could feel his strength. I held him in my arms and we kissed passionately. He kissed me all over from the top of my head to the bottom of my feet. He turned me over and straddled me and continued the kissing, making sure he hit every spot possible. I was in sheer ecstasy. I was glad that I was with such an experienced man. He rolled me over on my back and laid himself on top of me spreading wide my legs with his. I could feel his erection searching for the spot. When he was sure that I was ready, he entered me tenderly, not wanting to hurt me. He wanted to pleasure me in every way. He took his time and was so patient that I thought I had died and gone to heaven.

As our passions grew, he knew just the right time to enter me more deeply, but very slowly, inch by inch, and then pulling out just a little. Every time he did this, I arched my back not wanting him to exit me. He was teasing me with pleasure, making me want him as much as he wanted me. I wanted him deeper and deeper. Finally, he reached that spot where he knew that he could not go without sheering my virginity. He slowed a little and waited for some sign from me all the while nibbling at my breasts and my ears and my whole neck.

My passions were rising ever higher. I was practically squirming in that bed. I wanted more. I wanted all he had to give. I gave a little thrust and then another. He met me time and again. We were like two animals in heat—uncontrollable, unstoppable. This had to be it. Now he was thrusting a little harder and a little faster. I loved it.

Then it happened. He went even further in me. He broke through. I could feel a little pain, but the ecstasy was overwhelming. I knew he could feel it too. It was so pleasurable to him that he moaned differently now, lower and with less breath. We were both panting and gasping for air. We coupled passionately and wildly. Finally, he could not stop himself anymore. He could hold back no longer. With wild abandon, his thrusting turned into a pounding as fast and as hard and as deep as he possibly could. My legs were splayed high and wide. I wanted him to have it all.

Suddenly, his breathing became shorter and shorter. He looked me straight in the eyes. His face was very red and sweat was pouring down from his head. He let out a long moan as he thrust deeper and deeper, but slowed to an even rhythm and continued for what seemed an eternity. He had climaxed. I had not physically, but emotionally I had many times from the first moment he entered me. My heart had raced and I had known such pleasure that it didn't even matter to me. Anyway, only later would I even know of such things for girls. But for now I was certainly satisfied and knew that I would be satisfied many more times in my life. I had a taste for it now. It was in my blood.

We lay in each other's arms a long time just kissing and feeling and touching and caressing each other. Finally, we fell asleep just lying there together like that. We hadn't said a word in hours since we had first began our lovemaking.

Chapter Five

You Want to Marry Me?

Of course, all the girls knew that I did not come back to their room that night. The next morning they found Eddie and I eating breakfast in the little motel dining room. We were ravenous, having skipped dinner the night before, banqueting on each other instead. They all said, "Hello," very nonchalantly, but rolling their eyes at each other, smiling and giggling all the while.

I knew my secret was safe with them. Some of them had been up to the same thing. After all, this was 1967. The nation was in the middle of a sexual revolution, especially among teenagers. It wasn't exactly uncommon behavior, but for us it was. All my girlfriends and I had the privilege of a private education, but had also been somewhat shielded from the world. We had no idea of what was really going on. The hippie generation and "free love" had not come to our town and never did. We had never been exposed to drugs. We thought cigarettes and beer was being wild. But we had all known all the last year that lovemaking was going to happen soon to each and every one of us. So even though we all blushed a little, they were glad for me.

Some of them were even a little jealous. They could see Eddie had eyes only for me and wouldn't let go of my hand for even a minute. We ate and giggled. We even acted so silly as to feed each other, but we laughed so loud and so hard that the food would just fall out of our mouths. We couldn't even swallow. Finally, we finished, and I am sure the manager was glad when we left. He gave us a dirty look. Even that didn't make me feel cheap. What was all this talk about feeling cheap and being used, a vulgar slut and a whore after your first time? I didn't feel any of those things. I was in love and the whole world was mine to have. I was loved. Eddie had told me so. During our most intimate of moments, he had whispered very softly in my ear, "My darling, I love you." I virtually floated on cloud nine the remainder of that week. But the eventuality of going home finally came at last. The week was over and home we went, I with the girls, Eddie in his car alone.

At home, I was asked the usual questions. "Did I have a good time? Who did I see? What did we do?" My father finally asked me about Eddie. He said, "Cynthia, by the way, I didn't see Eddie at the store this week." I had not planned for this.

I said, "Oh, really, Father, he must have been working the early shift."

"No," he said suspiciously. "I don't think so. His manager said that he was on his vacation for spring break. He thought he had gone to the beach. You didn't happen to run into him down there, did you?"

I lied. "No, Dad, I didn't."

"Okay, if you say so," was his only reply. Now I was suspicious. I went to my room and really started to worry. What would happen if he found out?

A few days passed and things around the house seemed calm enough, but I knew something was brewing, possibly a storm. One afternoon as I was checking groceries, my dad came into the store. He never came there when I was working. As a matter of fact, it was my mother who always did all the grocery shopping. I was shocked and so surprised to see him. He waved hello as he went by. He headed to the back of the store. He was looking for something or somebody. Finally, Eddie spotted him, and as usual in that friendly Eddie way he walked right up to my father and held out his hand and greeted him with the biggest smile.

"Hello, Mr. Thomas," he said. My dad had been pretending to look at some steaks, something we never had, and suddenly looked up as if he was surprised.

"Oh, hello, Eddie," he said. "How are you?" Their conversation seemed to be going along smoothly, and then something happened. The conversation started to heat up and I could see my father towering over Eddie and pointing his finger directly in his face. My father handed Eddie something small and shiny. The conversation ended abruptly. He left the store walking exactly by me. He neither looked my way nor said a word to me as he left the store. I was so afraid. I was trembling.

I couldn't leave my stand. It wasn't time for my break. Another hour passed and I just had to stand there and smile and be nice and check out all those damn groceries for all those little old ladies and listen to all their complaints, but I thought each and every one of them gave me a little different look, a knowing look. They seemed to be saying with their expressions, "Yes, dear, we knew all the time that it would probably be you. You would be the one. Not our girls, of course." *What is going on around here that I didn't know about*, I thought. I was already paranoid, and that cloud on which I had been walking was getting thinner and thinner.

I nearly bolted to the back of the store when my break time came. Eddie was already there. I was already in tears, dreading the most awful thing that I could imagine. I fell into Eddie's arms sobbing. Eddie already knew what I was thinking. He said, "Cynthia, your father confronted me directly."

"What did he say? What did he want? What did he ask you?" I asked through my tears.

"Listen, Cynthia. He found out somehow that we were seeing each other during spring break."

"How? How could he find out?" I cried.

"I don't know," he answered. "Somebody, probably one of your jealous girlfriends snitched to her mom, and you know how it goes after that," he said calmly.

"He asked me if I was the one who got you pregnant," he said. "I tried to be furious, but I was just comical instead. I told him that I didn't know that you were pregnant. I think he was bluffing," he said.

"Now, listen, honey, he is just nosing around, sniffing around for information and making a fool out of himself. He has no real proof that we even saw each other then. You're not pregnant are you? Remember, I was there," he said with a little proud smile.

"I most certainly am not. I shouldn't be," I said with certainty. It was then that I remembered that we hadn't used any protection. Kids usually didn't then. It was an old myth that you couldn't get pregnant the first time that you had sex.

"Well, what did he give you? Show it to me," I demanded.

"Just this," he said, as he held up a cheap little gold wedding band. "He said that if it was me that I was going to have to marry you, or he was going to kill me," he said and just smiled and smiled.

"Why did you take it? That's the same as admitting our secret to him," I stammered. I was so mad.

"Oh, I don't know," he said. "It was all that I could think to do at the time.

"Give it to me," I said. "I'm gonna throw it right in his face. Why that bastard. When I get home, I'm going to kill him."

"No," he said. "You're not, Cynthia, or you will give the whole thing away, and he would have won. Just be as cool as a cucumber." That was his only advice.

I had years of violence training. I was ready for him. I would make him pay for trying to ruin the only beautiful moment in my whole entire life. And Eddie wasn't helping. He was practically strutting around like a rooster. He was giving the whole secret away. That's when I realized that Eddie was still just a kid and wasn't taking anything to serious.

I left work early that night and told the manager I was sick. He just smiled understandingly and said to come back when I felt better, to take all the time I needed. He nodded at me with a sly little smile as I left the store.

I tore into the house furiously.

"Where's Father?" I demanded of anyone around.

"Why Cynthia, you're home early. Is anything wrong, dear?" asked mother in her own smug way.

"Where is he?" I asked, again.

"Oh, I think that he might be out back hoeing in his garden, if you know what I mean," she said with a little too much emphasis on the word "hoe." It was as if she wanted to call me a whore, but didn't. My paranoia was running rampant. I ran through the house and out the back door.

There he was just sitting comfortably in his lawn chair as if he was waiting for me, and had been expecting me. "So, I can see by your worried expression, that my suspicions were right from the start. You are pregnant," he said with superiority.

"I most certainly am not. And I am furious that you are going around asking everyone about me. Doesn't that kind of questioning embarrass you, Father?" I asked.

"Not so much after the deed is done," he said. "Now I have to save face for the family by acting like the concerned father. You know, play the role."

"Well, you can just stop asking questions and stop telling Eddie that he is going to have to marry me," I screamed at him. I threw the ring right in his face and caught him in the eyeball. I'm sure that it hurt. It surprised and enraged him.

He jumped up from his chair, kicking it and everything else between he and I out of the way. He grabbed me by my arm and screamed for the whole neighborhood to hear, "See the whore that strikes her father." He held me tight and slapped me hard across the face. He slapped me a second time, and then I did the only thing that I knew to do. I had learned it at school. I kicked him in his groan, at exactly grand center. He let go of me and grabbed his crotch. He screamed and groaned as he fell to the ground.

Mother came running out of the house screaming for help, "Help. Help me, please. My whore daughter is trying to kill my husband." I knew that the neighbors had been listening through the fence, and that surely they would all come running to see the ruckus

I bolted. I ran to my room and threw a few things into a bag. I ran from the house, but not before picking up my books. I was never coming back here alone, but I was going to finish school. He wasn't going to break me.

I stayed at a girlfriend's house that night. I did call my mother and tell her, but I wouldn't tell her where, only that I was safe. She said, "Okay, dear, if you would rather stay with total and complete strangers than with you own family, then, that's your decision. There's nothing that I can do about it." I was sure that she preferred it that way, anyway. I knew she didn't love me and hadn't in a long time, not since I was a little baby, and she had to love me to show my father and the whole world how wonderful she was. It was all about her, then, not really about me.

Graduation was approaching fast. I finally went home. I was expecting responses from my scholarship requests. To my surprise, no one said anything when I came back. It was, as if they didn't care if I stayed or left. Mother didn't speak to me at all. And, all my mail had been bundled up nice and safe. All she did was hand them to me. In all there were three scholarship awards, all full tuition, books, boarding, and all that I would need.

I didn't tell anyone at first. I would wait and make them suffer. That night I studied all my offers. I reread all the brochures from the three universities. I made my choice. I would accept the scholarship from the university that was as far from here as possibly could be. I was going to put as much distance between my parents and me as possible. I chose a small but prestigious university named St. Alban's University. It was located in upstate New York. And from the south, that sounded very far away. And, it was co-educational. It would be good for me, and it would just kill my dad.

Several days later, mother presented me with two new dresses. One was a formal for prom, for which I didn't have a date. It had a full skirt, but a very cinched waist. I could only guess that she thought Eddie would be taking me. The other dress was especially pretty. It was an ivory silk print on print, cut in the oriental style with a little stand up collar. It was tight. I liked it, but I thought that it was a little tight. "Oh, that's they way it's worn, dear," Mother yelled back to me from the kitchen. "I'm sure that it is perfectly proper for your graduation dress. Oh, and don't let me forget, we have to go shopping for some very high heels to go with it." Something was up. Was she trying to make me look like her version of a tramp? Or what?

The last month of senior year was going by much to fast. I missed my period. It worried me a little, but it wasn't especially unusual for me to skip a month. I was sure that it was a safe time when Eddie and I had had our encounter. Still, somehow, I just felt heavier, fuller. Paranoia really set it. I didn't tell anyone.

Eddie and I continued to see each other at the store, but I certainly wasn't allowed to date yet. I was to have a date for the prom, but I knew if my father knew that it was Eddie, he would forbid me to see him and everything would be ruined. I told him that I didn't have a date, and that I was just going with some of the other girls who didn't have dates. It was becoming the fashion of the day to go out in groups anyway.

So I went. Naturally, Eddie met me there and we had a wonderful evening. We left early by the side door. He took me to the nicest restaurant in town. Some of the other kids were already there, so I was sure that my father would eventually find out, probably sooner than later.

We ate our dinner quickly and left immediately. Eddie had a little romantic rendezvous motel already reserved. This time we undressed quickly in front of each other, neither blushing. We jumped right into bed and quickly got down to basics. We were both pleasured quickly, and held each other securely for a long time. But it certainly wasn't like before, like the first time. I guess it never could be. But we left the little motel happy, hand in hand, just like two young lovers.

We made it back to the prom just in time. The girls were waiting for me and we were running late. They brought me home immediately. They all knew of my father's famous temper. I barely made it in before midnight; I had only a minute to spare. He was waiting for me.

"Well, Cynthia, did you have a good time?" he asked.

"Yes, sir, I did," I answered politely. "Good night, Father, I'm tired and I'm going to bed." For some silly sentimental reason I stopped and turned around. I tried to give him a little good night kiss.

"Oh, I know only to well what kind of a time you had, your little slut, you whore," he hissed as his fist hit me squarely in the jaw. "I followed you and that little squirrel, Eddie. I know you two went to that seedy motel and screwed your lights out. I saw you leave together hand in hand."

I had fallen to the floor, but I wasn't screaming. That wasn't the first time that he had ever hit me with his fist. I was sure that my jaw was broken. I tried to stand, but his other fist hit me on the other side of my face. As I hit the floor, I knew that he wanted me dead. He was really trying to kill me. For some reason, I couldn't find my voice. I looked down. My dress was full of blood. I was in a daze. I fell into unconsciousness.

When I awoke in the hospital, the dress had been taken off of me. It lay crumpled and bloodied in a little chair, and I was in hospital scrubs.

"Why am I here?" I asked.

"Now, now, there, you just lay back down and take it easy. You've had a rough time," said a pretty little emergency room nurse. I lay down trying to remember. I remembered being with Eddie. I remember getting home on time. Then, it hit me. The last thing that I remembered was Father's fist coming down on my face. I was scared. I started to cry.

The doctor came in and asked me what had happened. I told him that I didn't know. I told him that I had gone to a party and had too much to drink, that I must have fallen.

"It must have been a long flight of stairs to do such injuries as these," he said calmly. He told me that the police had found me wondering down the side of the main highway, which led here to the hospital. Did I want anyone to call my parents? "No, no," I said. "I live alone."

Obviously, my father had finally completed his threat. He had finally thrown me out of the house and into the street. The doctor also told me that I was lucky to be alive. I had a minor concussion, but no broken bones. My face would heel. I was being kept overnight for observation. Eddie walked in at just that moment.

"Also, I am sorry about your baby," he said.

"My baby?" I asked. "What baby?"

He answered calmly and as friendly as he could, "The baby you have been carrying for about two months. Didn't you know you were pregnant?" Eddie turned pale and just stood there. I introduced him as my husband. That way, surely the hospital and police would not call my parents.

"No, no, it's not possible," I said with astonishment.

"I am sorry for your loss, but you will be able to have other babies, lots of babies if you like. You are going to be okay."

I just wanted to get out of there. I insisted that I be released. Thank God one of the neighbors had called Eddie's dad, and Eddie had come looking for me. He swore he would kill my dad. I begged him to stop. "Just get me out of here," I begged him. He paid the bill in cash. He took me to his house. We were both in too much shock to talk about losing our baby. His mother and father took me in and put me to bed.

The next day, when I knew that my father would be at work, my girl-friends and I packed up my things and I left that house forever, at least I swore it would be forever. I thanked God that mother was not at home either. She was off walking somewhere. Later we would come to learn that the correct term was wandering. Sometimes she was just wandering off in a daze, going where she did not know. My younger brother and sisters started coming in from school. I quickly settled them into their homework and started a quick supper. I could do this last favor for them. I gave them a quick talk and told them that I was going away to college, but that I would see them again one day, and that I loved them. I gave each one of them a special hug and a kiss. I wanted to get out of there before my father came home.

I didn't stay with Eddie's parents very long, although they did make me welcome. I choose to stay with a girlfriend, Nancy, the same one I usually stayed with that whole last year in high school. Her parents were under-standing, but didn't want to interfere.

By the time graduation day came around, my face was almost healed. Nancy and I tried to cover the bruises with makeup, but you could still tell. I refused to be in any pictures. My parents did not attend, but Eddie did. Afterwards, he took me out for a nice dinner. He had graduated the day before but had waited to celebrate with me.

We had our long awaited talk during that dinner. We were not ashamed of what we had done. We mourned the loss of our baby, but we were young and it didn't hurt too much. We knew that it would bond us together forever in that little way. Our only knowledge of that was what the doctor had told us. We went on to talk of other things.

I told him about St. Alban's. He told me that he had been turned down for every scholarship for which he had applied. If he went to college, it would have to be from his own savings, which were not much to speak of. I insisted that he must go every semester he could, even if he had to get a student loan. "I know that it will take the rest of our lives to pay it off, but we'll manage somehow," I said without thinking.

"You said us," Eddie asked.

"Yes, sure, you and me. You don't think that just because I am going off to school, that I am going to let you get away do you?" I asked with a little laugh.

"I'm glad you said that," Eddie replied with a big smile. "I thought for sure that this was a farewell dinner."

To my surprise, Eddie got down on one knee and pulled from his pocket a little ring box. He opened it. It held the most gorgeous little diamond ring. "Will you marry me?" Eddie asked solemnly. I was so surprised. I didn't know what to say. "Well, are you going to keep me down here on my knees forever?" he asked.

"Eddie, please, sit back down," I pleaded. "What are you thinking of? We can't get married now. I have to go away to college. We both need to get our education."

"And, my darling, we are going to do all those things, but I want to make sure you are mine," he said softly. He kissed me sweetly and tenderly on the lips. "I want us to be engaged," he said. "We can get married whenever you say the word."

He looked so pitiful sitting there and so sad. I just couldn't say no. Of course, I wasn't sure, but I said yes anyway. He was elated. He slipped the little, cheap thing of a ring on my finger and he beamed. He lit up the room with his face and that charming Eddie smile.

The next day he drove my few belongings and me to the bus station for the long ride up north. It was going to take several days on the bus, but the bus was the cheapest way I could go. I would have to horde the few thousand dollars I had managed to save from my cashier's job. I didn't want to have to work and study at the same time. I was going to apply myself and get that degree as fast as possible.

As Eddie kissed me goodbye, he told that he loved me, that he would wait for me, that he had never loved any other girl but me, that it was going to be me and him forever, together. I swore the same to him and that I would never take off his ring. We both meant what we said, and in our hearts, we believed it.

Chapter Six

The Loss

I loved college. I met lots of nice kids there. I enjoyed the intimacy of this small, exclusive university. There were almost as many teachers and assistants as there were students. I loved all my courses and chose *business* as my major. I loved the campus and all the people in the little shops. It was so Ivy League. I thought that surely I was in a dream. It was like it was all out of a storybook. I found college work to be quite different and a lot harder that my little high school down south. But I took a short course at night called How to Study in College. It proved enormously helpful. After that the A's and B's started flying in on every test, every assignment, and I made the dean's list the first semester. I made friends with everyone I could. Everyone was so nice and sincere and helpful. The whole town of St. Alban's became like a family to me, for the college was the town and the town was the college. I never missed being away from home.

I was a little ashamed of that because I didn't miss Eddie as much as I had thought I would. Of course, I still loved him, and I still wore my engagement ring. He had written to me and told me that he had dropped out at mid-semester. He just didn't get college. He said that he didn't have the brains to be college material, at least, that is what his counselor told him, and Eddie believed him. He had gotten a little job as a mechanic and was planning on going to night school to be a *certified* mechanic. He wrote me, "I know that this disappoints you, honey, but it is the best thing for me. It may be a grease monkey job, but when I graduate from this little industrial training school, I'll get a raise, and good mechanics are hard to find, and they make good money. You'll see. I'll make you proud of me yet." He didn't have long at his one chance. Within a month of leaving college, he got his draft notice from the army. He hadn't thought about that. Without his college deferment, he had to be drafted. The war in Vietnam was raging on and on. The number of American men going over there was increasing everyday. And the number of dead men coming home was increasing also.

As soon as I got the letter, I called him. I desperately wanted to go to him. I cried and cried on that phone. I felt that I was losing him forever. "Oh, don't worry about me, baby," he said bravely. "It's only for two years. I'll be back before you graduate college. Maybe, I'll like it so much that I'll make a career out of it. A lot of men do, you know. I promise I'll write you everyday."

"I know. I'll write you everyday too," I said sadly.

"I love you and I miss you," he said.

"I love you and I miss you too," I replied. What else could I say? He was being so brave. He was still such a kid. He thought he was going off to camp. He was really going off to the worst of all horrible wars yet. His best time in the army was his sixty days in boot camp. He wrote me everyday and called every week. His last day there, he called me to tell me that he was going overseas. The war was ever escalating. He had been trained as a radioman. We both knew that he was going to the front of the battle. We both cried a little, and finally said good-bye. He vowed his love for me and swore that he was coming home to me and we were going to be married and have a family. I assured him that I would be waiting for him. In my heart, I knew that I would never see him again.

I was wrong. He was only in Vietnam thirty days before he was shipped home. He wasn't shipped home in a box. He was alive, but badly injured. He had been caught up in a fiery ambush and stepped on a land mind. He lost both of his legs and most of his right arm. His face was hardly recognizable. He wasn't really expected to live. His mother called me with the bad news. I told her to tell him to hang in there, that I would be home in the spring, and we would have a beautiful Easter together. I never got another letter from Eddie. I continued to get progress reports from Eddie's mother. She wrote me about once a month. It seemed that Eddie needed constant care. Our beautiful Easter wasn't to be. His parents just couldn't give him the care that he needed. He was in such pain, and the drugs drove him crazy, sometimes in a daze, sometimes paranoia struck so hard that all he could do was scream and make grunting animal sounds. He was wild then and out of control. His parents committed him to a veterans' convalescent home. Almost no one ever came out of those places any better than they went in.

As soon as my last class was over for the spring break, I ran all the way to the bus station with my little suitcase in hand. I had carried it with me to class along with my books all day long. I didn't care if I looked stupid. I wanted to catch the first bus. Those two and a half days on the bus gave me some time to think about the situation. I tried to prepare myself for the worst scenario possible. I wasn't prepared for what I found at all.

I arrived late in the afternoon. I went straight to the veterans' convalescent home. It was more dismal that I thought. The building was a short, squat ugly thing streaked gray. There was no lawn, only a few scrawny trees here and there with a few aluminum outdoor chairs. As I walked in, the smell of the place nearly knocked me down. It was some awful combination of disinfectant and urine. I was nauseous. I was sure that I was going to be sick.

An attendant approached me. "Can I help you?" she asked, coldly.

"Yes, I'm here to see Eddie Morgan.

"Who?" she asked. "Who did you say?"

"Eddie Morgan," I answered.

"Well, the name doesn't ring a bell with me. Are you sure you are in the right place, dearie?" she asked, not in the least bit interested. She didn't even look up at me.

"Yes, I am damn sure," I said losing my patience. The violence was rising. "His name is Edward Morgan. He is a Vietnam veteran, and he has been here about three months."

"Okay, okay," she said. "No need to get all huffy about it. I'm sure that he's here somewhere." She looked through several file cabinets, and finally found his chart. "Here he is," she said proudly. He was just misfiled. That's all. I mean, it's not like we lost him or anything." She said this laughingly, as if it were all a funny joke. I was silent, but livid. *What kind of awful place was this?* I asked myself. "Follow me," she said with a ballooned authority.

We walked up several flights of stairs, and down a long corridor to the very last room. She opened the door.

"Oops, not here," she said.

"Why isn't he here?" I asked in amazement.

"Oh, he's here all right, just not in this room," she replied, not worried in the least. "They move this type around a lot, and most of the time the chart is never up to date." I thought about this as I followed her from floor to floor, up and down dirty corridors. If they couldn't keep up with his correct room number, how in the world could they keep up with his care, his medications, anything? We finally found him, but only by his chart. He was in a ward with fifty other beds.

"Here you are, Mr. Morgan. And, how are you doing?" she asked the man lying in the bed as if he could really answer. "Well, I'll leave you two alone for now," she said, glad to be rid of me.

As she walked away, I just stood there in a state of bewilderment. It was an awful place with leaking windows, and walls with pealing paint. Poor Eddie lay there in a bed of filth and the whole ward smelled of it and the others. The sheets showed that he had lost both his legs, and where his right arm should have been was just a nub oozing with puss. His hair was long and tangled and wild. His beautiful strawberry blond curls were now limp with frazzles of grayness. His face was really unrecognizable, but his chart said that it was he.

"Eddie," I said. "It's me, Cynthia." He was silent with his eyes shut. He didn't move or stir. Only the breathing motion of his chest indicated that he was alive. He face was scarred horribly and was the color of ash. His muscular build had been reduced to a few bones and little muscle. He was a pitiful site, and I guessed barely alive. I decided to take a look at his chart hanging loosely at the foot of the cold medal bed. I was shocked. He was on every imaginable narcotic available, all of which were prescribed for pain. No wonder he was out of it. They were keeping him knocked out, because it was easier for them to manage him, easier for them to wait and to let him just die there. I called for the nurse, which I realized was just an attendant. There were no signs of any real nurses or doctors. I questioned her as much as she would let me about his care. She finally tired of me and said that I could wait for the doctor. I sat by Eddie's side until midnight. No one came to care for him. He was on painkillers and intravenous feeding. I finally left feeling totally dejected and lost. I would come back the next day. I told the attendant what I thought about the place. I lied and said that I was a lawyer for the family, that I would be back at 10:00 A.M. the very next day, that she was to have the attending physician available at that time. With a little shrug she said, "Hon, I just work here. I don't run the place. I wouldn't count on it if I were you, but I'll pass your message of concern on to the administrator." I thanked her and left.

When I walked in the next day, they had been expecting me. Eddie's bed had been changed. He had been bathed and his hair had been shampooed and cut a little and tied back. They had reduced the pain medication, and the doctor was talking to him with the greatest of concerns. Eddie wasn't saying much, still being drugged. He was totally helpless. As I approached, Eddie turned his head in my direction and his eyes caught mine. They seemed to light up a little. The doctor noticed and turned around to face me.

"Hello, I'm Dr. Thompson," he said with little emphasis. "I've been assigned to your friend here."

"His name is Eddie Morgan, and your are correct, sir, he is a friend, a very good friend, and he is my fiancé," I answered with a little menace trying to show what I thought of this place and him. "When were you assigned?" I asked. "This morning?"

"Well, actually, last week," he replied slowly. I've been on vacation and have just arrived back here this morning."

"I want to speak with you privately, but I want to visit with Eddie now," I said a little kindly. Obviously, he had managed to make some progress since last night. At least Eddie looked clean and was almost lucid.

"Of course. I'll be just down the hall whenever you are ready," he said with a little pat on my arm. *Patronizing asshole*, I thought. But he was all I had to go on, so I just took it for Eddie's sake.

I turned to Eddie. I took his hand. "Eddie, it's me, Cynthia. Can you hear, my darling, my dearest? What are they doing to you here?" Eddie opened his eyes and just stared at me. Tears started to stream down his face. He tried to speak, but couldn't. He just sobbed and sobbed and held my hand firmly. Finally he spoke. He barely could say, "Stay with me. Don't leave me for a while."

"Of course I'll stay. Of course I will," I said. I held his hand and every so often he would open his eyes and squeeze my hand and nod his head just a little, as if to say that he was glad I was there. After a while I knew that he had drifted off to sleep. I slipped down the hall to talk to the doctor.

The first thing I asked him was, "When and where can we take him from this awful place. What are you doing to him here? This is terrible. This is awful. I won't leave him here any longer than necessary."

"Please, Mrs. Morgan, have a seat," he said gently.

"I am not Mrs. Morgan," I answered. "But I am Eddie's fiancé."

"Oh, I see. It would be so much easier if you were Mrs. Morgan."

"What do you mean?" I said. "I don't understand."

"Well, poor Eddie has sort of been dumped here. This is not the first place to which he has been admitted. The first facility was so much closer to his parents' home. He has been shipped around to several places like this, I'm afraid to tell you. You see, the government keeps finding places for people like Eddie that is cheaper and not necessarily better. His care is expensive. Each facility eventually convinces some bureaucrat to transfer him to a 'better' facility. Each one feigns that his care would be so much better some place else. You understand that each facility has its own budget."

"What is the best place for him?" I asked plainly.

"Probably in some private institution, but I don't believe the funds are available from the family," he answered bluntly. "Naturally, if you were married, that would be an entirely different matter. There would be more funds available. Too bad you don't have any children. That would add even more dollars to Eddie's care."

"I just don't understand why he can't get the care and service that he needs anyway," I said with disgust.

"Like I said, it's a matter of money. If you two were married, then the family benefit plan would kick in. You would have your own personal income as his wife and those funds could go to better care for Eddie. Too bad you didn't marry before he left."

"But, we can be married now, and that would make it better for Eddie?" I asked.

"Well, technically, yes, I suppose it would. But, my dear, are you sure your feelings for him are the same now as before? You have seen him. He will never be any better."

I was infuriated with this man. "My feelings are the same as they have always been. I don't care how many limbs you cut off or what you do to him. I love him. I do. I always have, and I always will. There are all sorts of rehabilitation. And, don't talk to me of my feelings. You're not a priest, just a doctor, probably just an intern. What do you know of these feelings?" I asked.

"But, my dear, are you sure you want to be saddled with a man for the rest of your life who has no legs, and only one arm, and we are still not sure how well he will recover psychologically?" he said. "You know that he will never be able to have children."

"Listen, doc, I intend to do whatever is necessary for that poor boy out there in order for him to receive the best possible treatment and recovery possible," I said with determination. "I believe in him. Now I suggest that you start doing the same, or else Eddie never will. Now, are you in or are you out?"

"Well, even though you are not the lawyer you pretended to be, I must say that I am impressed," he replied. "I could lose my license for saying all that I did, so I guess I better side with you." He spoke with a smile and gave me some hope for encouragement.

"Okay, that's better," I said. "What is the first thing that we need to do?"

"Well, he is still in a lot of pain. Keeping him on the narcotics is only temporary. It could eventually kill him, so I suggest that the first measure is to gradually lower the dosage of the painkillers. We need to start some small amount of rehabilitation. This is not going to be easy, and you will have to stay with him night and day. He really needs someone with him at all times. You know when something like this happens to you, you lose a little of your sanity, but I believe you can bring him back. I really do," he said as he looked at me tenderly and with a new type of admiration. I didn't know what to make of it.

"And the marriage, how soon can we do that?" I asked with my head lowered.

"The sooner the better," he said. "But first we have to sober him up somewhat, and that means lowering his pain medication. I don't know if it will be days or weeks."

"Thank you for your candor, Doctor. I'll call his parents, and see what we can work out," I said meekly. I knew that he knew that I knew that what we were proposing wasn't exactly written in the standard medical textbooks, but if that was what it took to make Eddie even a little better, then I was ready.

I went directly to Eddie. To my surprise he was awake. I didn't try to explain the whole plan to him. I just told him how much I loved him. And that I wanted to marry him immediately. He managed a hint of that old Eddie smile.

"Really," he asked.

"Yes, Eddie, right away," was all I could manage without breaking into tears.

To my surprise he said, "Okay." Then he fell asleep. In a moment of desperation I thought what a foolish girl I was being. How was I going to manage all of this and keep college too? I just couldn't throw all that away. It was our only future.

I called his mother immediately. She understood completely. She and her husband would make the plane fare somehow and would be there as soon as possible. I stayed with Eddie for the remainder of the day. I could tell that the doctor had already started lowering his pain medication. He was trying to estimate and meet Eddie's threshold of pain. By the next morning, I believed in my heart that his recovery had already started working. He was awake more, but couldn't take solid food as of yet. He felt better after his sponge bath and clean pajamas and managed to say so in a sort of frail way. But every now and then, he managed that little Eddie smile and a wink, and then he would drift off to sleep again. All that day he was awake more and more, and he slept soundly throughout the whole night.

By the end of the third day, I was exhausted. His parents came in the very early afternoon. We all spoke with the doctor, and then we went to see Eddie. His mother cried and I quickly walked her out into the corridor. His father was a little stronger and gave soothing encouragement to Eddie. He stayed until he drifted off to sleep again.

"Cynthia," he asked me, "do you know what you are really giving up here for Eddie?"

"Oh, don't think, for one minute, that Cynthia is in this alone," spoke up Eddie's mother. "Neither Eddie nor we have any other choice. Cynthia does, and we must be grateful and do our part, also. Cynthia will marry Eddie. His benefits will increase and he can get the help that he really needs. We can get him into a better place and then another if necessary. You are going home and continue your job, and if you have to, get another job at night. Cynthia is making a great sacrifice for our son, and we are going to help. I am going to stay here with Eddie. Cynthia will go back to college." I protested, but she insisted.

His father spoke, "I just want to ask Cynthia one question, Mother, and that is do you really love him, I mean, like this, Cynthia?"

I knew what I had to say, and I said it. I said it for Eddie's sake. "Yes, sir, I do. And I am prepared to stand by him for the rest of his life, but for now, I need your help."

"That's all I needed to hear. We were at our wits ends. That is why he is here. We didn't know what to do," he said. "Both Mother and I are grateful and we always will be." He cried and held his wife and me in his arms. We all cried a little. It was a life challenge, and even with their help now, I knew that I would outlive them, and then all the responsibility would be mine.

We were silent for a while, just starring at Eddie and praying. "My dear, you go now and get some rest. We will stay," said Eddie's mother. Just then the hospital chaplain came in and was most uncertain of this marriage. To my surprise, Eddie's mother was more clever that she appeared. She had to talk him into performing the marriage as soon as possible.

"Well, three days is the earliest, and we will need blood tests," he said rather sternly.

"It will all be arranged, I'm sure," she said as she ushered him away.

"Okay," she sort of whispered to me. "It is all set for Wednesday, 9:00 A.M., here at his bedside. Now, off with you. Get some rest and we will see you tomorrow, daughter. May I call you daughter?" she asked.

I was startled. The word "daughter" meant something entirely different to me, but her husband looked at me so imploringly. I was their only hope. "Of course you can," I said.

As I left the hospital a light rain was falling. A chilly wind was blowing. I had hope and I had despair at the same time. I could be brave in the front of battle, but as soon as I closed the door to my motel room, I fell on the bed crying. I needed a father. I needed a mother, and I would not have them. I could not. They were gone forever. Eddie's parents were going to be the closest thing that I was ever going to have as parents anymore. I washed my face and recovered. I was reconciled to go through with this. I washed my hair and went to bed. I forced myself to sleep.

The next day, I felt changed, but better. Eddie was struggling bravely with the increased pain, but he knew he had to do it. He had to appear lucid for the brief ceremony tomorrow. We only had one day. After that we could up the dosage just a little and then start to bring him out of it a day at a time.

Wednesday morning came only too soon. I dressed in a somber summer dress. I hadn't counted on the weather changing so soon. I pulled on my old school parka and walked all the way to the hospital. Everyone was waiting for me. The news had spread fast throughout the hospital. Many of the nurses and the aides had made Eddie's bedside look a little better with a couple of arrangements of flowers. Eddie's parents had bought him a new shirt, tie, and a coat. He could sit up in bed just a little.

The chaplain performed the ceremony with no pomp or circumstance. It was over in two minutes. I signed the marriage license first, and Eddie signed with an X. He had been right handed and would have to learn to sign with his left hand during rehabilitation.

There was no cake, no white dress, no champagne, no wedding bells, and I guess we had already had our wedding night a year before. His dad was the first to leave. I had to leave the very next day. I had already missed a week of school and still had that awful two-and-a-half-day bus ride back to college. Eddie's mom had been befriended by one of the nurses and was to stay with her for a while.

That afternoon the doctor and I sat down and made all the necessary paper arrangements, registrations, and more than I can't remember. He had turned kindly. He was so young, being just a few years older than I was.

The next morning, I arrived to see that Eddie was awake and a cute little nurse was trying to feed him some baby food. The doctor had changed his painkiller to a non-narcotic, and Eddie seemed to be the better for it. The little nurse excused herself so that we could say our good-byes. "I must go, now, Eddie," I said. "I must go back to school. Mother is here and is going to stay with you until you are better." He wasn't able to say anything, but he tried. I kissed him tenderly on the mouth and he returned the favor. The savage beast still beat in him. I was so startled to hear him say, "I'll see ya'cutie." That is what my father had often said to me. It was unsettling. I told him that I loved him, to work hard, and that I knew together we could make this work. I cried all the way down the hall. What have I done? I thought. I was just standing outside of the little shabby chapel of the hospital. I went in to catch my breath. It had been some time since I had prayed.

I told God that this was not how I had it planned. Why had this happened? Would anything go right in my life? I prayed for Eddie, to let him recover to his very fullest. It was all I could manage. I broke down crying. Suddenly, I was startled by a hand on my shoulder. For a moment, I thought I was having a vision. I turned and looked up through my blurry tears. To my surprise, there stood the young doctor.

"There, there, now. Cry all you need to," he said. He sat down beside me, and I crumbled into his arms. He held me comfortably and we stared at all the little candles and the pretty statues and the gold cross over the little altar. After a while, he said, "Would you like to light a candle for Eddie?"

"Yes, yes, I would," I said. He held my hand as we walked down the little side aisle. He stopped under the picture of the Mother of Perpetual Help. I didn't know exactly why, but that is where we lit a candle for Eddie. We paused for a moment in prayer. Then, he walked me out.

"Are you leaving now?" he asked.

"Yes, I must. I'm late for school, being gone all these days," I said as I dried my tears. "You know something, doctor, I don't even remember your name. I am so embarrassed."

"Please don't be, Cynthia. My name is William Thompson. And I am not an intern here. I am the attending physician. But I don't always plan to work here. In a few years, I will probably go on to a more prestigious position, possibly even Chicago. I was born there, and would like to return. But, enough, about me, I am driving you back to school myself. It will cut the bus time in half." I protested. But he insisted. We drove for the whole day and arrived quite late that night. By the time we arrived, we knew quite a bit about each other, and I felt more kindly towards him. I was afraid that he was falling in love with me. That frightened me. When he left, I was grateful, but relieved.

For my sake, he called me everyday for the next month. Naturally, he wanted to report on Eddie's condition. Everyday he gave me a little more encouragement. He said that he and Eddie were talking more and more every day. I was all Eddie could talk about He didn't want to talk about himself or his loss. By the end of the second month he had arranged for Eddie to have his own phone, and we talked daily. His recovery was proceeding as scheduled, but he still refused to talk about his injuries. He refused to even meet with his psychologist. Young Dr. Thompson advised me that Eddie was at a turning point, and that I should come at the end of the term.

As the end of that May 1969 neared, Eddie seemed to talk less and less. He was beginning to realize the extent of his injuries. A serious depression set in and his downward spiral began. He refused to eat. His pain increased. Once more the intravenous needles were inserted in the thin veins of his arms. He was hardly awake anymore. His mom was exhausted and at her wits end. She called me frantically, "I am afraid we are losing him. Can't you possibly come a little early?"

I spoke to the Dean of Women and was exempted from most of my exams since I had all A's. As soon as I could, I packed that same little suitcase and caught the bus. Two and a half days later, I was back at Eddie's side. He was weak. He could hardly hold his head up. He opened his eyes, and looked at me pleadingly.

"Cynthia, are we married?" he asked.

"Yes, my darling, we are man and wife," I replied softly.

"No, not man and wife," he murmured. "You know what happened to me. You have seen me now as I am. How can I be any husband to you or any body? You know that we can never make love again."

"Darling, there are so many ways to make love. That doesn't matter. What does matter is that you get better, so we can be together," I said as well as I could really mean it. My voice could hardly convey my conviction. He looked at me pitifully.

"That is what you all want for me, but that is not what I want for you. If I can't be the man that I once was, I will not live like this. I would rather die, and I am sure that I will."

"No, Eddie, I won't let you," I said with little tears running down my face.

"I love you, Cynthia, and now I want to see the doctor," was all he could say.

He and the doctor had a short chat. Eddie had made his demands clear. He wanted to be unhooked from all the machines. No more needles. No more forced food. No more painkillers. "What can I do?" Dr. Thompson asked mother and me. "He is now of sound mind. We have got him so close; close enough to realize the reality of his situation and the sacrifices that you are all making for him. He doesn't want to live this way, and doesn't believe in any future for himself. He wants to die. As I see it, it will be either here or somewhere else closer to his home. He could make himself proceed in six to seven months to a point where he can check himself out of here and do what he wants. He doesn't want you to put him through all of that, and he doesn't want you two to go through that either. He really feels that his life is over. Cynthia, he wants to see you, now."

I went to his bedside. "Eddie, you are a coward," I said threateningly. "You will live." He was silent. His mother came and pleaded for him to try. Dr. Thomas finally came in and gave Eddie words of encouragement and hope.

Finally, Eddie said, "Okay, I'll try. But I am tired. Now I want to sleep. Stick me with the strongest stuff you have got, doc, I am in a lot of pain, you know." His mother and I said our good nights, believing that he was in good hands now, and on his way to a recovery. The doctor ordered more narcotics for the pain intravenously administered. The nurse assured us that she had seen worse cases than this, and from her experience she thought that this was a cornerstone in Eddie's recovery. "Both of you go get some rest. Come back tomorrow. I'll take care of Eddie," she said with such assuredness.

As we left the hospital together, Eddie's mother and I talked of the next step in Eddie's recovery. As soon as he was strong enough, he was to be transferred to a rehabilitation hospital in upstate Baltimore. It would be a long trek for me, but she was sure that between the two of us, that we were all going to pull Eddie through this and make a life for him. She had a mother's hope, a hope that I had not yet experienced. We were both disappointed. Eddie didn't live to see the light of the next day.

After the pain killer had been hooked up to Eddie's arm and the nurse was sure that he was okay for a while, she left him alone. He was awake enough to turn the little valve all the way on.

Poor Eddie was buried in the little Rosewood Cemetery in our hometown, courtesy of the Veterans Administration. His parents and I rode the bus down south together. We talked little and it was a tiring trip. They invited me to stay with them, and I was glad to accept. Very few people turned out for the funeral. It was just sad.

Chapter Seven

A Quick Widow

My parents never called me during that day and a half of the funeral. I never called them, either. They knew Eddie was dead and that I had married him. His parents phoned in the obituary from the hospital. I knew my parents wouldn't come. I did manage to meet the kids just as they were coming out of school. I was so glad to see them and we all had hugs and kisses all around. I managed to give Jonathan a little money. I returned to St. Alban's that very night.

During that long bus ride to my college home, I had a long time to think, to grieve, and to cry. I even prayed a little. It didn't do much good, but I tried anyway. Every man that I had ever loved had left me in some way, first, my father and now poor Eddie. I felt lost and abandoned, left alone, not wanted, and washed out and just not any good for anybody. I was really a quick widow. That's just exactly what I was. I was in the depths of despair. I had had such high hopes for Eddie and me, but I think mostly for Eddie. Marrying him was a last act of a desperate, idealistic nineteen-year-old girl. I didn't know if I would ever love again. I didn't know if I had a choice to love or not, to be in love or not to be in love. I knew that I loved my brother, Jonathan, and my two little sisters Janie and Marie. I prayed for them. I knew that I must continue my struggle to live if not for myself, then for them, and that would be for us. I wasn't alone after all. I loved my brother and sisters, and I had to have them with me just as soon as possible. I had to finish college at a record speed, and then I had to have a career on a fast track to big time money. It had to happen that way, or there would be no hope for them at all, and maybe none for me either. So, my struggle to continue was for us all. I counted the years until we could all be together. Jonathan could join me in two years, Janie in three years, but for poor Marie, it would be eight long years. How would they all manage? My mind raced for answers. "Oh, I can't think about that now. I'll go crazy if I do. I'll just have to think about that tomorrow. Somehow, it will all work out. I believe it will," I said to myself. I had to have something to believe in, something to hope for, and something for which the struggle would be worth.

I must have fallen asleep during the night on the cold, lonely bus. When I came to, we were just a few miles from St. Alban's and with the sleep I felt rested. I knew that I had a plan. I felt renewed.

A month later I realized that I could initiate the plan to save my siblings earlier than I had anticipated. I received in the mail a letter of condolence from the Army, and to my great surprise a check for $20,000. It was mine as Eddie's heir, his widow. It was the price he paid to die. Somehow, I just didn't have any more energy to cry. I invested the money wisely and hoped that it would double or maybe even triple in value. It would have to be college tuition money for my little ones left at home. It was the only way to save them.

During that second year of college, not one of my friends knew that I was a widow, or that I had lost a child. When the conversation of my childhood came up, my imagination went wild. No one could have ever believed that it was so sad. I embellished every minute of as if it was the perfect childhood any child could ever have. I was loved, nurtured, wanted, coddled, and my home was the picture of perfection, with a loving mom and an adoring father. No one ever asked why I never received any mail or phone calls or "care packages" from home. I guess they just didn't think. I had made many close acquaintances, but I was afraid of making any really close friends. I didn't want all the ugly secrets of my past to be known.

On weekends, I started to visit a little bar across town, just to take a break from the studies. I don't know why, but when I went there I always made myself look like a real tart, with the teased hair, tight sweater, and short skirt, a real pickup. I convinced myself that I just needed to be somebody else for a few hours.

I met several nice men there, but I never told them who I really was, never gave them my real name, and never let them drive me home. I just wanted to be in a fantasy world for a while, and I wanted to see if men still wanted me. I still wanted to be wanted. It wasn't long before I found out for sure.

Late on a Saturday night, I walked in the bar. It was called Lucky's then. That night, I felt especially cute, cheap looking, but cute inside. I was just going to have one or two beers, maybe play a round or two of pool with some of the boys there, probably turn down someone, and just go home. It didn't happen that way at all.

As soon as I walked into the place, I locked eyes with the most handsome man I had ever laid eyes on. I was a little ashamed. I had always thought Eddie was the most beautiful one. I sat at the opposite end of the bar. It was not crowded yet. The man looked directly at me and tipped his glass at me. The bartender asked me what I wanted to drink. Naturally, I told him, "Oh, just the usual." He would know that I would have a draft beer. It was the cheapest thing to have there. The man would know that I was a regular since I was on such friendly terms with the bartender.

I sat there drinking my beer alone. I looked around the place. There wasn't a soul in there that I knew just then. "Oh, why does this have to happen to me," I asked myself. I decided to leave. I got up slowly and started for the door.

"Leaving so soon?" I heard someone ask over my shoulder. I stopped for about a half step and then kept going. With a few more steps I would be out the door and safe from the animal attraction that I felt for him in that first instant that I saw him. *What is wrong with me*, I asked myself. *I am a new widow, for God's sake.* I knew that didn't mean anything.

"Hey, stop. I asked you a question, missy," he said loudly before I could make it to the door. I could feel him directly behind me. He had only taken three strides for him to make it clearly across the room. I turned around with my heart racing. My eyes rested only on his belt buckle. He was so tall. He towered over me. He was wearing a coat and a tie, as if he had just left work. I looked up. His shoulders must have been a mile wide. He was naturally tan with brownish blond hair with most of it mussed and hanging down over his forehead. His blue eyes locked with mine. He was definitely older than I was, probably by about ten years, I thought.

He just stood there staring at me. "Where are you running off to in such a hurry?" he asked.

"Oh, I have to get home. I am late already," I lied.

"Could you do me a favor and just have one drink with me," he asked politely. I knew that it was a come on, but I just couldn't resist.

"Well, just one, but then I really have got to go," I laughed.

We sat at the bar. I thought it would be safer than a booth, which he had suggested.

"Okay, missy, it's okay with me," he said.

"Please, don't call me missy. My name is Cynthia, and if you want to call me anything you can just call me that," I said a little tersely.

"Cynthia, that is a nice name," he said. "Do you have some nice college boy friend that calls you Cindy?"

"No one calls me that, no one. Do you understand?" I said hurriedly.

"Okay, Cynthia, I get it. I get it," he said smoothly. "But you still haven't answered my question."

"Well, what was your question? I'm sure I don't remember," I said a little frustrated.

"I simply asked if you had a boyfriend," he replied.

"I guess if I said yes to that, then I would look pretty cheap in a place like this all by myself," I replied a little harshly.

"On the contrary, I think you look real pretty, really pretty, indeed," he said. I was silent. I didn't know what to say. "Look, if you have to go or you want to go, you can. You don't have to stay here and have a drink with me," he said. "Leave if you want to."

The bartender arrived and said, "Oh, are you staying, Cynthia. I thought I saw you leaving. Any trouble here?"

"No, Andy, everything is all right," I assured him.

"Well, then, the usual?" he asked.

"Absolutely, not," my uninvited escort said. "Have you ever tried a Courvosier and soda?" he asked.

"No, I haven't," I said with a little smile.

"Then, you shall have one now," he said. "Bartender, two of the same, and make them doubles. I don't know if I'll have the opportunity to drink with Cynthia again or not. Tonight may be the first and last night." We both laughed a little. The drinks arrived and we both relaxed a little.

To break the odd silence, he said, "Well, I know your name, but you don't know mine."

"Oh, I am so sorry, sir," I said quickly. "How rude of me. What is your name?"

"Well, now, that is better," he said with a broad smile that made my heart jump. "My name is Dan, Dan Callahan, and I am very glad to meet you."

When he talked like that, his voice was smooth as butter. It made me take quick, short breaths. We had one drink and then another. Before, long he knew that I was a student at St. Alban's and I knew that he was the manager of a little department store in town, Grahams. It was family owned and operated. It had been in business for over fifty years. The Graham family was the leading socialites of St. Alban's, which didn't have very much society life, but whatever there was, the Grahams were responsible for it. I had never shopped there. It was very exclusive and very expensive. But I loved the clothes in the windows and I admired them whenever I passed there.

We talked a while longer and drank a while longer. The more we drank the more we talked, and the more we laughed. He had a broad booming laugh that seemed to fill up the place. We were both getting a little drunk. Finally, he turned to me and asked, "Can I ask you something personal?"

I was so relaxed and having such a good time that before I could really think, I said, "Sure, Dan, ask me anything." He motioned for Andy to bring us another round of drinks. I didn't protest.

He said, "Cynthia, what is a nice girl like you doing in a place like this?" I was shocked and caught completely off guard. He was finally getting right down to the question. He saw the shocked expression on my face. "I said it was personal," he said. "You don't have to answer or explain to me what you are dong here. I can only guess that you come here for the same reason that the rest of us do, to find some company. Is that it, Cynthia?"

I felt ashamed. He could feel it. I could only look down at my lap. "Here, here, now," he said. "I didn't mean to ask the question of the century." He took my hand in his and tried to give me a little look of comfort. My heart was racing wildly. This was the moment we had both been waiting for all night. I knew it and he knew it. He was just being nice about it. I could walk out that door right now, but I knew it would do no good. He would find me again, or I would find him. *Why not tonight?* I asked myself.

I sat up very straight on the bar stool and crossed my legs so that they showed off the really high heels that I had on and my long legs. It must have been some action that I had seen in a really old movie. I stuck out my chin and looked him right in his eyes. With a little tilt of my head, I said, "What am I doing here? Well, probably the same thing that you are, sir."

"Cynthia, please, I should think that at this point in time you could drop the 'sir,'" he said. "So, then, shall we go? My car is just outside."

"Sure," I said, bravely. "Why, not? But, let's finish these wonderful drinks first."

So, this was going to my first "pickup" date. I really didn't care. He was so handsome and someone important, and most of all he wanted me. At least, he wanted me tonight. I said that I didn't care that it was just a cheap pick-up, and I meant it. I was so desperate for someone to want me even for a few hours, and even if it was just for quick sex. I had no idea if it was going to go anywhere. I didn't ask any questions. The word "love" was never mentioned. I knew that it was just a carnal urge, and decided to ride it. And ride it I did.

I have to admit that I was somewhat impressed when he opened the door to his car for me to enter. It was a brand new black Cadillac with red leather upholstery. It was the most beautiful and luxurious car that I had ever seen. *So, he has money,* I thought. *I hope he doesn't try to pay me. But, hey, it is just as easy to date someone rich as someone poor.* The alcohol was really kicking in.

We drove to a small apartment complex just at the edge of town. It had been built in the 1950s and was rather quaint with ivy growing up the walls and wonderful manicured bushes lining the walk. I felt quite elegant being escorted into his apartment. *It is like something out of a movie,* I thought to myself again. I was in a sort of a fantasy world, where I was sure all my dreams would come true. I felt wanted. I felt safe. It felt exciting to be with this man, a total stranger. It was also the thrill of anonymous sex, that is, sex with a total stranger. I felt exhilarated. I was doing all the things that Father always beat me not to do. *Well, Father, if you only knew,* I thought.

His apartment was one flight up the stairs. I was sure the landlady had opened her door on the first floor just to take a peek. As we walked in I noticed that it was superbly furnished with the best of everything. It was a small, one bedroom apartment with a little kitchen. It was lovely. Suddenly my admiration of the place was stopped short. Dan grabbed me from behind and pulled me to him. He kissed me passionately and a little too roughly on the neck. I tried to play along. I pulled free and faced him.

He grabbed me by my shoulders and forcibly started French kissing me. I didn't mind, but he was hurting my mouth a little. I tried to kiss him as hard as I could, but I could hardly move my head. He held it firmly as if in a vice grip. I couldn't move. He practically dragged me into the little bedroom and threw me down on the bed. I didn't know what he wanted. I thought that maybe he was going to rape me. I was terrified and I was drunk.

He stood over me and undressed. He straddled me and undressed me, one piece of clothing at a time. The final unveiling came when he slipped off my panties with his teeth. Then he started to lick me with his tongue all the way up the inside of my leg just to that special spot and stopped, then he licked the inside of my other leg in the same fashion. I was in sheer ecstasy and fear at the same time.

I had never thought of sex like this. I felt that he was going to lick me all over and then, maybe, take a bite out of me. Then he started kissing me on the mouth and down my throat to my breasts. He was a little rough with his tongue and his teeth and his hands going all over me. I was not accustomed to this. Eddie and I sure never had sex like this. It was certainly unusual to me, but it was so pleasurable that I was his captive unable to even ask him to stop.

He held me by my hands and raised them over my head. He continued to nibble and lick any place he could as he moved his hot tongue downwards. I felt like I was being eaten alive as he did. He spread my thighs wide and dove in face first with wild abandonment. I had to stifle a little scream. I had never experienced such rough oral sex before this time. Eddie had always been so gentle. While doing so he spun around positioning his full erection at my mouth. He kept pounding my face with it. Finally, he came up for air and said, "Take it, Cynthia. Take me in your mouth." I knew what he wanted. I was a little afraid. I figured that I didn't have much of a choice. I was a little afraid that I would be to embarrassed or that he might hurt me.

I took him in my mouth. He was much longer and rounder than Eddie. He was huge and he was rough. He was choking me. It was like he was screwing me in the face. I turned my face to the side and took no more. That didn't stop him.

He held my hands over my head again and lay flat against me. He plunged himself into me as fast and as hard as he could. He pounded the hell out of me. It hurt and it felt good at the same time. I felt helpless and that he was in control. I was wild with passion. It was rough, sort of like being beaten. *This is probably what I deserve*, I thought. *Okay, then. If it is what I deserve, I'll just take it the hard way.* I started to bite his neck I wanted to participate too. He slapped my face with his free hand. I was stunned. He grabbed my right breast and twisted it roughly.

"Don't do that, Cynthia," he said between beating breaths. "Don't do anything, except what I tell you to. Do you understand me?" I turned my head to the side and started to cry.

He slapped me again and grabbed my breast harder this time, until I let out a little scream, all the while continuing to pound me with his engorged penis. "That's right, Cynthia, moan and groan and even scream a little if you want. Let it all out baby. Tell daddy all about it. You love it. Don't you? You feel that pounding deeper and deeper down there between those college girl legs." I could hardly breath. I knew I couldn't speak. He grabbed my breast again and said, "Answer me, my little bitch."

I was in such pain and pleasure at the same time. I just gave in to it. "Yes," I said between clinched teeth. "I love it. Pound me harder. Spread me wider."

"That's a good girl, Cynthia, just get into it and you will not be able to get enough of it. You'll grow to want it more and more," he said between long grunts. "Just let your sugar daddy here please you inside and out."

And he did. I began to enjoy it. I had endured rough treatment from a man all my life. I could endure this. It was like floating in space. I just gave in to it and let him be in control. As I started to cooperate, he relaxed some. He didn't slap me anymore that night, and he didn't twist my breast any more painfully. It took him hours, but he was gentler and gentler, but held me tightly with rough passion. He moaned and groaned, and said "Oh" I don't know how many times.

Suddenly, I could feel him tensing. His whole body seemed to merge with mine. He was one huge muscle from head to toe. He was tight. His was breathing heavier and his moaning became lower. I knew he was going to climax. I closed my eyes and tried to feel every inch of him and realize every bit of what we were doing. I felt a sort of rumbling start deep inside of me, deeper than ever before. My breathing increased. I realized I was moaning, too. I arched my back as he thrust harder and harder. We climaxed at the same time. I thought he would never stop, but, finally, he slowed. His breathing slowed and the pounding became easy motions of smooth in and outs that went on endlessly. I thought that we were finally at an end. I was wrong.

I could feel him enlarging even more. He had never exited me. He started a rhythmic, smooth and easy fluid motion, massaging me down there back and forth, back and forth. It felt like he was on a determined mission. I was beyond panic or even wanting to make him stop. I didn't want him to stop. I didn't know he could go on and on. I was way beyond ecstasy at this point. I was downright itching for more and more and more. He had had his way with me and he wasn't going to stop.

With one final pounding thrust he gave out a loud moan and fell still on top of me. He had climaxed a second time. We lay there together for only a moment drenched in each other's sweat and body odor, that musty smell that only comes from having sex. He rolled off of me. "Wow," he said. "What time is it?" He swung himself off the bed and started to dress. "Come on now honey," he said. "Hurry up and get dressed. I've got to go. It's late. I'll drive you over to the campus."

I didn't know rather to be mad or happy, sad or ecstatic. Where was the tenderness? Where was the love? I wasn't going to kid myself. There had surely been none of that. We had seduced each other in the bar. I had even dressed up looking for it and gone to the place where I knew that I could get it. I didn't know that it was going to be this rough, but I sort of liked it. And I sort of hated it. But I was drawn to him. I knew that he was a powerful man, and I had felt his power. I had tried to love my father; maybe, I still did, even though he had beaten me. And, this man, tonight, he had beaten me, too, and had brought me pleasure along with it and the other. I had not even tried to make him stop. He had dominated me. He had brought me to my first climax. Was this attraction for Dan Callahan a sort of love?

We drove back to the campus in silence. He finally said, "Well, honey, how was that? Did you enjoy yourself tonight?"

I turned and stared him directly in the face and to my astonishment took his hand and kissed his face softly and said, "Yes, I did."

"Good," he said. "Always glad to know I still got it." He said nothing else. He just puffed on an old cigar that he had lit and gave me a little wink with a nod of his head. Eddie used to do that, but differently. This man was glowing in his own prowess. Eddie had always been so sincere about how I felt. This was so different. He nodded at me again as if it was time for me to go. I opened the door to the Cadillac and stepped out. As I shut the door he drove off. I barely got it closed. He seemed to be in a hurry. I would soon find out.

As I walked back to my dorm room, I thought, *Well I guess what they say about widows is true. I sure am one, a quick one, a quick widow for sure.*

As soon as I entered my room, I took a steaming hot shower and scrubbed myself hard all over. I quickly toweled myself dry and found the oldest pair of pajamas that I owned. I jumped into bed and forced myself to sleep. I tried not to think of what I had just done. I would try not to think about it tomorrow.

Chapter Eight

In the Light of Day

When the morning light hit my face, I knew that I must be sick. I had never had a hangover before. I tried to get out of bed. A sudden soreness ached between my legs. I was sure that I must be paralyzed. I could hardly stand. I managed a cold shower. I washed my hair, rolled it and dried it with my little cap hairdryer. I repainted my nails a soft pink, and my makeup was just a soft touch of blush on the cheeks with a soft pink lipstick. There would be no mascara of heavy lashes today. I fixed my hair in its natural wave, and choose to wear a simple slip of a dress, a light blue smock with a white turtle-neck shirt underneath. I wore nude hose with a pair of black flats. I almost looked matronly, but the blush of youth was still on my cheeks, and the wear and tare of the night before hardly showed at all. I made all my classes. I smiled and spoke to everyone I knew. I was determined that last night wasn't going to be the ruin of me. That experience happens to all women sooner or later, I was sure. I had brought it on myself. I could still be me, sweet, innocent, caring, and loving.

During that second year of college I turned twenty years old. I was no longer a teenager. I guessed that I was fully an adult now. I could no longer blame the foolishness of being a teenager for the blatantly stupid and maybe even dangerous thing that I had done. Spring of 1970 brought on new burdens. It seems that my scholarship money was only going so far each semester. My financial counselor, Dean Whitman, called me in for a chat.

"Now, Cynthia, look here, there is nothing to worry about," he said. "But there may have to be some rearranging. For starters the sorority house is not filled. I have made arrangements for you to move out of the dorm and move in there. There will be some savings on expenses. Of course, you will have to do a little work around the place, like answer the phone, just general stuff, nothing too heavy or hard. It just shows that you care, a sort of token of your appreciation for free lodging and boarding. In addition, I have secured you a part-time position at a very exclusive and old store in the town, Grahams. Have you heard of it?"

Well, what goes around comes around, I thought to myself. "Yes, sir, I have," is the only thing I could manage to say without laughing at the total situation and myself.

"In addition, I have managed a little job for you here on campus. We are expanding our computer science department. You know the time to start in that field is now. Why the following decades will depend on people like you with a great brain, an aptitude to adapt, and a willingness to learn. You will work directly with the dean of that department. It is just a little modest pay, but Cynthia, learn all you can. It is a great opportunity for you. Well, with you academic achievements and the way that you approach your studies, I should think that you would have no trouble at all fitting these things into your schedule," he continued. "Oh, and by the way, I am truly sorry that your scholarship funds aren't covering everything. Sometimes that happens. We expect money and we don't get it. I am sorry. I personally think you can manage, Cynthia. The entire faculty and I expect great things from you. I know you are going to be great."

"Thank you, Dean Whitman. Thank you for the chances, the opportunities, and the connections. Your help and encouragement mean a great deal to me. I am sure that I will be able to manage and keep my grades up, too," I said bravely. As I left his little office, I didn't let it bother me. He seemed to think that all would work out, but it would take extra care and time on my part to keep my grades and work. I didn't know how I was going to handle Grahams with Dan working there, too. I would just have to hold my head up high and be brave about it. Maybe he would be more embarrassed than I.

As soon as I returned to my dorm room, some of the sorority girls were already there to meet me. They helped me pack, and I moved into the sorority house that night. During those days, it was expected of girls to be nice to other girls, especially if one was in need. Those girls had to, or they would have been seemed mean, and that would have meant unpopular. All those girls talked about were boys and hair and nails and makeup. I didn't mind at all. It was kind of cozy. Later that evening as I was just getting settled, I heard my named called from the girl on phone duty. "Cynthia, it's for you she yelled up the stairs." I couldn't imagine who it could be. No one knew I was here. I had not even thought to call Jonathan and tell him. I would have to call his friends house and relay the message anyway.

"Hello," I said with a little hesitation.

"Hey, girlie. I hear you're coming to work for me, now," the voice on the other end of the line said with a little laugh. It was Dan Callahan.

I steadied myself and said, "Well, I am coming to work for the store."

"Honey," he said. "I am the store. Don't worry about anything. I'll make it all easy for you. I make it easy for all my girls here, you know. I have already spoken to my personnel director. See him tomorrow. You are to work whatever schedule you need and that doesn't interfere with you studies. Who knows what the future will hold for any of us. I may need you someday."

"Thanks, Mr. Callahan," I said.

"Cynthia, don't you think that the 'Mr.' part is a little formal at this point in time?" he asked.

"Look. Mr. Callahan, I think that we should keep this on a professional level from now on, since I will be working for the store. I'm sure you understand. Good night," I said and I hung up the phone not waiting for some smart reply. I could tell in which direction that phone call was going. Just being there already compromised my position. I would have to keep up a guard. I knew this wasn't going to be any fun.

I called a friend of Jonathan's, and within a few minutes Jonathan was calling me back, collect, of course. I was searching for every nickel, dime, or quarter in my little leather coin purse. We only talked for three minutes. I managed to tell him of my changes. He managed to tell me very little about home, but I was sure it wasn't very good. He was now working at the old grocery store just like I had. He was saving all the money he could and was still making straight A's. I told him to start immediately to apply for scholarships and to certainly apply to St. Alban's. I would do whatever I could to help him get in to this college so that we could be together. It would only be one more year.

The next day I dutifully reported to Grahams Department Store after my last class. I met the personnel director. I was shocked. He was giving me the "eye" as if he might be trying to make a move on me. I avoided eye contact with him, anyway, as much as possible. He just smiled and said, "I'm sure you and I are going to get along just fine. By the way, report to Women's World tomorrow at 9:00 A.M., sharp.

Why? Why would he treat me like that? Then I remembered that men brag. I swore if that Dan Callahan had been talking about our little rendezvous, I would beat him to a pulp, no matter what. The next day was Saturday. I was to work eight hours.

As soon as I entered my department I sensed trouble. I was introduced to the other girls and women working there by the manager, Mrs. Primrose. Then she took me over to the side of the department for a confidential talk.

"Now, Cynthia, I am not going to lie to you and tell you that you were my first choice, but, you see, I didn't have any choice. Everybody has a boss, and I was told to take you. Remember the most serious rule of all rules in my department. There will be no fraternizing with any of the other men working here or the men customers. Do I make myself perfectly clear, Cynthia Thomas? There is going to be no slander, gossip or scandal in my department. Remember you are starting on a thin line already." At that time in walked Dan Callahan. He was trying to be so cool. After the good tongue-lashing I had from Mrs. Primrose, I didn't know if I was glad to see him or not.

"Good morning, Cynthia," he said just like he knew me. "Good morning, Mrs. Primrose."

"Oh, good morning, Mr. Callahan," she said all flustered as if she were just a junior high school girl.

"Mrs. Primrose," he continued," I am sure that Cynthia is going to work out wonderfully. She will be a big help to you and your department."

"Oh, Mr. Callahan, thank you so much. I am sure she will," she said as she blushed and smiled all the while twisting her little embroidered handkerchief

She introduced me to one of the other girls there, Cathy, to show me around and help train me on the cash register. We spent most of the day together and I managed to help all the customers I could. Finally, Mrs. Primrose called me into her little office and said, "Cynthia, there is someone that you should meet." I couldn't imagine who it could be. Just at that time in walked a very tall, blond, and distinguished looking older woman. I estimated her age at about forty.

"Cynthia," she said. "Please meet Ms. Graham. She is the storeowner. All new employees meet her personally."

"How do you do?" she said as she offered her hand.

"It is a pleasure to meet you," I said with great politeness and admiration.

"Likewise, I'm sure," she said as she turned to go. I was a little startled and wondered if I had said something wrong. Mrs. Primrose just sat there with a little sly smile and her head cocked to one side. "You may go now, Cynthia. Our business here is concluded," she said. For some reason I felt embarrassed, but I didn't know why.

When I went back to the department, Dan walked by just to catch my eye. He started doing this several times a day. It made me nervous, but somehow I started to miss it when he didn't. I even started to look forward to it. It was some sort of a game that he was playing and I was his unwilling participant.

Several weeks went by and everything seemed to be coming together. Working and going to class was hard, and I had to study whenever I could and sometimes late into the night. I was starting to be tired a lot, but that was normal for college life. Soon it would be summer, and most of the students would be leaving. I would be paid a little more for staying on in the sorority house and I would have it all to myself. I only had a two-week reprieve between semesters. I had to attend all the summer classes I could so that I could graduate as soon as possible.

My schedule at Grahams was increased to full-time, but the hours were worked around my classes. This meant that I would often have to work the mornings, attend three classes, then go back to work in the evenings. I would have to help close the store.

This was a hectic schedule and Dan was always hanging around. Every time I got into the employee elevator, he seemed to appear out of thin air. I would never speak. He would just look at me in a jeering way. Finally, he approached me. I was just leaving the store and was walking back to campus. His shiny black Cadillac pulled up along side me, just as Eddie's car had done so many years before. "Hey, cutie. Do you want a ride?" he asked.

"No, thanks. I like the walk," I said. He stopped the car and had to run to catch up with me.

"Hey, Cynthia, it's me, Dan," he said as he grabbed my arm.

"Listen. Don't you ever grab me again. And, if you are going around Grahams spreading rumors, I'll sue you for slander," I said fiercely.

"Hey, hey," he said. "I'm just offering you a ride home. As for the other, it sounds to me like your paranoia is working overtime."

"You mean, you didn't say anything to anybody?" I asked innocently enough.

"No, of course not. In a town like this you have to keep that sort of thing quiet. If you know what I mean," he answered. Just then a car passed. It was Mrs. Primrose. I was so embarrassed.

"Now, look what you have done. That's my boss who just passed," I said. "You know that there is no fraternization between the men and women at the store. It will probably cost me my job."

"Look, Cynthia. Don't worry about Mrs. Primrose. She knows not to meddle. Anyway, I have got to get home, too. Now, do you want a ride or do you want to walk the rest of the way in this hot summer heat," he said with his superior authority.

"You're sure it is just a ride?" I asked.

"Come on, kid, get in the car. I'm melting it's so hot," he said.

I got in the car and we were perfectly quiet all the way back to the campus. He was acting like a perfect gentleman. As he stopped the car and I started to get out, he put his hand on my knee and asked me, "Can you get away on Tuesday night? I know you have to work late that night. Maybe we can go back to that nice little bar where we met."

I took his hand off my knee and said, "Thanks, but no thanks." He said nothing. He just gave me this "why not?" look and just stared down trying to look so sad. I was tempted, but bravely got out of the car and gave him a little wave. I ran into the sorority house as fast as I could.

That night I replayed that scene over and over in my head. There was something just not right about it. Finally, I realized that he had said, "I have to get home, too." I wondered why. It didn't sound right. Something was funny about it. I slept restlessly that night.

That hot summer of 1970 blazed through June and July. Dan continued to ask me out. I continued to decline. He started hanging around my department more and more always asking me to lunch. One day I finally said yes. I would use this opportunity to tell him to leave me alone once and for all.

The phone in the department rang at about 11:30 A.M. that Friday. Mrs. Primrose answered, "Good morning, Women's World, Mrs. Primrose speaking. How can I help you?"

"Well, a very good morning to you, too, Mrs. Primrose," replied Dan. She instantly blushed.

"On, Mr. Callahan," she giggled. "What can I do for you?"

"Send Cynthia Thomas to the back of the store," was all he said. She hesitated. She was the most jealous, old biddy anybody ever met.

"Well, she is with a customer just this minute. How can I help you?" she asked. She was taking any shot she could.

"You can help me by taking over her customer. Ring the sale on her commission number, and send her back here immediately," he replied not so politely.

"Well, yes, sir, of course, if you insist," she answered.

"I do," he said as he hung up the phone.

"Cynthia Thomas," she shouted. I was so startled that I dropped the dress that I was showing one of my regular customers. I excused myself and walked over to Mrs. Primrose. Before I could say one word she said, "Report to Mr. Callahan at the back of the store." She stared straight ahead, unwilling to look at me. She was brimming with a dismissive attitude.

"But, why? What is this about? What does he want?" I asked.

She turned only to give me a dirty look and said, "Cynthia, I'm sure that I wouldn't know anything about those matters." She emphasized the words "those matters." I simply turned and walked slowly to the back of the store. As I walked down that center isle of the store I felt like everyone was staring at me, but no one was talking to me. Suddenly I was dizzy, a little nauseous, and I thought surely I was going to faint. It was just like that time at home after the knife incident. I felt as if I was walking in slow motion.

By the time I hit the big, double doors to the back of the store, I had managed to put on my brave face. However, my heart was racing and I was breathing heavily. I was sure that I was wet all over. The cool air of the back receiving room was a little refreshing but stale. This is where all of the new merchandise was received into the store. Now it was empty, except for him. Dan just stood there with that stump of a cigar in his mouth puffing away and ringing his hands.

"Well, what do you feel like eating?" he said suggesting something vulgar.

"What do you mean?" I asked.

"Oh, I just thought we could have lunch or something quick," he replied.

"This certainly wasn't my idea," I said. "Anyway, I can't go until twelve."

"Don't worry about it. I'll fix your time card. Anyway, you're with me," he said, as if I was just so stupid.

"You infuriate me, Dan. You really do. Let's just go," I said.

Other employees were starting to come in, and we were being noticed.

"Okay, now we're cooking," he said. "Look, I'll go get the car and pull way out in the rear parking lot. You wait five minutes in the ladies room, and then you come out."

So we were going to have to sneak out. None of this was making any sense to me. I was so frustrated that I just said, "Okay."

He took me to a little Mexican restaurant not too far from the store. I was hoping none of the other executives would come here for lunch. I had never eaten Mexican food, so I was at a double disadvantage: first, he was a store manager, secondly, I didn't know how to order.

"Would you like me to order, Cynthia?" he asked.

"Okay, if you want to," I replied.

"Well, then, let's just have the buffet. It's cheaper," he said. I was feeling cheaper by the minute.

As soon as we sat down to eat, I started right in on him saying, "Look, Dan, what is this all about?" He said nothing. He just ate and ate and drank his beer until he was finished and had satisfied himself thoroughly. I hardly touched my food.

"Look, Cynthia, we are both adults. You wouldn't have come to lunch with me if you didn't want to see me," he said.

"See you? See you," I said. "Why, I see you all the time. You are always hanging around the department and leering at me. Every one is noticing, and this lunch will probably get me fired."

"No, you are not going to get fired. I told you not to worry about that," he said. "Now I do have something to tell you. That one time when we were together, I was a little drunk, and I am sorry about the slaps and I hope I wasn't too rough."

I was absolutely floored that he would even have the nerve to approach that subject. "Look," I said. "Forget about it. I don't want to talk about that. We were both a little drunk, but you are right about one thing. No one is ever going to slap me again and get away with it. Do you understand that?"

"Sure, honey," he said.

"And, don't call me honey or cutie or anything. As a matter of fact, not ever call me again," I said with as much fierceness as I could manage.

"But I will call. I will call you Cynthia," he said. "I can't seem to stop thinking about you. Do you know the best part about our little date?" he asked with a sincere smile.

"I am afraid to ask," I replied.

"It was when were sitting in the bar just talking. Talking like we were the oldest friends, like we had known each other all our lives," he said. "It is true, Cynthia. It has been a long time since I have been able to talk so openly with any one, especially since my mother died two years ago."

I was so scared. I was really beginning to believe he was sincere.

"Can't we go out tonight and have a few drinks, and just talk, that's all, Cynthia, just talk. I need some one to talk to," he was practically pleading. "Can't you have just a little humanness in your heart, Cynthia, just this once."

I gave in and said, "Okay, but not tonight. Summer finals are over next Friday. We will go after the store closes."

"A whole week?" he asked.

"Yep, that's it. Take it or leave it," I said.

"Okay, next Friday," he said.

"But, you won't tell anyone, will you, Dan?" I asked.

"Why, you little hypocrite. You don't mind being sought after, wined and dined; you just don't want anyone to know. Never mind, dear, your secret is safe with me," he said sarcastically.

"And, stop hanging around the department all the time, too," I added.

"We'll just have to see about that part, Cynthia. You see, my dear, I do work there. It's my job," he answered smugly.

"Then, don't look at me, and certainly stop all that leering," I answered. He said nothing and we left the restaurant.

He said nothing on the ride back to the store. He had assumed this superior air of confidence and conquest as if he had achieved his goal. "I don't know whether to love him or hate him," I whispered to myself as I put my purse away in the ladies' locker room.

"What did you say?" asked Mrs. Primrose. I was shocked and jumped back just a little.

"Oh, Mrs. Primrose, I didn't know you were standing there."

"I know my dear. I know," was all she said as she stuck her nose up at me and walked out. That made me mad. On one hand I had some one wanting me to do something that I really didn't want to do, and on the other hand I had someone telling me that I wasn't going to it. I had to make a choice. Mrs. Primrose wasn't it.

So, this is the way it is going to be. *Screw it all,* I thought. *No dried-up old prude like Mrs. Primrose is going to run my life for me. I make my own decisions. I will keep my date with Dan.*

During the next week, I began to feel a little better. Dan stopped hanging around so much, and I actually started looking forward to our date, but I wasn't going to let it evolve into another sexual encounter. "No, absolutely, no way," I told myself. "Absolutely, not." My thoughts kept going over the first time. I admitted that part of it was adventurous and pleasurable, and he promised no more slapping. I was getting in a good mood, the first in a long time. I thought that I should be worried a little, but I just wasn't.

Finally, that Friday night came. We closed the store as usual. I knew to meet Dan at his car parked in that special out of the way spot. I was glad that he respected my position in the store. If I were to be seen leaving with him, I could be fired even if he said differently. After all he was just the manager. It was not like he owned the place.

We drove to a little bar outside of town, one that I had never been to. Everyone seemed to know him; I realized he was a regular. There were very few women, but there were many beautiful young men. Some can over to just say hello, but he had attention for only me.

After we had settled into our first drink he said, "Cynthia, I am enjoying our conversation, but I have a confession to make." My heart skipped a beat. He took my hand and looked me straight in the eye. "I am just crazy about you. I told you before that I can't get you out of my mind. I always want to be near you, to be with you, to have you close to me. Cynthia, you are very important to me. You are an important person in my life, and my life would be empty without you in it." He stopped and just looked at me.

I took a long drink. He did the same. He said, "I've been wanting to tell you this for some time. Now, I feel that a great burden has been lifted off my shoulders."

To my surprise I wasn't as shocked as I might have been. Somehow I must have known this was coming. Maybe I had even encouraged it without knowing it. I should have never taken that job at Grahams. *It is my entire fault*, I thought. *This poor guy has gone bonkers over me, and I let him.* I felt responsible. I had to do something to let him down gently, but did I really want to. If I decided to date him, I was sure I could find another job even if I had to check groceries again.

"I understand, Dan," I said. "I myself have had those same feelings for someone else long ago."

"You do?" he asked with a little smile.

"Yeah, I do," I said as I held his hand in a sort of firm little shake.

"Well, I feel better already," he said. "Bartender, another round here. And buy a round for those two guys over there."

"Sure thing, Dan," said the bartender.

"Dan," I said. "How do you know those two guys over there, and how come so many of the others seem to know you fairly well?"

"Oh, I used to come in here a lot. You know, it is out of the way and quiet, and everyone is so friendly. It is just a friendly out of the way place. I like to come here when I need to have a few drinks and relax. It's just a place away from everything and everyone."

"You mean, away from the store?" I asked. "I know it keeps you very busy. It must be stressful for you."

"Oh, yes, the things that I have to endure there and my job is so big and I am responsible for almost every aspect of the stores success," he was quick to agree.

We had our second round of drinks. "Come on, Cynthia, lets go," he said. I need to relax." I was feeling pretty proud of myself that I had handled the situation so well, in such a grown up manner. On the drive home, it did occur to me that he had not asked me how I felt about him. I guess he must know that we are just friends. I was satisfied with that. I didn't want him to feel worse than he already did.

I noticed that we weren't going in the direction of the campus. "Dan, the campus is back there," I said.

"Oh, Cyn, I thought we would just go to my place for one last drink, you know as friends, anyway, I have a surprise for you," he said a little mischievously.

"Well, I don't like being called anything but by my real name, Dan. I am sure that I told you that. Just call me Cynthia."

"Oh, honey, don't spoil the fun. We're having such a good time. Don't be a party pooper," he said as he steadied the car on the road. I didn't know then that he had had three or four drinks in his car waiting for me. "Hey, Cyn, reach under that seat and get me that bottle." It was a bottle of Scotch. I handed it to him. "Unscrew the top for me will you, Cyn? I mean Cynthia," he asked. He was high and feeling good. I didn't want to spoil it for him. So I did. He took three of four long gulps from the bottle, and then handed it to me. "Here," he said. "Cyn, have a little taste. It won't hurt you. Let's keep the party going." I was just in the mood to take a dare already, so I took a little slug. It burned like hell going down, but it had a smooth manly taste about it. I liked it.

"By the way," I said. "Where are we going?"

"Why, to my place naturally," he said. "That's where the surprise is, Cyn."

I just gave up trying and refused any more drinks from the bottle. We were almost there anyway. He seemed perfectly normal as he parked the car. I waited for him to open my door for me. He didn't. He didn't even look back. He just said, "Hey, Cyn, are you comin' in or not? Get the lead out."

He wasn't exactly being abusive, but he was definitely rude. Well, I would stay just a few minutes then leave. Tonight will be the end of it. He can move on.

When I walked in to his apartment he fixed us both a couple of drinks and then one more. "Wow, that's enough for me. I have got to go," I said.

"But, Cyn, honey, I haven't shown you your surprise, yet," he said. I knew he was drunk. His face was red, and he had a big smile from ear to ear. He pulled from his jacket pocket a brochure for an Acapulco, Mexico vacation, the reservations and the plane tickets. "Surprise, Cyn, you've earned it," he said. "What do you say? I know you have two weeks between semesters. Anyway, it is only for two nights and three days, just a weekend trip. I'll make sure you get time off from the store."

I was absolutely speechless. I was floored. Sure I wanted to go. I could just picture me in Acapulco. It would be so glamorous and cool, and a nice break in my life for the first time. "Can I give you my answer tomorrow?" I asked.

"No," he said jokingly. "When you get out of the line you lose your place." He was joking with me.

"No, really," I said. "I'll have to think about it. I'll let you know tomorrow."

"No," he said. "Tell me now." He was tickling me under my chin.

"Well, if I say yes, there will have to be some ground rules," I said.

"What rules, Cyn? Come on, be a free spirit for a change. You are so tense and tight all the time. Relax a little." He got quiet. He took my hands in his. "I really want you to go. I feel like I owe it to you. If you go, it will make me feel a lot better. We got off on the wrong start and I want to make it up to you, as a friend."

He looked so doggedly dejected. I hadn't the heart to say no. Without thinking I said, "Okay." He was so excited. He picked me up and swung me around in the air. We both laughed and laughed. He hugged me tightly.

"Oh, Cyn, you have made me so happy. Thank you. Thank you for saying yes," he said with excitement and sincerity.

He set me down, but didn't let me go. He held me close with my head on his chest. I could feel those big muscles bulging under his jacket. His manly musty smell was intoxicating, mixed with the drinks, the trip to Acapulco, and the moment felt so special. I lifted my head and kissed him on his lips. His lips caught mine and sought more. Our tongues became entwined as we held each other closer. Our passions rose higher and higher. It wasn't planned. We were both just caught up in the moment. Soon we were both undressed.

As we lay in that little bed of his, I noticed how gentle he was with me. He was telling me with his body how much he appreciated me. He was very patient, and the foreplay went on for what seemed an eternity. He was waiting for me to move our love play up to the next level.

"I really need to get back," I said.

"Back to what?" he asked. "Do you really have to get back to that empty old sorority house? You'll be all alone, and so will I."

I could feel his passion rising again and again. He was almost daring me. I didn't answer. I should have, but I wasn't sorry when I felt his aroused passion start to enter me just a little then stop. He just held me there, waiting for some response.

I could hold back no longer. It was true. I was longing for it, for him, from him. I arched my back and lunged forward, engorging myself with him all the way with all he had. He gave out a little moan and so did I. We both started that rhythmic motion that is only known by two who are on the same path of ecstasy. I took all he gave. This time he was so gentle and passionate.

I could tell that he really cared for the way I felt in this act. Again, we climaxed together. I have to admit: The sex was good.

We only lay there a minute enwrapped in each other's arms. He gave be a little peck of a kiss on the check and rolled out of bed. "Come on, Cyn. Let's go. I have got to get going and so have you."

"Can't we stay here like this for just a few more minutes?" I asked.

"No," he almost shouted. Then he caught himself. "I mean that we both have to go and get our rest. You know we both have a long day at the store tomorrow," he said as if to explain.

I had just finished my second psychology course. I thought I was so smart. "He is great at the talking," I said to myself. "And he is good at the listening and the sex, and he is generous and gentle, gentle, now, that is. But I think that he must have a fear of real intimacy. That must be it, and I am not going to make him feel bad about it. It is just a man thing. Given a little time, I know I can make him enjoy it with real intimacy."

The next weekend we flew to Acapulco. It was a long trip. We enjoyed every minute of it together. We were becoming lovers, but had not told each other that we loved each other. As we flew over the luscious tropical green jungle the Acapulco airport could be seen for miles. Straight ahead we could see the blue waters of the Pacific Ocean. The little city of Acapulco was perched on the beach and had grown straight up the cliffs of the steepest mountain I had ever seen. It was filled with luxurious hotels and wonderful tiled villas. We swam in the warm waters and lounged by the pool of our little bungalow hotel. We drank margaritas all day. In the afternoon we took our siesta along with the natives. The afternoon time would only be the first of our encounters for the day. Later, at night, we would always make it last longer.

We mingled with the other tourists and shopped until I couldn't shop anymore. I had taken Spanish in high school and one year at St. Alban's, so I naturally acted as translator. I thought I was so sophisticated and cool. It wasn't until much later that I learned that all the shop owners and anyone connected with the tourist trade already spoke English fluently and were just being polite and trying to sell me more and more.

That weekend was the best time of my adult life at that time. I thought I was in love. I hoped that Dan loved me. I knew he was passionate about me. I thought he cared.

Soon enough we were back at work. I was tired and exhausted, and I wasn't exactly glad to see Mrs. Primrose. As soon as I entered the department she left. Cathy came in. I said, "Good morning, Cathy," just as I always had. She didn't even speak to me.

"What is going on around here that I don't know," I asked her.

She said, "Well, if you don't know, then you are the last to know." She softened a little and said, "We'll talk on our break." I could hardly wait until

10:30 A.M., our break time. She met me in the employee lounge and already had lit her cigarette and had gotten a Coke for her and one for me.

"Come on outside," she said. "Look, I don't want to butt into your business or anything, but you asked for it, so here is the news. Cynthia, everyone in the whole store knows you and Dan were both missing these last three days including Friday and Saturday. Don't you think that looks a little suspicious? And, your skin, you are so tan, so suddenly. And, when Dan comes in and he is so tan, well, dear, everyone already knows, but I must tell you this. Last year, it was I he took to Acapulco."

"Well, what happened? You two did break up. Didn't you?" I asked.

"We didn't exactly break up or anything. He just stopped coming around, and I knew that I had had my trip and he had had his thrill and that was that. I didn't have much hope that it would be anything more than that."

"And, how did you manage to keep you job if that is against company rules?" I asked.

"Well, certain people, who will remain anonymous at this point, prefer to turn their heads and look the other way," she said.

"You mean, Dan pulls the shots around here at the store," I said.

"Well," she said. "You see, dear, let's just say that he gets away with a lot, you know. Anyway, I have been here three years, and to my knowledge he has taken a different girl to Acapulco every year. I haven't the slightest desire to know what went on before that. But he gets away with it. You were just the next in line. You know how it is. Don't you, Cynthia? You do know, don't you? You do know who he is? she asked.

"Know what?" I asked. "What else could there be?"

"Oh my gosh!" she said. "You really *don't* know, do you?"

"Know what?" I repeated.

"Oh, my God," she said. "You *really* don't know. Well, listen here sister; I have said more than I should have said already. You will find out in time. I am sure. I'm not going to be the one to tell you. Oh, no, not me. I need this job. Bye for now. I'll see you inside."

With that she just turned and practically bolted through the door. I could hear a little laughter coming from inside. I was very confused. I could understand that Dan had another life before he met me, so did I. But what was this other thing. I would soon find out.

I went back to the floor and assumed my clerks position in the department waiting for another customer. I saw Ms. Graham looking through some scarves, and I went over to help her. "Good morning, Ms. Graham," I said. "How are you this morning?" She looked up at me with a peculiar expression on her face.

"Oh, I guess I'm okay, Cynthia, but it seems, dear, that I should be asking you that same question."

What an odd reply, I thought to myself. "Oh, I'm just fine," is all I could manage. "Can I help you pick out anything?"

"Oh, no, dear, I have already made my decision. I will take this one. It goes so well with this new Channel suit. Don't you think so, dear?"

"Yes, it's beautiful," I said.

It was a strange conversation, but I thought it was going fairly well. She was the owner of the store, after all, and I was just her clerk.

"Will you just take it then?" I asked.

"My dear, Cynthia, everyone pays in one way or another, even I. Here is my charge card."

Out of the corner of my eye I saw Dan barreling his way down the main isle. He saw us and stopped. He turned as if to talk some business with another manager. He lit a new cigar, all the while keeping his eyes on both of us.

I took her charge card and read the name. It didn't say *Ms. Graham.* It did say *Mrs. Dan Callahan.* I was totally shocked. I blushed. I tried to steady myself. I rang the sale wrong twice. I was so embarrassed and ashamed and furious at Dan all at the same time. I finally got it right and handed her the scarf after putting it into a little tissue and a gift box, and then into the bag. I knew Mrs. Primrose was watching the whole story unfold from behind a little curtain in the back of the department. I could hardly think.

"Cynthia, if you continue to use so much tissue and gift boxes and bags on one little scarf, you'll put us out of business in a month," said Ms. Graham with a little laugh. "And, might I compliment you on your tan. It looks lovely on you. But I must say that by the light of day, you look so much older than in the dark of night." I was really confused, now. I hadn't the slightest idea of what she might be referring with that last comment of hers.

"By the way, leave the store early today," she said. "I have already authorized it with Mrs. Primrose. I want you to have tea with me at my house. Come around 4:00 P.M. I have something very important to discuss with you."

"Yes, Ms. Graham," I said. I knew she knew. She had to.

She left the department just as lightly as she had entered. I could see her gliding down the aisle speaking and smiling with every one. She was putting on a brave face. She knew the whole story, and knew what a slut I was, and what a lady she was and would continue to be. When she and Dan met in the middle of the store, they did not speak. She simply touched him on the arm and gave him a little smile with a nod. I had to hand it to her. She had guts. She had grace, charm, and style. And she was a savvy businesswoman. I had cheated her by giving myself to her husband. She knew it. I knew it. She knew that I knew she knew it, and yet, she still had the braveness to surge on. She didn't crumble and fall to pieces, as I would have. That day I began a great admiration for a great lady. I loved her and I felt a little sorry for her. I never dreamed that I would know her the rest of her life.

Dan never even came near my department for the rest of the day. He ran like the real coward he was.

Chapter Nine
A Friend and a Career Opportunity

$\mathcal{I}$ left the store early and borrowed cab fare from Cathy. I had the jitters all day. I was so nervous, but I knew that I had to go through with it. She was going to tell me what a real slut I was, that I was fired, and that if I tried to see her husband again, she would have me thrown out of town. My imagination was soaring. Finally, I was going to arrive at her front door.

As the cab drove down the long drive I noticed acres and acres of finely manicured gardens with ponds and statuary everywhere. Even the front steps were flagged on either side by two life-size bronze lions.

I was surprised that the house was so huge. It must have been the biggest house in town, and certainly the finest. It was constructed completely of stone from the local quarry. The long flight of front steps covered the whole first story, so that when you entered the house, you were already on the second story. The house soared to four stories with several wings on each side. I was in a daze, and certainly at a disadvantage. I would just have to take my punishment. I had done wrong. I had been done wrong. I was sure that I was to blame, not Dan. I should be punished, maybe even prosecuted by the law. I didn't know what to expect. She was the rich wife. I was the poor wench. The poor wench usually lost. That much I did know.

I only had to ring the bell once and a livered butler opened the door immediately. He said coldly, "Please, follow me." I said nothing. We walked through several rooms and down several halls until we found the place she was sitting. It was the solarium, a giant of a room with plants everywhere from all over the world. In the center a fountain splashed playfully. It was filled with filtered sunlight. It seemed peaceful and a joyful place. There was assembled in one cozy corner a sitting area of two white rattan chairs and the matching settee. Over the back wall was a full size picture of Ms. Graham on her wedding day. She had been beautiful then. I certainly felt small and insignificant. I wished that I were a bug so that she could just step on me and get it over with. I was full of dread.

As I was escorted in, she arose from her chair. She had been arranging calla lilies in a beautiful crystal vase. She was dressed in a flowered chiffon frock of mauve. Her grayish blond hair was pulled up high and she wore simple but elegant earrings and necklace. Her hands were beautiful mani-cured with the softest of pink nail polish. She wore only one ring, a large five-carat diamond solitaire; it was obviously her wedding ring. She was making a real statement by her very presence, and she hadn't even said one word yet.

"My dear, do come in. Please, have a seat and relax," she said with grace. "Albert, you may serve the tea now." She was kind to her servants, never demeaning, I knew that much already. I knew that they must be loyal to her and probably hated me.

"What lovely flowers," I said as she completed her arrangement.

"Yes," she answered. "They are lovely, aren't they? Appropriate for any occasion. I carried them in my wedding bouquet. Since then, I have always insisted that they grow here all year. Our greenhouses are full of them."

The tea was served in silence. Albert was dismissed. "Please, dear, do have some cake," she said calmly. "It's my favorite, almond cream. Doesn't that sound deliciously sinful?"

I didn't answer. I just took a little slice of cake and tried to balance the cake and the tea at the same time. It was a little awkward. She was going to make me start the conversation so I said, "That is such a beautiful painting of you."

"Oh, my dear, that was done more than thirty years ago when I was just a young girl of twenty and just recently married," she replied. "It was a remarkable resemblance of me then, but I am no fool, I know that there is none now. Thirty years can bring a lot of changes in a woman, Cynthia. Don't you agree my dear?"

"Yes, I'm sure it can," I answered.

"My first husband insisted that I have my portrait painted," she contin-ued. "He said that he always wanted to remember me as I was on my wed-ding day. As the years went by I always knew that I would never be lucky enough to find another such as he who loved me with every fiber of his being. He made me very happy for many years even though he was twenty years older than I. We stayed in love all those until the day he died." She stopped and I thought I saw a little tear in her eye. I sipped my tea.

"Did he die suddenly?" I asked. She stared at me coldly. I knew that I had asked the wrong question. It was too prying. "Oh, no I am sorry. I shouldn't have asked," I said.

"Oh, dear, it's perfectly all right," she said softly with grace and charm. "You can ask me anything. I feel like we are going to know each other very well. I don't mind telling you. It was the cancer. But he died peacefully in his sleep. There was no cure in those days, no hope at all. It was quick, his death, so quick that it left me in a vacuum. I tried to immerse myself in Grahams. It had been in the family for such a long time that I felt that I had to keep it going. My husband's father and mother started the store together when they were just newlyweds. Naturally, I had never worked. I knew absolutely nothing about business, especially retail selling. But I hired the best of every one, from managers to the architects who remodeled the store and really brought it up to date for its time. That was fifteen years ago. I was thirty-five years old and already a widow. That's when Dan came on board so to speak. And so, that brings me to the very topic about which I wanted to talk to you."

I was raddled. She had bridged the gap so quickly, that I was startled. I almost dropped the china teacup and saucer.

"Here, dear, let me take that for you," she said as she stood. She placed them on the tea service, and stood beside her portrait.

"As you can see, Cynthia, I am not that same girl of thirty years ago. But I am no fool. I have had two husbands, the first older and the second younger. I have tried both, but I have loved each differently. I can't say that I loved Dan the way I loved my first husband. They don't make men like that anymore. We were only together for fifteen years, and they seemed to fly by. It went too quickly. Did you know that Dan and I have been married for fourteen years?"

"No, I didn't," I said.

"You may be wondering why I marred so quickly after being loved the way I had been," she said. She gave me no opportunity to answer. She was telling a story, her story. It was all going to have some meaning soon. I knew it.

She continued, "Well, I will save you the trouble of asking. I will just tell you. Fourteen years ago, I was approaching middle age very quickly. My first husband and I had no children. I wanted a child desperately and Dan was so damn handsome. I don't know if I charmed him or he charmed me. Oh, of course, he knew he was marrying a wealthy widow. He knew he would have a job for life, that being the store and me. I knew that. But for some reason I just didn't care. I was floating blindly, and I wanted to feel safe again. I didn't know how to be a woman alone. I wanted a man to be in charge of things, but this man I could control. I had to have control. There was too much at stake to lose to just turn everything over to him. We even have a premarital agreement. I was desperate, but I wasn't stupid. Women can't be stupid, Cynthia. We always have to plan, to think, to fight!"

71

"Please, please," I said. "Please, don't go on. You tell me too much. It's too personal. This must be too painful for you."

"Life is pain, Cynthia," she answered quickly as she sad down, again. "Life is many things. I know you know that. But I must continue. I want you to know the whole story. Dan was hired as a department manager. He worked in men's clothing. As I said, he was so damn attractive, and I was so lonely and in need. He was irresistible, even for me. The wedding was quite a shock to everyone. But I did wait until one year after my husband died to announce our engagement. We were married shortly after that. You see, Cynthia, I am a woman who always insists on maintaining appearances. I am a woman leader in this small community, a woman leader among men. Naturally, I am part of society. You young folks don't understand the importance of that. A woman's good reputation is always her best asset. Without it you can go nowhere. If it weren't for me, there would be no St. Alban's College. You see, Cynthia, there is more to being rich that just being part of the country club set. I personally have raised millions for that college, that lofty institution of higher learning. I even have an honorary doctorate. But I didn't do it alone. Being a member of society, I had influential friends, rich friends. I made sure that I was on every charitable board of directors in this county. That is why we have a special children's wing at the hospital. With wealth also come responsibilities. For a widow, it is harder. That is another reason I needed a husband. I wasn't about to be courted by every old bachelor or gigolo who came along. Dan was the perfect pick, if not the perfect match. Oh, I guess in the beginning it was exciting. You realize I had been a young girl of your age who married a man twice my age the first go around. We had good times romantically, but twenty years does make a difference. When I married Dan that part was so different for me. He brought out the animal woman in me. It was a way of postponing the inevitable point of middle age for a few years anyway. He exhilarated me. But, you will see that as women age they just look old. When men age they mature and become even more handsome. It happened with me. It happened to Dan. Naturally, he was drawn to other women. We were only married three years when he took his first lover. I thought I would suffer and I did until I knew that it had to be me to make the decision. I could either suffer with him or without him. I was only going to suffer so long. I made that pledge to myself. Women suffer enough, Cynthia, without prolonging it, so I confronted him."

"He said to me with a little smile, 'I deny everything and admit nothing.' He looked like a deer caught in the headlights of a truck. Naturally, he denied it until I showed him the pictures. I had hired a detective from out of state. He said that he would agree to a divorce quietly. That I did not agree too. We sort of made an arrangement. I didn't feel like looking for another husband. By this time I knew that children for me was out of the question. I wasn't going to have his child, and time was running out for me. It would have been risky at that age anyway. But Dan always did right by me in all his duties, as a good husband should. You understand that part, don't you dear?"

"I think so," I replied.

"He has never left me lonely or wanting, if you understand my meaning," she said.

"I do," I said.

"And, he has always kept his private time discretely," she continued, "that is until recently."

I blushed and felt so ashamed. I was sure that I was red from head to toe. My father had been right about me all along. I am a man chaser, a slut, and now a husband stealer. I am getting just what I deserve, and she is giving it to me in the most severe manner possible. She is baring her soul and most intimate secrets so eloquently to show me how painful I have made her life. I am a miserable person. I just wanted to say I was sorry and get the hell out of there. I knew that I was too miserable and terrible a person to even be in her presence.

"But, now, my dear, we must speak about you. We must speak about you and Dan." I wanted to say everything, but she would give me no room to speak.

"First of all, do you love him?" she asked. "Are you in love with him? Do you want to marry and spend the rest of your life with him? Do you think that you can't spend another minute without him? Do you have that much passion for him to sacrifice the rest of your life to be with him?"

She was so forthright that I could hardly speak. She was an amazing woman. She had not rehearsed this scene in her mind. She was speaking purely from her heart and her experience and wisdom. I felt like I was in the presence of a goddess. I had such respect for her and shame for myself.

I could only say, "Honestly, no. He is not in my plans, but how did you know?"

"Come, come, my dear. I told you that I was no fool, and I can read Dan like a book. I always know when he is about to stray. You see, my dear, you are not the first, as I have said. But I guess you have a right to know, after all I don't usually invite employees to have tea with me here in my home or anywhere. You must know that I am usually at the store until quite late and I have eyes everywhere. Of course, the whole store knew how he was flirting with you. The first I knew about you and Dan was the night you met him in the outer parking lot. I saw you get into his car with my very own eyes. I followed you. I have never followed anyone before. I must confess I felt a little sneaky. I knew he had a little place somewhere. I had just never wanted to know before. The whole scene was obvious. And, then when you both went to Mexico together it was just to much from which to hide."

"I see. Thank you for telling me how foolish I have been," I said. "I deserve this humiliation and I am so sorry."

"On the contrary, my dear, I didn't bring you here to humiliate or punish you. I brought you for several reasons. The first reason is to tell you that I had no choice. Dan just got sloppy this time, and the time before you, that was last year. And the year before that it was the same. It is partly my fault, I should have put a stop to it sooner. You will know one day dear, that the older you become the more you think you can endure, the more you should endure. I have tried to make many excuses for Dan over these many years, but now it is too late. He has dropped all discretion. He has not kept his end of the arrangement. In addition, I believe that he is an alcoholic and possibly addicted to drugs. He may even smoke marijuana and take cocaine. I have had someone watching him for some time. His own selfish desires and stupidity are making the name of Graham dirty and dishonorable publicly. His behavior, and, to some extent my own for letting it go on far too long, is almost a laughing stock of the community. The name of Graham means a great deal to this community and this state. There is a great deal more to the situation about which you are unaware. There are far too many little people who depend on our reputation for their living and income, as you do my dear."

"You mean, because I work for you?" I asked.

"Well, that, and because of your scholarship," she answered.

"My scholarship," I replied. "What has my scholarship got to do with all of this?"

"As I have said," she continued, "my late husband and I made that college just what it is, exclusive, that is, exclusively for bright, young academic achievers who deserve to go there and for some who might not be able to afford the tuition of more privileged children. Didn't you know you received a Graham Scholarship?"

I beat my hands on my knees and hung my head down so that my hair covered my face. I cried, "I am so stupid. I never put the two together. You have been paying for my education while I was having an affair with your husband. I am an awful person."

"Not so awful," she said. "I have a little confession of my own. I have not been totally honest with you. I knew about you and Dan before that night in the parking lot. I saw you two together as you left that wretched little bar on the other side of town the very first night you two met. I knew that he was getting restless again. A jealous woman is not something that I am proud of being. But I am not now. I have been at fault too. I had you investigated. I was furious when I found out that you had a Graham Scholarship, so I had the funds reduced. I shouldn't have done that. It only threw you and Dan together more. I never dreamed that the Dean would arrange a job for you, especially at Grahams. It was stupid of me. I wasn't thinking that you have to make up for the loss of funds somehow, and so it is I who will be the first to say I am sorry. You are just a child becoming a young woman. I am sorry you had to be caught in the middle of what is really our problem."

"No, no," I interrupted. "It is all my fault. It is always the woman's fault. I should have said no on that first night."

"But you are so wrong my dear," she said. "Women are always too easily persuaded to assume that all the bad things that happen in the world are somehow their fault, and the men let us do so. You must unlearn that immediately. Cynthia, we live in a man's world. Think about it. It can't all be our fault. Men play the game too, you know."

"Thank you for being so kind about it, Ms. Graham," I said. "Naturally, I will resign my position at the store. I understand about the scholarship. You had to do it. I won't see Dan again. And, I will manage somehow. I must finish my education. If not here, then, maybe I will have to go home."

"Go home?" she asked. "Cynthia, I already know that would be a death sentence to you. I told you I had your background investigated. I know pretty much about everything in your past as well as your present situation, and if there is more, then you can tell me when you are ready. You see, dear, I have a plan and it involves your future. If you were to suddenly disappear from the store and the campus, it would only make matters worse. It would only make the obvious more obvious. I am a Graham. I know how to handle these things and I have confidants to help me. No, my dear, it will not be you to disappear. It will be Dan. I will send him on a long trip. When he returns he will know that he is divorced. It will be quietly handled and he will be adequately compensated, compensated to such an extent that he will never quibble over one penny, nor will he ever see you, St. Alban's, or me again. He will then just disappear. I have no doubt that he will. I have no other choice. I knew as soon as you said that you really didn't love him, that you could live without him. I know now that it was only a fling for you. Don't worry, my dear. I have not suffered too much, and you shouldn't either. And, I don't plan to suffer. Life is too short. Who knows how much time we each have left to live. My life will be fine without Dan Callahan in it."

"I am so sorry and ashamed, I don't deserve a second chance," I said.

"It is the only way, my dear. Now, here is what you must do. First, I will have Albert drive you directly to the sorority house. Do not answer the phone tonight or tomorrow. Do not answer the door. I am sure Dan will try to contact you. He will be on a flight to London within the next twenty-four hours. You will continue your classes at St. Alban's. You scholarship will be refunded. You won't have to work at Grahams for the money, but I want you to work there for me. We must be seen together there in a business-like and friendly manner. With Dan gone, and you and me tight as thieves, the situation we will create will be so confusing for everyone that no one will know what the real truth is. Can you do that for me, Cynthia? Do you think that you can tolerate the company of this old woman for a while? Will you help me in this endeavor? God knows it is I that needs you now. Ironic, don't you think so, dear? Who knows what the future holds for any of us. Grahams may become a career for you."

I looked at her and she looked at me and we both laughed at the same time. "Yes, it is ironic," I laughed.

"So, you will help me handle it in this best way?" she asked me sweetly.

"Yes, I will do it," I answered. "We women have to stick together."

"That's exactly correct, my dear. You are learning already. You will see that it is the only way," she said.

She rang for Albert and he drove me back to campus. I felt shamed, but I felt shamed in a corrective manner. There was no screaming, no hitting, no beating, and no belittling of another human being. She had kept her dignity, and she had helped me keep mine. She was correcting the situation in a take-charge manner with grace and determination. Instead of being made to feel like the other woman, she had almost made me feel like a daughter to her. I had great admiration for her, even love. I wished that one day I would be more like her. I have always known that it was at this point and because of her that I really began to emerge as a woman. I was thankful then, and I was thankful for many years to come.

Chapter Ten

My New Life

My new life changed me in ways about which I had only dreamed. I managed to make it through the weekend. Dan did try to contact me. The phone at the sorority house rang off the hook until I finally answered it.

"Hello," I said in a small meek little voice.

"Cynthia, hello. It's Dan," he said. I continued in the same voice saying, "Sorry, she's gone."

I hung up the phone and just stood there in a stony silence. After my visit with Ms. Graham, I thought I knew what I wanted and that didn't include the company of Dan. But just hearing his voice sent a titillating vibration throughout my body. I wanted to touch myself, but didn't. What was this control he had over me? Why does he make me feel like the sexiest woman alive? Why do I want to jump into bed with him every time I hear his voice? All these thoughts and feelings came flooding back into my mind and touched the very essence of my soul. It frightened me that I could be so easily controlled by someone else, especially him who I really didn't trust. It had been hard to just hang up the phone like that. I knew that I had to do it. Late Sunday afternoon he came to the sorority house. Thank God only I was there. He knocked and knocked and knocked and then went around to the back door. I watched him from behind the little thin curtains of my room.

I wanted to run to him. To drag him inside and pull his clothes off right there in the front hall. It was all I could do stay in my room. I locked the door. I didn't know why; that wouldn't keep me from going out, and Dan couldn't even get in the house anyway. I remembered locking the bathroom door once after a terrible beating by my father. Locking the door then kept him out. In someway locking the door to my room now helped me stay calm and sit still and be silent. His knocking and pleading for me to open the door was tearing out my heart. Or was it just an overwhelming battle with lust? I was so thankful when he left.

I lay in my bed that night trying to cope with a multitude of emotions. I missed Dan already, but I knew my future depended on the agreement that I had made with Ms. Graham, and the future of my little brother and sisters depended on the same. I knew that I had made the correct choice, but it hurt.

Albert drove me to the store early Monday morning. To my surprise, Ms. Graham was already in the car.

"Oh, good morning, Ms. Graham," I said a little surprised.

"Good morning, Cynthia," was all she said. When we arrived at the store, I went to my department and she went to her office. I was nervously watching everyone as I thought they were doing to me. Dan did not arrive that day. He would never arrive at the store again. I knew this and Ms. Graham knew this, but no one else knew this. I was so paranoid that I could hardly think straight. By midmorning, Ms. Graham appeared in my department and motioned for Mrs. Primrose and I to approach.

"Mrs. Primrose, I'm afraid we are a bit short-handed this morning upstairs in administration. I going to have to borrow Cynthia for awhile," she said as she laid her hand on my shoulder.

"But, of course, Ms. Graham," she said.

"Come along Cynthia. We have a lot of work to do," said Ms. Graham. Mrs. Primrose knew something was amiss. She just didn't know what it was. In time the whole store would know. Dan wasn't ever coming back, and my position at the store was growing. But Ms. Graham was arranging the evolution of this whole situation so cleverly that it all just seemed like a natural progression. Eventually, everyone at the store would understand what had happened, but by that time it would all be old news, but it would always be a part of the history of Grahams, and that was that Dan had finally picked the wrong girl and she ended up taking his place. Everyone would always smirk just a little about this, and every new person ever hired would be told the story. That is why Ms. Graham started my store education in the personnel department. I would be directly responsible for processing every new application. Every new employee would know that I had something to do with them being hired. I would be somewhat empowered. My duties at the store grew to such proportions that I only returned to work directly under Mrs. Primrose twice and that was just for appearances during that first month.

School started again and I was swamped, but not a day went by that I didn't think of Dan. Would I ever see him again? Would I ever have the chance? I only had small bits and pieces of time to even think about such things. I had increased my course schedule at school; I had to graduate just as soon as I could. By Christmas I was considered a senior. I needed two more semesters to graduate. I devoted all my time to the store and school. Jonathan would be coming in one more year. Ms. Graham had already promised a scholarship for him, but I didn't tell him. I wanted him to apply for himself and for it to be awarded to him on his own merit. It would have been the same anyway. He had great grades in spite of what home was like.

During those precious moments when I could talk to him on the phone he assured me that he was handling everything there, and that everyone was all right. He wouldn't give me any specifics, and I must admit that I didn't pressure him for too much information. I didn't want to know too much. I would have been helpless to do anything about it.

By New Year's of 1971, everyone at the store knew that I was Ms. Graham's right-hand girl. By this time I was spending every free moment I had at the store. I never dated, although several boys asked me out. I just wasn't interested. And I was exhausted. All my energy was spent at school or at the store. I didn't care really. It helped distract my attention from missing Dan. I didn't want to miss him, but I did. I didn't know why. But Ms. Graham was a constant companion by now.

She insisted that we be seen discussing business while walking down the main aisle of the store asking my opinion on everything from merchandise to the showcase windows. She wanted everyone to see just what she had done. She was protecting her pride by showing everyone in her world just how much she didn't care about Dan, and how important I was to her now. She was playing the irony game and it worked. Everyone there acted towards me just the way they were supposed to act; anything less would have been an insult to Ms. Graham and that would have cost them their jobs. "After all, she fired her own husband," was the general statement around the store.

During the spring of 1971, Ms. Graham fell at the store. She broke her hip and had to have hip replacement surgery. That surgery was extremely risky at that time. I had to assume full responsibility for most of what went on at the store. That was the hardest part. Without Ms. Graham I was just another clerk. She had given me no title, no real position of authority. She knew this. The first day in the hospital after recovery from her operation she summoned the assistant general manager and all the department heads and me, little Cynthia nobody, to her bedside. I was the first to arrive.

"Oh, Ms. Graham, how are you feeling?" I asked.

"How do you think I am feeling?" she said, "absolutely miserable is how I feel. More importantly, how do I look?" She had had her hairdresser come to the hospital and fix her hair and put on her makeup. She wore a silk brocade bed jacket of steel blue.

"Ms. Graham, you look beautiful," I said.

"Cynthia, stop patronizing me. I can't use it. What I can use is your honest opinion. You know that I have called this meeting against my doctor's orders. I have to look right for it and for you," she said briskly.

"You look fine," I said. "Maybe we could prop you up with a few more pillows."

"That's the kind of information I need. Now you are getting the gist of it," she said.

One by one, all who had been summoned appeared and gathered around her hospital bed. There wasn't one person who didn't bring a vase of flowers. They didn't exactly know what to expect, but they did want to show their courtesy, and they wanted to protect their jobs.

"First of all, I want to thank all of you for coming here today. Secondly, I want to assure you that I will be back at the store within six weeks," she said. Everyone congratulated her on that and on how well she looked

She put up her hands in protest and said, "Enough of that. We are here to discuss business, the business of the store, my store, and your jobs there." Silence fell around the room. Everyone was waiting while she paused just a moment.

"While I am gone, operations at the store will continue as usual. Everyone will be in charge on his or her own departments. Mr. Jones, you as assistant general manager will continue to coordinate all of the store activities and you are to work shoulder to shoulder with Cynthia Thomas as if she were I. Cynthia will be my eyes and ears while I am recuperating. You will no longer be working for Ms. Primrose. Cynthia, anything that requires my signature, any mail and all of the store receipts of the day will be brought to me here no later than 6:30 P.M. each and every day by you. Does everyone understand?"

Everyone agreed wholeheartedly.

"Furthermore, I have a personal favor to ask of Cynthia and I want all of you to be aware of it," she continued. I was shocked. I had no idea what she might ask me. "Cynthia," she said. "I hate to ask such a big favor of you, but it is as much for the store as it is for me. I am going to be released from the hospital in three days. A rehabilitation specialist will come to the house everyday to aid in my recovery, but I simply can't run the house and the store and manage my recuperation by myself. Do you think you could be a dear and move into the house with me for just a little while, just until I can walk again and have my strength back?" You could have heard a pin drop in that room. I'm sure that I heard a little gasp from someone.

Naturally I said yes. I really didn't have a choice. "Of course, Ms. Graham," I said. "Anything you want, I can do."

"Albert will be at your disposal night and day. He will drive you and your things from the sorority over to the house. He will drive you to school and the store and to the house everyday. He will be your assistant in what ever you need," she said slowly and for everyone to hear.

"Well, that is all for now. Please, return to the store and remember this: You represent Grahams and Grahams represents you," she said as she dismissed everyone. "Oh, Cynthia, could you stay just a moment longer?" she asked.

After everyone had left the room, she said, "Here is a key to the house. Albert is parked outside. Please, go to the house. Here is a list of things that I need."

"Of course, Ms. Graham," I replied.

"Cynthia," she said. "I don't want anything to interfere with you school work, so I have hired a general tutor to help you in your studies. There will be no discussion about that. Do you have any questions for me?"

"Well, yes, I do," I said. "Why are you doing all of this for me?"

"Doing what, my dear?" she asked.

"Promoting me at the store, the private tutor, moving me into the house, what is this all about?" I asked.

"My dear, I guess you will have some advantage from all of this, but, Cynthia, you know that my first concern is for the store. And right now, really, you are the only one that I can count on to tell me the truth. You are the only one I feel that I can trust, almost like a daughter. It is just an instinct, but I have always tried to act on my own instincts and usually I have been correct," she said honestly and from the heart. I could tell, she was looking straight into my eyes and holding my hand firmly. "Is it to much for you, my dear? If it is, I will understand and you will be not be obligated," she said as she laid her head back on the pillow.

Suddenly she looked a lot older than a woman approaching fifty years of age. She had let her hair go naturally gray, and her makeup looked a little forced. I was suddenly afraid that she might die. I realized that if she did die it would be a great personal loss for me. I felt sorry for her. With all her wealth and riches, she had no one on which to rely except me. That was sort of pitiful I thought. She had hardly known me a year, and yet, we had been through so much together, and she was beginning to think of me as a daughter. How terrible that she didn't have any children of her own I thought.

She opened her eyes and looked at me as if she could read my mine and said, "Don't feel sorry for me, my dear. If I had a real daughter, she might not even want to do it, might not be able to do it. But I know you can. So you see that you are even closer to me than some daughters are to their own mothers. I depend on you in ways that you don't even know about yet."

I started to cry. It was just too much for me. "Of course, I can do it all. It is an honor and a privilege," I cried.

"There, there," she said as she patted my hand. "I know you can handle it. It won't be so bad as all that. You see, I have great things in store for you, my dear, and no damn hip is going to stop me now. But remember this. Don't overstep you boundaries of power at the store, just listen and learn and by all means smile, be confident. I need you now more than ever. One day soon, we will sit down for tea and have a long talk about all of it. But for now, I must rest. Please, go. Albert is waiting for you."

I walked down that long corridor of the hospital to the elevator waiting to take me into another world. When I stepped out, there was Albert, cap in hand, waiting for me. I don't know why, but he took my hand and led me to the door as if I were a princess. All my stuff had been professionally backed and was waiting for me at the sorority. All the girls were there to bid me goodbye. We all hugged and kissed and said we would get together at school for lunch, that I really wasn't going away. I guess we all knew that I would never be the same again.

As my meager belongings were piled into the trunk of the black limousine, and Albert opened the door for me into the back seat, I turned for one last look at the house and girls and I knew that college life for me would never be the same. I knew that this was my graduation day.

When we arrived at the mansion, I wasn't allowed to carry anything upstairs. "Oh, no, Miss Cynthia," said Albert. "I can do that for you. Ms. Graham would want it this way. You go on in and get settled. I am sure dinner is waiting for you."

"Thank you Albert," I said. I felt like the lady of the manor even though I didn't want to. *I don't deserve all this*, I thought. *What is happening to me? How did I get here?* It all seemed so mysterious and dreamy.

As I entered the foyer, Hilda the housekeeper was there to great me. "Good evening, Miss. Let me take your coat for you. Come along with me. I'll show you to your room," she said graciously. She led me up the long curving staircase and I realized that the house was even grander than I had ever remembered. It was enormous and richly built from stone and marble, with fine paneled walls and Persian rugs everywhere. Crystal chandeliers hung from the ceilings. My room was the same with an enormous canopied bed at one end and a little writing and sitting area at the opposite end, all centered around a fireplace, which had just been lit. There were several tall vases of roses and calla lilies. The walls were lined with pinkish, water-stained taffeta. The bedding matched perfectly. The hardwood floors beamed beautifully, and the large Oriental rug was at least two inches thick. Attached to this room was my own private bath with all white porcelain tiles. On the bathroom counter I found French soaps and perfume, along with bath beads. There was a small vase of flowers there as well. I couldn't help but to think of Mother and her cheap bath beads. Here I was, a real nobody, and I was being lavished with the richest of riches. *At least she married, had children, had a husband, had her own home*, I thought, *at least she tried to be a good wife and mother in the beginning.* I just knew that this must have been. What had happened to her? I knew the answer, of course. I felt worthless. It was all so over overwhelming. It was suddenly all happening much to fast. I was snapped out of my dizziness by the ringing of the phone. Could it be Dan, I wondered?

Had he heard about all of this? I was afraid to answer the phone. It stopped ringing.

A second later there was a knock on my door. It was Hilda. "That was just me ringing, Miss. Dinner is ready. You'll find your clothes in the closet over there behind that panel of a wall. If you have any outside calls, they come in on the house phone downstairs. Don't worry about pesky calls. I will always tell you who it is before I put them through to you."

"Thank you, Hilda," was all I could think to say.

I touched a little knob on the wall and the panel slid open. To my surprise, there was a whole different room. It was a dressing room with a little skirted table in the middle and full-length mirror opposite it. All around the room were closets and drawers each revealing different articles of clothing. There was a whole closet full of business suits, some for daywear and some for evening. There was a closet just for blouses, mostly white. Another closet held several evening dresses, some short, some long. Another closet held dresses for work. Every conceivable article of clothing was there in my size.

I picked a simple black dress and put it on. I presumed that in this house you dressed for dinner. I didn't want the help to know that I was just a nobody from a southern hick town who didn't know how to act any better, and I was acting. I didn't know anything about anything.

As I came down the stairs, Hilda met me. "Oh, Miss, in all the excitement, I forgot to tell you that Mr. Hamilton is here. He always dines with Ms. Graham on Thursdays. He's her attorney, you know."

"No, I didn't know, but thank you Hilda. We'll be right in to dinner."

I entered the living room and introduced myself to Mr. Hamilton. I explained the situation to him and assured him that Ms. Graham was perfectly okay and would be home in a few days. He was a little upset that no one had informed him of her accident. I assured him that from now on he would be. We had our dinner and he excused himself early. I was glad when he left. I am sure he felt a little awkward too.

As I prepared for bed, Hilda came in to turn down the bed covers. "So, that's Mr. Hamilton," I said.

"Oh, miss, I am so sorry. I should have called him and cancelled the dinner plans. It is my entire fault. I hope it wasn't too much of an imposition on you to go through with it."

"No, not at all," I said. "And for the record, I see no need to rearrange the schedule of the house. I can play hostess until Ms. Graham comes home."

"Oh, thank you miss. That makes it easier for all of us," she said with a little bow as she left the room

I felt tired and wonderful all at the same time. I put on the beautiful dressing gown that Hilda had laid out on the bed for me. I danced around the room as if I were Cinderella. I caught a glance of myself in the full-length mirror and was startled. *Who is that woman*, I thought? "It's me, I said to myself, just plain old Cynthia Thomas, a real nobody, just dressed up and acting like somebody." I quickly took off the beautiful gown and carefully laid it across a chair. I put on my old, usual white cotton nightgown and climbed into bed. Laying there in the dark I started to wonder just exactly what was happening to me. Was it all for real, or just a dream? It was all too good to be true. I pondered this for a long time unable to sleep. I wondered if Ms. Graham really needed me. Did she really not have anyone else, or was she just killing me with kindness? Maybe it was my duty. Maybe I owed it to her. Maybe I owed her big time. After all, I did have an affair with her husband, and that was the final straw that broke her back and ended their marriage. Oh, I was that awful girl my father said I was. *Whatever is happening here, good or bad, I must deserve it*, I thought.

I got out of bed and began to wonder around the suite. I noticed that there was a little door behind the wingback chair beside the fireplace. It was the first time that I noticed it. I walked over to it and turned the big, brass knob. The lock clicked in the silence and I jumped back just a little. The door swung open only to reveal a narrow little hall with another door at the end of it. I walked in and opened the other door. To my astonishment, I was standing in the room of what had to be Ms. Graham's bedroom and suite of rooms. There were pictures of Dan everywhere, one was even a full portrait, oil on canvas. There were dozens of snapshots in various sizes and all richly framed in silver and gold. By her bed there was a professional photo portrait of Dan. The walls were full of pictures of Dan, pictures of Dan playing tennis, swimming, horseback riding, pictures of them on trips, probably their honeymoon. It was almost like a shrine. On the valet there hung a man's suit, dress shirt, and shoes. I recognized these to be Dan's. I swung open all of her closet doors, but there were no other clothes of his. Another door led into another adjoining room, which must have been his, as it was decorated for a man, so masculine. I snatched open the closet doors, but they were empty. As a matter of fact, this must have been his private quarters, but there remained nothing personal of his. It was as if the room had just been abandoned. It was all a little too weird.

I left this room just as quickly as I could. As I walked through her room I noticed the picture of Dan on her bedside table. A little drawer was ajar. I couldn't resist the temptation to open it. What I found astonished me. It was a little tape recorder with a tape sill in it. I touched the play button and heard my own voice. It was the whole conversation of my first tea with Ms. Graham. She had recorded the whole conversation. But why, I wondered? Why would she do such a thing? When I heard the part where she said, "He will just disappear," a chill ran threw me. Had she divorced him or had she had him killed? Was he trying to seek my help when he was pounding on the doors of the sorority house and calling every few minutes?

I ran back to my room and flew into bed and pulled the covers up to my chin. *Just what is going on here?* I wondered? "Oh, I can't think about that now. If I do, I'll go crazy. I'll think about that tomorrow." I told myself that it was just my paranoia running rampant. I lay awake until the early hours of the morning. I must have slept some. The next thing I knew the sun was streaming into my room and Hilda was standing over me with my breakfast tray.

"Come along, Miss. Rise and shine. I'm sure you have a full day ahead of you. Albert is already waiting in the car to take you to school and then to the store. You'll meet with Ms. Graham at exactly 6:30 P.M. and then home. Your tutor will be here this evening."

Everything was being arranged for me. Was it a little too perfect? I thought it might be. Was I safe? I wasn't sure. Was I being bought? I thought, *maybe yes.*

Chapter Eleven

Jonathan Comes In

The next few weeks flew by so fast that I hardly had time to think of anything. Before I knew it, Ms. Graham was home from the hospital and her rehabilitation instructor came every day. She was progressing nicely, but it would take another few months before she would be able to return to running the store.

Everything at the store seemed to be running smoothly. I was there almost the whole day. My being there seemed to be perfectly normal, but I could tell there was resentment from everyone who worked there, especially the assistant manager, a little old squat man named Mr. Jones. He thought that since Dan was gone, the job of manager should have gone to him. He let me know it in no uncertain terms.

"But Mr. Jones, this is just temporary until Ms. Graham comes back," I assured him. He didn't believe me. Working side by side with me as equals was really chafing him, but he was trapped. He had made Grahams his whole life and was eligible for retirement in only five more years. Everyone thought that he secretly had had a crush on Ms. Graham for years and years.

The rest of the staff was nice enough, but I could tell there was talk behind my back and I could catch little sneers turn into smiles as I walked down that main aisle of the store. It all made me so uneasy. I guess they all thought I was just there to be a little snitch.

Everyday I attended my classes. Every afternoon I managed the store, and then reported to Ms. Graham at home. She still wasn't able to go back to the store. The summer of 1972 came soon enough and by Christmas I would be graduating. That May, Jonathan graduated from High School. He called me on the evening of May 1. My phone rang in my room. Hilda said, "Miss, there is a Mr. Jonathan Thomas on the line. Can you take his call?"

"Oh Hilda, you know that's my brother, of course, I'll take the call," I said. "Hello, Jonathan, is that you?"

"Hey, Sis, it's me. How are you?" he asked.

"I'm, okay, I guess. I am really tired. You know this is kind of a weird situation here, with school and the store and taking care of this house for Ms. Graham, well, it's a lot," I said.

"Well, then," he laughed. "I guess I will just have to go to college somewhere else."

"What do you mean?" I asked.

"Well, if you are too busy," he answered.

"What's that got to do with anything? Jonathan you got it, didn't you?" I asked.

He burst out laughing, "Yes, I got the Graham Scholarship. Just as yours in running out, mine is kicking in."

"That's great," I said.

"Cynthia, I don't exactly know what is going on up there, but I know you had a lot to do with me getting the scholarship. Whatever you had to do, I know that I can never be able to repay you for it and I will always be grateful," he said. He sounded as if he might cry.

"You can repay me by coming up here and show these Yanks what a fine southern man you must be," I said. It had been three years since I had seen him. "I'm dying to see you," I assured him.

"Me too," he said a little sheepishly. "Sis, I have another favor to ask. It would mean a great deal to me if you could come to my graduation." I was stunned. This had never occurred to me. I was silent. I didn't know what to say. "Sis, did you hear what I said," asked Jonathan?

"Yes, honey, I heard you," I replied.

"It would be good if you could come home for graduation and maybe see the girls," he said. "It would be really good," he said again.

"Jonathan, is everything okay there?" I asked. "Are the girls all right? Is anybody hurt or anything?"

"No, nobody is hurt. I can't exactly explain. It would just be good if you could come," he said. He sounded a little downhearted and sad and like he was just taking a stab in the air.

"I'll see what I can do, honey. I can't promise," I said.

"Okay, then, I'll send you the invitation," he said. "I know you'll be there, Cynthia. It would be the best present you could do for me, and the girls. Thanks, bye, now." He hung up before I could say anything else, then I heard the click. I knew that someone had been listening in on the conversation.

During dinner that evening, I mentioned the call to Ms. Graham. I said, "Ms. Graham, I received a phone call this afternoon from my brother Jonathan."

"Oh, yes," she said. "I am so glad that he will be studying at St. Alban's next year."

"Then you know about the scholarship?" I asked.

"Why, of course, my dear. We discussed that over a year ago, now. It was decided then that Jonathan would have a scholarship. Besides, after reviewing his records it appears to me that he is just as smart as you and has the grades and if you add in the family situation he was well deserved to be granted it."

"What do you mean by saying 'the family situation'?" I asked.

"Cynthia, you and I have already been over this before. Must we rehash that again, now, over dinner?" she replied. "I'm sorry, my dear. I had to know for myself. You knew that I already had some information before I took you in to the store. We talked about that. Naturally, when Jonathan's turn came up, I had to know more about the family, your family, and I can tell you that it has not gotten any better. The sooner we get him out of there and here with us the better it will be for him."

I was silent for a moment, and then spoke. "It's my fault. I should have gone home more often, taken some action. I'm such a coward. I just left them there on their own. How bad is it?"

"Well, I wasn't going to tell you just yet, not until I had substantiated more evidence, but it seems that Jonathan has been raising the children himself, going to school, managing the house and just doing everything," she said sadly.

"But Mother, what about Mother?" I pleaded.

"Well, I know she is there. I think alcohol may be involved," she said. I was silent.

"I am so ashamed," I said finally.

"Cynthia, look at me, girl. It is most definitely not your fault. Why you are just a child yourself, barely a woman. How can you blame yourself?" she demanded.

"I could have taken them and run away, or something. Oh, I don't know. Now, I am really worried," I said nervously.

"Nonsense, if I had thought there was any real danger, I myself would have taken some action," she said.

"Well, Jonathan wants me to come to his graduation in two weeks," I said. "Don't you think that I should go?" I asked.

"I think we should both go," she said sweetly as she patted my hand. "Don't worry my dear. There is nothing that I can't make right. Now, let's eat our dinner."

"Thank you, Ms. Graham," I said.

"And, my dear, don't you think it is time that you called me by my given name? It is Carolyn. My name is Carolyn. It would please me very much if you would call me by my name, at least here at home. Of course, at the store, only Ms. Graham would be proper. You know that I want you to stay on here at the house a little longer, at least. I am still not quite up to a full day at the store yet, and I really need you now."

"Thank you, Ms. Graham, I mean, Carolyn. Thanks a lot."

The next two weeks were busy for all of us. I finished the semester and once again I was on the Deans List of Honor students. I don't know how I did all that I did. Carolyn was trying to stay longer and longer at the store, but her hip was giving her problems. She would have to have more rehabilitation and rest at home, but she insisted that she accompany me to Jonathan's graduation.

The day finally came, and we flew home first class. A long, black limousine with a burly driver named Burl met us at the airport.

"Good afternoon, Ms. Graham," he said.

"Good afternoon, Burl. You are to take us directly to the graduation, and you remember our conversation about the rest."

"Yes, Ms. Graham. I have that all arranged."

Once we were seated in the back of the limousine I asked her, "What else is going on here that I don't know about?"

"Well, Cynthia, I thought it best not to tell you until we got here. Now is as good a time as any to tell you. After graduation, Jonathan is going to take us to the house. We will see for ourselves just exactly what the situation is. I don't think there will be any resistance. We will have Burl with us and a few of his friends will be near by if there is any ugliness. Don't be so naïve, Cynthia. I know you know what I am talking about, but I am trying to make it easy for you. Don't make me put the situation into words. I don't want to insult you and your family. You will know what to do when the time comes."

I didn't know what to expect at home, or what she was planning for us to do. I didn't have much time to think about it. Within a few minutes we were at the school and Jonathan spotted us immediately.

He came running across the campus. "Hey, sis. How are you?" he asked as he gave me a big hug and kiss. "It is so good to see you and have you here again." Burl helped Carolyn from the car.

"Jonathan," I said. "This is Ms. Graham. Ms. Graham, please meet my brother, Jonathan."

"It is a pleasure to meet you, son. I have so looked forward to this moment. I can't tell you what it means to me. Thank you for having me here," she said so honestly that I thought she was going to cry.

"Come on in, and I will show you to your places," he said.

As we walked in, Carolyn couldn't stop talking about him. "He is such a handsome boy, so tall and good looking, and so polite. I can tell he is older than his years." She looked at me knowingly.

As we took our reserved seats I noticed that the two seats next to us were empty, and were reserved for Mr. and Mrs. Thomas. "Oh, don't worry about that," Jonathan said. "They're not gonna show. Meet me after the ceremony. I have to go now." He smiled broadly and hurriedly he gave us both a little kiss on the cheek.

"Quite the charmer," said Carolyn as we settled in for the beginning of the graduation.

All through the ceremony, those two empty chairs next to me made me more nervous than ever. What if they actually showed up? How embarrassing that would be for everyone. In my heart I secretly imagined that they did attend Jonathan's graduation. I would be so proud to see my mom dressed up and looking so pretty as she did when I was a very little girl. Father would be as handsome as he was when they first got married. I used to hold their wedding picture for hours and just stare at it. They had been a beautiful couple. What had gone wrong for them I wondered? Why did he take it out on me? Why had she acted all those years as if nothing bad was happening there, especially to me? Why didn't she help me?

"If you don't stop reminiscing about the past, I do believe, dear, that you are going to cry," said Carolyn.

"Why, it's as if you can read my mind," I said.

"I can, dear. I can. I'm really just an old lady with a little experience who doesn't want to see you sad. Now cheer up, the program is about to begin."

With that said, the old piano began to play the same old graduation march, and in walked the graduates, with the girls on the right and boys on the left. That was so like the Catholic schools then, mixing the boys with the girls as little as possible although it was a coed school. It didn't stop me, I thought. Then I thought of Eddie, and I did shed a tear for him. Carolyn nudged me with her elbow for me to pay attention. Jonathan was just walking by. He looked our way, and I stood for second to take his picture. He was beaming proudly from ear to ear. I saw Carolyn give him a little wink and he blushed the color of azaleas in the spring.

The program lasted less than an hour. After the diplomas were given out, the special awards were announced. Naturally, Jonathan received the Graham scholarship, but to our surprise he was also announced as valedictorian of his class. He gave the graduation speech. He started his speech in the usual way, welcoming and recognizing the special officials there. But it was the end of his speech that has always been so special to me. He said, "In conclusion I dedicate this speech to my sister Cynthia Thomas, whom I have always held in high esteem and for whom I have always had the greatest admiration." I was so shocked and surprised. I couldn't help myself. I broke down and cried. Carolyn handed me a little embroidered handkerchief to wipe my tears and she patted my hand trying to console me. It was such a lie. In reality I had abandoned him and Janie and Marie, just left them there in that house of despair with no one to really love them or take care of them. I had left them and gone off and had wild sex with a married man, and now I was his wife's confidant and best friend. I was living the high life while they were just barely struggling to get through another day alive and without going insane. I was a slut. My father had said so. I was also selfish. I told myself that. I was so ashamed of who I was. How could I make it all right again? What could I do?

I was deep in thought when Jonathan brought me back to the graduation, "Hey, sis. Perk up. Let's get out of here."

"Jonathan, is there any where special you would want to go to celebrate?" asked Carolyn. Why hadn't I thought of that? I was certainly so selfish, thinking of nothing the entire time but myself.

"No, I just want to go home and see how Janie and Marie are doing," he said.

We drove the short distance to the house. When the long black limousine pulled up to the house, I could see those same old nosy neighbors peering out from behind those same thin and dingy little curtains. *Well if we ever gave them a show before, this sure is going to be one*, I thought.

Burl was the first one out of the car. He came around to our side of the car and opened the door for us. I was the first one out. As I took a little step backward to make room on the sidewalk for Carolyn, I could hear our squeaky screen door open and close with a clatter. I looked around only to see in horror my father in a dirty, old undershirt and his white boxer shorts. He looked like he hadn't shaved or bathed in weeks.

"Hey, Dad," said Jonathan as if nothing were out of the ordinary. "You sure missed a great speech, and look I made valedictorian."

"You sissy boy. You take of that cap and gown off and get yourself in here and shut up those other two brats from their squealing," he said. "And who are these two fancy women you have brought with you? Ah, I see one of them is your slut sister. And, who is that old broad with her, her pimp?" He was so drunk that he almost fell off the porch.

I was mortified and afraid. He came barreling down the steps with both fists clinched. Jonathan stepped in front of me to shield me from him. Father just slapped him with a left hand across the mouth and Jonathan went sprawling across the front yard. He grabbed me by my hair and started to shake me calling me whore, slut, bitch, and much worse that I have blocked most of it out of my mind. I remember Burl shoving Carolyn back into the limousine, and then he took Father down with one fist square to the middle of his face. My father had the most shocked look of his life on his face. He tried to stand and barely made it to his feet when he came at me again. Jonathan sprinted across the yard still in his graduation gown and jumped on his back beating him with both fists on either side of the head. With one hand Burl pulled Jonathan off Father, and with the other hand he hit Father again in the face. He then proceeded to beat the living hell out of him. Father just kept getting back up. Finally, he didn't. He just lay there in the dirt and grass with himself exposed and not caring. Now there were real witnesses to his true beastliness. These were real people who cared about me and who cared about Jonathan.

Carolyn said, "Let's go, Burl." I was so dazed. I didn't know what she meant. "Come on, Cynthia, I can just imagine what we will find inside." She grabbed my hand and we ran up the steps and into the house with Jonathan trailing behind us. Burl stood guard over father who was cursing so loud and so furiously that it took another slap across his face to shut him up. He fell into an alcoholic stupor and just passed out. *Too bad he didn't pass out before we got here*, I thought.

Once inside the house, it didn't seem so bad. Of course it was shabby and worn, but it was clean. "I tried to clean up a little before graduation," said Jonathan whose right eye was beginning to swell and his cut lip was bleeding all over his chin and neck and all the way down his neck onto his new white shirt.

"Janie, Marie," I called. "It's me, Cynthia. Come on out. Everything is okay."

Jonathan ran to his room and pulled out three suitcases. "Come on, sis. They aren't here."

At that moment, Mother came staggering out of her room. She had a bottle of bourbon in one hand and a crowbar in the other. She was a mess. Her hair hung in dirty clumps. She wore no makeup. Her dress was soiled with what I did not know. She had a crazed look on her face. Both of her eyes were black and blue and the left one was swollen shut. She had been beaten. "Come on back, you crazy son of a bitch," she screamed. "Come back in here you coward so I can kill you." She took a few steps towards us.

"Mother," I said. I don't think she recognized any of us.

"Get out of my way," she said with clenched teeth. "You social workers have been here before. I'll kill you too. You took my Cynthia, but you are not getting my baby girls." She took a long drink from the bottle. She steadied herself and took a long breath. With one swift action she raised the crowbar and charged us swinging the crowbar back and forth in front of her. It lodged in the wall. She tugged to free it only to lodge it again in the other side of the hall wall. Then, she just started hitting anything in site. She tore the whole living room apart before Jonathan could stop her. He grabbed the crowbar from her hand and she just went limp in his arms. She was unconscious. He sat her in Father's chair.

"Come, Cynthia," said Carolyn with a trembling voice. "It is time to go."

"I'll say it is," said Jonathan as he hurried to the car with the luggage.

We had just pulled away from the curb when we saw Father running towards the car with the crowbar. He managed to smash the window where I was sitting before Burl could speed the heavy limousine away. I screamed. Glass flew everywhere. A large piece of glass flew across the seat and cut

Carolyn's hand. Jonathan and I were both screaming then, and Carolyn almost fainted.

"Where to first?" asked Burl. He knew we would need an emergency room at a hospital.

"Go straight through town and hang a left at the last light," I said. "You'll see the hospital on the right."

"No, no. We must go on with our plan," said Carolyn.

"Plan? What plan?" I asked.

"We thought it best not to tell you, Cynthia. But we had to plan this carefully. You know, to keep it legal, to have the law on our side," said Jonathan.

"Who is *we*, and what is the plan?" I asked nervously. "Carolyn, what is going on here?"

"Well, my dear, Jonathan and I have been in touch for some time now. He was keeping me posted on what was going on at your parent's house. You will remember when you first came to me that I told you that I had some knowledge of what your life had been like. I had no reason to believe that it was going to change and I knew you still had Jonathan and the two girls there. It was his last call to you that really alarmed me."

"I knew someone was listening in," I said.

"Please, don't fault me, Cynthia. Don't you see? I had to. If I had asked you straight forward, I didn't think I would get a really clear picture."

"Oh, it is all my fault," I said. "I should have stayed. I should have stayed and protected Jonathan and Janie and Marie from all that awfulness. I'm sorry, Jonathan, I know that I have failed you."

"Stop, Cynthia. And stop that crying," said Jonathan in a commanding manner. "We can't use you now in that self-pitying manner. We need you clear-headed and calm, or else this is going to look like a kidnapping."

"A kidnapping?" I asked. "What kidnapping?"

"That's the plan Cynthia. It's okay for me. I'm eighteen. But Janie and Marie are underage. We can't just take them with us." I must have looked so confused.

Carolyn said, "Cynthia, Jonathan is coming home with us, and so are Janie and Marie. It has all been arranged. I have been in touch with the state capital. I have connections there in the Justice Department. The whole situation at that house has been under investigation for months. Tonight's exposition was just the icing on the cake, so to speak. Both your father and mother are being hospitalized tonight. When they become sober they will be charged with child neglect, maybe even child abuse. I know we can prove neglect, and that will be enough for Janie and Marie to become wards of the state."

"Wards of the state?" I asked. "I don't want them to become wards of the state, or orphans or anything like that."

"Cynthia, calm down," said Carolyn. "This hysteria of yours is just exactly what we expected. I told you they were coming home with us."

"We can't just take them. Can we?" I asked.

"Well, yes and no," said Jonathan. "You see, Cynthia, I have already reported the neglect to Social Services. This time, thanks to Ms. Graham, I called the right people. It's true Mom and Dad are being hospitalized this minute. They have been drinking for weeks, twenty-four hours a day. They started drinking when you went away to college. Every year it has escalated. They realized that I was graduating, and the closer it got, the worse things became at home. I had done everything that I could do alone, Cynthia. You weren't there. How could you possibly understand? This morning, I took the girls to a friend's house. Janie and Marie go to school with his little sisters, and I know the parents well. I, also, had to have a safe place to go once in a while just like you did, Cynthia. He beat me, too." He started to cry. It was all too much for him. He was just a child himself.

"Oh, my darling, my darling," I said. "When I think of you there all by yourself, alone with those monsters, I could just kill myself." I hugged him and covered him with kisses.

"I think there has been enough killing for one night," said Carolyn. "Now, Cynthia, listen to me. This is how it has to be. You have to be calm, and you too Jonathan. The girls are all ready to be taken into protective custody, but we don't want to alarm them. There cannot be a scene. We are just going to pick them up. You will be the surprise. You will introduce them to me as your boss. They will be delighted to ride in this limousine. But we will have to make one stop at Social Services. It will not be at some cold office. We will go to home of a friend of mind, Judge Harris. He lives just inside the county line. The Social Services officers will be there. They already know the story and have been well informed of the situation. As I have said, I have already been in touch with the Justice Department. Jonathan has made his statement in a sworn affidavit about the treatment of the girls and himself. His statement should be enough now that he is of legal age and a part of it himself. My statement can only contain what he has told me as adult, and what I have witnessed tonight. That may be enough to get the girls out of there permanently, but your statement would seal the deal." She stopped. She had a little look of distraught on her face. "I know that it may be difficult for you. I am only telling you so that you will be aware of what may be asked of you. The girls will only be told that they are going on a little trip. I am sure that with you and Jonathan along that they will not protest. If we tell them too much, we don't know how they will react."

"Don't worry about it, Cynthia," said Jonathan. "The judge is only going to ask you yes or no questions. You won't have to give any graphic details about what happened to you. I have already done it. I know you can do it too, sis."

I was silent. It was all happening so fast. Thirty minutes ago we were all smiling and clapping and joyous for Jonathan's successful speech. Suddenly, within the last half hour, both Father and Mother had attacked me, along with Jonathan. All those old memories came flooding back to me again. I started to tremble. I wanted to scream for help. I felt like I was suffocating. I didn't have much time to think about it. Before I knew what was happening the car had pulled to the curb in front of a little bungalow in a much nicer part of town. When Jonathan got out of the car Janie and Marie came running down the front steps to see him. They were all over him with hugs and kisses.

"Sorry you two couldn't come to my graduation, but I do have a big surprise for you," he said as he pointed to the car.

"That's your cue, Cynthia," said Carolyn. "Now, get out of the car with a big smile, all happy and everything." She gave me a little nudge.

I took a deep breath and checked my lipstick in the mirror. I put on a big smile and stepped out of the limousine. As soon as they saw me, Janie and Marie can running down the tiny sidewalk, and fell into my arms.

"Oh, Cynthia," said Janie. "You are so beautiful. I'm so glad to see you." Marie was silent and a little shy.

"Marie," I said. "You do remember me, don't you?" It had been almost four years since she had seen me and she had been just a little girl, now she was just a shy young teenager.

She looked up at me with those shy little eyes, and with a babies voice said, "Yes, I always knew you would come. You are my princess who has come to rescue us." She stood perfectly still and held my hand waiting. She had been trained well by my father. I could just imagine him yelling at her, "Girlie, don't speak until you are spoken to, and don't move a muscle until I tell you." I remembered it well. I was sure it must be very fresh in her memory. She was in a sort of a state of shell shock.

"She's been like that for about a year, now," whispered Jonathan. "Just go along with her. Let's all get in the car."

We all piled into the car and I introduced the girls to Ms. Graham and Burl. Marie said, "Oh, you must be the queen and you must be her guard. Finally, you have come to rescue us. What took you so long?" She said it with such a matter of fact way and with such seriousness that I had to cry a little. What great horrors she must have suffered to make her escape into our old and worn fairy tale books of knights in shinning armor, of kings and queens, of fairy tale princesses, and, also of men in black and the dragons of bygone days. She was so composed and serious about it all that it added an eeriness to all that was happening.

"Don't worry, my little princess," I said. "You are safe now. Nothing bad is ever going to happen to you again." Both Jonathan and I were crying just a little trying to hold back the big tears we knew would come later. Marie was asleep just like a little child of six or seven years by the time we reached the edge of town and the Judge's house. We had to rouse her to bring her inside.

The judge had a little private talk with Carolyn in his study before we were all ushered in. We met the two social workers. The judge asked me certain questions to which I only had to answer yes or no, saying just enough to free the girls and not too much to embarrass or shame me. I signed certain papers along with Jonathan and Carolyn. We were gone in less than an hour. I never knew if it was all exactly legal. I was somewhat suspicious that money must have been involved. But I was sure that we were safe. We were free to return to New York. The girls would be in the custody of both Jonathan and me since we were of legal age and the closest living relatives. Carolyn was proof that proper shelter and food and education would be provided for the girls.

We flew back to New York on a little private plane that could land just a few miles from St. Alban's. Very little was said by anyone on that long return trip. I am sure that we all slept a little. I know the girls slept the whole way. We were all exhausted. Both Jonathan and I had an overwhelming sense of relief and disbelief. What if Father and Mother tried to get the girls back, we wondered?

We worried for nothing. They were found guilty of child neglect and sentenced to five years in the state penitentiary. We would be safe for a while. We didn't know if we would ever hear or see them again.

Chapter Twelve

A New Adjustment

We soon fell into a new pattern of living, and that was our first summer together. It was a fun summer. Jonathan started St. Alban's immediately just like I had done. He and I went together everyday, then to the store. Jonathan would work there in sales in the men's department. Carolyn and I continued to run the store. It was readily apparent that both the girls needed therapy, but we didn't call it that then. We just told them that we going to visit a friend and have some little chats. Janie progressed beautifully. She was fifteen and very pretty. She wasn't as mature as other girls her age, but she readily talked about her life at home. She always professed that she loved her father and mother, that they were just sick. She hoped that someday we could all be together again. Her ability to talk about her home life helped her put some of the horror behind her. Marie's recovery would take years. She was trapped in the mind of a nine-year-old girl. That was her age when I left home. Time for her had simply stopped. With me went her hope and her feeling of safety. She had not progressed since then. She had lost all hope when I left home. She had sent herself into a fantasy world of beauty and salvation to escape the horror of that house. I blamed myself for leaving her. No one ever thought to offer counseling to Jonathan or me. We were dysfunctional functional. We didn't know it then. It wasn't called that then. We had learned to bury the hurt and grief, the shame and the guilt. We were young adults and we had to act the part. But we had to be the saviors and the survivors. In order to save ourselves and Janie and Marie, we had had to fight for our lives and theirs, to put ourselves between danger and them. We had had to bury deep within our own beings the agony of being born to those two parents. We hoped that we could contain it there. He and I never talked of it.

I was so glad and relieved to have him and the girls safe with Carolyn and me. Our futures were bright and promising. I felt like a breath of fresh air and decency had descended upon us.

That was a glorious summer of 1972. Soon I would be graduating from St. Alban's. Jonathan would have four more years. The girls would be in a good private school with at-home tutoring. They were both behind in school. They had a lot of catching up to do. When the summer semester ended for Jonathan and I, Carolyn announced that she was taking the "family," as she now called us, to the coast for the last two weeks of summer. She had a beautiful beach house, and she hadn't been there in years. "Honestly, Cynthia, I was just afraid of going there and being alone. This is all a great help to me too, you know," she said. I was so grateful to her and I was beginning to really love her. In some ways I knew how Marie felt. Carolyn had been my Queen who rescued me, and she had given us a new life. In doing so she had also found a new life for herself.

It was a wonderful way to end that first summer together. The beach was warm and the water cold. None of us kids had ever been on a vacation. We had never seen the ocean, must less swam in it. The four of us acted just like kids for two weeks. We stayed in the water most of the time. We ate and swam and slept. In the warmth of the afternoons we would lay a little quilt outside on the big covered porch and the four of us would lie down together and snuggle and take little naps. I still remember the cool breeze from the overhead fan and the soothing sound of the wind chimes, and the waves pounding on the shore just a few yards away. I could always see Carolyn sitting in her summer frock in her favorite wicker chair just a few feet away. She would look over at us and smile. It made me feel safe.

Too soon it was all over. My last semester in college, I had to take eighteen hours in order to graduate by Christmas. It was a grueling schedule. I was at the store less and less in order to keep up with my studies. Jonathan was spending more and more time with Carolyn at the store. His first semester at St. Alban's was fairly easy for him. If he had any hard studying to do, he didn't mind staying up most of the night. He seemed to have boundless energies. He made friends very easily at school and at the store. All the girls were crazy to date him, but his dates were few and far between. He didn't seem to mind. Carolyn helped him pick those special times, such as a homecoming dance or winter formal. He never had trouble finding a date.

The first few weeks for Janie and Marie at their new school, Thornwall School for Girls, wasn't as difficult as we could have imagined. Janie's adjustment was a lot easier than Marie's. Janie immediately became one of the best students, but she was a little shy with the other girls. Carolyn and I decided that a complete makeover was necessary to help her fit in a little better. One Saturday Albert drove her to the store. Carolyn and I treated her like a little queen. Our first visit was to the hair salon. Her long hair was cut in a new and more stylish look, the mod look she called it. Both Carolyn and I held our breath while all that beautiful hair was cut and we watched it fall to the floor. Janie didn't mind at all. She suggested some "highlight." All the other girls at school seemed to have something a little different from each other, and so we agreed. Her brownish long hair was now a light brown with some blond highlights cut in a short bob with a few wispy bangs.

Our next stop was the "Teen" department. She needed everything from underwear to socks to pajamas, play clothes, casual clothes, and a few dresses. Everything that she picked was in the best of taste and of the latest style. She looked good in everything and very mature for a girl of fifteen. All the boys were giving her the eye, the once over.

"Janie," I said, "you know, of course, that all the boys and some of the men in this store are giving you the eye."

"Oh sure," she said.

"Do you know what that means?" I asked.

"Oh, yes, they all want to do me," she replied. "But, sis, you don't have anything to worry about. Remember that I went to the same school as you. I know all about the facts of life. Believe me, I am not going to let any boy ruin my life. Don't worry, boys and sex and things like romance are the last things on my mind. I will never let anyone dominate me. That's what men do to women. They bend them, change them, break their spirit, and make them their slaves. That is not what I want. I would rather be alone. But I have ambitions, and I am smart. I intend to make good use of the discipline you and Carolyn are offering me, but I am going to throw myself into my studies and education. I will be completely independent and never dependent on anyone ever again, especially a man. Oh, I guess it would be fun to get dressed up in some of these fine clothes and go on a date every now and them, like to Homecoming dance, or prom or something special like that. Cynthia, I will probably never marry. I don't see children in my future. I have to be the only one controlling me. I have great ambitions to be somebody special, to offer something to the world of kindness and refinement, and to be some creative, contributing person to make the world a better place. I'm not sure what that will be at this time. But, I intend to make good use of all the tools and opportunities that you and Carolyn are making available to me. I know that I will meet the right people to break the glass ceiling. It may be a man's world now, but, times are changing, and I am not going to be held back by anyone, man or woman, or a child. Do you think that is mean?"

"No, I don't think that is mean," I said. "I think that is very courageous. Don't let anybody ever take away from you anything that you want. Work as hard as you can, but don't underestimate the importance of a best friend.

Sometimes, a girl needs a best friend to talk to, to turn to when no one else will do. We don't have a father and mother anymore. I guess we haven't for many years. It is sad that we don't have a good mother and father to turn to, to grow old with, to help us make our way. Janie, Carolyn and I are here for you anytime. All you have to do is ask. I'm sorry, that is the best I can do. I will always be your sister and you will always be mine. You can always depend on me. I may have to depend on you. In many ways, you are already more mature than I am. But do enjoy these teenage years. They don't last long. Always remember to add a little fun."

We gave each other a little hug right there in the middle of the store. Carolyn had been standing a few feet away. She turned towards us and we all gave each other a hug. Everyone in the store seemed warm after that. They knew we were making our own family and they respected our struggle to survive.

Marie's situation was somewhat different. It became painfully clear that at-home schooling was the only answer for her at this time. She had not ventured too far from that mind of a nine-year-old. She was well into her twelfth year. Girls her age were all into makeup, hair, clothes, boys, and dying to go to parties and wear the clothes of their older sisters. Carolyn and I also gave the same treat to Marie as we had to Janie. Marie could not choose anything for herself. She kept wondering into the children's department and wanted to try on frilly little dresses with lace and ruffles. We finally gave in and found one that barely fit, but the seamstress seemed to understand and assured us that she could make it fit for a while anyway. Carolyn and I would let her wear it at home, and would gradually encourage her to wear the clothes that we choose for her. We were not going to let her look ridiculous outside of home. As that fall ran fast towards Christmas she became more and more interested in school. She was making very good marks. She was gradually coming out of herself and back into reality. We could only make her feel safe on her own terms. With a little kindness and a lot of patience, both Carolyn and I spent a lot of time with her and we could see her start to blossom into a beautiful young girl.

Carolyn suggested that we have little parties for her and Janie. We invited their schoolmates and some of the children of the people who worked at the store. Slowly, but surely, they both progressed.

By Christmas excitement was running high. Business at the store was booming. Carolyn was working full time and overtime again. She was there from morning to night, and then she gladly left things to me when school was over. She looked forward to going home to be with the girls. She went home several times a day as did Jonathan and I to check on Marie. And one of us was always there when Janie came in from school. She was always full of gossip of what was going on there. Soon we were turning her tales into little dramas and at night we didn't have to watch television. We entertained ourselves. We studied and we enjoyed the peaceful safeness of our new home.

I managed to graduate at the top of my class. I received the Graham Achievement in Excellence Award, a scholarship for continuing my education, but I also received the St. Alban's award of "Community Involvement." It was the last award that really got my picture in the local paper. I was listed in that year's Who's Who of top college graduates. The newspapers picked up the picture and the commentary ran across the country. I didn't think anything of it then, but after the first of the year a part of my past was going to catch up to me. It was going to be someone that I had never expected to hear from again.

Chapter Thirteen
Higher Education

Carolyn offered me a job at the store as head buyer, but she understood when I told her that I wanted to use my Graham scholarship to get my MBA, Master's of Business Administration. The University of Chicago was the closest and the best university for those studies, and I was determined to continue learning more and more about computers. I knew they were going to be the wave of the future. I promised her that I would come home as often as I could, now that I had someplace to come home to. I received overwhelming support from her, Jonathan, and Janie. They were all overjoyed for me, but sad that the summer and fall and Christmas had all gone too fast. That was the only time we had to try and make up for almost four lost years. Marie was a little more apprehensive. She didn't want me to go. She was adamant about it. I knew the abandonment feeling that she surely was having. I spent most of the last week spending everyday with her. We went to the movies, shopping, and to what we called "The big ladies lunch." We would get very dressed and take the train into New York City, have lunch at the Palace Hotel, which was the grandest hotel in those days. Then we would take in a play. She would be asleep on the train on the way home. These were special days for her and I have never forgotten them. By the time I was packing to go to Chicago, she even wanted to help me. That last night was fun for us.

After dinner we all got into our nightgowns or pajamas, even Carolyn, and proceeded to pack all my bags. We were sort of having a slumber party.

After awhile Hilda came in with a little cake and ice cream, which we devoured. We were having such a good time, until the phone rang. I can still hear Hilda's voice. As she answered the phone she knew it must be wrong. She was always having premonitions like that.

"Miss Cynthia," she said. "It's a man calling for you. Don't take it, Miss. I have a bad feeling about it. They won't say who's calling."

"Don't be ridiculous, Hilda," I said. "I haven't the slightest idea who it could be. Hello," I said.

"Is this Cynthia Thomas?" some man asked.

"Yes, it is," I said gaily. "Who's calling?"

"Here, I got her on the phone," I heard the voice say.

Another man's voice said, "Cynthia, is this Cynthia Thomas?"

"Yes, this is she," I replied. "Who is this, please?"

"Are you so high and mighty now, girlie, that you don't even recognize your old man's voice?" It was my father. "Did you think I couldn't find you? We do have newspapers in prison you know." I was silent. I couldn't say a word. Carolyn could see the fearful expression on my face. I waited to answer until she picked up the phone in her room. He said, "When I get out of here I am going to kill you. Ha! Ha! Ha!" He was laughing himself silly. Carolyn was signaling me to continue to keep him talking so that he would identify himself further.

"Father," I said." "Is that you?"

"Yes, it's me, girlie. And I meant every word I just said," he answered.

"Hello, hello," pretended Carolyn. She was acting like she had just answered the phone herself. "Who's calling, please?"

Without thinking he said, "Who the hell do you think it is, you old bitch? This is Mr. Arthur Thomas, father of Cynthia, Jonathan, Janie, and Marie, those children you stole from me. And I guess I have the privilege of speaking to the kidnapper herself, the famous philanthropic Ms. Graham. Guess what, Granny. I gonna kill you, too, when I get out of here."

Carolyn hung up the phone and motioned for me to do the same. All the kids wanted to know who it was. We told them that is was nobody, just a wrong number. We ushered them off to bed. As soon as they were all settled, Carolyn called me into her room.

"Don't worry, my dear," she said. "I still have a few tricks up these old sleeves of mine." She pulled out the little drawer of her nightstand. There was the same little tape recorder that she had used to tape my first visit to the house. She played the phone conversation back. She had captured most of it on tape. "I think we have enough to add about ten years to his sentence," she said. "Remember, I still have connections. No one threatens my life and the lives of those I love."

"I hope not," I said trembling.

"Don't worry, my dear," she said. "I can fix everything. But I may have to file adoption papers for all of you, especially Janie and Marie."

"Do whatever you think best," I said with clenched teeth. We called in Jonathan. It was decided. Ms. Graham would adopt Janie and Marie. It would be for their protection.

By the time Easter 1973 arrived, Father's sentence had five years added to it for threatening the lives of Carolyn and I. The adoption was completed the very next day for Janie and Marie. I was grateful to Carolyn, but I felt like I was losing a little part of Janie and Marie. I was relieved to know that they would now be safer. Something about the adoption worried me. Both Jonathan and I had to give our consent. We never thought that we had a chance to adopt them. It was apparent that even though we were of adult age, that we were still dependent on Carolyn for everything. I had trusted her this far. I would have to trust her a little further.

I was enjoying the University of Chicago. Carolyn had helped me get a job as an assistant buyer at one of the biggest department stores there, Bennington's Department Store. In reality it was just an internship. I worked for the assistant buyer of women's clothes, Mrs. Howard. She was just another Mrs. Primrose. We really didn't click.

Bennington's had chains across the country and owned several other stores under different names. Carolyn thought that I had a future in retail. I wasn't that sure. I was sure that she wanted me to get my MBA as quickly as possible and return to St. Alban's to manage Grahams. That was her dream for me. I wasn't sure that it was my dream for me. It worried me that she may want me to repay so many debts of help. I started to doubt all that she had done for me. Was this some game she was playing with us? I had never met anyone like her. Would a day come when she would "drop the other shoe"? I finally decided that I was just having an anxiety attack or just being paranoid. Everyone was always talking about having a psychological condition. It sounded like an every day occurance. I vowed that I would stop having those kind of uncertain thoughts, and to be more confident, more assertive.

But with every passing day I began to reflect on all that happened to my family and the long lasting affects that must be influencing my life. I always knew Jonathan and Marie and Janie had been affected. I had never really stopped to think about myself. I always thought that I had survived intact, that I had escaped unscathed by being smart. My educational opportunities had allowed me to escape, but I was still scared. I had never healed. I worried about my siblings. I knew Janie and Marie were in therapy once a week. I wondered about Jonathan. He seemed to be fine. He was having those same euphoric feelings that I had been having since escaping from home. But would a day come for him like I was having now, the flashbacks of the beatings, the feelings of abandonment by mother, and now the nightmares. They were becoming more regular, almost every night. With the move to Chicago, I didn't have Carolyn and my siblings and the advantage of working at the store that I really loved. I was alone. I had lost my support group, Carolyn and my siblings. Living in this big city was very different than my small southern hometown, and certainly different from St. Alban's. Now I had time. Carolyn had thought that I would enjoy this time to myself. It was supposed to be a time to relax and to study and to get more experience in the retail business. But it was too much time to think about the past. I felt like I was falling apart.

I started to fill my every waking hour with some activity. If I were tired of studying, I would jog around the university. I started staying later and later at Bennington's. I seriously started thinking about continuing school through the summer, but I would make a trip home first then come back to Chicago. By the end of the spring semester, my grades had dropped to all B's; I didn't have one A. My counselor at school thought that I was taking on too much, and should take the summer off. I vowed to keep remembering my spirit by believing in my dreams and myself, and my dreams for my brother and sisters.

I applied for summer school anyway. I was really a wreck. I had let my appearance go to the dogs. I only had two more weeks of school. I took a Saturday off from work. I called in sick. I felt so guilty about lying, but I needed time to get myself together. I made a beauty appointment and had my hair cut and restyled. I did some clothes shopping. I had a facial and a manicure and a pedicure at a little shop right across the street from Bennington's. I felt like a little sleuth slipping in and out of there. I hoped no one from the store saw me. I was supposed to be sick. I slept all day Sunday. By Monday morning I felt much better.

I don't remember much about that Monday. I know that I had classes in the morning and that I went to work around 1:00 P.M. As soon as I entered the office I noticed that my boss was talking to a new man. As I got closer and closer, I could see more clearly through the glass door of our office. I recognized him from the back. I started to tremble. A hot flash sizzled through my body. I knew that my hair must have been standing on end. I stopped in the middle of the aisle.

"Is everything all right, Ms. Thomas?" asked our little secretary, Miss Charlotte.

"I'm not sure, Charlotte," I said. I started to turn around and never come back to the store again. As I did so I heard my name called.

"Oh, Cynthia," called my boss, Mrs. Howard. "Could you come in for just a moment before you go down to the floor?" I was caught. I felt trapped. But what could I do?

I slowly turned around, swallowed hard, took a deep breath and walked with sheer determination into our office. "Oh, Cynthia, I am so glad you are here," said Mrs. Howard. I knew she was a two-faced bitch and she was probably trying to spring some trouble on me. She was never glad to see me. I was scared to death, but I had to take it. "Cynthia, I would like you to meet our new store manager, Mr. Dan Callahan." He turned slowly and faced me. He let that come-and-get-me smile spread across his face. He had already known that I was working there. I was sure that Mrs. Howard had mentioned my name, or that somehow he just knew. He had always been like that, always a step ahead of you. I knew I was going to faint. I was completely caught off guard. As I reached out to shake his hand my legs just buckled and I could feel all the blood drain from my head. I was breathless. The last thing I remember before I hit the floor was being caught by Dan. I just fell into his arms.

When I awoke, I had a cold cloth on my forehead. And I had been laid out on the little sofa in our office. "What happened?" I asked as I sat up.

To my surprise they had just left me there, alone. I felt so stupid and ashamed. Mrs. Howard probably thought something was really wrong with me, like maybe I was pregnant or something. In the movies, all the young pregnant women fainted sooner or later, and some gallant man, usually their husband, would catch them in their arms and be all concerned and worried. I had been left alone with a cold cloth. I thought that it was very rude of them to just leave me. Then I remembered. *Oh my God. Thank goodness they left,* I thought to myself. *It was Dan Callahan who caught me, and now, he is also my boss. He is the store manager.* The whole scene replayed itself in my head. I felt worse than ever. I was really trapped, now. I needed this job. Carolyn had gone to a lot of trouble to get it for me.

As I got up to leave, Mrs. Howard came in and said, "Cynthia, I see you are feeling better. You can go on down to the floor. We are a little short-handed today, and the women's department is very busy. By the way, why did you faint? You're not in any trouble or anything. Are you?"

I was so embarrassed. I could have guessed she would ask. "Of course not, Mrs. Howard," I said sternly. "And, by the way, I am not that sort of girl, anyway."

"Well, of course, dear, if you say so. If there is anything you want to tell me or talk about with me, you know my door is always open to you," she said with sugarcoated honey words that I didn't believe for one minute.

"Thanks, I'll keep that in mind," I said as sarcastically as I could. I left our little office immediately. I went to the ladies room and washed my face with cold water and had a soft drink. I reapplied my makeup. It was a little too heavy, but I couldn't stall any longer. I had to get to work. I knew Dan would be strolling along any minute.

I spent about two hours in the department, and then I took a break. As I was walking down the main aisle, naturally, with my luck, I ran into Dan. Literally I ran right into him. I had stopped to look at some sale sweaters that were so pretty. When I turned around, I almost knocked him down. He caught me by the arms. He had positioned himself directly behind me.

"Oh, I'm sorry, Cynthia," he said so sweetly. "I didn't see you there."

"Of course you saw me there. That's why you made me run into you," I said as I jerked myself free. I just stood there red faced and furious.

"Oh honey, I don't mind at all," he laughed. "Although it does seem like you are making a habit of it today. But, please, be my guest. Run into me anytime. How about tonight?" We were making a scene. People were beginning to look.

"Thanks, but no thanks, Mr. Callahan," I said. "I am sorry. It won't happen again. You can be assured of that."

I walked off, just to hear him laugh as he was talking to the buyer of men's furnishings. I looked back. I was so sure they were sharing a little off-color joke about me. I went to the employee lounge. I needed a soft drink. *What I really need is a good shot of whisky*, I thought. I hadn't thought about drinking alcohol in years. Not since Dan had left town and I had moved in with Carolyn. And now, here he was. I had made a fool out of myself once, and then he purposely ran into me, and now I was thinking of drinking. How was all of this happening in one day. I couldn't wait to punch the clock and go home. I needed to talk to Carolyn. I had to ask her what to do.

As I rummaged through my purse for change, I heard a voice from behind me. It was Dan. "Need a quarter for the machine, Cyn," he asked in a sort of low-down voice, slinky and inviting, as if I was still a nothing and didn't even have a quarter for the machine, and he was still this big, strong, handsome man that could just sweep me off his feet.

"No, thank you," I said. "I can manage."

"Yes," he said as he eyed me up and down unashamedly. "I can see you have managed very well for yourself. You are looking better than I remember. But my memory may need some refreshing. How about it, Cyn, want to refresh my memory tonight. Come on, Cyn, it will be like old times."

"You and I had better step outside right now, or I swear I am going to slap your face and start screaming," I said.

"Okay, okay," he said. "You know I'll go wherever you want me to and do whatever you want me to do." All I could manage to do was to roll my eyes and give him the meanest look possible.

"Come with me," I said.

"Oh, good, my car is parked just outside," he said. "Maybe you want to get in the back seat for a few minutes." He was being insufferable and people were overhearing him.

"No," I said loudly. "I don't want to get in the back seat of your car, and I don't want to go out with you. But I am taking you outside to get a few more things straight with you."

We walked outside and around the corner of the store. As soon as we stopped, I turned and slapped his face. "Hey, hey, baby, you still like the rough stuff, huh?" he asked. He caught me by my arms and pulled me to him and kissed me roughly on the mouth. "Don't fight it, Cyn, my memory is coming back now. Come on baby don't fight it." His hands slid down my back and he was trying to pull up my skirt. I fought him off with a right punch to the eye. By now he wasn't playing anymore. He was enraged. He was furious. He lunged at me, and I kicked him square in his nuts as I had once done to father. As I ran to get away, I heard him moan and fall to one knee. "Oh, come on, Cyn, I know you want it." He had absolutely no pride, no shame. He had grown bolder and had become more reckless.

I was determined to finish my shift. I returned to the floor a little flustered, but managed to ring up a few sales before the store closed at 6:00 P.M. About 5:50 P.M. the phone in my department rang, and another girl answered it. She said, "Oh, Cynthia, it's for you. It's Mr. Callahan." It sounded like she was singing it across the whole department. Her voice was booming in my ear.

"Tell him that I have already left the store and gone home early," I said softly.

"Oh, honey, he won't believe me. He's calling from right across the floor. If you look around the corner of that column you can even see him over there smoking his cigar and hanging on the phone," she said a little too hurriedly. As she handed me the phone, she gave me a little sassy look as she smacked her gum. She had the nerve to say to me, "Careful, hon. He's a real tiger, you know."

The situation was getting worse by the minute. I wanted to fly out of that store, but I still had to count the money and bring it upstairs. I knew Mrs. Howard would be waiting.

"Yes," I said. "I thought I made myself perfectly clear this afternoon."

"Well, yes, you did," he said. "I guess you did try, but unless you want to be charged with bodily assault, you will get your little ass to the back of the store and meet me at my car. We have some talking to do." He had said this as a threat. I was silent. Then he softened his tone. "Oh, listen, Cynthia, I'm sorry everything went all wrong for us, and I don't want to interfere with whatever you are doing here. And I am sorry for the way I handled myself today. I behaved badly. I was a bad little boy. I apologize. Now, does that help?"

"Well what do you want?" I said.

"I want to take you to the best restaurant in Chicago," he answered. "I want us to have a great meal together, have some champagne, a few drinks. I want to make it up to you. I feel bad about everything. Can't you give a guy a chance to make it right, just a little."

He was practically begging me, and he was perfectly purring over the phone with that oh-so-smooth voice of his. He was a real charmer. What could I do? Now I felt bad for him. It had been so long since I had been anywhere nice. I was tired and hungry and dying for a drink.

"I'm not going to let you off the phone, until you let me make it up to you," he said confidently.

"Okay," I said. "But know this, Mr. Dan Callahan. This is business and only business. You behaved badly today. And, if you don't want a sexual discrimination suit filed against you and this store, you had better keep you hands to yourself and no sexual overtures."

"Oh, sure thing, hon. Great. You can depend on me," he said happy as a schoolboy. He hung up the phone. I knew that from his response that he still didn't understand. But I had to make him understand. I didn't have any choice. I could tell he was just going to get worse. I had to have this dinner with him to put him in his place once and for all.

I met him at the back of the store. I didn't think anyone saw me. It reminded me of that time almost four years earlier when I had met him in the back of Grahams in just exactly the same way. It looked sneaky, like we were trying to hide something. I knew he was doing it on purpose, just hoping someone would see me getting into his car in the dark.

"I'm glad you could make it, Cyn," he said.

"Look Dan. First of all my name is Cynthia Thomas, not Cyn. You can call me Miss Thomas like you should. You are the boss and you owe me that courtesy."

"Okay, good, I got it," he said as he pulled away from the curb squealing his tires just like a pissed-off teenage boy. His face was red. He was already mad and this wasn't going well at all. We drove silently to the restaurant.

Once we were seated he ordered a double Scotch and water. He ordered the same for me without even asking. As usual, he was trying to be the commander. He lit a fresh cigar, which he knew I hated. He was quiet until the drinks came. He told the waiter to wait. He drank the first one down in one gulp. "Keeping them coming. I have a thirst tonight," he said. The waiter returned with another. As Dan settled into his second drink and had time to smoke on his cigar, he seemed to relax just a little. He looked up at me with a sheepish grin on his face and said, "Cynthia, I want to tell you a story, about what I have been through these last years."

I said nothing, but just looked at him thoughtfully. He started, "When I was forced to divorce your stepmother."

I interrupted, "Oh, she is not my stepmother."

"But didn't she adopt all of you, you and your brother and sisters?" he asked. I knew he was searching for information.

"No, not at all," I said. I didn't know how he knew about the adoptions, but he was giving himself away. He had been doing some research, maybe even hired a private detective.

"Well, anyway, after the divorce," he said, "I left with a pot full of money. I thought I had it made, but, I guess I blew it, so to speak." He laughed. "I wanted you to run away with me and take a trip around the world. I wanted to show everyone that I had won me a little prize like you and I wanted to show you off all over the place. You know I practically knocked down the doors to your sorority house that night. Pretty soon after that, two police-men escorted me out of town. Well, I thought that was okay. I was loaded with money. I went around the world alone, but I wasn't alone, if you get my drift. I spend money lavishly. I finally landed in Chicago. I even made some land deals with Dennis Tripp. You know the Tripps of New York. Well, everything they touch turns to gold, so I invested everything I had. I doubled my money in six months. I invested heavily in real estate here in downtown Chicago. I made it big. I own several office buildings and one Hotel where I maintain the suite on the top floor. I'm only working at Bennington's to have something to do. Anyway, everyone knows they can catch me there, and I don't like having to maintain a secretary or an office. I can do that at the store."

"You mean, Dan, that you maintain your own private business at the store?" I said.

"Sure, as long as I do my little duties there, no one needs to know, and I don't think anyone would care if they found out," he said. "So, you see, it was quite by accident that I found you there. It must have just been fate that we would see each other again. I always hoped we would. As long as you were in St. Alban's I had no chance of seeing you. Carolyn had you ensconced there."

"But you candidly admit that you haven't been lacking for company," I asked. "So, you couldn't have been pining away all these years over little just me."

"Hey, if you haven't noticed it, Cynthia Thomas, I am a man, and men have needs."

"Yes, I know you are a man and men say they have needs. What has it been, Dan, boys, women, or both?" I said rather sarcastically. "Not that I care, you understand."

"Oh, Cynthia, you always did read me like a book," he said. "But you can't blame me can you? I mean I am sure you have been seeing other men."

"No, not really. I have been too busy with school and...and other things," I said. I didn't want to give him any more information than I had too.

"Cynthia, what I am trying to say to you is the truth. I am not trying to hide anything. It is true. I do like some kinky stuff. But the others, I mean I never loved them," he said.

"Love?" I asked. "When did love ever have anything to do with you and me?"

"Cynthia, it is what I call love. I have never had a woman who I felt real-ly understood me. But I knew you did. I could feel it in the way you always responded to me."

"That was just overwhelming passion," I said. "Overwhelming passion going on between a pretty college coed and a man obsessed with sex and approaching middle age. That's not love, Dan."

"Well, it was something. I wanted it to be something. I tried to take you away with me for Christ's sake. I didn't ask any other girl to go with me," he replied as if he were pleading a court case.

"Let's just order, okay?" I asked.

"By all means," he said. He ordered more drinks.

We didn't say very much throughout dinner, but he kept looking up at me and smiling.

"What are you doing?" I said.

"I was just enjoying looking at you. You are so beautiful, and I made you laugh. You are so beautiful when you laugh, Cynthia," he said. "I have never forgotten how beautiful and how smart you are." He was really laying it on thick. And I was already one drink ahead of myself. "Admit it," he said. "You are having a good time."

"Well, as long as you're nice," I said. "I guess so."

"Someday I want you to say that you enjoy being with me as if you really meant it," he said softly. "You know I have never gotten over you. I think I must have been in love with you from the start. I remember how damn good you were in bed."

"See there, Dan," I said. "That is just exactly what I wanted to talk to you about. You equate having a damn good lay in bed with love."

"Well," he said. "I love a damn good lay in bed, and when I find one I want to love it and hang on to it, and take care of it as long as it may last. That's not love?"

"Dan, I don't think you get the real picture here. Now, I am going to say what I came here to say, and then I am going home. First, I am not in love with you, and I never have been in love with you. Secondly, I am never going to be in love with you." He ordered more drinks. "Thirdly, I am in Chicago to get my MBA and more experience in retail and, by the way, we need some computers at the store. We need to start with this thing at the beginning. Computers are going to revolutionize the way we and everyone else does everything, even the way we live and socialize. That brings me to the store and you. I don't intend to have a repeat scandal like before. You have to respect my position. And I will respect your distance from me. Our relationship has to be only on the professional level, or I promise you I will cause you more trouble than you can handle. I need this job, and I am determined to see it through and to make some needed changes around the store. It is in dire need of being updated, and I have experience in that. I am the one who is going to do. It is going to be my final thesis. You can challenge me, or you can be part of the winning team. But remember, this is strictly business and professional. No more funny stuff like today."

"Wow, what a woman you have become," he said. He sat back in his chair and looked at me as if for the very first time. He was admiring me. He smiled. "Well, I guess I really messed up this time. I lost this deal, and I was hoping we could make up and start over," he finally said.

"No, we can't ever go back," I said a little too sadly. "I mean that we must maintain this as strictly business and on a professional level," I repeated.

"Is that really all, Cynthia? Is there no hope for me at all?" he asked.

I stood and he helped me with my coat. "No, Dan, no chance at all," I said.

"Well, could we just consider this round one, which has been won by you?" he asked.

"No, Dan, this is no contest. I laid my conditions out on the table, plain and clear."

"Well, let me make myself clear, Cynthia," he said as he took my hand. "You have grown up a lot. You are a real woman who could be on her way up the corporate ladder. You have a lot of smarts up there in that pretty little head of yours, and you are abreast of the needs of the time. I know that you and I can make a lot of positive changes in the store and we will. We will make that dream come true for you and you can make it a thesis. Hell, for all I care you can write a book about it. But you have to know one thing. I want you. I have always wanted you. I have never wanted another woman as badly as I want you this very minute." He took a rose out of the little vase. He wrapped his handkerchief around it and presented it to me. "Let this be the first of many tokens of my love for you," he said with a little bow. "Now, let me show you my penthouse. It is just upstairs. This is my hotel that I told you about."

"Dan, don't you ever stop?" I asked. "You have got to take me seriously. I am going home. Thanks for the lovely meal. We will just have to see how things go at the store tomorrow."

"Well, then let my driver take you home," he said.

"Okay, I guess that would be proper," I said.

He walked me arm and arm to the front of the hotel. His driver was waiting there for him. He opened the door for me and I got in. Then he started to get in, but I stopped him.

"Oh, no," I said. "Your driver is taking me home. You are already home. Remember, Dan, you live here." I closed the door and locked it and told the driver to pull away.

It had been an exhausting day and night, but I had to admit to myself that the dinner had been fun. We had jostled with words back and forth all night. But I believed that I had gotten my point across and he had agreed to cooperate and help me. He hadn't changed very much I said to myself. He was still as handsome as ever. Four years had even made him more attractive. He was graying just a little at the temples. He still had a head full of golden blond hair, and I guessed that he always would. He looked more distinguished. Any woman would be happy to have him, and I was sure he could pick and choose. I didn't understand fully the part about his enjoying other men. I had not been taught about the bisexual concept in school. It wasn't a topic of everyday conversation. I would have to find out more about that. But he had almost admitted it. He was a devil, and I knew it, and I knew that the devil meant temptation. I giggled a little to myself. It had been a long time since any man had made a play for me. I couldn't even remember that far back. I was a little proud about the way he said that he wanted me. I told myself to put that entire sort of thought out of my mind.

I awoke at 3:00 A.M. I came out of a deep sleep of a dream about being with Dan. We had been naked and warm in a big bed and he was telling me that he loved me and no other. But the phone was ringing and I guessed that was what had awakened me. "Hello," I said a little sleepy.

"Cynthia, it's me, Carolyn," she said. I felt instantly guilty, guilty for something that I hadn't even done and had no intention of doing, guilty for having a dream in my sleep.

"Oh, Carolyn," I said. "Is everything all right?"

"No, dear, I am afraid I have bad news for you. Your father is dying. The prison called here for you. They want you to come down there immediately. I have arranged your air fare from Chicago. You will have to change plans in Atlanta, and I shall be there to meet you dear. I don't want you to go through this alone. You have been through enough already. I insist. I will be waiting for you at your gate."

"Thank you, Carolyn. Thank you for everything. I will see you there," I said.

"Okay, dear. Don't worry. Everything is going to be taken are of, and everything will be all right. Good bye now." She hung up the phone and so did I.

I knew that I wouldn't sleep any more that night. I was already hung over from all the drinks with Dan. Then it hit me. This poor woman, poor, kind Carolyn, always thinking of all the others and me, she was the very woman with whom I had just had dinner with her ex-husband. And he had been flirting with me all night. I had resisted his temptations, but I had enjoyed it. Guilt, guilt, guilt. I was such a bad girl. I felt so guilty. I felt guilty for leaving home and my little siblings so long ago. I felt guilty for Carolyn always having to help me and being my friend. She really had to be a mother to me. I felt guilty for Dan being in such longing for me. I knew that it was my entire fault. My father had told me that all my young life. Everything would be my fault, that I was a slut and just no good, that I was a home wrecker. It seemed like all he had said was coming true, and I hated him even more for it.

Chapter Fourteen

Out in Real Life

I was so glad to see Carolyn at my gate in the Atlanta airport that I broke down crying. I wasn't as collected as I thought I would be. It has been an intense time for me. The combination of school, fighting off Dan, the job, and now my father's death was so overwhelming that I felt seriously ill, and I must have looked it.

"Cynthia, darling child, everything is going to be all right," said Carolyn. I held on to her as she led me to our connecting gate. They allowed us to board first since we were first class passengers and I was obviously not well. I felt like I was on the edge of a nervous breakdown. "Here, Cynthia. I want you to take one of my little pills. It's nothing heavy and it won't knock you out. It will just help you calm yourself. Believe me, it will help you feel better." I took one pill and ten minutes later I was asleep. I slept all the way home. When we landed, the driver and car that Carolyn had arranged took us directly to the prison. It was another two-hour drive. I was exhausted and I know that Carolyn must have been feeling the wear and tear of the trip by now herself. But she would not leave me.

When we entered the prison gates I told them who I was and why I was there. "We have been expecting you, Miss Thomas," said the guard at the gate. "Please sign in here, then proceed to the main administration building." Another guard there escorted us to the prison hospital. I had never been inside a prison before, and I was sure Carolyn hadn't been either. I was a dreary, dirty, and scary place. Everything was pealing of paint. I was sorry that Carolyn had to go through this and I felt guilty for her having to be there with me. I certainly didn't deserve her.

We entered the hospital and the nurse showed me to my father's bedside. He was in a ward of about sixty other beds. All of them were filled with dying or sick prisoners; each one was handcuffed to the bed with only one hand free. I stood by the bedside of my father and Carolyn stood beside me. I insisted on that. The nurse pulled a dingy little curtain around the bed for a little privacy, not that I cared.

"Mr. Thomas, your daughter is here to see you," said the nurse as she tried to rouse him. He opened his eyes and looked at me. For a second I think he was dazed. Some minutes passed before he was somewhat clear headed. Those minutes seemed like hours, but the time helped me turn into an anchor of steel. I felt stiff and unsmiling, cold and hard.

"Cynthia, you really came," he said.

"Yes," I said. "The prison said that I had to."

"Did they tell you I was dying?" he asked hoarsely.

"Yes," I said coldly.

"Cynthia, I am glad you made it. I have been hanging on waiting for you to get here," he said with a heavy breath. His breathing was slow and laborious. I knew that he didn't have much time left. I didn't answer him. I was silent.

"Cynthia, please tell me something. Do you hate me?" he asked. I could tell Carolyn was startled. I didn't move. I let the question sink in and it was minutes before I answered him. He closed his eyes.

Finally, I said, "Yes, I hate you."

He opened his eyes and said, "I know that I have no right to ask you this, but I will. Please, don't hate me. I know that you have every right to do so. But as you can see I am an old, sick man, lying here dying. Have you no compassion even though I am your father?"

"You are only my father because of one mistaken night of passion with mother," I said. "I know you never wanted me. I wasn't planned, and it was no joy when Mother had me. There couldn't have been, or the two of you would have loved me and you didn't. You never did, and I don't believe you do now."

"Maybe, I don't deserve to hear my oldest daughter, my first child tell me that she loves me, but, maybe, you could say you forgive me," he said slowly. His eyes were only half open.

"No, I will never say that to you," I said loudly. Carolyn caught me by my arm to calm me. "I haven't loved you since I was a very little girl and I did everything to try and please you, and for that you beat me," I said. "I don't love you, you bastard. I hate you. And I hate Mother for conspiring with you. And, I will never forgive you, so don't wait for me, go ahead and die. I don't care."

"Cynthia, if you can't give me a little peace of mind before I die, if you can offer no kindness from your heart, then, please, just let me tell you this," he said softly. "Maybe, it will make a difference in your life. You are right. You weren't planned. In fact, you were an accident of passion. Your mother and I had to get married because of you. She was pregnant before we got married. But Cynthia, we tried to have a family. I remember, in the beginning when we only had a two-room apartment, we tried to be happy. We tried to think that our future would be bright. Life had sort of jump-started us before we were ready. When you were born, you were so beautiful, so small and helpless. I guess your mother and I were always a little ashamed of ourselves for what we had done. We didn't mean to pass that shame on to you. We tried to protect you. We tried to warn you. We tried to teach you better than what we had done. We didn't want that for you. So, we were overly strict with you. That was only because I was always so afraid that you would make the same mistakes that we had. We knew that you were growing in to a real beauty of a young girl and you were so smart and had such a bright future ahead of you. Cynthia, we were jealous of your chance at life. We had thrown our chances away with one night of passion. We blamed you for that. We were wrong. I guess everything we did was wrong from the day we conceived you. Everyday of our lives just seemed to get worse, and they did. We thought we had a happy little home for a while. When Jonathan was born, I was so proud of him because he was a boy, our first son. I thought that because he was a boy he would do better than me. I wasn't as hard on him as I must have been on you. I thought it would be easier to train him to be a man, but I didn't know how to train you to protect yourself from men who I knew would certainly prowl you for sex. I knew that Jonathan would always be able to take care of himself. I wasn't sure about that for you. So your mother and I tried for another boy. We thought with two brothers you might be okay. But we failed and had two more girls. I won't lie about that now. We were disappointed that Janie and Marie were born girls and not boys. I guess we never recovered from that and we must have let them know our disappointment in so many ways. There is only one thing that I can do now, Cynthia, to try and help you, and that is to say that I love you now. I am glad you were born. I am glad that all of my children were born. And I am sorry for all the many ways that I have harmed you." He stopped talking. He closed his eyes and his breathing was very slow. He reached for my hand and held it as tight as he could. I pulled back in alarm and fear. I was trembling with rage. He opened his eyes and said, "Well, Cynthia, is there nothing you can say to your old pop?"

"Yes, there is something that I can say," I said. I leaned over the bed and talked softly into his ear so that Carolyn could not hear me. "I am glad you are dying. I plan on celebrating on a grand scale when you do die, hopefully, tonight. I have a big man waiting for me back in Chicago and we are going to celebrate by having wild and kinky sex and drink several bottles of French champagne, and I will never think of you again. You will not have a burial place. There will be no monument for anybody to ever grieve you or know that you were alive. All remembrance of you will be erased. Your body is going be burned to ashes, and when they give them to me I am going to throw them in the first garbage yard I can find. There will be no tears for you. That is where you belong, with garbage. I do hate you that much. And there are two things that you will never hear from me, that I love you and that I forgive you. You will never hear those words from my lips. So don't hold on too much longer. I don't want to waste my time here with you any longer than I have to. Go on and die, you bastard." I was hard and cruel. I thought saying those things would make me feel better, but they didn't. I only felt more guilt, but I refused to cry and held a look of defiance on my face.

He looked up at me for the last time and said, "Then I have really failed you."

"Yes," I said. "You didn't protect me from your sins. You only made it worse."

It must have taken all his remaining strength, but before I knew what was happening, with his free hand he reached up and slapped my mouth so hard that my lip was cut. It bled all over his bed and me. "There, now I can die in peace, but I will haunt you in death forever," he said.

He slumped down in bed and closed his eyes and rolled his head away from me. Carolyn pulled me back and rushed me out of the ward. The nurse insisted that she sanitize my lip and gave me a cold compress to stop the bleeding. I said nothing. I went into a daze. I think that I must have slipped into shock. I felt cold all over and I went limp beside Carolyn. The next thing I remember was waking the next morning in our hotel room. Carolyn had grabbed an attendant and they both carried me to the car and up to the hotel room. She had called a doctor herself and arranged for him to come there. She didn't want me in any more hospitals that night. Carolyn could always make those things happen. I never knew how.

My father died that very same night while I was in shock. I dreamed that I saw him as an old man, with long greasy hair and a beard. He was dressed in rags. He was falling, falling and spinning downwards into a dark, cold hole. Maybe his wish was coming true, that he would haunt me in death. I remembered this as a shock when the prison warden handed me a little plastic sack with a box containing his ashes. I gave them back to the warden and said, "Don't you have some place here that you could bury them?"

"Yes," he said. "We can take care of that for you. Once, again, let me offer my condolences for your loss." With that I began to laugh and laugh and laugh. I became hysterical and screamed and fainted.

When I awoke, Carolyn and I were back in the car headed for the airport. "Here, Cynthia, take one of my pills," she said. I did as I was told. I slept on the plane, but Carolyn flew on with me to Chicago. She told me that

I had two choices. Either I could come home with her and get the rest and recuperation that I needed, or she was going to give it to me herself in Chicago. I told her that I wanted to go home. I fell asleep. She thought that I meant Chicago, but I had meant St. Alban's. When I awoke the next morning I was fairly groggy. I still felt sick and ill. I was back in my own apartment in Chicago and Carolyn was trying to get me to eat some breakfast.

I realized instantly that Carolyn and I and Dan were in the same city. I couldn't go back to sleep. I had to have a plan to get Carolyn back to St. Alban's. I didn't have the luxury of being sick. I ate a little breakfast. Carolyn helped me with my bath and laid out some fresh pajamas for me. I made myself look as presentable as possible. I brushed my hair up into a ponytail, and put on a little makeup. I put on a smile and entered the little living room. I wanted to assure her that I was okay so that she could get back to the children and St. Alban's. She couldn't find out that Dan and I were working together, and that I had even been out with him. I was afraid it would be too much for her, and that she would leave me and stop being my friend. I was afraid to be without her in my life.

"Carolyn, I can never thank you enough," I said brightly. "Thanks for always being there for me. You know that I depend on you. I am so grateful."

She stopped me with her interruption saying, "Yes, I know that you do, dear, and you know that I would never keep anything from you," she said. Was she telling me that she already knew about Dan and me? I must have blushed or gone pale or something. "Dear, you look a little weak," she said. "Come and sit down. Have some more juice."

I did as I was told. I sat there waiting.

"Now, Cynthia, I know you are going to be all right. But I do have something to tell you. I couldn't help but overhear your comments to your father that last night. You understand that I wasn't eavesdropping. It was just that I could hear. I couldn't help it. I heard you. But I am not here to condemn you or shame you or correct you. I won't be a judge and jury for you to say that you were right or wrong to say the things that you said. I will say that it was a sad moment in your life, and it wasn't the proudest moment in your life for me. But, by hearing what you said, I know that you are carrying hate and nonforgiveness around with you in your heart. Those are both heavy burdens and they will affect everything you do for the rest of your life. I pray that you will relieve yourself of them. I will pray to God for you that you do. I hope that you will pray to God to relieve you of these burdens, or they will drag you down to nothing and you will never truly be able to love again. I say this because I love you. I love you as much as if you were my own child. I wish you were." She stopped and dabbed her eyes with her little, dainty handkerchief. She was never without one.

"Thank you, Carolyn. I love you too. I know that I can depend on you. I will pray. I will try," I said. "Thanks, for worrying about me, but I know you have a plane to catch."

"But, Cynthia, I can stay as long as you need me," she said.

"I will always need you, Carolyn, but you can't stay that long. Now go along and give all my love to the kids. I will call them tonight and try to explain the death the best way I can. Don't worry, I won't burden them with my troubles in this matter. I won't ask them to hate or anything like that. I will ask them to try and remember any good moments that they had together. And I know that you will have better words for them than I could ever imagine. Go home and help them through this."

She left on the afternoon plane. I saw her off from my apartment. As soon as she was out of sight, I called Dan. I knew that it was wrong to do so, but I needed a man then to lean on. I needed something that Carolyn couldn't give me. I felt so weak, so alone and vulnerable. I needed to feel like a woman. I just had to do it. I couldn't help myself. I knew he was the wrong man, but he was the only one I knew. And, I knew that he would be there and that he would come for me.

"Cynthia, I am so glad to hear from you," he said. "I was so sorry to hear about your dad."

"Stop the condolences," I said sternly. "Just come get me. I'll be waiting." I hung up the phone.

I dressed in a little black cocktail dress, black suede high-heeled shoes, and a little black mink coat. I looked sexy, and I looked rich. I brushed out my ponytail and twisted my long hair high on my head, letting a few wisps of hair curl around my ears. It was entirely too early in the afternoon to go out dressed like this, but that was my intention. As soon as he and the car pulled to the curb, I ran down the steps. He had brought the limousine just as I had hoped. He opened the door for me and I stepped in. I was going to go on with my life and forget my father ever existed. I was going to succeed, and I was going to use Dan Callahan to get to the top. I refused to be helpless little Cynthia any longer. If I had to lie and cheat and steal, I would do so to get to where I wanted to be, on top. I would break that "glass ceiling" of the corporate world, and when I had enough of Dan, I would dump him. He would never know what hit him.

Chapter Fifteen

I Climb

I didn't sleep with Dan that night or very soon after that. But I let him escort me around town and introduce me to every powerful person he knew, men and women. Of course, everyone thought I was sleeping with him. I didn't care.

Some of the most powerful people I met were gay; some were straight. I didn't care about that either. Everyone had a purpose, and everyone could be used. I networked constantly without shame. I was delightful and charming. Soon my phone was ringing off the hook. I engaged an answering service to handle all the invitations. There were parties every night, gala openings, charity events, museum and art showings. Fairly soon, my picture was in the social pages of the newspaper at least once a week. I was known as the new woman of the seventies. I was a workingwoman and a woman continuing her education. My updating of the store and my knowledge of computers over-whelmed everyone, but I never forgot and I never let any one forget that I was a woman. I dressed smart every minute of every day. I started having my hair and makeup done professionally every morning, and if I needed, in the evenings too. I had Dan hire me a social secretary/companion. He moved me out of my little apartment and into an apartment suite across the hall from him. My secretary/companion was a woman younger than me, just out of secretarial school. Her name was Julie. Dan and I figured out a way to pay her salary from the payroll of Bennington's. No one ever questioned our motives. We were on a roll.

Of course, I wanted her to live with me. I needed her night and day I told him. That would help in putting off his advances just as long as possible. He had to buy out the lease from the man and woman living there, but I didn't care about that either. "Throw them out on the street, for all I care," I said laughingly and recklessly as we sat in the bar one night having our second or third round of drinks. And he did just what I wanted, all the time waiting for the repay. He moved them out the next morning and moved me in. Now he had direct access to me, but I still resisted his advancements. I knew someday I would have to repay him or destroy him. I didn't know from one day to another which would come first.

As that awful spring ended and the long Chicago summer started, I needed a break. I still had two more semesters to finish my MBA. I would continue during the summer; nothing was going to stop me. By May of 1974 I would have my final degree. Between now and then I had a lot of hard work to complete, both at school and at the store. But I decided to go home to St. Alban's for two weeks. I needed Carolyn and my siblings, my family, my only family. I had missed them terribly, and I needed to be with them now. I hadn't spoken to them since I called to tell them that father had died.

Albert met me at the little airport in St. Alban's and I was so glad to see him, but to my surprise Carolyn had brought the children. I was so happy that I cried, and I could have hardly called them children. During this last year since Jonathan had graduated from high school, so much had happened. He was still trying to be the man of the house and I guessed that he always would. He must have grown at least a foot taller, and his hair was almost shoulder length. He was still growing into a very handsome man.

Janie and Marie had made even greater strides. Janie had made straight A's that last semester. She had two years more of high school to graduate, and I was sure she would go on to St. Alban's. Marie wasn't talking baby talk anymore, but she was nowhere near the maturity of a fourteen-year-old girl, at least not mentally. Physically, she was maturing into a beautiful woman with a curvaceous body and luxurious black hair. Her body was way ahead of her mind. Carolyn caught me staring and our eyes locked thinking the same thing, *How were we going to control this? Marie would soon have the body of a woman and we were hoping the mind and brain to go along with it.*

"Oh, Cynthia. Oh, Cynthia," said Marie. "Why must you stay away so long?" She nestled close to me like that of a little child.

"She's just being dramatic," said Jonathan. "She's okay. Really she is."

Marie sat up straight and said, "I most certainly am not okay. I am not okay in any shape or form. I am more than okay. I am an original. I was born differently than ordinary people, and I shall always be forced to live so." She raised her hand to her forehead and played a little forced faint into my lap.

Janie said, "Her therapist thought that dramatic lessons would help her come out a little."

121

"My therapist is a twit and really knows very little about who I actually am," said Marie with as much drama as she could muster. "I am who I tell him I am, and that is whom he must deal with." We all laughed at this then, but had not idea where it would carry our little Marie in the future.

"Really Cynthia," said Marie. "How long can you stay? Can you stay forever and be our real mother?" I was so startled. One moment she was a drama queen, and the next moment she almost sounded normal.

"I am here now, and here is where I will stay for two whole glorious weeks," I said. "Guess what my little chickens? I do hereby proclaim this the start of our vacation. Oh Carolyn, do say we can go to the beach?"

"Don't worry, Cynthia," she said. "I am already a step ahead of you. Why do you think we are going in this direction? Of course, we are going to the beach this very minute."

A huge cheer could be heard inside the car, and we all acted like spoiled little children, laughing and pinching and hugging and kissing each other. We headed to the beach, and for a brief period, all seemed peaceful and calm. Carolyn was doing a great job with the children. During this time I made a point of spending an individual piece of time with each one of my darlings.

Jonathan was doing fine in school, but he wasn't dating. "Don't worry about that, Cynthia," said Carolyn. "He is still adjusting. Be glad."

Janie had made many friends in school and her grades were good. Of course she was still too young to date, at least Carolyn and I thought so. This didn't seem to be a problem for Janie; she seemed not to be bothered by it. She brought friends home from school, boys and girls, but they were always the outcasts. Her friends were the boys and girls that no one else wanted to be with. Carolyn assured me that they were nice kids and always made decent grades. They just weren't the "in" crowd. Carolyn said, "Oh, they are like the little stray dogs and cats that some children always bring home and want to keep."

"Oh Cynthia," Janie said one day. "Can my friend Davey come out to the beach for a few days? Can Albert bring him out?"

"Well," I said. "Let's ask Carolyn, shall we?" Naturally Carolyn had no objections. When Albert swung the big car up and around the winding driveway to the beach house, a beautiful young boy hopped out. But I was so shocked at his appearance that I had to run inside. His face was black and blue. He had been beaten.

"Don't worry, Cynthia," said Carolyn. "Sometimes boys just play rough."

Davey was a bright and handsome young boy of sixteen. I remembered myself at that age and shuddered. He and Janie seemed very close, too close. "Oh, don't worry about me and Davey, he's gay," Janie said candidly. "But he is my best friend." Davey would wash and roll Janie and Marie's hair, he would polish their nails while lying in the sun. He would brush out their hair and tease and style them both. He was a natural at it. He even picked out their clothes for dinner when we ate out.

During his days there with us, I learned a lot about him. He was gay. He openly admitted it. He longed for a boyfriend. We were his only confidants. "I've never told another living soul," he said, except Janie. "Don't worry about these few bruises," he said. "I've been getting them for years, but this summer I'm taking classes in kick boxing and ballet. Hey, maybe Janie and I can come and visit you in Chicago. You don't know any cute boys you can fix us up with, do you?" Janie and he laughed and laughed about this and rolled all over each other trying to contain themselves.

"Well," I started.

"Don't worry, Cynthia," said Carolyn. "It is a rhetorical question. You're not supposed to answer." With this said, all the kids including Jonathan and even Marie burst into laughter. It seemed that they had a better understanding about this than either Carolyn or I did.

Carolyn and I took long walks along the beach together with the kids trailing behind. "Carolyn, you are doing such a wonderful job with the kids. But I feel so guilty about not being here."

"Don't worry," she said. "You soon will be. Jonathan is a big help, and Janie is mature beyond her years. She understands things that you and I never have. In a way they are teaching us. As far as Marie is concerned she is coming along nicely in school, and next year I am hoping that she can go on to high school as a freshman. During this past April and May, Janie took her along some days to introduce her to some of the girls to start to get the feel of things. Marie just adores Janie, and she is trying so hard to fit in with the school. The important thing is that Marie understands that she is catching up and she wants to. Of course, home tutoring will continue for both as long as necessary. Both Janie and Marie continue therapy with their counselor every week. I don't know how long this will continue, but they can go indefinitely. But let's talk about you, Cynthia. How are you getting along?" She paused and stretched her long lanky arm around my shoulder and pulled me close to her.

"Well, Carolyn," I said. "I am terribly exhausted. I can't remember when I wasn't working or in school. And there is something eating a hole inside of me that I must tell you about, but I am afraid."

"Now, Cynthia," she said. "We have been through too much together to hold back anything, now. Dear, you know that you can tell me anything." She gave me one of those long, warm, motherly looks and a little squeeze with her arm.

"It's about the past," I said. "And, I am afraid that it may be painful for you, because it involves part of your past, also."

Carolyn stood still, frozen in time. "It's about Dan Callahan. Isn't it?" she asked as of a blow had struck her from behind.

"Yes, I am afraid that it is," I replied.

"Oh, I should have made some provision for this when you were listed last year in *Who's Who*," she said nervously twitching her handkerchief in her hands. "What made me think he wouldn't see your picture in the paper? It's my fault. I should have known better than to think that he wouldn't try to come back into our lives, and between us. Well, he is not going to get away with it, with anything. Tell, me everything. Start at the beginning. Don't leave anything out. He had better not be pestering you."

"Well, yes, he is pestering me, a little," I said. "Carolyn, he is the store manager at Bennington's."

"A store manager?" she asked. "With all his money, why would he want to be a store manager at Bennington's?"

"Because, he found out that is where I am working," I answered humbly. "Plus, he owns real estate all over Chicago. He's very rich and very well connected. Oh, Carolyn, I am so sorry and ashamed and embarrassed."

She stopped our walk and looked me straight in the eye. "Child," she said, "have you done anything about which you should be sorry, ashamed, or embarrassed?"

"Oh, no. Nothing like that," I said.

"Then you have nothing to be worried about with me," she said. "And, even so, I would have forgiven you."

"But we have to work together everyday. He and I are working on a special project that will eventually be my thesis, and I just can't back out now. We are updating the store, including taking computerization the whole way. It is going to make a great thesis, and I intend to turn it into a book."

"Well, that's a wonderful idea," she said. "What can I do to help? Do you want me to get rid of Dan for you? I can, you know, if you want me to." She said all this with a little mischievous smile as if the two of us were plotting something awful together. It occurred to me that that was the second time during which we had known each other that she had mentioned "getting rid of Dan."

"No, it's not that easy," I replied. "It is a project that we must work on together. With his connections I can complete the project in time for graduation in 1974. After that, I'll just drop him."

"Spending that much time with Dan is going to be a lot harder than you think, and if you are stringing him along, as I suspect you are, you foolish girl, then dumping him takes on a whole new meaning. Just remember that there are certain ways to make this work and still get all the glory for your self and dump him afterwards," she said. "But you must never give in to his sexual advances, which must be coming your way. I know that putting this whole matter on a strictly professional manner didn't make a dent in that dense head of his. Did it?" she asked.

"No," I replied dejectedly. "He is still trying to get me to go to bed with him, and I think half the store must think that I am."

"Cynthia, I am a lot older than you and a lot wiser with more experience. Let me think about this and come up with a little plan of my own. Okay?" she asked. "Of course, I'll tell you all about it before we put it into place."

Later that night she came to my room. "Oh, Cynthia, you are going to think that I am a wicked old woman. But I thought I had taken care of Dan Callahan once and for all. How foolish I was for thinking I could get rid of him with money. He is a dangerous fellow. I have discovered that he may have underworld connections. I am not sure about that, but I have sources that have told me that he often associates with the most unseemly characters who have drug backgrounds."

"Just as I suspected," I said.

"Well, listen to this," she said. "You may be quite right to need him and his connections to pull off your plan, but to disquiet his amorous efforts in your direction, we must replace him with some young man. He must be a wonderful man, closer to your own age. It will be a set up, of course. You don't have to fall in love with him or sleep with him. He won't work at the store. He won't work at all. He will come from a wealthy, Chicago, socialite family, a family that is looking for his bride so that he can continue the family name. Someone Dan has never heard of and with whom he has no connections. This young man's reputation must be indisputable, and I think that I have just the person, but I pity the poor boy. He is sure to fall in love with you. Dan, of course, will sulk at first. Just ignore that. Eventually, he will try to match you with some floozy that he will flash around town. No one respectable would be seen with him. Then he will huff and puff, and try to berate you and your new boyfriend. Intimidation was always his best effort, but you must stand firm. Keep reminding him that your relationship with him is only professional."

"Well, who is he?" I asked. "I know that you must already know yourself."

"His name is David Caruso, and he is gorgeous. He just passed the state bar exam and is practicing with one of the top law firms in Chicago. His background is impeccable. Some say that his ancestors landed on Plymouth Rock. His parents are dear and near friends of mind. He and they have agreed wholeheartedly to our little plan. They have friends who know Dan. Seems he broke their lease at his hotel and had them removed from the penthouse floor."

"Yes," I said. "That was for me." We both laughed.

"Well, what goes around, comes around," we both said in unison. We talked on into the night planning little scenarios. It was too soon that I would have to return to Chicago, Dan and the store, and school.

Chapter Sixteen

The Plan

As soon as I arrived at the store the plan was put into action. Without his even knowing why, Dan received an invitation to a large reception for David Caruso. He was being introduced as the newest member of the firm. I knew that Carolyn must have been working behind the scenes.

"Oh, Cyn, you have to go," said Dan. "Everyone will be expecting you."

"Dan, I can't possibly go to any parties now. I have only just arrived back from vacation. I am way behind in school and the store needs me more than ever." We were having our morning coffee in his office and going over the plans for the day. Fairly soon the Chicago store would be complete; at least we hoped by spring that it would be. "Anyway," I said, "I already received my invitation separately. See, one just for me."

"But I can't just walk in there alone without you. Everybody will be expecting us together," he said.

"Well, they are just petty and narrow minded and all they want to do is mind every body else's business," I said.

"Well, if you're not going, then neither am I," he said.

"Oh, I will probably make an appearance," I said, nonchalantly. "Why don't you go ahead, and I will just meet you there."

"Well, I do hate to miss a party such as this. There is no telling who will be there," he said. "But you are sure you will meet me there?"

"I'll do my best," I said. With that, he was satisfied. We worked through the day at break-neck speed. I had classes all afternoon.

Jo Whom It May Concern

I arrived at the party just as it was about to crescendo, not to early, not too late; it was perfect timing. The drinks were just taking hold of everyone and dancing had begun. I spotted Dan talking to some young debutante. I was instantly jealous. I wondered why. Across the room a tall man was taking David Caruso around and introducing him to everyone. I presumed it was his boss from the law firm. I waited until he approached Dan and the two were introduced. David was just left there to talk to Dan and the young debutante just disappeared. I had my hair piled high on my head with a little green ribbon. I wore a cocktail dress that was ballerina length just to the ankles made out of dark green satin with matching netting over the top. It was narrow at the waist and accented my bosom. Matching green lace covered my shoulders and back and fell to three quarter length sleeves. I looked more like something from 1959 than 1973. Actually, I have always had a keen interest in vintage clothing. Carolyn had worn this little number on her first date with Dan. She had sent it to me hoping that it would fit, and it did. We both knew that it would confuse him just a little. I looked sensational in it.

Here we go, I thought. I squared my shoulders, raised my chin, and walked very slowly over to where they were talking.

"Well, Dan, aren't you going to introduce me to the man of the hour," I said with the sweetest smile that I could muster and a little tilt of my head. Dan was speechless. "Hi, I'm Cynthia Thomas.

"Hello, I'm David Caruso," he said as if we had rehearsed it. "I've heard a lot about you."

"Well, then David, that gives you the advantage, because I know absolutely nothing about you," I said gaily. We both laughed. Dan was still staring.

"Would you like to dance, Cynthia?" asked David.

"Sure, and thanks for asking," I said, giving a drop-dead look to Dan. We were off. I had hoped that I hadn't spread it on a little to thick. I didn't want to give the plan away on the first night. For the remainder of the evening David and I danced and talked, but I managed to slip away unnoticed before Dan could catch up to me. I felt like Cinderella at the ball. It was being sneaky and a little underhanded. I stopped at a pay phone and called Carolyn collect. After thirty minutes of telling her how well it sent, we said good night.

The next day at the store, Dan was completely business-like, but he couldn't help mentioning the previous evening just before I was to leave at noon. "That was quite a little display you put on last evening, Cynthia," he said surely.

"Why, I haven't the faintest idea about what you are talking," I said in my best southern accent.

"I guess you're going to fuck him next, right," he said. The cold sound of his voice stopped me dead in my tracks.

I turned around and said loudly, "That wouldn't be any of your business, now would it, Mr. Callahan?"

127

"Well, how do you think that makes me look," Cynthia, he said. "Everyone knows that you are my girl. Do you think I am going to let some young punk just march around in here and take you away from me?" he asked.

"I'm not going to argue with you about it now, Dan, or ever," I said. "You know perfectly well that I am not your girl. I never was, and I never will be. Tell me why would the likes of me take up with the likes of you, with you and your punks. Know this, Dan Callahan, if I ever have the time, I will date whomever and whenever I want. I suggest you do the same. As you know, I always keep my doors locked at night and my secretary is just next door. I have always suggested that you look elsewhere for whatever stuff pleases you. And, don't think of sabotaging the renovation project of the stores. Don't forget, you are the boss. If it goes down, so do you."

"Don't worry, my pretty, I'll find my solace somewhere else," he said. "There's plenty of stuff out there for me, and it is just mine for the asking. I'll have something new every night of the week." With this said, he picked up a paperweight and threw it at me. It smashed the glass wall of his office. Everyone saw his anger. I ran from the store and was so glad to see the campus when I drove up.

But Dan had other plans for me. He never mentioned David again. David and I dated several times a week. Of course, I told him over and over how grateful he was for being so gallant. Naturally, he was in on the scheme. "It is my pleasure, Miss Thomas," he would always say with a little bow. Just as Carolyn had predicted, Dan was seen more and more in the seedier bars of town and never with the same person twice. Sometimes he took a male clerk to lunch, but he had his favorite female clerk also. He made sure everyone saw them together in the store everyday.

He and I continued to work together on the project, which was nearly finished. He never pestered me any more, but I still felt uneasy around him. By Christmas the store was complete and everyone was trained on the new computer system. There were fewer mistakes everywhere in the store. We could track any item or a line of items from the time it was ordered until the time it was sold. Inventories were a breeze, and we could already envision what styles we would want for our next season. Accounts payable and accounts receivable, payroll, employee insurance—everything was automated on our new system. We really were the model for the age of the fully computerized department store. We also managed not to have any lay-offs. We found jobs in the store for everyone. We even sent an advance team of those people who wanted to relocate to our next store. Most of these employees received promotions and new titles were invented. This team was something that Dan and I didn't have the luxury of when we started the renovation at the main store in Chicago. Bennington's of Chicago had the best Christmas ever. It was a big success and I had already started my thesis in a rough draft. The renovation of the store was a news item for weeks in Chicago, and once again my picture, along with Dan's, was in the paper. He loved it. I hated it. It was good publicity for the store, but it reinforced the general opinion that I was going to the top so fast that I must be having sex with him. I "dated" David Caruso as often as possible and was sure to been seen in public. Soon I would have my MBA and I would be out of there. Where I would go I didn't know. However, Dan had other plans.

In January he called me to his office. "Cynthia, good to see you," he said with a little laugh. He eyed me up and down as usual. "I have some good news for you. You and I are going to take a little trip to our new store. It can wait until you have your spring break. But be prepared to work. The advance team isn't working out as we had planned. It is going to take you and me to finish it."

"I couldn't possibly go then. I will have more schoolwork than ever. I will be working on my thesis night and day," I said.

"Well, it is a must do, unless you want it to be a failure," he said. "I'm sure the papers would just love to hear all about it."

"Dan, don't make me go," I begged. I was so humiliated. Things had been going so well. Now this. I had never begged him before. I had always managed to have the upper hand. While I was in the Chicago store, I could supervise the renovation, but this was different and I hadn't counted on it.

"Well, either you are part of the winning team that you have created or you bow out now," he said with a little sneer.

"Oh, I'll be there," I said. I went directly to my own office and called the new store. Bennington's had bought a little mom and pop operation out west. It was big enough to be a Bennington's, but the employees had no idea about computers. Not one employee had ever been to Chicago. Our team and their team didn't even seem to speak the same language. So Dan had found a flaw in my plan, and now he was going to try and make me his pawn. I would have to go.

I called Carolyn. "What can I do?" I asked her.

"I suggest that you come home to St. Alban's immediately where you are loved and safe. Don't go with Dan," she said. "Play it safe, Cynthia."

"If that store falls through the roof, my thesis will be ruined," I said.

"Nonsense, my dear. You have already proven you thesis. Turn it in early and come home immediately," she said sternly.

"Oh, Carolyn, you just don't understand how these things work. I have to go. I just have to."

"Whatever you do, never be alone with him," was her only other advice. Reluctantly, I went.

Chapter Seventeen

His Plan Works

I worked furiously every night on my thesis. I had it in its final form. I would be able to submit it with a few revisions after spring break. Going to the new store would add a new challenge and a new dimension to it. My school counselor liked the idea and encouraged me to incorporate the renovation of the new store as the telltale finale to my thesis. "Sure, anybody can see how that can work at a big existing store in Chicago, but if this type of renovation and computerization can work in a newly acquired retail operation taking it from small time to big time, you will be wanted from coast to coast as the only specialist in this field," he said. "Cynthia, you and I have discussed many times that times are changing very rapidly, and you know that consultants can set their own pay. You will be doing something that you enjoy and you'll make a mint doing so. You will really be on your way, and the book is sure to follow. I'll make sure of that."

It all sounded so glorious. Suddenly, I wasn't afraid anymore. It was all going to work out. I called Carolyn and told her that I had decided to go. "Be careful and be smart," she said.

Dan and I spent two weeks working furiously at the new store talking to the old employees and encouraging them. We tried to teach the advance team patience. We produced new manuals on the concept for the existing employees to understand. We retrained the advance team on how to deal with them. We practiced our people skills as best as we could. Together our knowledge and skills paid off, and our public relations front eased tensions on both sides. We got all of them back on track again. Soon we were back in Chicago. Dan was exhilarated. I was exhausted. My fears had been for nothing. Dan had been the consummate professional and a perfect gentleman. My guard was down.

As we exited the Chicago airport, Dan asked if I would have dinner with him. "Cynthia, I've got a great idea. Let's paint the town red tonight, just you and me," he said. "Come on we deserve it. We'll go to the best restaurant in town. What do you say? You have to admit it, I was good." I started to say no, but he was right. He had been on his best behavior, and I was feeling a lot less pressured to be alone with him. We had worked hard and we had succeeded. We did deserve a break.

"Okay," I said. "I'll meet you in the lobby in one hour, but I have to be home early. I have lots of notes for the secretary and I want to go over them with her before we open the store tomorrow."

"Sure, who knows, the sun may not even come up tomorrow," he said. "Don't worry about it. We'll be home early."

This part didn't make much sense to me, but I knew he had had a few drinks on the plane, so I just blew it off. I was so looking forward to a really good dinner, and together we could bask in the light of our achievement.

When I entered my suite at the hotel, Julie was nowhere to be seen. *Oh, well, I guess she just went out. I'll see her later,* I thought. I showered and changed and threw on a new little cocktail dress that I had been dying to wear. I looked a little tired, so my makeup was somewhat heavy. *What the hell, I thought, it's just Dan. He won't care.*

I met Dan in the lobby bar. I don't know how many more drinks he had while I was changing. But he still had on the same old suit he had worn for two weeks. He looked a little shabby. But again, I didn't say anything.

As we stepped outside, I noticed that his car and driver were nowhere to be found. We took his car to the restaurant. *That is a little odd also,* I thought. When Dan was drinking we always took his limousine. I was too tired to think much more about it. The restaurant was called Marshall's, and it was my favorite. Everyone knew me there. David and I had always gone there for dinner.

"Oh, good evening, Miss Thomas," said the host, Pierre. "Please come with me. We have your usual table reserved just for you."

"Thank you, Pierre. You are so sweet, as always," I answered.

"They seem to know you pretty well here, Cyn," said Dan with a slur in his words. I was beginning to wonder if this had been a good idea or not. "I don't recall ever bringing you here before tonight," he said. "Oh, it must have been your Prince Charming, David Caruso, who oozed you in here." He was drunk and beginning to get ugly. I thought about leaving, but didn't.

"Well, if you must know, Dan, it was I who took David here," I said as sweetly as possibly. I didn't want him to know that he was really beginning to tick me off. "Some men ask their dates where they would like to go.

131

Unlike you who just tell them," I replied. "And, don't call me Cyn. How many times do I have to tell you that?"

"Okay. Okay, honey," he slurred. "Let's at least try to keep up appearances."

"I wasn't the one trying to start the argument," I said fiercely. The people at the next table were beginning to look our way. "Look, maybe, this wasn't such a good idea," I said. "I'll just leave."

As I started to get up from the table, Dan grabbed my wrist and pulled me across the table. I jerked my hand back away from his and he was so uncoordinated by now that his hand hit himself in the face. Several people laughed. He said, "And, you think that you can just leave me sitting here? Why, you have got a lot of nerve, Cyn. Sit down. We are going to have a nice meal, and then we'll just see about the rest of the night. You know that old saying, 'I do think the girl doth protest too much.' Really, that means that she wants it badly and is just to prudish or selfish to say it. At least I am honest, Cyn." He ordered another round of drinks. I didn't care. I needed a drink about them. He was back to his old self and being insufferable. I was having a terrible time, but was determined not to make a scene.

We ordered and dinner was served. I didn't enjoy it very much. "Just what did you mean by saying 'after dinner we'll just have to see'?" I asked.

"Well, Cyn, most men and women who have spent so much time together as we have, especially the beginning; and men who take women out for dinner expect a little something afterwards. It is the same old man and woman thing that has been going on for years. Don't pretend you don't know how to play it. This is me, Dan, you are talking to. Don't play with me," he said. I was silent.

It was true. Sometimes late at night, especially when I couldn't sleep, when my hands uncontrollably searched for my private parts, I did think of Dan. And I had a wonderful time with that fantasy. Then, in the light of day, I was always glad that it was not him again.

Dan ordered after-dinner coffee with a mint liquor chaser. He knew that it was my favorite. I was already feeling a little lightheaded and just wanted to go home. Dan lit a cigar. He always had big fat Cuban cigar. From where he got them, I never knew. He practically used them as props. He was lingering over this dinner and drawing it out forever. I should have left and gone home, but I stayed. He ordered more drinks. We drank them and moved into the lounge. He snuggled me into a little booth and ordered more drinks. That night we had been drinking gin and tonic with a twist of lime. He always said that it was his summer drink. "Gin always brings out the meanest part in people, Cyn. Don't you agree?" he asked. He had always tried to be so elegant, and he always failed so miserably. "Cynthia, I must confess that I have been lonely without you. No one else even comes close to you, men or women," he said.

"Gee," I said. "Thanks for that."

"I'm afraid that soon you will be leaving me and Chicago," he said a little morbidly.

"What, the 'Big Cahoona,' who can have anybody he wants, any time, any place," I said sourly. "You're afraid? I don't believe you."

"Yes, I am afraid that I may never see you again, ever. Sometimes, late at night when I think about you, well, I just have to do it. I get off on you, just thinking about being with you. You probably think that is a sick thing to do. But it relieves me. Only then can I sleep." He reached over and touched my hand and said, "Promise me one thing, Cynthia, promise that wherever you go and whatever happens to me, that we will always be friends. I am a part of you as you are a part of me and that will never change. We have been through too much together. I'll never truly let you go. You will always have a piece of my heart."

I was touched. I almost cried a little tear for him. I grasp his big, gnarled fists with my fragile little hands and said, "Oh, Dan. You do trouble me so. What can I ever do for you? You have accidentally been a big part of my life for so long, some of it good, some of it bad. But, I have never seen you like this before tonight."

"Just spend one last night with me Cynthia," he said. "That's all I ask."

Before I could say no, he pressed his huge body against mine in the little booth. He French kissed me. It was warm and passionate. I had been in charge so long now, that I was actually enjoying having someone else in control. His big body felt so overwhelmingly hot on my small frame. I couldn't have moved if I had wanted to.

"Let's get out of here," I said softly. He called the waiter for the check. I was surprised that he paid with cash leaving only a small tip.

"Cynthia, let's not go back to my hotel. Let's go someplace we have never gone before," he said. "Somewhere special."

"Anywhere, let's just go," I said a little drunkenly. The valet pulled his big, black Cadillac around to the front of the restaurant. Again, there was no tip, and I noticed that what was once a very beautiful car was now rusty and dented, even the bumper was a little crooked. I was silent. I didn't say anything. I was too much in the mood to spoil anything.

He drove me to a place that was just an apartment. He said that it was a friend's apartment. I didn't see anything special about it. I was a little disappointed. I was expecting champagne and caviar. He didn't even turn on the lights. "The bedroom is in there, Cyn. Go on in and I will be there in a minute."

Where were the moonlight and romance, my champagne and roses? This was hardly the way to fall in love, or even a romantic evening. I undressed slowly and slid between the sheets only to find a packaged condom. My mood was failing fast, but my heart was pounding and my head was reeling, and I was hot inside and out. Suddenly, Dan appeared, completely naked. He had such a beautiful body. He was already fully erect, so huge. He had always been hung. He carried a large silver tray. It was filled with my favorite caviar, chocolates, and three long stem roses, and a chilled bottle of champagne with frosted champagne flutes. He was being romantic after all. My heart melted. We drank the champagne and we fed each other the caviar, one bite at a time.

"Cynthia," Dan said. "Kiss me softly with you lips and your tongue." I wrapped my arm around his neck and played with his hair with my long nails. I kissed him softly. He responded softly. I pulled him over on top of me and spread my legs. I was so eager, but I was to wait. He kissed me softly and then a little harder. I responded every time. My legs were going wild sliding all over him. I wanted him in me so badly. I could hardly wait.

"Wow, wow," he said. "Slow down. We have all night." He nibbled at my ears, sliding his wet tongue down my throat and up the other side. He sucked my breasts and licked between them. He licked his fingers and slid them all the way down my belly and entered me one at a time. He licked me all the way down and entered me with his tongue. He spun me around, so that I could take his aroused gorge in my mouth, which I did hungrily. We were like animals. We couldn't get enough of each other. Emotionally, I think I climaxed almost immediately. He continued and so did I. While he was doing so he lifted the champagne bottle and poured it all over him and me. Now while we were sucking and licking, we would taste the remaining bit of the champagne. He spread my legs open wide, and entered me with his fingers. My body writhed and my back arched and I must have moaned for what seemed like moments, but was only a few seconds. I knew that he was going to enter me himself any moment, but he didn't. He threw the champagne bottle on the floor and turned me over on all fours with my butt facing him. I was letting him guide me into anything that he wanted me to do. His desire was my desire.

He pulled out from a bag on the floor, what was commonly called adult sex toys. One was an unusually very large dildo, much larger than a man could ever be in this fashion. I had never had this before. He lubricated me fully and also the dildo. "Now, Cyn, just slide down onto it. Take all the time you want. Make it pleasure you."

I was on my knees and leaning forward on my hands. Dan held the toy and I slid down on it between my legs, slowly, very slowly. I backed out and let it tickle my tip, but I wanted more and more of it. Each time I slid further and further onto it until the whole thing was as far inside of me as I could make it go, and I was spread further open than I had ever been before. The base of the toy must have been ten inches round. I road it up and down, and in and out. Dan handed me a little bottle of liquid and said, "Here, honey, sniff this." It was amyl nitrate. My head exploded and my loins burned hotter with desire. I rode that dildo so hard that I was sure that it would break in to two pieces.

While I was still in my ecstasy, I could feel Dan lubricating my anus, as if for an examination. I was fearful, but if I stopped now, would he beat me? Suddenly, I could feel his cold finger entering my butt, again and again, first just the one, then two. Then he entered me with his penis.

"Easy, buckaroo," said Dan. "Just take it easy and enjoy it. Take another hit from that little bottle." He reached around and held it under my nose. I inhaled deeply. I went wild with desire. I plunged downwards on the giant dildo. I was fucking myself and Dan was fucking my rear. I was wild with passion. I was out of my mind. Dan came very fast in this way and pulled out quickly. He withdrew the dildo from me and lay me down gently on the bed.

"Wow, Cyn, that was really wild," he said. He hadn't asked me, but I had not been ready to stop. He simply presumed that since he had hit his ecstasy point that we were finished, but I was glad it was over for now. We lay there for a few minutes exhausted and still drunk. I drifted off to sleep, but I could feel him applying a warm wet towel all over me as if he was bathing me like a little baby. He pulled warm, soft sheets around me and we both must have drifted off to sleep.

I must have had a nightmare, I awoke around 3:00 A.M., screaming and sitting straight up in that bed.

"Darling, what is the matter with you? Hush, now, hush," said Dan soothingly.

I lay down next to him only to remember my dream. In it Dan and I were having the most normal and happy sex in the usual position with him on top. As I gazed up at his beautiful face with all those golden curls, his faced turned into that of my father saying, "Now, Cynthia, you will really know how to please a man, and I know you will please many." I was so ashamed. I realized that I had been enjoying it in the dream. I didn't have to force myself to sleep. I was still so drunk that I must have just passed out.

He had been right in his drunken prediction. I guess he had it planned all along. We didn't see the light of the next day, except by moonlight. When I awoke, he was still sleeping. It was 7:00 P.M. and someone was knocking at the door.

Chapter Eighteen

My Name Is

I answered the door wrapped in a sheet. "Hey, I'm Junior," some young boy said. "Are you two still at it? Dan said that you were pretty wild." He just walked in.

"What do you want?" I asked.

"Well, if you must know, ma'am, this is my place and I live here," he said.

I spun around and almost lost my balance. My head was aching. "Hold on there, buckaroo," said Junior. "Come on over here and sit yourself down, and just collect yourself." Where had I had that term "buckaroo" before now? "How about some coffee," he said. "I make the best in town, cappuccino, latte, straight black, whatever you want. You know a friend of Dan's is usually a friend of mine." He smiled.

"Sure, great, whatever," I said. "Look, where's your phone? I have to make a call." He showed me that it was just on the wall where I was standing. I called the store, and apologized with some lame excuse that Dan and I had gotten in very late and we were both down with a twenty-four hour bug, that I would see them in the morning. "Oh, by the way, how did we do today over last year?" I asked.

"Twenty-six hundred more that last year."

"Okay, thanks. See you in the morning."

Dan was still sleeping. I could hear him snoring from the other room. "If you want, you are perfectly safe to take a shower," said Junior.

"Thanks." I headed for the bathroom and dropped the sheet to the floor. As the hot steamy water hit the back of my neck, the full realization of the episode of the night before blinded me with the truth of it. For some reason I didn't feel very guilty. I wasn't sure why. I guess I had wanted it to happen. I did feel a little dirty. Then I remembered the dream and the full reality of it hit me. Had it only been a dream, or was it a dream of a real happening of the past. I didn't ever remember being raped by my father, no, not that. I did hate him, but I didn't hate him that much. If that had been true, I would have had to kill him and probably mother too. I couldn't deal with that. I convinced myself that it was only a nightmare and vowed never to think of it again. I wondered if I would ever really be able to have normal sexual relations with a man and not have that dream. Then I thought of Carolyn. She must never know. All these secrets were piling up inside my head. I thought that I would surely go over the edge and into the loony bin, maybe a trash bin. Hey, maybe that would be a good place to call things that you what to loose from a computer, but keep in a safe place. I decided that I would keep my secrets in my trash bin, and remember the term later, much later. Junior called me from the tiny kitchen.

"Hey, buckaroo, our coffee is ready," he said cheerfully. He made my head ache even worse.

"Hey, you! My name is Cynthia," I said. "Don't call me buckaroo." I felt guilty. I had said it too harshly.

"Okay. Okay," he said as he barged into the bathroom.

"Hey, what's the big idea, Junior," I said as I pulled up the sheet.

"I'm sorry. It's just that we're kind of loose around here. One thing for sure, you can't wear that sheet home, and secondly that pretty little dress is ruined. I already tried it on. Hope you don't mind. But, it reeks of alcohol and it has one strap broken and the zipper is busted. I might know somebody who can fix it though, but it won't be today."

"You tried on my dress," I asked.

"Sure, I try on all my girlfriends' clothes. I do drag down at the Tightbottom Bar. I'm a bartender there."

"Listen, Junior, I'm not your girlfriend. So don't go getting any odd ideas about me, and don't try on my dress again. Just stuff it in a bag," I said. "And, where's that coffee?"

"Here it is, ma'am," he said as he served me the most delicious cappuccino that I had ever tasted. He must have known that I had a hangover. The coffee had a little liqueur in it. I could taste it. He surely knew a hangover when he saw one.

"Here," he said. "These ought to fit you." He handed me a full bundle of young boys clothes complete with a little pair of cotton briefs and a T-shirt, a white button down collar long sleeved shirt and a pair of jeans. They all fit perfectly, and they were freshly laundered. I felt clean again.

"Thanks, Junior," I said. "Sorry I was so mean. How do I get out of here?"

"I'll drive you myself, but first you need some food, I can tell. I'll make you an omelet that will melt in your mouth."

"I think that I have had enough in my mouth for one night," I said with a laugh. He laughed, too. I liked him. "But you can make me an omelet at my place," I said.

"Sure, let's go," he replied. I just left Dan sleeping there. He never awoke that night.

When we reached the hotel, I said, "Pull around back. I don't want to go in the front." He did as he was told. We took the back elevators up to my suite.

"Wow, how luxurious can we get?" he asked a little sarcastically with a laugh.

We entered and there to my amazement sat Julie, my secretary. She had waited all day. She had a very bewildered look on her face when I introduced Junior. "Go on and go home for the day, Julie. Come back first thing in the morning. Thanks for waiting, but you should have gone home hours, ago." She left with a few mumbled words.

"Find your way to the kitchen, Junior. I still want that omelet," I said. "I am going to shower and shampoo my hair." Being back in my own apartment made me feel safe and I locked the door. I could hear Junior banging around in the kitchen. I didn't know why, but I felt instantly comfortable with him. I showered and shampooed. I put on a new cotton terry robe and wrapped my hair in a towel. When I came out, Junior had set the table and prepared a full breakfast meal.

"All for you, ma'am. Please be seated," he said.

"Careful," I said. "You're going to spoil me. Oh, you sit, too. I insist."

The two of us had that wonderful omelet dinner and he briefly told me his life story, and I shared very little of mine. We never mentioned the name of Dan Callahan. Junior was only seventeen years old. He said that he had always knows that he was gay. His parents kicked him out of the house when he told them last year. "Thank God I was sixteen, then. That's when I start-ed working at the bar. I lied. I told them I was eighteen. I started doing drag then too. You know, for the extra tips. I don't want to be no girl. Believe me. I am all boy, I mean, man. That's why I share that little dump with two other guys, and you know who drops by from time to time. Oh, don't worry. He's not my type." I undid my hair and he was ecstatic. "Wow, do you ever have beautiful hair," he said. It was shoulder length by now, and I had just had it highlighted. "Oh, please, let me do it for you.

"You would do it for me?" I asked.

"Sure, honey, a girl's got to pinch pennies or she is sure to get pinched if you know what I mean," he giggled.

We went into my big bathroom and he was all agog. "I can do wonders in here. If I can't, then I should get out of the business," he said. He added a little mousse to my hair and curled each strand individually. He sat me under the hair dryer for only thirty minutes while he gave me a manicure and pedicure. Before I knew it, I had ruby red fingernails and toenails to match.

He took down my hair and hot curled each handful until I had a head full of curls. I had never had curls before in my life. I had always worn my hair up or just straight in its natural wave. "Well, that's okay for business, I guess," said Junior. "But for going out, you have to look especially elegant." He pulled up a little bunch of curls from each side of my head and tied them with a little black ribbon on top of my head with the other curls cascading down onto my shoulders. "They're sure to ask for your ID tonight, Miss Cynthia," said Junior.

"Why? Where are we going?" I asked.

"Tonight is my night off and I am taking you out to your first gay bar," he said. "Where else, luv? We're going to the Tightbottom. It's my home away from home."

Junior and I surely did go out to my first gay bar that night. I had a blast. We danced and laughed and he introduced me to everybody. It was fun to feel young again. I hoped that I would know him for the rest of my life. He was such a good kid. I made him bring me home at midnight. I am sure that he must have gone back out. I went to sleep, happy that I had had such a sudden diversion and so much fun and with a man. He was a man who was comfortable with women and comfortable with himself. I had never met such a man before and I never did again. He was to be a part of my life for some time to come, but not as long as I would have wished.

I snuggled in bed that night in my oldest flannel gown wrapped in my favorite goose down comforter. I took the phone off the hook, and was thankful that Dan didn't come around knocking.

I was wrapped in a feeling of contentment that I had never known. I had had sex that was supposed to be forbidden, but for now I didn't feel guilty. I had also made a new friend, Junior, and he was a man. I admired him. I was determined to make a place for him in my life.

Chapter Nineteen

MBA

I had to rush through the next two months to finish everything. I couldn't see Junior, but I talked to him at least twice a week. I told him that I had a big surprise for him in June and for him not to make any plans. Unfortunately, Dan thought that he was in love with me. He courted me. He brought me flowers and candy and tried to make more dates for dinner. I knew he was hoping for more nights of sex. I was sure that I certainly didn't have time for that. "But, Cynthia, it has already been two months. I ache for you," he pleaded. But I stood steady. I was too close to finishing school for another night of that. After that one night, I really didn't get my head clear for a week.

Graduation was the next day, and I was so glad and relieved. Carolyn and the children were coming in just to see me receive my degree. I hadn't invited Dan or told him the date of the event.

I didn't feel very sorry for Dan. I was sure he was getting his fair share. But something else was happening to him. He began to gain weight. He would forget to shave. He would have to leave for meetings in the middle of the day. Some days he didn't come into the store at all. He was on the verge of being fired. He looked shabby all the time. I knew before he could tell me.

I came home from work the night before graduation to find all my belongings packed and out in the hall of the hotel. The key to the lock didn't work; it had been changed. I tried my key to Dan's suite and it also didn't work. It too had been changed. I went down to the manager's desk. The usual man wasn't there. In fact almost all of the help looked new. The manager apologized profusely, "I am so sorry, Miss Thomas, but the hotel has been bought. We had to move your things out."

"But what about Mr. Callahan? Where is he and where is his things?" I asked.

"Well," he answered hesitantly. "All his personal belongings have been confiscated by the district attorney's office, and they are looking for him and his car. You understand, he has been bought out, lock, stock, and barrel. It was a hostile take over. Somebody just bought out all his debts. I am afraid that he's broke and down to his last nickel."

I was shocked and scared. I was so embarrassed. "I'll need a suite for the remainder of the month. I'll pay cash in advance. What's available?" I said with a steely smile.

"Well, we have a small parlor room on the third floor," he said. "The bigger suites have already been taken. We'll be lucky just to fit you in there."

"Just move the boxes in. Don't bother to unpack," I said.

I called Junior immediately. He hadn't seen Dan in days, but promised to help me search for him. That night we hit every bar in town, starting from the bottom up. It didn't take us very long to find him in a little run down bar in the worse part of Chicago. When we walked in he was doing two lines of cocaine and shooting back straight tequila with two tattooed men sitting on their motorcycles right there in the middle of the bar. Nobody cared.

It was all we could do to get him out of there safely. I threatened to call the police. The two motorcycle men wanted him for themselves. A brawl was about to occur, but Junior stepped in and said, "Now, gentlemen, I'm sure we can all see that this man is sick and no good for fun tonight, but if it is a little fun you are looking for just come with me." They were so drunk they said okay and walked outside with Junior. Five minutes later Junior walked back in with the two and they roared up their motorcycles with a smile and sped away.

"Don't ask," said Junior. "Let's just get Dan home."

We piled Dan into the backseat of Junior's old 1965 Caddy, and he and I jumped into the front. Junior pulled Dan's car around to the back of the bar and out of site. I can't describe what condition that Dan was in, but he was ready to party. I knew that he was surely drunk; he stank of alcohol.

"Why, I ain't so drunk, Cyn. I've seen you. Well, I seen you," he said. He couldn't think of the next words to say.

By the time we got back to the hotel, he was singing as loud as he could.

"That cocaine was probably mixed with another drug like 'angel dust' or something," said Junior. He helped me get Dan out of the car. Dan stood up straight and walked directly through the lobby with the same old dignity as if he still owned the place. I don't think that he remembered that he had lost it. Junior helped me get him in the elevator.

"Thanks, Junior, I think that I can handle it from here," I said.

"Cynthia, you don't know Dan when he is like this," said Junior.

"That's okay, hon. I am sure that he is going to pass out any minute," I said.

"But Cynthia, when you mix alcohol and cocaine," was the last thing I heard Junior say before the elevator doors closed.

As soon as we were alone, Dan grabbed me. He was as violent as I had ever seen a man, and so powerful. I didn't know where it came from. He ribbed my blouse off and all my little pearl buttons fell to the elevator floor. I slapped him. He stumbled back silently stunned. I was on my hands and knees trying to pick up the little buttons when he kicked me in my butt with his boot. I hit the floor and instantly could not breathe. I had the wind knocked out of me. I was helpless. He picked me up by my hair and threw me against the wall. He started to maul me. I frantically tried to fight him off. I couldn't reach any of the elevator buttons. Unfortunately it wasn't stopping on any of the floors. It must have been so late that no one was around. The doors opened on my floor. Dan didn't even notice that we weren't on the penthouse floor. He ripped open my purse. Everything spilled to the floor. I grabbed the key.

"So, you thought you could sneak down to your own little party suite," he said. "You think that I don't know tomorrow is your graduation, your big day. You might try to be free of me then, but tonight you are mine, Cyn, all mine. That's what I was doing when you found me. I was trying to round up some party fellows to help us celebrate. It sure would have been a pretty picture seeing you spread eagle and handcuffed to the bed with all three of us taking turns."

I ran out of the elevator and he was directly behind me. He tackled me. I was sure that I was going to faint. I didn't have any breath to scream. I was just crawling to my door which was just inches away. If only I could get in and lock him out. He grabbed the key from my hand and managed to open the door. With one hand he picked me up by my hair and threw me into the room.

"Well, what is all this?" he growled. "You're all packed and ready to run out on me."

I found my voice and the nice fresh feeling of oxygen filled my lungs. "Dan, you're crazy," I said. "We are both in this together, you know. We are both locked out of our suites. I barely managed these two little rooms for us," I lied.

"What the hell are you talking about?" he screamed as he backhanded me across the sofa.

"Dan, I think you know more about this than I do. You're broke. You've spent too much money on everything. You lost the hotel, and probably everything else. You'll be lucky to still have your job at Bennington's if you don't settle down and sober up before morning."

142

"If I haven't been attending to business as I should have been, then that must be your fault. You're just a tease, Cyn. One minute you're off. One minute you are on. I have wanted you for two years that you have been in Chicago, and you think that one night two months ago when you were drunk is the end of it? Well, if I have lost everything because of you, then, I don't think that you should have anything either. I'm going to get what I want tonight. I am still Dan Callahan tonight, and tomorrow can hang itself."

I tried to run from the suite. Reasoning with him wasn't working. He tackled me again, and my head hit the edge of a small table. Blood gushed everywhere. He picked me up and set me on a small dresser and smashed me back against the gilded mirror. The glass shattered all around me. He punched me right in the eye with his right hand. I was stunned and flew across the room. He jerked me up by my arm and twisted it around my back. I grabbed his long hair with my free hand and screamed as loud as I could. He was just using me as he would a punching bag. He let go of me and I fled to the bedroom and locked the door. All was silent.

I peeked through the keyhole. To my horror Dan was moving everything in the parlor up against the door, all the furniture, all the boxes, everything. He was wild. He was barricading us in. I knew that one of us wasn't getting out alive. As I stumbled to the bed and picked up the phone, the door to my room crashed in.

"No locked door is going to save you tonight, Cyn," said Dan with a menace that I had never heard from him before.

I had just managed to dial the front desk. "I wouldn't do that if I were you, Cyn," he said.

I screamed, "Help, he's trying to kill me."

Dan pulled the phone cord from the wall and grabbed the phone. He hit me with it against the side of my head. I could hear Junior pounding on the door of the suite. "Cynthia, Cynthia, unlock the door," he screamed.

"So, it's the little tweety bird of a boy who has been getting all the good stuff," Dan whispered in my ear as he ripped off my slip and bra. "I knew he went both ways, but, Cyn, how could you choose his little tweeter over my big hammer? You are a slut. I must be broke to have fallen to your level."

"Don't touch me," I screamed, fighting him off. "I'll kill you. I'll kill you," I screamed, kicking and clawing. I managed to punch him in the nose and his blood spilled all over me. With my long fingernails I gouged at his eyes just managing some good scratches.

I looked around the room wildly. I thought about jumping out of the window. *Would suicide be better than this?* I thought blindly.

I was barely managing to crawl across the floor while Dan was ripping off his pants. He was holding me by one ankle and I was smashing his face with the other. It didn't seem to matter. He still had on his shirt and tie. *How ridiculous this must look,* I thought. I was so crazed that my screams turned into fits of laughter. I was crying and screaming and laughing all at the same time. *This isn't happening to me again*, I thought.

Dan threw himself on top of me as I lay struggling on the floor. He ripped off my skirt and pantyhose. I was screaming for my life. I could faintly hear Junior and other voices pounding on the door. Dan pinned me to the floor and thrust himself into me. I screamed in agony. "You really know how to play the game, Cyn. You know us men like it a little rough now and then," he said.

"Now you really know how to please a man, Cynthia. We like it a little rough now and then," I heard the voice say, but it wasn't the voice of Dan. I looked up through my blooded eyes and tears. To my horror I saw the face of my father, and I heard his voice say, "Now you really know how to please a man, Cynthia."

He was pounding me harder and harder. A rush of long ago hidden memories flooded back to me as the pounding continued. "Just spread those leg, girlie, and relax. Your old pop is just teaching you the real facts of life. This is how men really like it, and you will learn to crave for it too."

I was so horrified and panicky that I knew that I must be hallucinating. I tried to live through it by doing what I was told. "Just lay still and relax," said my father's voice. I was trying to be a good girl. I was in a daze. I couldn't believe that this was happening. I stopped fighting and was trying to relax as I was told. Then I saw the face of Dan and the pain shooting through my body brought me back to stark reality. He was raping me, but why had I seen the face of my father and heard his voice?

A shot rang out and both our bodies jumped at the same time. My shoulder was on fire and Dan was being pulled off of me. I barely managed to reach up and pull the spread off the bed. I was trying to cover myself. Junior was at my side instantly. He covered me. I thought that I must have still been hallucinating because I was sure that I saw Carolyn walking in with a gun in her hand. Two policemen rushed in behind her; but I was sure that I saw Carolyn's face. That's when I blacked out.

I awoke in the ambulance on the way to the hospital. I couldn't believe what I saw. Carolyn was sitting there besides me holding my hand. Junior sat beside her steadying her. "Don't talk, now, dear. You are safe," Carolyn said.

Safe, I thought. *When have I ever been safe?*

I looked at Junior. He was crying just a little. "I'm sorry, Cynthia. I should have never left you alone with him," he said through his tears.

I tried to speak, but couldn't. My whole head was bandaged. I was groggy and slipping into a haze. "You're sedated," said Carolyn. "Just close you eyes. I am going to make sure you are safe."

Chapter Twenty

Graduation

I awoke the next morning in the hospital. Carolyn was sleeping on the cot next to my bed. Junior was sleeping in a little chair with his head resting against the wall. I lay there for a minute wondering if I was still in a dream, a dream with my father in it; but I realized all too soon what had happened when I tried to move. The first pain hit me between the legs. Junior awoke first, then Carolyn.

"Lie still, dear, the doctor, will be in soon enough. You have been through quiet an ordeal," said Carolyn. "I am sorry to tell you this, but the police will also want a statement. I am afraid that you are going to miss your graduation ceremony.

Then it hit me. Today was my graduation ceremony. My thesis had finally been finished and accepted. I was to receive my Master's in Business Administration degree today, and here I was in the hospital hooked up to IV's. I could hardly speak, so I just stopped trying. The big clock across from my bed indicated that it was 7:35 A.M. Graduation was scheduled for 10:00 A.M. I couldn't think about or deal with what had happened last night. I didn't understand all of it anyway; I didn't want to remember it. I just wanted to get out of here. I wasn't going to miss graduation. I had worked too hard not to walk up on that stage and be handed my diploma. Somehow I had to think, to plan. Junior would have to help me get out of here, and then I would gladly come back. I didn't know what I would say to the police. I didn't exactly know what I would say to Carolyn. She prob-

145

ably knew more of the truth than I did anyway. I would have to get the whole story from Junior.

I tried to speak, but couldn't. Junior handed me a little pencil and a pad. With my one good hand I wrote. I insisted that Carolyn go to the cafeteria and have some breakfast. Naturally, she refused, but in a mad frenzy of writing I insisted.

"Maybe you better just go on down," suggested Junior. She agreed.

"I could use some coffee," she said. "But when I come back, then you must go," she said to Junior. "I don't want her left alone."

As soon as she was out of the room, I furiously wrote on the pad. "Junior, must get me out of here. I won't miss graduation. If you won't help, I will do it alone."

"Cynthia," said Junior. "You are lucky just to be alive. You have a minor concussion; plus, your whole arm, hand, and wrist have been badly sprained, nearly broken. Cynthia, you were shot in the shoulder. The bullet just grazed Dan and hit you. You have to stay here. It is the best place for you."

I wrote furiously on the pad, "I won't miss graduation. If I have to crawl every inch of the way, I will. I will go to my graduation. You have to help me." Junior was hesitant. "Please, please, help me," I wrote with my one good hand.

"It's against my better judgment," he said. "But, if we are going, we had better go now. I'll be right back." Junior disappeared out the door.

I pulled the IV out of my arm myself. I had underestimated how painful that would be and almost passed out. I was just getting out of bed when Junior reappeared. He had on a pair of green scrubs and a little robe for me. He was pushing a wheel chair. He helped me in and off we went.

"Better put your head down, Cynthia," said Junior. "I'm going to have to lie enough just to get us out the front door. I called a friend of mine who lives just behind the hospital. She's a real drama queen. So don't be surprised at anything, and, for Christ's sake, don't try to speak. I can do everything."

To my surprise, when we wheeled down the hall and past the nurses station, no one said a word. Only a male nurse was there, and he was dozing off himself with his head in his hand. It was either a very late shift for him or a very early one. "Too bad about that," joked Junior. "He was kinda cute."

We made it all the way down to the lobby, when we noticed a pair of policemen coming in with a plain-clothes detective. "Betcha, they're here to see you, my little princess, I mean Cynthia," said Junior. I do believe that he was enjoying this. He wheeled me around and out the back door to the court-yard. As soon as the cops were out of site, back around we went and out the front door. "Hey, Mercedes, over here," said Junior.

A very tall girl wearing a wig and way too much makeup drove up in a little, old car. Junior helped me in and introduced me. Soon we were safe and in her apartment. It had taken all of ten minutes to get me there.

"Cynthia, this is Mercedes," said Jonathan.

"Nice to meet you, Cynthia," said Mercedes as she pulled off her wig. To my surprise she reached in her T-shirt and pulled out a pair of falsies. "In here just call me Michael," she said. "As you can see, I haven't decided to have the operation yet or not. Sit down, lie down, or do whatever you need. Junior, you help her. I'll make us all some breakfast." With that said, she disappeared behind a beaded curtain that looked like it had been a dress at one time or another.

I was reeling with dizziness. I was glad when Junior laid me down on the sofa. "I have some pain pills if you need them," Michael yelled from the kitchen.

Junior helped me with my bandaged head so that I could at least speak. "Okay, tell me everything," I said as best as I could.

"Only on one condition," said Junior. "You keep you mouth shut and just lay there and rest while I tell you the whole story." I shook my head okay.

"Well, you must remember that Dan attacked you," he said. "That is my fault. Oh, Cynthia, that is my fault. I am so sorry. I should have stayed with you." I shook my head no and felt even dizzier. I laid my head back.

"Junior, don't do any confessing, now. You'll only make her feel worse. She just wants the facts," yelled Michael from the kitchen. "This is no time for you to fall apart. Save that for later dear, and I'll be there to catch you."

"That's not funny," said Junior.

"Look, just tell what you know. I am dying to hear it myself. Oh, sorry, girl. I'm just naturally nosy," said Michael.

"Well, it seems that Carolyn came in for your graduation, but the kids stayed home," said Junior. "Why, I don't know." *Thank God for that*, I thought. I was so relieved that they weren't involved with this.

"Seems she was staying in the hotel. Hey, wasn't she supposed to stay with you?" asked Junior. "Well, when she couldn't get into your suite and saw all the boxes, she just barely was able to get a little room on the third floor, same as you. She was waiting up for you and heard all the commotion. I came flying up the stairs and almost knocked her down. It was awful, Cynthia. Almost everyone on that floor was standing around just doing nothing. They were just listening to the fight and you screaming. Not one person was trying to help. One guy was serving drinks. Another had lit a cigarette and was just standing there listening."

"Well, I pushed through the crowd. The door was locked. I kicked and kicked until it finally broke. When I realized it was blocked, I screamed for the other guys to help me push it in. Come on, you idiots. Someone is being murdered," I yelled. Carolyn had already run back to her room to call for help."

"It took three of us to make a little space for me to get through," Junior continued. "After I was in, the others just kept pushing and they all piled in. That's when I saw Dan raping you." He stopped talking and hung his head in shame. He started to cry. I reached out to him. "It was horrible, Cynthia. I felt so helpless. I had never been in a fight before."

"Here, hon," said Michael as he handed Junior a little pill with some orange juice. "This will calm you down so you can finish."

"Thanks, Michael. You can be a real friend, even if you are a bitch most of the time."

"Honey, just finish your story," said Michael.

Michael handed one to me. I didn't care what it was. I was hurting. I took one of the pills too, and the orange juice tasted delicious although my jaw ached.

"I saw Dan on top of you. You were naked and screaming that you would kill him. He was saying that you really knew how to play the game. He kept pounding you. But I knew he was raping you. I just ran into the bedroom and jumped on his back and that is when I heard the gun go off. That's why Carolyn only grazed Dan and hit you. She didn't have a clear shot. Carolyn is the one who fired the gun; I guess it was hers. It is my entire fault. I am so sorry, Cynthia. I should have been able to do more, to defend you. I never knew that Dan was that mentally defective. I knew he was kinky, but not deranged."

Michael came in and put his arm around Junior and tried to console him, but he cried and cried. The reality of what had happened was just hitting him. We were both victims.

Michael said, "I may do drag, and maybe I do have a sexual identity crisis, but I am also a second-year law student. Both of you better get your stories straight, and we better go get this Carolyn person. Who is she anyway?"

Junior and I looked at each other in horror. I wrote on the little pad, 'She's his ex-wife.'

"Oh, my God, you poor babies. This could look very kinky to the police," said Michael.

I tried to speak. "Junior, go get Carolyn. She is probably worried to death. Bring her here, but don't let anybody else know."

"No, Junior should not go back to the hospital," said Michael. "But I'll bet you I can get her out of there without a hitch. Just give me a minute. Cynthia, you write the note to Carolyn that she is to come with me, that I am a friend, and that I will take her to you. I'll be ready in five minutes."

Junior and I just looked at each other. We ate the breakfast Michael had made. With that and the little pill I was feeling a little bit better. To our surprise, Michael appeared in a full nurse's uniform—wig, make up, stocking shoes, and all. He looked like a real woman, just a little tall, but really beautiful. "You can never be too prepared," he said with a little grin. "Wish me luck." He took the note and he was off.

Thirty minutes, then forty minutes, went by. Suddenly he and Carolyn came walking in. Carolyn was furious with me. "What in the world is going on here?" she asked. "Who are these people to you, Cynthia? Where is the phone? You do have one, I presume?" she asked Michael.

"Yes, Granny, I do," he said as he pulled off his wig. Carolyn gave a little shout and sat down hurriedly. "But I am almost a lawyer. I also have a nursing degree, so Cynthia is perfectly okay here. The hospital is just there. And we are all going back there after graduation. Let me explain the situation to you a little clearer than it may seem to you. You all must have to have the same identical stories to tell the cops," continued Michael.

"First and foremost, the three of you have to decide how you all know each other. Cynthia, you have to decide if you are going to press charges against Dan or not. With an ex-wife involved, and you working with him, and, of course, Junior here, to those deadheads at the police station, you may all end up in jail. Dan could easily be the one to walk out a free man. I can just see the papers now, EX-WIFE CATCHES COLLEGE COED WITH HUSBAND, TO BE TRIED FOR ATTEMPTED MURDER. Or, how about this one," he continued, "COLLEGE COED WORKS HERSELF TO THE TOP BY BEING ON THE BOTTOM." I can think of a million of them. If this Dan has any friends left at all, and he probably does owe money to the underworld and they always want their money, it could look like your fault, Cynthia. Poor Junior would have to testify, and we don't want his previous record coming out in court, turning tricks, selling grass, small stuff, but still stuff. I don't know the half of it, but you three better start thinking. This is not all on Dan—of course it is, but with the right lawyers and the right judge, things could go wrong for all of you. That's all I have to say. Now, I have to pick out something for Cynthia to wear to graduation. Let's see, I think I have a little black suit, somewhere." With that he was off and left us to ourselves.

"Cynthia, for the first time I feel indebted to you," said Carolyn. "After hearing all that, it was probably a good idea that you got me out of there. If this were turned the wrong way, it could be bad for St. Alban's, Grahams, your reputation and career, not to mention mine, and of course, we are already indebted to Junior here and Michael. I think that I should call my lawyer in New York."

"No," yelled Michael from the back of the tiny apartment. "That would only make you look like you are already on the defensive. You have to figure out some truth that clears Dan. Unfortunately, that's the secret. When this is all over and settled, just let Junior and I settle with Dan. We know what to do."

Carolyn and I talked for the next two hours, while Michael tried to make me look presentable. We could hear more and more police cars approach the hospital. We were sure that they were looking for me and Junior and probably Carolyn, too. We had no idea what Dan had told them.

We decided that we would deal with Dan later. Carolyn's part would be played down. We would tell as much of the truth as possible; we would not lie. We just wouldn't tell the whole story. Carolyn was correct about everything and more. We had to think about Jonathan and Janie and Marie. If the press got a hold on this story, all our pasts would be dragged out like dirty laundry. We had to think of ourselves and protect the children.

We decided that Carolyn was in town to attend my graduation. Which was the truth. She did have a permit to travel with a gun. She had simply seen what was happening, didn't recognize Dan as her ex-husband from behind in all the confusion, and just shot to protect me. After all, he was only grazed. If she had wanted to she could have blown his brains all over the room. She had always been a good markswoman and won many awards. When she saw that it was Dan, she would say that she was horrified, and that she had already reconciled my working with Dan to present my thesis; that she had even helped give me a reference to work at Bennington's. She would also have to say that she knew nothing about our being in love and planning to be married; that the whole incident had been misunderstood.

I would say that I had been worried about Dan being missing, had gone to that bar and that this boy, Junior, had helped me get him home. Junior would play the hero. Upon arriving back at the hotel, we had had a quarrel, that Dan was upset over losing the hotel, and that the whole thing got out of control. I would not press charges against Dan of rape. Dan would not press charges of attempted murder against Carolyn. Both Dan and I would pay for all damages to the hotel.

We played the little scenario out for Michael and he thought it might work, but said if Carolyn had any legal connections in Chicago, that she should get on the phone now in order to keep the story out of the papers. In the end, the cops would look benevolent and not like dopes along with the District Attorney. Dan's other legal problems with the District Attorney's office could also be taken care of by spreading around a little extra cash to the right people. It was too late to save his real estate holdings, including the hotel. Dan would have to pave his way at Bennington's for him to stay on; that was all he had left. We had a good feeling about it, but how to get the information to Dan. "Oh, don't tell me I have to play nurse, again. Not to that maniac," said Michael.

"No, not you. I'll do it," said Junior. "With a painted face, they will never know it is me, not even Dan. But for starters, I can promise you this. He will have to leave town, because when all this settles, Michael and I are going to make sure that he is the most unwelcome man in any of the bars in Chicago. With his cravings, he'll have to leave town. But you know what, people like that always end up landing on their feet."

Junior looked like a very young nursing student. He got in and out of Dan's room a lot easier that we thought. Michael wrote up all the conditions in as good a legal jargon as he could to make it legal, and Dan signed it without a hitch. We were all so relieved when Junior returned. We sat quietly for a moment letting all that had happened sink in a little.

"I was just wondering how to protect others from him," I said aloud, mostly to myself, but the others picked up on it.

Carolyn spoke up first, "We'll deal with that later, dear. Now, let us clear our minds, and try to get with this graduation."

Since only the doctors were looking for me now and the police had left, we felt fairly safe. Dan had been discharged from the hospital and no charges were pending. He would have to put in some time at the store just to keep his job. We didn't worry any more about him just then.

I didn't want to go back to the hospital before graduation. Michael and Junior helped me dress. Junior took Carolyn back to the hotel and she picked up something for me to wear. I told everyone at school that I had been in a car accident. They all felt so sorry for me.

Junior wheeled me right up to the front. As soon as I got that diploma, I left the campus. Carolyn, Junior, Michael, and I headed back to the hospital. I was glad that it was over and that I had my diploma. My school counselor had already told me he had the outline for the book, and that when I was feeling better we could start the real writing of it. I was elated, but tired.

I was shown to my hospital room. I undressed and put on a little pink gown that was Carolyn's. Junior and Michael left and went home. Junior assured me that he would be safe. Carolyn stayed with me and insisted that all she needed was a little nap. The nurse came in and hooked me up to the IV, the usual so that I wouldn't get dehydrated, and gave me a little pain shot. I was just about to fall asleep when the doctor came in.

"Hello," he said as he glanced at my chart. "My name is Dr. Thompson." His southern drawl sounded familiar. I looked up from my hazy sleep. "So you are Cynthia Thomas. You look so familiar to me. Say, you're not from down south are you?" he asked. "I had a patient down there when I worked at the Veterans' Hospital."

I thought I recognized him. "Yes, I am," I said. "I am not from Chicago. You knew me then as Cynthia Thomas and Mrs. Eddie Morgan."

"Well, I am so glad to see you again," he said as he took my hand. "I've always wondered what happened to you and hoped that we would meet again." He gave a little laugh and looked back at the chart. His mood seemed a little lighter. I noticed that he wasn't wearing any wedding ring. I glanced over at Carolyn. She gave me a little wink.

He came back to check on me after 8:00 P.M. He wasn't wearing his usual doctors white coat. He wore a bright red knit shirt and khaki pants with loafers. He was so handsome even out of his whites. "How's my little patient tonight," he asked as he took my hand.

"Well, I am a little groggy, with all the pain medication," I said.

"We can taper that off in a few days," he said as he took my pulse.

"What does Mrs. Thompson think of all the long hours you have here at the hospital?" I asked coyly. "It is awfully late you know. I was almost asleep."

He said, "You should be asleep and not asking so many questions." He turned to go. He stopped for a moment at the door. He turned and said,

"And, by the way, Cynthia, there is no Mrs. Thompson. Now rest, sleep, and I will see you bright and early in the morning." He left singing a little song.

I looked over at Carolyn. She smiled. I felt safe again.

Chapter Twenty-one

In Order to Publish My Book

I enjoyed my two weeks in the hospital. I could have left after one, but Dr. Thompson insisted. His name was Bill, Bill Thompson. I didn't know if patients always fell in love with their doctor, but I knew after that first day that I could surely love him. He had only gotten more handsome during the past years. He was almost thirty years old by my calculation and just beginning to gray at the temples, yet his hair was wavy and shiny black, cut short. He was as tall as ever, well over six feet. He was so trim. He loved tennis and played racquetball every day.

Upon Carolyn's insistence, I had to tell him about the real circumstances of that night. I was so embarrassed when he told me that he would have to take more blood samples to run venereal tests and a pregnancy test, plus he wanted me checked thoroughly by my gynecologist. He insisted on some psychological counseling. I couldn't do much about the blood tests, but I assured my counselor after two weeks that I was sure that I would survive. Inside, I knew that I had been dealt a terrible scarring emotionally. *So what,* I thought bravely, *they have been adding up since I was a little girl.* I didn't take the advice given to me to join a battered women's group who had encountered similar things. I just wanted to forget all about it and get on with my life. I never told anyone about seeing my father's face. I convinced myself that that was just a bad and terrible dream.

I resumed my work at the store. Dan had been fired. I didn't ask why. I simply presumed that he had been his own undoing: coming in to work late, not showing up at all, leaving early. I heard that he had even shown up one day around noon drunk with alcohol on his breath. "He looked like he had worn that same suit for weeks," I overheard a salesgirl say.

Carolyn had wanted me to return to St. Alban's for safety. I had objected. "But, why, Cynthia? Why stay now that all this has happened; and you have your MBA. I have a beautiful home for you and the children need you, and I especially need you now. I am not getting any younger, and the store is wearing me out."

I agreed to come home for my two-week vacation. Carolyn was a little hesitant about having Junior come along. "Carolyn, after all he has done for the both of us, especially me. I owe it to him."

"But, to expose his element to the children," she said. "I don't think that is a good idea."

"Carolyn, the children are already being exposed to men like him," I replied. "They know more about that lifestyle that we do. We are the ones who have to understand. Junior and Michael are two of the nicest men I have ever met. They would do anything for me. They lack the freedom that we have, the real freedom to move through society with no fear of being beaten, ridiculed, or even killed. They face discrimination and contempt everyday of their lives. They're lucky to just make it through another day. That is why they band together. We are the one's who are out of touch. Surely, you have met at least one gay man in your whole life."

"Yes, I have," she said solemnly, "and more. I just didn't want to acknowledge their existence. I guess they are in every walk of life. Of course, you are correct, Cynthia, Junior may come as well as Michael. We'll just have a gay old time of it." I looked at her with a sour smile.

"It was meant as a joke, Cynthia," she said. "In my day the word gay meant something entirely different." She gave me a big hug and we held on to each other for a long time. I needed it and I think she did also.

"Then, to make the two weeks even more interesting, would it be too terribly awful of me to invite Bill to come down for a couple of weekends?" I asked.

"Well, naturally, you'll need to have a follow up with your doctor, so, yes, of course," she said with a little twinkle in her eye. "But, before we leave Chicago, we are going to find some suitable housing for you to live in when you return." She was correct, but it was also her way of changing the subject. A subject with which she just wasn't familiar, and one that made her a little anxious and afraid. I could no longer stay at the hotel. It wasn't safe. I secretly believed that Dan was still around, somewhere.

That summer of 1974 was even more glorious than the year before. Although they didn't say it, I believed that Junior and Michael had probably never been out of Chicago until then. They had both been born there and there they had stayed.

The first thing I did when we got to the beach was to buy them both some decent clothes. "Oh, no," I said. "Men's things only." We had gone shopping in the little town nearby, and to my surprise both Junior and Michael ran into several of their friends who were vacationing there from Chicago. Junior had stopped me to look at a dress in a store window and said, "Cynthia, this would be a killer dress on you."

"No," I said. "We are here to shop for you." But they both insisted and so I went inside to look at it.

Neither Junior nor Michael was the least anxious about being in an exclusive shop just for women. Before long, they had piled up three dresses that they said, "were must-haves." To please them, I bought all of them. Naturally, one was a little black cocktail dress with long sleeves, a high collar and a full skirt. I was just drawn to it for some reason.

"Come on you guys, let's finish shopping for you," I said. "And we'll buy something for everyone waiting back at the beach house too." We had a whole day of fun shopping. One thing these guys had was taste, good taste.

Bill came down several times during those two weeks, which stretched into three. I had called Bennington's and was told to take as much time as I needed. He spent two whole weekends with us. He played more on the beach with the kids, which now included Junior and Michael, than I did. Carolyn always watched from the shade of the big wrap around porch. She was always knitting something. "You know, Cynthia, I have to keep my hands busy," she would always say.

It was a wonderful time. The house was filled with all of us. Carolyn and I shared her room. She had a little twin bed fitted into one corner for me. I was glad. I could resist any temptations with Bill, not that he offered any, but he was my constant companion when he was there. I knew we were falling in love.

Junior and Michael shared their own room and bath. Carolyn thought that best for some reason. Jonathan had his own room. Janie and Marie always shared their same room. Poor Bill was regulated to the little attic room that Carolyn hurriedly had converted into a small bedroom with a bath. It was finished just in time.

I called my counselor several times and sent him several ideas on my book. I was going to make it my next project. He never mentioned Dan, and neither did I.

The little romance that I had expected to develop between Jamie and Junior never happened. Jamie and Junior and Michael were always a team, but they seemed to blend in so well with Jonathan, Bill, Janie, and Marie. Carolyn and I were sitting on the little porch one day watching all of them play on the beach. "I guess this must be what having a lot of kids feels like," she said with a smile. "During their stay here, I have a learned a little something about each one of them. I do believe that I am falling in love with each and every one of them."

As usual, she was correct. We were just like one big happy family. Jamie and Junior and Michael never hid the fact that they were gay, but they always tried to make everyone feel comfortable with who they were. All of us learned a lot that summer at the beach.

During our last night there, Carolyn ordered a formal dinner. She had grown especially close to Junior. "Junior, will you say grace for us," she asked. He looked around sheepishly and said, "God we acknowledge you for who you are in your almightiness. We ask you to forgive our sins, as we ask you to forgive the sins of those who sin against us and you. Oh, Lord, we give thanks for this food and all that we have and all the bounty of the whole world. We ask you to bless those who are present tonight, and the fellowship that we have found here. Please, give us the grace to be shining examples of acceptance, understanding, love, and forgiveness that is necessary to make the world a peaceful place in which to live." He finished and looked down. All were silent for a moment and all eyes were on him. We all felt a little bewildered and humbled by his prayer.

"Well, I may be gay, but I am no heathen," he said with a laugh. With that said, the meal started and Carolyn even opened two bottles of her favorite wine. We did have a gay old time that night.

Too soon, the three weeks were over and we were all thrown back into reality. I think that we certainly underestimated then the power we had of being together. I know that I felt even more fractured when I got back to Chicago. I had so much for which to be thankful. When I arrived at my new apartment, it had already been redecorated. Carolyn had done it again, and I was a little resentful that I had not had the chance to do it myself. It was a small place, but it was perfect in style, grace, and taste. I immediately knew Bill would be comfortable there when we dated.

Janie and Marie were going to the high school in St. Alban's. Janie would graduate in one year. She was already working at Grahams along with Jonathan and Carolyn. I was so thankful for that. Marie had thrown herself into the full workings of the drama club and was the best Juliet they ever had for their fall play. I was just sorry that I couldn't make it.

If all that I had gone through was going to have any lasting value, any meaning whatsoever, I had to continue my work at all the Bennington stores. My counselor at school said that if I wasn't totally involved in the renovation and computerization of them, that my book would have little merit. So back to work I went. I would have to start traveling extensively to oversee the change in each store.

My last night in Chicago, Bill took me to a small Italian restaurant in a part of Chicago that I had never seen. It was the Italian district, or had been. I didn't even know it existed. The restaurant was as quaint as it could have possibly been.

When we arrived, we were greeted at the door by an elderly gentleman in a beautiful suit, an old suit, but made of beautiful blue wool cloth and freshly cleaned. "Hello, Dr. Thomson. Welcome back to Mario's," he said. "You have been away too long, shame on you" He even shook his finger at us.

"Hello, Mario," said Bill. "It is good to be here, again." We were shown to a little table near the window. All the tables had red and white tablecloths with melted candles in Chianti bottles. Pictures of Italy lined the walls. You could tell from the smells coming from the kitchen, that the food was good here. The place smelled of Italy. It was small and cozy. Mario's wife, Rosa, even came out of the kitchen to welcome us, especially Bill.

"Oh, my baby, why have you stayed gone so long," she said as she wiped her hands on her apron. Obviously, she was the main chief. "You have stayed gone too long this time," she said as she put her big chubby arms around him and kissed him on both cheeks.

"And, who is this beautifully dressed lady you have brought to our little humble eatery?" she said smiling.

"Mama Rosa, this is my fiancé, Cynthia Thomas," said Bill. Mario rushed over. I was flabbergasted. I was sure that he didn't mean to say the word fiancé. I just blew it off in all the excitement.

"Not the beautiful Cynthia Thomas that I see in the society columns all the time," she said.

I was so embarrassed, that I am sure that I blushed. "Well, yes, that is I," I said. Mama Rosa helped herself to a chair and sat down with us.

"Oh, you young girls of today are so lucky, don't you think, Mario," she said as she tugged at his sleeve. "In my day, we didn't have your chances. We just got married and with a little luck, we made it through. Of course, my own marriage was arranged for me. Did you know that I never met Mario until the night before the ceremony, right here in this little restaurant? His father owned it then. Oh, but I don't have any regrets. Mario has been a good husband, and Bill has been like a son to us. High time you settled down yourself, young man, Dr. Thompson," she said as she gave Bill another big wet kiss on the forehead. "You think about what Mama Rosa says."

"Come along, Mama," said Mario. "As usual, you have said too much already." They argued in Italian all the way back to the kitchen, but you could tell that they were still very much in love. Pretty soon a bottle of Chianti arrived at our table.

"My name may be Dr. Bill Thompson," he said. "But my mother was Maria Gonzales Alonzo. She and Mama Rosa were girls here together. Did you know that I grew up in this neighborhood? That is why I returned here, to be close to my family."

"Yes, I know that. You said so on one of our dates at the beach," I replied. "And would you like a large family, too."

"Not as big as my family," he said. "You know there are eight of us kids. Mom and Pop struggled all their life to see to it that all us amounted to something better than they had. And they were successful. My sister is a surgeon. You know that I am an internal specialist. Five of my brothers are lawyers and have their own law partnership. And the baby is in the seminary. He will be ordained in two years. My mom and dad are still alive. Someday you will meet them. It seems that we are ready for anything."

"Yes," I said. A little silence fell around us. We drank the Chianti in silence and our meal was served. We never saw a menu. Mama Rosa had just decided that we would have the veal parmesan.

"Bill," I finally said. "Why did you introduce me as your fiancé?"

"Oh, I am sorry about that," he said. "I hoped that that would be a surprise." Suddenly a large arrangement of red roses was delivered to the restaurant, and I could see Mario heading our way with it. He set them down on edge of the table and left without a word.

Bill stood up and came around to my chair. He knelt on one knee. He reached in his pocket and pulled out a little ring box, and said, "I had it planned so beautifully, Cynthia. I'm just a clumsy fool of a doctor I guess. But I know that I love you and that I want to spend the rest of my life with you." He opened the box. It held a one-carat diamond ring set in platinum. "Will you marry me, Cynthia?" he asked me. "I know that we will have good times as well as bad times. There may even be times when we both want to get out. I pray that we will always stay together. But, I know that if I don't ask you now, it will break my heart."

I was so stunned that I didn't know what to say or do. "Well, this ring isn't doing anybody any good in the box," he said. He slipped the ring on my finger. Everyone in the restaurant was staring at us, even Mario and Mama Rosa were peeking around the kitchen door.

I felt compelled to say yes, then no, but to everyone's relief I just said, "Yes." The restaurant exploded with applause. "Oh, Bill," I said. "The roses are so beautiful and the ring is exquisite. Your proposal wasn't clumsy. It was perfect. How was I to say anything but yes. You don't give a girl a chance."

"You slipped away from me once many years, ago," he said tenderly as he held my hand across the table. "I'm not going to let that happen again."

"But Bill, I don't know what kind of a wife or mother I would make. You know this is so soon after, that is, after my, my 'accident.' Do you know what I mean?"

"Cynthia, I love you," he said. "Do you love me, too?" he asked.

"Yes, I do," I answered. "I knew that I loved you that night in the hospital, and that love just grew through the summer, especially when I saw how you were with Carolyn and my brother and sisters, and, even Jamie, Junior, and Michael. You know we consider them all our family, and Carolyn and I will always do whatever is necessary to protect and take care of them. None of us are perfect and we all have our problems. Are you sure that you want to take us all on?"

"Are you kidding, you haven't even met my family yet," he said.

"Yes, I know, but, well, that is, we are somewhat opposites of your family aren't we?" I asked.

"Yes, and that is why I love you even more," he said. "Loving Carolyn is easy along with your brother Jonathan, whom I think is a swell guy, and Janie and Marie are going to be just fine. You'll see. As far as your gay friends are concerned, I bet you didn't know that I roomed with a gay fellow in college. Of course, I'm not sure he even knew then. All the girls were crazy for him; he was so handsome and charming. I always suspected that he might be. I'm not sure why. I just did. There are so many gay people around today. I think that we know. We just choose to ignore them. That's probably wrong. Hey, how did we get so long winded on that subject? You really still haven't said yes."

"Yes, I will marry you, Bill." He stood and kissed me across the table.

"Cynthia, you have made me the happiest man in the world."

Our little romantic dinner ended and there were hugs and kisses all around from Mario and Mama Rosa who couldn't stop crying. "Oh, don't even think of paying this bill," said Mario as he tore it into tiny pieces that he let tumble to the floor.

That night we took a long walk around the old neighborhood, and made plans to introduce me to his family. "Bill," I said as we walked arm in arm. "You know that I probably don't want to be a stay-at-home mom, that I have to do this book, that I want to be a career woman."

"Darling, nothing matters, now," he said. "Work, don't work, write, do anything you want to do. All that matters is that we are going to be married. And I am the luckiest man on the planet." He was riding high on that emotion.

He told me more about himself that night than he had ever done before. He didn't come right out and say it, but I do believe he was still a virgin. I didn't ask and he didn't tell, but he mentioned several girls that he had taken on dates, but that they were never anything serious. His parents never approved of any of them. I was his first love, he said so.

On the other hand, he knew almost everything about me. "Bill, there is only one question that I want you to answer," I said.

"Of course, darling, anything," he replied.

"Can we have a long engagement, at least a year?" I asked. He looked a little disappointed. I felt so guilty for that. He had been so good to me. "I want to get the book finished and over with, and besides, I'm not sure that I am ready for, well, you know, ready for any sort of sex. There, I have just said it. Is that okay?"

He stopped walking. He took me in his arms and said, "Cynthia, can I kiss you? Are you ready for that, I mean a real kiss? Not just the little on the cheek kiss that we have been having all summer?" I held him even tighter. He kissed me ever so gently and smoothly on my lips. I could feel his tongue, but he wasn't being forceful. He made me want it and I did. We must have stood there for several minutes, because the little lace curtains at the window of the brownstone building that we were standing in front of began to flutter and move. We could tell that we were being watched.

"Come on," I said with a little laugh. "We better move on."

As we walked on, he said, "I'll answer your question like this, Cynthia. The wedding can take place next month or next year, when ever you are ready, my dearest, but I think that I have the right to know and so do you. Do you want to be engaged to be married? Do you want to be engaged to me? Yes or no. Tell me, now. For that answer I can't wait."

"Oh, yes," I said. "I do."

"Good, because I want to be engaged to you too," he said. "But there are four things that I want you to do for me," he continued.

"What could that possibly be?" I asked.

"First, I want you to go into therapy. You have got to deal with some of the horror that has happened in your life before you can really take on any more lifelong obligations. I can set you up with the best psychiatrist or psychologist there is in Chicago. Do you have a problem with that?"

I hung my head in shame, "No, I know I need it."

"Good," he answered. "And I will go with you to every session that you need me to. Secondly, finish that book just as soon as you can," he said.

"I'll make it six months or less," I promised.

"Thirdly, come home with me, tonight, and meet my parents," he said.

"But Bill, I am not ready for that. I'm dressed all wrong. I need to freshen up, at least, I don't have the right clothes."

"Excuses, excuses, excuses," he said. "Then, if not tonight, when?"

"Would tomorrow be rushing it too soon?" I asked with a blush and a little giggle.

"No," he said. "That's perfect. And, fourthly, darling, don't worry about the sex between us," he said gently. "I want it, of course, but only when you are ready."

"Thank you Bill. That is the nicest thing you have said tonight," I said as I gave him another kiss. "Now, there is something that you can do for me."

"Anything, just name it," he replied.

"Call us a cab. My feet are killing me." We both laughed at that, and were back at my apartment in just a few minutes. I kissed him tenderly on the lips, and I could feel his response. I knew then that I wanted to be with him for the rest of my life just at that moment, and I could tell that he felt the same for me.

As his cab rolled away from the curb, I felt lonely instantly. As soon as I was inside, I called Carolyn to tell her the good news. She was ecstatic. We talked for hours just like schoolgirls. I was happy and so was she. Bill and I were in love. The kids were coming along nicely. Everything seemed to good to be true. And it was.

When I arrived at Bennington's the next morning, I was called to the manager's office to discuss the renovations at the other stores and to make a schedule. I was horrified. I was to do all of them within one year. "It's not possible," I said.

I was told that I would have to do it or they would just get someone else, after all, they had all the documentation from the first two. The orders came straight from headquarters, there in Chicago. After three hours of discussions, arguing, and trying to be reasonable, I quit. If they wanted me to do the work, they would have to hire me as a consultant. My asking price was $200,000 or they could get someone else. We finally settled on $150,000, and I would only be responsible for three more stores: San Francisco, St. Louis, and New Orleans. After that, we could renegotiate if both parties agreed.

"Oh, Cynthia, I am so glad that we have come to these terms," said the assistant manager as he walked me out into the hall. "You know, I have always been on your side. If there is anything that I can do."

"Yes, sure, thank you," I said. I just wanted to get out of there.

"By the way, where can we messenger over the contracts and any other papers," he said a little too eagerly.

I stopped walking dead in my tracks. To ask that question he must have known that I wasn't living at the hotel any longer. I kept walking. "I'll call you later," I said. I went home. I needed time to think about that last statement. I called the store and told the manager that I would receive all my department mail at the store, and that I would need an office there, that would have to be part of the deal. It only made sense. I wasn't setting up a private consulting firm. Naturally, someone else had taken my old office.

I didn't see Bill that night. He was on call, but we did manage a short conversation. I was a little disappointed. I would have to meet his parents another night.

I went to the store the next morning and the assistant manager showed me my new office, which was just a small space converted from part of the warehouse. It had a desk, one chair, a file cabinet, and no window. I was so disappointed. I wasn't on the executive floor any longer. It was practically an insult and I knew it. *Oh, well, how bad can it be. I'll be traveling, anyway,* I thought.

On my desk were the consulting contracts, which I signed and sent upstairs. The other package was labeled "Packard and Callahan." The name Callahan came reaching out for me so as to choke me. I had to sit down. I opened it slowly. Inside there was nothing except a short note which read, "Congratulations, Cyn. If you are reading this then you must have gotten the job. You didn't think that I was so stupid as to be fired and leave all these drawings and design plans just laying around did you? No, I drew them and when I was fired I took them with me. Everyone knows about it. I threatened to sue, and those candy-ass lawyers who work for you all know how my lawyers would be working on them if they hadn't agreed. I was fired as store manager, but the Board of Directors knew that the other stores would never be ready in a year without the original drawings, so I had them by the 'shorthairs.' Ha! Ha! They weren't about to trust a woman to get the job done." The note continued, to my horror.

"I have them and you don't. I agreed that I would work with Packard Brothers as part of the deal. You know they are the largest and finest design firm in Chicago. Packard and I have formed a small, exclusive company called Packard and Callahan. I know that you have already signed your consulting contract with Bennington's. The Board loves the idea. You are there under contract to oversee the renovations. I am out of their hair as store manager, but I have the plans and will be working with Packard Brothers. It couldn't have worked out better for the store, the board of directors, or the stockholders. Everyone is ecstatic over the deal. All the key players are still in, plus a nationally prominent design firm. Naturally, I let them think the whole thing was your idea. So you see, Cyn, it looks like we are going to still be doing a little business together." The note was signed, "In with you for the long haul, partner, Dan Callahan." I was so stunned I thought that I had turned to stone. I jumped when my phone rang.

"Hey, Cyn, did you get my little package yet?" It was Dan Callahan.

"I can't believe that you have the nerve to call me," I said.

"Why not, we're practically partners," he said. "You can crash and burn, or you can still try and break that glass ceiling. Looks like you are going to need a little man help to get there, though. Let's talk about it over lunch. I've changed, Cyn, I really have, and you're the little girl that did it all. If you play your cards right you can probably get you picture on the cover of News magazine by this time next year."

My stomach turned sour, but I agreed to meet him for lunch. In a public restaurant he would be a fool to try anything, plus I brought along Julie, my secretary. I would never be foolish to be alone with him ever again.

I called Carolyn immediately. "You are a fool to go through with it, Cynthia," she said, furiously. "My advice is to come home immediately. We can work on your wedding plans and you can fly in and out of Chicago every weekend to see Bill. Stop while you are ahead. Have you forgotten that Dan Callahan almost killed you?" She was livid.

I told her that I would have to think about it, and that I would call her later, but my book depended on me renovating at least three more stores. These three stores were recent acquisitions by Bennington's, and their successful renovations were the proof that I needed to turn my thesis into a real book. I called my counselor, now my collaborator, at school. I only told him the skeleton of the planned framework about the three stores. He said that it was a perfect situation, and the book was going to be a surefire bestseller.

"It is just one more step to getting my book published," I told myself. I knew that I could never tell Bill until it was all over. I wasn't even married yet, and already I was keeping secrets from my husband. I felt guilty about everything. How did I ever get myself into all of this? It was all my fault. I would just have to grin and bear it. I would have to do it Dan's way, even if it meant defending myself. I was sure that I would.

I left the store and bought a .38-caliber gun. I loaded it with bullets in my car. I held it for a long time. It was a pretty little thing with a silver barrel and an ivory handle. It made me smile.

I would do whatever I had to do. It could all blow up in my face. I may even die, but I was sure to write that book. I would collect all the work from my collaborator and would start a whole new episode. If Dan killed me in the process, at least, I would have authorship of this much and almost all the credit. If I were killed, at least I would be remembered by this much. I was determined to be a somebody. I had to prove my father wrong. I was already a highly educated woman, and now a highly paid consultant of the seventies. I would seal my future by being a published author, a good wife of a prominent Chicago doctor, and a good mother. I would break the stereotype of women. I would have it all. I had already lied and cheated and been a little sluttish. I knew God had forgiven me, if only I could forgive myself, maybe with a little more luck I could make it, even if I had to kill Dan Callahan.

Chapter Twenty-two
Engaged and Married

I met Dan for lunch. In the cab I prepared Julie for a lot of traveling for at least six months. She, of course, knew nothing about the rape. I felt guilty for keeping her involved. What if Dan harmed her? Everything was turning so fast. There were so many questions and very few answers.

The restaurant was large. Even so, I could see Dan sitting right in the middle of it smoking his usual cigar and with a drink in front of him. "Well, hello, Cynthia. And may I say how lovely you are looking today. And, Julie, what a surprise it is to see you here," he said. He looked us both up and down as if we were wearing nothing at all.

"Julie will be joining us on our travels, Mr. Callahan. She has been so involved in the renovations so far that she knows just what we want."

"Oh, I am sure she knows exactly what we want," said Dan as he gave her hand a little pat. She instinctively withdrew it and looked at me helplessly. She was such a mouse. She looked like a little mouse that had been bitten by a snake. Dan's reputation was known all over the city.

"Excuse me," said Julie. "I'll be right back."

"Wait," I said, "I'll go with you."

"No, I'm okay, really," she said. "Just order me a Coke and a hamburger. I'll be right back."

"But little Julie," said Dan. "This place has the best steaks in town. Don't you want a big juicy piece of meat?"

Julie just looked at me hopelessly and walked off saying, "No, thanks, I don't eat big meals at lunch."

I started to get up and go with her anyway. I thought that Julie and I should leave. Maybe, I should think this whole thing over. Had Julie already had her own problems with this monster? Everything was going so wrong, so soon.

As I got up, Dan grabbed my hand and pulled me back down into my chair. "Don't be a fool Cynthia. And, don't make a scene. There are important people here that you don't even know about."

"She is a high-strung little nobody of a secretary," he continued coolly. "You don't fool me. I already know why you keep her around. If she makes you feel safe, then that is fine with me, but I have something to say to you that is going to surprise you, and I hope it makes the next six months go smoothly. If that girl, Julie, wants to leave, let her. We may never have this chance again."

"I want you to know, Dan Callahan, that I hate and despise you and I will hate you till the day you die," I said with as much malice as I could manage and still smile. I didn't want a scene either.

"Is everything, okay here, Mr. Callahan?" asked the waiter as he walked by our table.

"Sure, Johnny, sure," said Dan. "We just can't decide what to order." Obviously, Dan had brought us to a place where he was well known. The waiter walked off giving me the evil eye. I was so pathetic for even being there.

"Look, keep your voice down," Dan said. "Do you want people to hear you? Paul Packard is meeting us here for lunch. He is recently divorced and a little despondent. He isn't paying much attention to details. It was all I could do to get him out of his office. It was I that convinced him that he should meet you, that after all, he should know who he is doing business with. You're lucky, Cynthia. He is a very powerful and influential man here in this city. Please, don't say anything," he begged.

He was acting differently, now that Julie wasn't around. "Look I know that things got a little out of hand. I have no excuses for my behavior the last time I saw you. I was drunk and a little crazy on drugs, but that is all finished, now, Cynthia. I'm over all that now. I hope you are okay. I will forever be in your debt. This deal may be my last chance to save my ass, and I need your help. I am not asking you to forgive me. I am not even asking you to understand what really happened."

I stopped him right there. "What really happened? Dan, you raped me. There are witnesses," I said under my breath. But I could feel that he was desperate.

"I can't explain that part, now, Cynthia, but I will later. For now, I need you to get through this lunch like we are the best of friends. And really, I am glad Julie is along. It makes it look even better, more professional." That was the last thing that he could say before Paul Packard came through the door of the restaurant and was shown to our table.

As he was walking across the room, Julie ran right into him. "Oh, I am so sorry, sir," she said.

"Please, don't worry about it," he said.

Then there was that little right step, left step thing. They couldn't get out of each other's way. Someone stood up and accidentally pushed their chair into the back of Julie and she was pushed right into Paul's arms. Naturally, there were apologies all around. When Julie and Paul both ended up at the same table they both looked at each other stupidly. I must say that it was Dan who saved the day and introduced everyone. We all made such a big joke out of the whole thing, especially Julie and Paul. The ice was broken, and I was a little relieved. I don't remember one thing about that meal except that it seemed to take forever. We never discussed business, and Paul couldn't keep his eyes off of Julie. He was one of those men who just believed in fate. She said little and giggled through the whole meal. She and I said nothing in the cab back to the store.

This isn't going well at all, I thought.

Just as I entered my office, my phone rang. I practically jumped out of my seat. "Meet me across the street in the little corner bar," the voice said. It was Dan.

"Who the hell do you think you are? And, don't think that I am going to play pimp for your Mr. Paul Packard with Julie," I said. Julie entered.

"Did you call me, Cynthia?" she said.

"No, I am on the phone."

"Oh, okay," she said as she floated out the door.

"Look," said Dan. "You and I have to set things right. We have to get a fresh start on this thing from the beginning. A lot of doors could open for both of us. If you don't come down here, then I'll come up there."

"You wouldn't dare," I said.

"I would, Cynthia. I have something important to say to you for your own sake, regardless of this deal," he said sternly. "Now, come down here immediately and let's get this thing straightened out." He hung up. I knew he was serious.

I grabbed my coat and purse and made some excuse to Julie. I told her to meet me outside in thirty minutes. "I thought we could both use some shopping time," I said with a little smile. She was so pleased. I had never asked her such a personal thing before.

"Oh, Cynthia, thank you. I would love to. You have such great taste, and I…"

"Okay," I interrupted, "…thirty minutes."

"Sure," she said. "I'll be there."

I walked the seventeen stories down the stairs. I didn't want anyone to see me leaving the store, and I especially didn't want to be seen entering the bar.

"Well, did you call me down here just to sit there?" I said to Dan as I stood over him from behind. I wasn't in a good mood and I wanted to be mean and I wanted this to be over as quickly as possible.

"Oh, Cynthia, you startled me," he said as he stood and held the chair for me.

"Never mind that. I'd rather sit across from you than just beside you," I said sarcastically.

"Okay, Cynthia, play it your way. You deserve that much," he said.

"Oh, I deserve a lot more than that. I should kill you right here on the spot," I said furiously.

"Just sit down. I have to say what I have to say, and then you can do what ever you want," he said. "I know that you don't have to do this deal. I know that you don't have to write a book if you don't want to. I can plainly see that."

"And, how would you know that?" I replied.

"Why, who could miss that sparkler on your finger? I noticed it during lunch. Who is the lucky man?" asked Dan.

"Never mind that. Just say whatever it is you have to say," I said. "I have to get back to the store. Someone is expecting me in about twenty-five minutes. If I am not out of here by then, you will regret it till the day you die, I may have to kill you."

"Hey, Dan," yelled the bartender across the bar. "Did that dame say she was going to kill you?" he asked jokingly. "What kind of trouble you into now, you bad boy?"

"Don't be stupid," said Dan as he waved him off.

I was just bristling underneath my clothes; that is how mad I was. Dan could tell.

"Look, this is what I want to tell you," he said. "I know what happened that night. And I am not trying to make excuses. But Cynthia, you have only your version, and I have mine. I think that you have to hear my version to have a clear picture. I know that is all behind us, and I am grateful, but I am not sure that it is all behind you. The only reason that I am doing this is for your own good, because I am still in love with you. There will never be another woman for me, not like you."

I wasn't going to argue. "Dan, just say whatever. I can't promise I will believe you or that I am even listening to you, but I am here. Just say the words and I will leave."

"Cynthia, for starters, it was you who pulled me out of that sleazy bar. I was drunk and full of all kind of drugs, but you know me. I thought you wanted to play. I was outraged and embarrassed that I had lost everything, the hotel and you. I was all messed up. When you started struggling, I thought that was just the way you wanted it, so I was playing it a little rough. We'd had it that way before; you remember. But this time you were different. Halfway through the doing of it you looked up at me and called me 'daddy.' It was about then that Carolyn shot me. It was only later that I realized that you must have been hallucinating. Cynthia, you should have told

167

me long ago about your father. I knew you hated him. I just didn't know why. I should have figured it out, myself. He raped you didn't he?"

I turned the color of white paper. I was sure of it. My worse enemy knew my darkest secret, one that I wouldn't even admit to myself. How had everything gotten so out of control, so out of hand? Nervously, I stood. I steadied myself with my fingertips on the tabletop.

"It's a lie. What you say is a lie," I said, calmly. "What you say is worse than asking me for forgiveness, for understanding. You are just trying to pull me down to you level of filth. If you dare say that again, I promise that I will kill you."

"But, Cynthia, I only thought that maybe you needed to know that. You don't know this, but I am in court-ordered counseling. I was arrested in New Orleans for drunken driving. I don't even have a driver's license. I don't even remember going to New Orleans, or how I got there. It was last month when everything was going so wrong and right before our incident. I am remembering some things about my own childhood. Truly, I didn't mean for this to hurt you. I only thought it could help."

"You can only help me by never mentioning it again, ever. Never find yourself alone with me, or I may kill you," I said.

"Hey, Dan," the bartender yelled out again. "She said it again. She said she was going to kill you. Man you are bad." He was boasting for Dan. I never dreamed he could have heard me, or that Julie would walk in at just that minute.

I rushed across the bar and grabbed Julie by the hand. "Come on, kid, let's get out of here," I said to Julie.

"Hey, lady, you're ruining my business. Don't pull my customers out of here," the drunken bartender yelled at me as we ran in front of him. Dan was right behind us. I hailed a taxi.

"Julie, what ever possessed you to go in there?" I asked her frankly. I'll never forget her answer.

"Cynthia, I could hear you screaming from outside on the sidewalk about killing somebody," she said. "What were you and Dan Callahan arguing about?" she asked.

I was so embarrassed and ashamed. It was all my fault. I had been yelling and hadn't even known it.

I took a deep breath and turned to her. I smiled and said. "Oh, nothing, Julie, just business. You know how he exasperates me so. It's nothing. Really, it is nothing. Let's do that shopping."

Poor Julie, poor, little bewildered Julie. "Honestly," she said. "I was never so scared in all my life."

"It's nothing," I said as I looked out the window.

"Well, thank heaven for that. But, Cynthia, I do have some news and a favor to ask of you."

I turned to her. She was so such a little mouse of a girl. What could she have that was possibly news and what kind of a favor did she want? Everybody always wanted something from me. I was in no mood for this, but it was my only escape.

"Well, what?" I asked.

She said, "Paul Packard called not ten minutes after you had left."

Oh, my God, I thought. "What did he want?" I asked with great irritation.

"Oh, nothing from you, but he asked me out to dinner," she said. "I need you to help me pick out something special for tonight. It's our first date."

"Of course, my dear. We'll find something, together," I said. I wanted to be happy for her. I wasn't sure that it was a good idea, but I couldn't advise her not to go. I wasn't about to ruin her happiness. It was probably her first important date in her entire life. Then I remembered that I needed something special to wear also. I was meeting my in-laws tonight. I had to get my head on straight. I couldn't keep changing this fast from minute to minute. I was sure that I was going crazy. I thought about Carolyn and her little green pills and wished for a whole bottle just then.

As we rode around town the remainder of the afternoon, I really began to wonder about men and what they really wanted. Did they even know? If they didn't know what they wanted, how were we women supposed to really please them?

I dropped Julie off at her flat and wished her luck. I made it home just in time to shower and change. I shampooed my hair twice. Curled it and pulled a pink ribbon through it. I had bought a little pink evening dress. It was short at the skirt, but full. The bodice had a scoped neck and a respectable back. The top was full of pink sequins. I looked in the mirror and was horrified. I looked like I was going to a prom instead of a first dinner with my prospective in-laws. I was about to change, but almost everything in my closet was black. Then the doorbell rang. It was Bill and he was early. I would just have to go as is.

"Good evening, Bill," I said with all the charm I could possibly muster. He just sort of stared at me. I knew the outfit was all wrong for me and was probably to youngish looking, after all I was twenty-four years old, not eighteen anymore.

"Wow, you look great," he said. "Let's go, honey. The cab is waiting." I grabbed my black fur coat at the last minute and threw it on. It had been a gift from Carolyn for Christmas two years ago. I had never worn it. I had never worn black over prom pink. I knew that the look was wrong and I was sure to make the wrong impression. But I was wrong. Naturally, he had worn a suit. I had only assumed that his parents were rich since he was a doctor. I was wrong, again. They were not rich, but they lived in a nice apartment that was modestly decorated. It was not far from the restaurant, Mario's, where Bill had asked me to marry him. I was overdressed, and I knew it. But his parents could not have been nicer. Nothing was ever said about how over dressed I was. I ditched the fur in the bedroom as soon as I could.

"Dad," said Bill with a blush. "I would like you to meet Cynthia Thomas, my fiancé, about whom I have told you." His parents insisted on very proper English in the home.

"It is such a pleasure to meet you," said Bill's father with a heavy Italian accent. "Please, come in. Oh, Mother, Bill and Cynthia are here." Bill's mother pulled off her apron as she came out of the kitchen.

"I am so pleased to meet you," she said. They were both lovely and lovely to me. I could tell as the evening progressed that they cared a great deal about all their children.

I noticed a piece of the newspaper lying on a chair. Staring up at me was my own picture from some community event. So they already knew about me. I wondered if I knew all about me, but tonight love was all around us, and for the first time that day I breathed a little easier. For the second time since I had really known Bill, I had witnessed for the second night in a row what a loving marriage could be. His parents were really in love after all these years, as were Mario and Rosa. This was the environment in which he had grown up, so different from my own. I was hoping our marriage could be the same. I hoped our engagement would last long enough to be a marriage.

Chapter Twenty-three

St. Louis

The very next morning, Julie seemed like a different woman. She was bristling with excitement. Her date with Paul had been so romantic that she was floating on air. But every time we started to talk about the three stores, she had nothing to contribute. It was as if she really did not want to go. We had decided to have our morning meeting at Paul Packard's office. That would save Dan the embarrassment of having to set foot again in Bennington's, but that intimidated Julie. She didn't want to be pushy. She was playing by the old rule, which was, "don't say too much, don't be too pushy," in other words, "play dumb" and let the man take the lead.

"But you are part of the team, Julie. You have got to go and that is all there is to it. We are leaving for St. Louis this afternoon," I said. "Don't worry. This is your chance to impress Paul. You are a very smart and educated young lady. You have already helped Dan and I with the first two stores."

She didn't have much to worry about. Paul announced that he and Dan had decided that Paul should personally help supervise the next three renovations. I announced, to her embarrassment, that Julie knew as much as we did about what had already been done, and I encouraged her to participate at every stage. As we boarded the plane, both Bill Thompson and Paul Packard were both there saying good-bye to their girls, Julie and me.

Dan Callahan had no one. He was really alone. This really was his last chance. Middle age had not been kind to him. He was almost in his mid-forties, but with his abuse of alcohol and drugs, long nights, and wild escapades, he was aging badly. He wasn't nearly the same man of five years ago; he had really let himself go to the dogs. He had gained a tremendous amount of weight. He was already walking with slightly stooped shoulders. His blond hair had gone completely gray in the last year. He just didn't have that sparkle in his eyes anymore. Even after all that he had done to me, I still felt sorry for him. If what he had been trying to tell me about our "incident" was true, then, maybe, in his own twisted mind, he didn't think all of the blame was his. He was really trying to say that I was a willing participant. I knew that wasn't true, but I wasn't offended. I knew at this moment that from somewhere above the power of grace was descending upon me and opening my eyes to the power of forgiveness. I was never going to be under his spell again, but I wouldn't continue the hatred that I thought he had planted in me. I had enough hate for my father to carry around. I would not hate Dan, but I would not be tricked again.

As the days in St. Louis passed, I even started to care about him as a human being. He was a sad person trying to hold his own in a world of men half his age. Men who were better educated, in better health, and with fewer afflictions. The world was passing him by and he knew it.

One evening he asked me to have dinner with him. We had been in St. Louis a whole month, and he had been the consummate professional. It had been all business between him and me. I had noticed him a few times having dinner in the hotel, always alone. I just couldn't bring myself to say no when he asked me to dine with him.

"Would madam care to partake of a delicious dinner this evening with her business partner? Strictly business, you understand," he asked with a flourish. I started to say no instantly, but I could see that he needed the company more than the food. I said yes. But I would meet him at the restaurant.

"But a friend of mine drove my car here from Chicago," he said. "I don't like to be without wheels, but it has just been sitting here in the hotel garage. I haven't really had any place to go."

The new store was just around the corner, so all of us had been walking there.

"No, I think that I'll just catch a cab and meet you there," I said. I felt sorry for him, but I still didn't trust him. I didn't want to be trapped in a car with him.

"As madam wishes. Shall we say 8:00 P.M. at Phillips Restaurant," he said. It was a new and trendy place, not the best food. I had already tried it with the advance team, but I just couldn't tell him no.

"Fine, I'll see you there," I said as I walked off. I didn't see him for the remainder of the day at the store.

As I walked back to the hotel, I was sorry, now, that I had told Dan that I would have dinner with him. I was beat. It was already 7:00 P.M. I was going to be late. I had a quick shower and felt a little better. I didn't wear anything particularly flattering, just a gray suit with a pink blouse. I looked almost matronly. The cab ride took longer than I thought. It was already 8:45 P.M. when I arrived at the restaurant. Dan was waiting for me in the bar. He wasn't drunk, but he wasn't sober either.

We managed to get through dinner and mainly talked about the store and what we may do differently in New Orleans. He was cordial and didn't have any more drinks. Of course, I had none. I didn't want to encourage his drinking. I was glad when dinner was over. Dan asked for the check. He pulled out his credit card. The waiter came back.

"Sorry, sir, your card has been declined. Dan pulled out another and another, and they were all declined. Our bill was only $150 including our coffee and desert and Dan's drinks. Dan was outraged.

"Here, take mine," I said. Five minutes later we walked out of there.

"I don't understand what happened," Dan said.

"Don't worry about it," I replied. "Those things happen." I had no idea that he was in the process of filing for bankruptcy.

"Cynthia, now that you see that I can be civil, do let me drive you back to the hotel," he said.

"No, but thanks for asking. It is nice of you to think of me, but I am meeting some friends," I said. "I'll just catch a cab." It was a lie and he knew it. I felt so sorry for him and so guilty.

I waited for my cab as Dan called for the valet to pull his car around front. I was surprised that he hadn't tipped the boy, and I was again shocked by what I saw. What had once been a beautiful black Cadillac with impeccable red leather interior was now shabby and worn. The doors still had little nicks and scratches on them, and even the rear bumper was still a little crooked. What had once been beautiful leather seats were now dried and cracked and pealing. It was in worse condition than the last time I had seen it. I didn't say anything. I didn't want to embarrass Dan. He didn't act like he even noticed. I couldn't help but think that the car was falling apart, as Dan was also falling apart.

I asked my cabdriver to take me to a little place for a nightcap and a little music. I was just stalling for time. I had hoped that Dan wouldn't be around anywhere. I had a lively time there and made it back to the hotel around 1:00 A.M. When I walked into the lobby I noticed that the bar was still open with only one patron, Dan Callahan. I slipped past him without being noticed and went directly up to my room. I was so thankful that I hadn't had to wait for the elevator.

I don't know how long he stayed up and drank that night, but the next morning he showed up at the store only fifteen minutes late. He had on a new suit, but it sagged on him and the colors were much too bright, much too young-looking for a man of his age and position. His face was yellow as if he had jaundice. His eyes were completely bloodshot, but he worked a full day.

Dan could still do that. Working all day and staying out most of the night and drinking was one of his trademarks, but I had a sinking feeling that his days were numbered.

Within one month the advance team had everything under control at the St. Louis store. Julie, Dan, and I flew back to Chicago. I had my notes and could hardly wait to discuss them with my collaborator. I was dying to see Bill. Of course, we had talked almost every night while I was in St. Louis, and on those nights that we couldn't for one reason or another, I was sad.

Julie and Paul had talked everyday. She would tell me all the details the next morning. He had flown into St. Louis every weekend and stayed through Monday. They were definitely becoming an item. She had a definite crush on him, and I sensed that he was crazy about her. We had sort of become girlfriends, something that I hadn't had in a long time. Still, she only knew a little of me, and I knew all there was to know about her. I felt guilty about that. In a way, that wasn't really being honest, but if she knew the real me, I was afraid that she wouldn't like me. I knew that she adored me and looked up to me. I wasn't willing to tell all to risk losing that and disillusioning her. I didn't want to risk losing her friendship, even if it was all on my terms. I knew that it wasn't fair, but it was just the best that I could do.

Paul and Bill met Julie and me at the airport. We had long hugs and lots of kisses. Dan and Paul planned to meet Monday to discuss the progress and the next leg of the program, which would be the store in New Orleans. As Bill and Paul collected our luggage, Dan just stood there alone. There had been no one to see him off to St. Louis and no one to greet him when he came back to Chicago. I felt lonely for him. I had no idea what to do. Soon, his one bag came around and he just disappeared into the crowd waiting for a cab. His car had been stolen in St. Louis. He never saw it again

As Bill drove me home he said, "Gee, Cynthia, I sure am glad to see you. I missed you terribly."

"I missed you too, honey. I'm so glad to be home. I'm tired. I'll be so relieved when all of this is over."

He did most of the talking. He was as eager as a teenager; I felt as worn out as an old lady. When we reached my apartment he carried my bags upstairs. I started to tell him good night, but I just lay across the bed. The next morning I awoke. He had tucked me in bed and spent the night on the little sofa.

"Honey, I was so worried about you, that I just stayed over," he said. "I hope that was all right with you." I was so glad to see him that I just started crying. I had one of those crying spells that only a woman can understand. I told him that nothing was wrong, that I was just glad that I was home and that he was there and that we were in love and going to be married. I don't think he understood. He just held me. He made French toast with marmalade and served it to me in bed. He squeezed fresh orange juice. I was so lucky to have him in my life and I told him so. We spent the whole day together and that night as I soaked in the tub, he made me a home-cooked Italian meal. I was in heaven and enjoying every minute of it. *So this is what it is like to have a normal relationship with a man,* I thought. That night he went on an all-night shift at the hospital. I was sorry to see him go, but glad to have time alone with myself. I called no one. I just curled up in bed with my notes on the book and was happy for the first time in a long time.

The next day I called Carolyn. We spoke for a long time. I told her all about Julie and Paul Packard. She had only met Julie once when she was in Chicago. She sounded a little despondent, but assured me that all was fine on the home front. I spoke with Jonathan, Julie, and Marie.

"I miss all of you, but I promise that I will be home for Christmas," I said.

"And will you bring your boyfriend too?" asked Marie a little shyly.

"I'll sure try to, honey," I said. "But I can't make any promises. I'm going to see him tonight."

"Cynthia, finish up what you are doing in Chicago and come home just as soon as you can," said Carolyn. "We all miss you so much, and I am worried about you working with Dan, again."

"Everything is going beautifully," I assured her. "I promise that I will be home just as soon as the stores are finished. There are only two more to go."

As we said good-bye, I felt a little twitch in my throat. Was everything really all right back home? Were the children really doing that well? Carolyn had assured me that it was. The kids sounded fine. That old paranoia and guilt overcame me. *Carolyn is having to shoulder all that responsibility by herself,* I thought. But what could I do? I couldn't walk away now. I would just have to take her word for it. Maybe I could slip away to St. Alban's before Christmas. That night Bill reminded me that I had an appointment with my therapist the next morning. I said that I would go, and I did.

The next morning, I kept that appointment. I was scared to death. How much longer could I continue to assure my therapist that I was fine? I was glad that she was a woman. "Good morning, Mrs. Peterson," I said gaily. I thought that I knew how to play these visits. A good night's rest before hand was a necessary ingredient. A good breakfast and a long shower helped me feel my best, and I always dressed with the greatest of skill. Maybe, if I looked perfect, she would believe that I was perfect, and that is what I had always tried to be, perfect. As much as I hated my father, I knew that I always had to do my best, and for me that meant perfection, anything less was unacceptable. He had taught me that. I thought that was one of the few things that he did teach me that was good and of any consequence, that is, if you are perfect, they have to love you.

"Good morning, Cynthia," said Mrs. Peterson. "How are you getting along in your new position of being your own boss? Tell me all about St. Louis."

"Oh, St. Louis was wonderful. The store is going to be beautiful and everyone was so cooperative. My assistant, Julie, and I have turned into good friends. I suspect that she will be engaged before Christmas, and guess what? I introduced them."

I talked on and on about Paul and Julie. She already knew that I was engaged. She stopped me after three minutes.

"That is nice, dear, but I want to hear about you," she said. "Are you still having those same old haunting memories?"

"Oh, I guess everyone resents their childhood a little," I said. "Yes, I think about it a lot. My parents were strict, but I was a handful to raise properly. I got spanked a lot. So what? We have been over this before. Why do we have to keep rehashing the same old stuff? My life is turning out just the way I had always dreamed. I am well educated. I have a good job. I am my own boss. I have friends, and I engaged to the most wonderful man in Chicago, a doctor. But you know all of this. What else do you want to know?"

"Did any thing significant happened to you in St. Louis?" she asked. She knew there was more to my story. I was afraid that eventually she would find out.

"Well, the renovation of the store is going just great. And working with Dan is helping me a little, I think," I said slowly.

"Yes," she said. "Tell me more about that part of it."

During our sessions, I would never lie on a couch of anything like that. In fact she sat on one end of the couch, and I always sat in a chair, which was anchoring the end of the room. She was not too close and I was just far enough away to say whatever I liked and not feel too weak or threatened. I had come to her with a full history, courtesy of Dr. Thompson. Bill had insisted that she know everything. He had written a little summary of what he knew about my childhood and some of the things that had happened to me, especially my marriage to Eddie and my relationship with Dan. When I thought about this I wondered how in the world could he be in love with me. I was sure that I didn't deserve him.

"Well, I am worried about Dan," I said, trying to turn the focus of the conversation to him. "He is all alone and he looks terrible."

"So, you care about him," she said. "You care about the man that raped you."

"No," I said firmly. "It's not like that. It's just that we work every day together. It would only be natural that I would want everything to be okay with him. Don't you think?"

"It's not what I *think*, Cynthia. It is what you *feel*," she said.

"Well, he has been the most perfect, professional gentleman and he even took me to dinner," I said hurriedly.

"Why did you feel the need to have dinner with the man who raped you?" she asked.

"Stop saying that he raped me," I cried. "The only reason that I went to dinner with him was because I felt safe in a public place with him. I went alone and came back to the hotel alone. He insisted that he had something important to tell me. He wanted me to understand. We had talked about it before, but he wanted to be sure that I understood."

"Understand what?" she asked.

"To understand about our incident," I said. "Did it ever occur to you to think that maybe I brought it on myself? He told me that it was I who went looking for him in that sleazy little bar where Junior and I found him, that it was I who invited him up to my hotel room." I stood. I started to pace up and down. I rung my hands and found myself pressing them to my skirt just like my mother used to do. I didn't know what was happening. It was like I was about to vomit up all my life. I knew that if I kept going, all my dirty little secrets would come out and then she wouldn't want to see me anymore.

"Go on, Cynthia. What else did he tell you?" she said.

"Well, he admitted that he was drunk and drug crazy and he almost apologized for that. He said that he thought that I was just playing the game rough; that I wanted it rough. So, naturally, he just played right along. I think that he would have stopped if Carolyn hadn't shot him, because he said that I called him 'daddy.' He said that I stopped struggling and that I looked blankly up into his face and said, 'Yes, Daddy.'" I instantly turned cold. I turned to face her. I was sure that she was through with me. I hadn't intended to tell her that. I hadn't even intended to remember it, but she just sat there waiting for me to continue. I looked at her. She looked at me.

"Keep going, Cynthia. You are remembering," she said softly. I turned to look at her wall full of books. Maybe the answer was there among all those worlds of words. I took a seat on the couch with her.

"Mrs. Peterson, I know where you are going with this, but I honestly don't ever remember any sexual abuse from father," I said with composure.

"Cynthia, I never suggested that," she said. "You did, by believing what Dan said was true."

"No, no I didn't," I cried. "You are just trying to get me to say something that never happened. Sure he beat me up a lot. He was trying to protect me. He was trying to teach me. He was trying to keep me a good girl. He was trying to keep me from committing the same mistakes he had made. He was always afraid that I would get pregnant like mother." I sobbed. I just broke down and sobbed. We had been over this before. Why did she keep harping on it?

"Cynthia," she said as she took my hands in hers. "You are right. You never suggested that your father raped you. Dan did. Cynthia, listen to me very carefully. No woman ever wants to be raped or abused in any fashion. No woman deserves to be beaten by anyone. Your father may have been trying to protect you, but he did it all wrong. He beat you and made you feel like you deserved it. He just transferred his own guilt and your mother's on to you, and your mother let him. She didn't have to do anything. She was escaping her own guilt by letting him do all the work for her. She was wrong. She should have stopped him. When you thought that you had escaped all that, you picked up with a man, Dan, who just continued your father's ways, just a little differently. Men like him hunt women like you. Your father was wrong and so was Dan. Don't believe for one moment that Dan Callahan doesn't know what he was doing to you. He knew it was coming for a long time. He just waited and planned it. He enjoyed it. He wanted it to happen. When he got let off the hook, so to speak, his own feeling of power just increased. Don't empower him any longer. Don't confuse Dan with your father. They are two separate men. But Dan tapped into those feeling of inadequacy set in you by your father. He read you like a book and used you for years. If you want to forgive him in your heart, I think that you must. But making you feel sorry for him for what he did to you is just another way of continuing to let him control you and blame yourself."

Everything came crashing in on me at the same time. I had known this for years, but hearing her say it made it so real, really truthful. "Will you think about what we have talked about today?" she asked. "I think you should."

"Yes, and I will see you next week, even if I have to fly in from New Orleans. You do want to see me, don't you?" I asked. "You don't hate me. Do you?"

"No, Cynthia," she said with warmth and understanding. "You are my patient and I am always here for you. I know more than you think I know already. I'm just trying to get you to know it. You have truths locked away inside of you that you already know about, but just haven't had the full realization of them yet. And I want you to know that I think you are a fine person and an accomplished one at that, but it is not important what I think, but what you think of yourself. I also think that you should stay away from Dan Callahan. If what you say is absolutely true, then he may be a menace to others. During this next week I want you to think about what we have talked about here today, and I want you to think about the word 'forgiveness.' Is there anyone in your life that you need to forgive or ask forgiveness of? Now, you must go, my next appointment is waiting."

As I walked out of her office, I decided to walk home. The ten blocks would do me good. I felt like a burden had been lifted off my back. She knew a little more about me, and still she didn't hate or loathe me. She had shattered my front of perfection, but I still needed it as a cloak. Maybe I would need it forever, but little by little and layer by layer I was peeling back something. I was still so confused, but I felt lighter than air just at that moment. I decided to go with that and to think about the word "forgiveness."

When I returned to my apartment, I took a warm bath and started to organize more notes on my book. I was feeling good and looking forward to New

Orleans. We would be leaving for that sinful city in a few days. I wanted to have my head together. I would still have to deal with Dan Callahan for just a while longer. For some reason I felt that the center of power had changed and for the first time I felt in charge of myself. I was empowered, just a little, but empowered.

The phone rang and startled me out of my warm thoughts. I answered the phone and was irritated that I had been interrupted.

"Cynthia," said Carolyn. "I have news, my dear, your mother is being released from prison tomorrow. She is having an early release. The warden called for you here. It seems that your mother is sick and needs constant care. The prison doctor has diagnosed her with hardening of the arteries. She is symptomatic with dementia. She may have a year or less to live, maybe two years at the most. What shall we do?"

I was silent, stunned.

Chapter Twenty-four

Becoming the Parent

I must have been in a little state of shock. I was absolutely speechless. Just when I thought everything was going so swell, this ugly snake head had to appear and interfere with my life again. I hated to have to deal with it.

"Cynthia," she continued. "May I make a suggestion?"

"Yes, please. Tell me what I should do. I just don't know," I said.

"I know of a very good convalescent home near your old town. It is practically new," she said. "She could go there. The warden suggested it. You will have to sell her house. It has been closed for such a long time. I don't know what you can get for it. Shall I contact a realtor?"

"Yes, and can you arrange for an attorney?" I asked. "We never did probate father's estate when he died. There is probably more debt that actual assets."

"Of course, I will do all that I can," she said. "Anyway, the warden already told me that the prison would pay for the price of the home for the next six months. That is the remainder of her prison term, but he thinks a member of the family should be there in order to have someone to turn her over to. Do you want me to meet you?"

"No, you have done enough already. I want to speak with Jonathan," I said.

"Yes, my dear," she said with a sigh of relief. "I'll have him phone you as soon as he comes in. He won't be long. I am sure of that."

"Thanks, Carolyn," I said. "I love you, you know. You have done so much for me. How will I ever make it all up to you."

"Let's not worry about that now. You know that I am always here for you. And, I love you too," she said. I could tell she was about to cry. "Good-bye, dear, and I will have Jonathan get in touch with you as soon as he can."

I phoned Bill and told him what was going on and asked him to call Paul and Julie for me. I was going to be gone for a few days. He wanted to go with me, but I assured him that I could handle it myself. I managed my composure for a while, but I just got madder and madder. I knew I hated mother. I just didn't know how much. *Oh, why didn't she just die in prison like Father did,* I thought.

An hour later the phone rang. It was Jonathan and Janie. Janie wanted to come along too. "I'm coming if I have to pay for the plane ticket myself," she said.

"Janie, please, just let Jonathan and I handle this. We know what is best," I pleaded.

"You heard what I said. I am coming," she continued. "I am part of this family, too. I am old enough to help make decisions."

"Well, I don't want you to come. I don't think that it would be in your best interest," I said.

"Come on, Cynthia," said Jonathan. "I think she can handle it. It is not fair to keep her out. She is our mother's daughter, also."

"Okay," I said. "But, please don't mention any of this to little Marie. You all know how fragile she is. We will just have to tell her a little at a time, later on, but not now."

They both agreed and we planned to meet at the Atlanta Airport and fly on from there. I had to rush to get to the airport. I barely got the last seat on the plane in order to make the connection in Atlanta. When they met me at my gate, I was so happy to see them both.

"Oh," I said. "You are both so brave to meet me like this."

"Face it, Cynthia. We are not children anymore," said Janie. She seemed more grown up that she had earlier in the summer. Jonathan just shrugged his shoulders. On the plane ride home we decided to pick up Mother together and get her settled in the home. Then we would call Carolyn for updates on the lawyer and a realtor. We had little else to say although we all had so much going on in our lives. We were all afraid, and we masked our fears in silence.

The next morning we picked up Mother from the warden's office. She was dressed in exactly what she had been wearing during her hearing. It was one of her old, plain worn-out house dresses. She didn't have anything better then, and she still didn't have anything better now. She looked terrible— old and tired. The nurse had tried her best to fix her up a little. She had shampooed and curled her hair and applied a little lipstick. Janie was so upset when she saw her that she just broke down and cried. As they brought Mother in, we were shocked, but it was most terrible for Janie. She ran to hug her.

"Now, now," said Mother. "We'll have none of that, but you are my sweet grandchildren. I guess you can cry if you want to, but why all the tears. We are taking a little trip aren't we? Oh, I am so glad that you have finally come for me. I have been waiting so long, but where is your grandfather?"

The nurse motioned us out in the corridor and said, "I'll keep her for a few minutes, but the doctor wants to talk to you."

The three of us must have looked like the three lost souls of the county. The doctor said, "It is always hardest on the family, but you can see her condition. She is at her best early in the morning. She is at her worse late in the afternoon and evening. She suffers from confusion and memory loss. The convalescent home really is the best place for her. I am afraid that there is no training for family members. None of you live here. Just try to offer as much comfort and support as you can. Don't argue with her. The sooner you get her on over to the home the better. Here are some papers for you to sign and there will be more over there. Can I call you a cab?" That was all he had to say.

"That won't be necessary," said Jonathan coldly. "We have a hired car waiting for us." He was furious at this treatment. "This is just a little better than an animal shelter," he said as he guided us out into the hall. Janie lagged behind a little.

She asked the doctor, "Can we take her home first?"

"Oh, I wouldn't do that," he said. "It would only add to her confusion. Just tell her that she is going on a lovely vacation and that the home is a lovely resort. I've known your mother for a long time. I know she will cooperate with that."

The three of us said nothing. We just didn't know what to say to comfort each other, much less Mother. We rode to the home in silence. To our amazement Mother chatted all the way there. "Oh, your granny sure is glad to see all of you. Are we there yet? What a beautiful car this is. How long will be staying? Oh, you don't know long I have waited for you."

It was Janie who spoke first and for the most part. She said, "Granny, we are so sorry for staying away so long. We love you. We promise to visit you more often." She held her hand all the way to the home and made a little conversation with her. She knew that mother was in a fantasy world of her own. Maybe prison had tipped her over the edge of sanity. I was so ashamed and felt so guilty for not being more helpful. Jonathan took my hand and that is when I cried. He and I tried to hide our tears.

"Oh, you two are so beautiful together. How thoughtful of you to take me on your honeymoon," said Mother. "I never had a honeymoon. No, your old granddad just knocked me up one night and a few months later we had your mother, Cynthia. We had to get married."

I was mortified. Neither Jonathan nor Janie knew the truth of this, and I wasn't about to tell them now. Somehow, it just didn't seem to matter to me so much anymore. Seeing her like this was more than I could bear. I didn't know if I could love her. She was a complete and total stranger. She didn't even look like the mother I remembered, but I couldn't wish this state of mind on my worst enemy.

Mother talked on and on, and to our amazement, she had us all in stitches by the time we reached the home. She didn't mean to make us laugh. She was just being so hilarious with her talking. We certainly were not laughing at her or even with her. It was our only way of dealing with the situation. I guess we didn't want to cry, so we just laughed instead.

I know the administrator thought that we were the most insensitive bunch of children, because we laughed our way in and out of the home. He gave us the grand tour. It was no palace, but I guessed that it was better than most. Mother would have a private room in a confined and secure part of the place, at least, for the first six months. We stayed with her most of the day and only left her in time to see the house and to catch the plane. We had no idea how sick she really was.

The driver took us to our old house. We knew that it was probably in bad shape. To our surprise, there was a family living in our house. We knocked at the door and introduced ourselves. They invited us in. "Oh we sure do thank you for the use of your home," said the mother. "We were only out on the streets a few weeks, when your neighbor helped us move in here. Oh, don't think we been loafing off of you. We've been putting back a little rent all these years." She brought out twelve quart jars. They were full of money. "We reckon that amounts to several thousand dollars," said the father. There were several small children playing on the floor, just exactly where Jonathan and I used to play, and I recognized the little blanket. It had been ours. There was a knock on the door. Our old neighbor motioned me out on the porch.

"I am so sorry, you kids. Sorry about your mom and dad and well, just everything. The house was vacant about a month after your mom and dad left. No one was seeing to it. My church needed someplace to house this homeless family. Well, we just put them there. Ya'll had just left so suddenly. The church has been paying the taxes, and you can see they have been taking care of the place for you. I know they have rent money. We found a job for the father, and, well, months just turned into years. I do hope it is okay."

We all assured her that it was. We accepted the rent money as a down payment for the family to purchase the house and told them that our lawyer would draw up the necessary papers as soon as possible. Jonathan assured them that they should continue to put the same amount in the jar every month just in case. We all thanked them for taking care of the house and assured them that they could buy it. We would make sure of that.

I asked, "Would you mind if I just looked around a bit."

"Oh, of course not, honey," said the mother. "Come on and I will show you around."

"No, thank you. I want to go alone," I said.

Jonathan and Janie and I walked through the little house, which didn't take long. The family gathered on the front porch and the mother and the father sat on the porch swing that should have been there all the time. We never had one. Each of us lingered in our own rooms for a few minutes. We walked around the little yard, which looked better than it did when we lived there. Rose bushes flanked the front sidewalk. Neatly tended flowerbeds swept their way around the front of the house and there was a vegetable garden in the back yard.

"I think this is the way the house should have always looked," said Jonathan. Both Janie and I nodded in agreement. As we got in the car each of us felt our own loss in our own individual way.

"It should have been that way for us," I said. All three of us cried on the ride back to the airport. We hugged and held on to each other as best as we could in the back of the car. We weren't just mourning the loss of our family home, but to some degree we were mourning the death of our father and our mother even though she was still alive. She wasn't the mother we remembered. I was thankful for that.

"Well, I am sure glad Marie wasn't here to see this, but how in the world are we going to explain this to her?" I said.

"I don't know that we have to," said Janie. "I think that she already knows. She talks to people on the phone all the time. I think that it is them. Maybe she thinks that she is doing us a favor by not telling us."

"We'll have to relieve her of that burden," said Jonathan.

On the plane ride back, Jonathan, Janie, and I talked about some our fun times there together. That was a short conversation, as there were so few fun times. None of us mentioned the beatings and the wandering mother used to do. Silence fell over us all. I was sure that time was suspended and that the plane was just idling in the air. I was sure that we weren't even moving and that we would never land. It was a maddening long plane ride. When we changed planes in Atlanta, I went back to St. Alban's with them. I needed to be with them and to be with Carolyn and Marie. I needed time with my family. I took it.

I managed to stay for three weeks. Finally, it was time for me to go back to Chicago. I went back mainly for Bill. Carolyn assured me that she and Jonathan would oversee all the legalities of my father's meager estate, and, of course, keep me posted on Mother.

"My lawyers will handle everything dear. We will send the necessary papers on to you in Chicago. Read them carefully. Sign them and send them back. Try not to let this set you back." Then she said something that really struck me hard.

"Cynthia, you know that your parents and your old homestead are gone, dear. They have been for a long time. Time marches on. Have you ever heard of the old saying, 'to forget and forgive'? I think that is what you must do now. Try to realize that, and what you have now and what you are planning for the future. Don't dwell on the past. Learn from it and pass it on. You are here for a reason. You are on a path. You are so young and beautiful. You have so many choices ahead of you. You have your health and you have Bill, who worships and adores you. Don't worry, my darling, he knows that you are not perfect. Remember, he has been with you several important times in your life. You are no secret to him. I don't believe that your meeting him in Chicago was an accident. Your journey has been a hard one, but I am seeing greener pastures ahead for you. Don't you? Do you understand, dearest?" I nodded yes, and cried hard on her shoulder.

She stood at my gate until the plane was out of site. I knew that she would not leave the airport until my plane left the ground. Two hours later I was in the arms of Bill and I had new plans for a brighter future.

Chapter Twenty-five
Two Weddings

I was so glad to see Bill waiting for me at the Chicago terminal. I ran to him. He picked me up and twirled me around and around. "Bill," I said. "I have changed my mind. I don't want a long engagement. Can we get married in six months instead of a waiting a whole year? Tomorrow, I am going to try to sell my part in the renovation contract to Paul Packard. I think that I have enough to put together some sort of a book. I have done enough stores. I want out of that. I may still want a career. I'm just not sure what I want it to be. I believe that I have almost accomplished what I set out to do. I have proven my point that equality in the work place for women is a must and it is surely to come. It is not just a man's world anymore. I know that I can finish the book in about two to three months. I don't care how long it takes to get published. I will probably need an editor to help finish it anyway. Maybe I will be a novelist, write at home, and have lots of your babies."

"That sounds great to me Cynthia," he said. "Anything you want is fine with me. My practice is healthy enough to support us both and have as many children as you want. But if it is a career than you want, then I want that for you too. I will help you in any way that I can to achieve whatever goals you set out for yourself, but let's not throw caution to the wind. Let's both go to your therapist tomorrow and have a nice long visit. I want you as my wife, happy, healthy, and wise."

He took me to a grand dinner that night to celebrate. It was just the two of us. We did drink a little champagne. I thought that was okay; it was a special celebration. We planned the wedding and our honeymoon in Maui, the island of lovers. He held me tight and we danced until the band went home. From the top of the tower of the restaurant we looked out over the beautifully lighted city of Chicago. We kissed and held each other until they closed the place; we were the last to leave. We didn't want the night to end. We walked to the lakefront and found a late night coffee shop. Fairly soon, the sun was rising. It was a glorious sunrise over the lake that lit Chicago from head to toe. It was a beautiful site to behold. The next day was Saturday. We spent the whole day in bed sleeping and just holding each other. We knew that we would be together always.

Two days later I was on the phone scheduling a meeting with Bennington's, Paul Packard, and Julie. Paul assured Bennington's that his firm, along with Julie's help, could finish the other two stores. I promised that I would continue to be available for short term consulting. I sold my share of the contract to Paul Packard for the remainder of my contract, which was about $125,000. That was a lot of money in big business in those days. News magazine picked up the story, and I finally made the cover; although I hated the title of the cover story which was written by a male editor, "Women in Our Business, Yes or No?" He didn't exactly come right out and say it, but you could tell he still thought women's place was in the home, probably barefoot and pregnant.

I was okay with it after my book collaborator told me that a publisher, Women's Press, wanted my book idea. It was a publishing house owned and operated entirely by women.

They even had some male secretaries. I was ecstatic. They offered me $200,000 to write the book I wanted, and I was to have the help of an editor. I met with them the very next day and signed all kinds of papers and contracts. Finally, I was really moving.

After Paul and Julie returned from New Orleans, Julie called me. "Cynthia," said Julie. "Paul and I just got back from New Orleans. Can you believe it has been six weeks? The store is beautiful and you will love it. You'll have to come back down there with me for the grand opening."

I agreed it would be wonderful to see my ideas in print and in reality. "Julie," I said. "How is Dan?" She was silent for a moment. I knew that she had been suspicious about Dan and I. "Well," I said. "He was there. Wasn't he?"

She hesitated to say anything. "Julie, say something," I said.

"Well, Cynthia, I wanted Paul to tell you, but since you are insisting I guess that I will just have to tell you. He didn't show up. Paul hasn't seen him since we all returned from St. Louis." Once again I was shocked.

"I don't know why that surprises me. I'm not surprised by whatever he says or does. Okay, thanks for telling me," I said. "Please, don't think another thing about it. Let's all meet tomorrow night at Mario's for some delicious Italian food."

"Oh, Cynthia, that would be just great. I also have some news," continued Julie. "But I will save it until tomorrow night."

I didn't know what to think about Dan's no-show. Was he sick? Was he in jail? Was he dead? What had happened to him? I called Bill.

"Honey," he said. "Don't worry about that creep. People like that are prone to just go off on a lark, but they always surface and land on their own two feet. Leave it alone. Pray about it if you want, but promise me that you won't go playing detective. Call Carolyn if you want to talk about it." I did just that.

"Carolyn," I said. "The last time that anyone saw him was when he got off the plane from St. Louis."

"Don't worry, my dear," she said. "If memory serves me correctly, he pulled that stunt on me a couple of times. He is probably in some cheap hotel with an even cheaper floozy and when he realizes that no one is coming for him, then he will come to his senses and sober up and land somewhere else. Anyway, he is not our concern anymore."

"Okay," I said. "But I feel a little unsafe not knowing where he is. He is such a manipulator and doesn't believe anything that he does is wrong. Maybe we did the wrong thing in not pressing charges on the rape, ugh, the 'incident.'"

"Whatever," Carolyn said with a slight irritation to her voice. "All of that is over and done, finished. You do have your gun, don't you?"

"Yes, but I don't want to have to depend on that for the rest of my life. I don't want to have to carry it around with me always," I said right back at her.

"They have something new, Cynthia," she said. "It is called pepper spray. Go get some and keep it handy. You will probably never have to use it, but it may make you feel better. Talk to your therapist about it. I know everything is going to work out for the best. Please, take my advice. Forget about him."

I did call my therapist and scheduled a visit for that afternoon. We talked for only forty-five minutes. She agreed with Carolyn. "You will probably never see him again. He has run like the coward he is. He is just off licking his wounds somewhere after your last dinner with him. I think that you bruised his ego. He has probably taken up with some other woman by now. But if it makes you feel any better, I suggest that you take a women's defense class. Just call my secretary and she will give you all the details."

I did just that and started the class the next day. It did make me feel better. I must have taken twenty flyers and handed them out to everyone on the street advertising the class. But it did occur to me that no one agreed with my worries about Dan, especially my therapist. They made it sound like I had no worries at all, that it just didn't matter. I thought about this and decided that I had better call Junior and Michael. Maybe they knew something.

It was another dead end. Neither Junior nor Michael had seen or heard from. "It's like I told you, Cynthia," said Junior. "After Michael and I got through trash mouthing him all over the usual places, he just disappeared.

He is barred from all the gay bars. You know that there is a crossover clientele. Probably the word is out all over Chicago and he just couldn't take the heat. He's moved on, but people like him land on their feet some place else." I had heard that part before.

After that phone call I was determined to renew my gun permit and to carry my gun with me, and I bought some pepper spray. I wasn't about to let him or anyone ruin the little piece of happiness that I had created for myself. I was going to be happy but safe, and I looked forward to the dinner that Julie and I had planned for that night.

When she and Paul walked into the restaurant, I knew her secret. "Paul asked me to marry him on the plane ride back to Chicago. It wasn't that romantic, but who has time for romance?" she said as she flashed her two-carat diamond ring set in eighteen-carat gold and platinum. "I got to pick it out today," she said with a smile.

"Come on. Let's take a walk to the ladies' room so we can talk," I said with excitement. "You boys settle down and break open a bottle of champagne. Be good and we'll be back, soon."

"Oh, Julie, I am so happy for you," I said. "I'm sorry for all those times that I may have treated you like nothing but a woman secretary."

"Oh, no, Cynthia, it is you that I have to thank. If it weren't for you, I would never have had your knowledge, skill, or your experience, or the nerve. I have to confess that I have been studying you for years. I've tried to copy you in every way that I can. You know that I don't have the advantage of your educational background. I had to learn somehow, and, the best part is that Paul wants me working in the firm. We may even start a day care for children in the same building. Wouldn't that be cool? But we are getting married just as soon as we tell our parents and the bans are announced in church. It better be in two months, or I am liable to start showing. But, you won't tell anybody about that part. Will you?"

"You mean you are going to have a baby?" I said.

"Shh," she said with her finger over her mouth. After tonight, no more champagne until after the baby is born, not even at the wedding. I'm sorry, Cynthia. I know you and Bill were supposed to get married first, but I know you understand. I have got to go first."

"Of course, you will go first," I said.

"Cynthia, I never thought I would be asking you this, not the Cynthia Thomas of Chicago, but will you be my maid of honor?"

"Only if you will be my matron of honor," I said.

"It's a deal, sister," she squealed with laughter and delight.

She had really blossomed in the last two and a half months since she had met Paul Packard. It reconfirmed my faith in meeting the right man. I knew that I had, and I hoped that she had. I hoped that they were as madly in love as we were, and that they weren't just getting married because she was pregnant.

189

It was also Julie that reconfirmed my faith in the fact that women should be in the workplace with the same opportunities and equalities as men. Julie had been only a little mousy secretary, timid and scared of everything. She had always been told what to do and how to do it. Her exposure to opportunity opened a whole new world of possibilities to her. I would use her as an example in my book. It should be the same for all women. I was beginning to think that maybe my career would be to champion that cause.

During the next three weeks I worked closely with Julie on the plans for the wedding. I hardly ever thought of Dan, but I knew that he was somewhere and somewhere he was running around in my mind. It was a worry to me, but I had little time for that.

Julie would call me everyday and pick my brain for help at Paul's firm. I really didn't mind. She was giving me all kinds of ideas to weave into the book that I continued to work on and was nearly finished. My therapy continued and Bill went with me once. He had suggested it and my therapist had agreed. I thought that I was coming along delightfully as did they.

It was hard to imagine that in the course of a few months, so much had changed in my life after the 'incident' with Dan. Bill and I had become close friends with Paul and Julie. Somehow we were all connected. I was beginning to believe that there were no coincidences in life, no accidental meetings. Maybe Carolyn was right about that. Everyone in my life had helped make me the person that I was. I had always believed in me, but now I was really beginning to believe in myself. It was finally dawning on me that I wasn't responsible for everything and everybody, and that life didn't revolve just around me. I really started to care for other people and to try and to champion their causes and their concerns. I was learning to deal with feelings of guilt and lay them aside one by one. The term guilt took on a whole new meaning to me.

Before I knew it, it was time for Julie's wedding. She had the nerve to wear white, even though she knew she was pregnant. I was glad for her. Her dress was an empire cut. She really didn't look like she was pregnant. And she was ever so radiant. I was her maid of honor and Bill was best man to Paul. It was a big affair with a reception for over 250 people, most of whom I did not know. It was a fun day for all of us. It made Bill and I look even more forward to ours.

Bill and I planned a Christmas wedding. It would be held in Chicago, since his family lived there and he and I were well known there. I loved the theme of Christmas for the wedding. It was set for the first Saturday in December. Everyone would still have time to settle down and enjoy Christmas for what it was. Carolyn was ecstatic, but I was sure that she felt a little disappointed in not being able to do more of the planning, and that I had my wedding dress custom made and not ordered from Grahams in St. Alban's. Bill and I wanted to plan it all ourselves. It was to be a big affair. All of his friends and family, former classmates, and current associates would be invited along with my family, Julie, and Paul.

A week before Thanksgiving I finally handed the final draft of my book to my publisher. It wouldn't be out in time for Christmas. Nevertheless, she had big hopes for it. So did I. I had titled it *Women Where We Want to Be*. I waited anxiously for any word from my editor; however, my own wedding was just two weeks away. It was a busy time for all of us.

A golden fall had finally come to Chicago and quickly turned into an icy Thanksgiving. Bill and I went apartment shopping and found just what we wanted a week before the wedding. It was a large two-bedroom apartment in a high-rise overlooking Chicago. It even had a doorman. I was beginning to feel a lot safer. Both Bill and I closed our separate apartments and moved all our things into our first home. We started living there a few days before the wedding.

On our first night there we celebrated with our first home cooked meal together. We even opened a bottle of wine and settled down for a "picnic" in front of the roaring fireplace. It was cozy and warm. After dinner, he held me in his arms and kissed me tenderly on the lips. I kissed him back. We separated for a moment and looked longingly into each other's eyes. The intimacy was so special and so different from anything that I had ever experienced before. Bill and I were so easy and gentle with each other that the intercourse just naturally happened. Before long we were both naked and wrapped together in a king-size down comforter lying in front of the fire sipping our remaining wine having already spent our passion. Being with him for the first time had such a special meaning that I will not go into all the details, nor have I ever done so with anyone else. Those memories are only for the two of us. Nevertheless, I will say that I felt a new closeness had embraced us. We saw it in each other's eyes and felt it in our souls. From those moments on, every time we would pass each other we would touch. Holding hands in public is something that just came natural to us. It always reminds me of our first time together.

The Friday before the wedding, Carolyn and the children arrived from St. Alban's. There was no one else there for me to invite. I had been in such a hurry to study and graduate that I had not made the effort to keep in touch with the few friends that I had made there and at the store. I regretted that and was sorry. It had been a mistake, but I certainly thought that it would be in poor taste to try and find them now.

My little family all piled into the new apartment. Neither Bill nor I made any excuses about what bedroom was ours. The guest room went to Carolyn, naturally. She insisted that the children bunk in there with her. We bought them sleeping bags and they all sort of crashed on the floor as if they were having one big blanket party. I was so glad to have my family around me again. I felt safe and warm. Carolyn would play the role of my mother since we both felt that way. Janie and Marie were bridesmaids, and Jonathan was delighted to be a groomsman. I was so relieved that all the gowns and tuxedos fit everyone.

Time passed so quickly that day, and all too soon the quietness of the night filled the apartment. I don't think Bill or I slept a wink that night. We both slept fitfully, and awoke too early and felt tired. It wasn't a good way to start our wedding day.

Everyone was up at the crack of dawn, and to our surprise Carolyn had been the first. She had cooked a full breakfast of bacon and eggs, toast, and orange juice. A big pot of coffee awaited all of us. We all laughed at the irony of it. "Well," said Carolyn. "Cooking breakfast isn't exactly as hard a brain surgery, you know. You don't have to be an astronaut or anything like that to do it." We all laughed and laughed, and I think that it made us feel a little better.

All too soon the church bells of little church six blocks from our apartment started to ring out. The limousines were waiting for us downstairs. I was just putting on my bridal veil when Carolyn walked in. She said, "Something old, something new, something borrowed, and something blue, I hope." I showed her my stocking garter, which was blue. "Well, here is something borrowed," she said as she handed me a tiny jewel box. To my surprise, it held a little string of pearls. She adjusted my veil as she wrapped them around my throat and caught the diamond clasp at the back of my neck.

"My mother gave these to me on my first wedding day, and her mother had given them to her on hers. I have never worn them since then. They are old and borrowed, but keep them anyway." She also handed me one of her little white, lace handkerchiefs with the initial "g" embroidered on the edge. She always carried one with her, and she knew how much I admired them.

"Oh, Carolyn," I said. "You are such a dear. What did I ever do to deserve all the many kindnesses that you have shown to me?"

"Nothing, really," she said. "You just came along and stayed and grew and I just took a liking to you. You know that you are more than that to me. As I have told you so many times, you and your brother and sisters have been the fulfillment of my dreams. You really are my children. I believe God intended you to be, anyway."

"Oh, Carolyn," I said. "Thank you so much. I know that I can always rely on you. A girl would consider herself lucky to have you as her mother, and I certainly do."

"Now, stop all that gushing," she said. "If either of us says another word I know that we will both be crying. We will have to do our makeup all over again."

We both walked into the large living room and Bill and Jonathan and the girls had all gathered there. I gave each of the girls a little gold locket on a chain to wear in the wedding. The inscription inside each one read, "*to thine own self be true.*"

"Oh, Cynthia," they each cried. "Thank you." I don't think that in all their years they had ever had a really good piece of jewelry. They knew what it meant.

To Jonathan I gave a gold insignia ring. I had left the initial area blank. I had an idea that one day his name might be changed to Graham. Carolyn still wanted to adopt him. On the underside of the ring the inscription simply read, "*I love you brother.*" We were all about to cry when the ringing of the doorbell startled each of us. The head chauffeur was there to collect us.

As we rolled up to the church, Paul and Julie were waiting for us just inside the door. Everything was perfect. Bill's usher escorted Carolyn to her pew in the front of the church. She nodded to Bill's parents sitting across from her. Then little Marie started up the aisle a little too slowly. She wobbled a little in her first pair of high heels. Her groomsman met her half way down the aisle. Jonathan escorted Janie. Paul escorted Julie who was big with child. I hoped she would make it through the ceremony without having to sit down. The altar was so beautiful dressed in calla lilies and Christmas greenery with white ribbon. Julie and my girls were so beautiful in their dresses of dark green cut velvet with little lace collars. The groomsmen were so handsome in the black tuxedos. The church was filled to capacity with family and friends. Bill's mother was already crying. Bill and I had decided to escort each other up the aisle. My veil as traditional as ever with a little part of it pulled forward over my face and neck. As we reached the altar, I handed my bouquet to Julie. Carolyn came around and raised back my veil so that my face showed, a custom traditionally saved for the father to do. It was such a lovely ceremony that I almost wished it would not stop. Bill and I had written our own private vows to each other and before we knew it we were pronounced man and wife. I was no longer Cynthia Thomas. I was Mrs. Bill Thompson. As we turned around the preacher announced to the congregation, "May I introduce to you Mr. and Mrs. Bill Thompson." The church erupted in applause.

As Bill and I started down the aisle, I saw Junior and Michael give me a little sign. A lone figure was standing in the little vestibule of the church. To my horror it was Dan Callahan dressed in a tuxedo with a white carnation boutonniere. He was dressed as if he were a member of the wedding party. I stopped cold in my tracks. Bill looked at me and saw the astonishment on my face. I was as pale as a ghost. He looked up. I whispered to him, "It's Dan Callahan." But my Bill was already prepared for that. Two of his groomsmen walked ahead and escorted him out of the church and around the block.

I was so relieved, but shaken. Carolyn was suddenly by my side. "I don't think anyone noticed, dear, just keep walking," she whispered in my ear with her usual composure. "Everything will be fine."

As soon as we were on the sidewalk we were ushered into the limousines and off to the reception. "It was just like him to ruin my wedding," I shouted.

Bill was dumfounded. Carolyn grabbed my hand and said, "Not unless you let him, dear. Now, he is gone, and I assure you that he will not bother us again. Not today anyway." I calmed down and took one of her little green pills. By the time we got to the reception I had composed myself. With a little champagne I forgot all about it.

I was so glad that I had not used the little hall that went with the church for the reception. There would have been no security whatsoever, but Bill and Carolyn had seen to that. The reception was to be a surprise to me. It was held at the newest hotel in Chicago, The Frontwater Bay. It was beautiful. To my relief there were two policemen guarding the entrance to our ballroom. Admittance was by invitation only. There was a full orchestra. Flowers were everywhere. It was decorated so beautifully, and the catering staff had assembled for our entrance. I felt like I was a real fairy princess. There were tables upon tables of food, a full bar and several fountains of champagne. Much of the food was served on trays. It was as if I had stepped back into the nineteenth century. Carolyn had used that as the theme for the reception.

The wedding party formed a formal receiving line and all the guests piled in to great us one at a time. The orchestra played and played. It was a glorious time and soon all were enjoying the wedding banquet. Every course of food represented a different country.

Bill whispered to me, "Darling, do you like the food?"

"Yes," I said. "It is all so delicious, but it is all so different. There is so much of it and it is all from different cultures, from all over the world."

"That's because I want you to get accustomed to it, because when we leave here in the morning, we are going on a trip around the world. We will be gone for six months. My practice is being taken care of by my partners in the clinic. It was just a little idea that Carolyn and I cooked up. I hope that is okay with you. I didn't ask you beforehand."

"I am so surprised," I said. "But yes, I think I can manage the time off, but from now on we plan together."

"Good, that is the way that I want it to be too, just you and me, us together in the world," he said as he nuzzled my ear.

The reception continued and the dancing began. Before long I must have had thousands of dollars pinned to my dress. I am sure that I danced with everyone. It all got a little crazy. It went on for hours. Soon, it was time for me to throw my bouquet.

All the single girls gathered in the usual group. I turned around and tossed my bouquet over my head. To my surprise it was Carolyn who caught it. She tossed it to Julie who tossed it to Janie. Janie pulled one rose from it and tossed it over her head. Finally, one of Paul Packard's sisters caught it and kept it.

Bill said, "Honey, it's time for me to throw the garter." A little chair was brought into the center of the room and I knew the cameras were rolling and flashbulbs were going off. I raised my dress just so in a dainty fashion. Bill reached up under my dress, and to my surprise pulled out a pair of men's silk boxer shorts. He had shoved them up the sleeve of his coat. It was like a little magic act. The crowd roared with laughter. I was so embarrassed that I must have turned several shades of red and purple. I was also getting a little drunk. The champagne was flowing like water. Every time I turned around another glass was in my hand. Finally, the garter was taken down from my leg and over my white bridal shoes and thrown to the crowd of single men. I was so glad that Junior caught it. I was just glad that he and Michael were there and wanted to participate in the fun with us. Janie's friend Jamie had taken the train in from New York earlier that morning and had met Junior and Michael at the church. They had formed a little group all day. I was glad for them. Glad that they felt comfortable being there and Janie and Marie were well looked after by these young men.

Soon, Bill and I made our way through the crowd saying our good-byes and thanks to everyone. We said good-bye to the children and Carolyn. I knew that Jonathan with the help of Bill's brothers would see to their needs and safely escort them back to the apartment. Bill had already asked two of his brothers to stay there as well, just to make sure they were all safe. They acted as their bodyguards. Bill and I were to spend the night in the bridal suite. The hotel manager was escorting us through the lobby and everyone was looking and waving and smiling at us.

In all the confusion and excitement I looked around the enormous lobby of the hotel. It was huge and filled with palm trees and other tropical plants lighted by a skylight. It was a huge atrium with beautiful appointments. We passed the lobby bar and as I glanced in, I was sure that I saw Dan Callahan still dressed in his tuxedo having a glass of champagne with my father. My mother was crying in a seat alone. That's when I fainted.

When I awoke I was in the bridal suite bedroom. Bill was on one side of me and Carolyn was on the other. Carolyn was applying a cold compress to my head. I could hear the hotel manager saying, "Oh, there is nothing to be worried about. I am sure. It happens to a lot of our first-time brides." Carolyn dismissed him immediately.

I sat up and said, "Did you see them?"

"Who dear? What did you say?" asked Carolyn.

"Dan and Father and Mother in the bar," I said. I knew I sounded a little crazy and was instantly sorry that I had said it. I knew that I couldn't possibly be true.

"Now, now, Cynthia," said Carolyn as Bill stood there in total bewilderment. "You know that is quite impossible. Now, lie back down and rest dear. It is just all the excitement and nerves. You've had too much champagne." When I awoke I was alone with Bill.

"How do you feel?" he asked as he took my pulse.

"Better," I said. "Has everyone gone?"

"Yes, I finally convinced them that I was the doctor as well as your husband and that you were in safe hands with me," he said as he sat on the side of the bed and held my hand. He had changed into a blue suit. My wedding dress was gone. Carolyn had taken it with her.

"Cynthia, I have another little surprise for you," he said. "We are not spending the night here. We are leaving tonight on our honeymoon. That is, if you are feeling up to it. It was always part of the surprise. See your new luggage over there. Carolyn and the girls packed a lot of your things and Carolyn threw in a couple of more suitcases. Whatever else you need we can buy on our journey."

"Oh, yes, Bill," I said. "Please, it was a lovely ceremony and the reception was such fun, but please take me away from here. I think that it might be haunted."

"Yes, my darling," he said. "As soon as you are ready."

"Thirty minutes and we are gone," I said as I stumbled into the shower. The hot steamy water revived me and I felt better. When I came out of the bath, Bill had already opened one of my suitcases on which Carolyn and tied a little white ribbon. In it was everything I would need for the next few days. She was so smart. I jumped into the new and fresh clothes. I pulled a soft pink cashmere turtleneck over my head and threw on a gray pantsuit. A little pair of low-heeled gray suede pumps completed the outfit. Bill handed me the matching purse. It was filled with my passport, driver's license, credit cards, and all the money that had been pinned to my wedding during all the dancing.

"Looks like Carolyn thought of everything," I said. "Could you call the bellman for our luggage?"

"Yes, darling, he is on his way up, now," said Bill.

As we hurried through the lobby, Bill held me with his hand around my shoulder. As we were about to leave, I glanced over my shoulder and I was sure that I saw Dan leaning on one of the many columns smoking a cigar. I tried to convince myself that I was just hallucinating from the stress of the day. We entered the limousine and I was so glad to be out of there.

Within the hour our plane took off, and I held Bill's hand very tightly.

"Feeling better?" he asked.

"Yes," I said, "now that I am alone with you." I never told him about seeing Dan in the lobby on our way out. I was sure that I was just hallucinating. I excused myself and went to the little bathroom. I took another one of Carolyn's little green pills, freshened my face, and combed my hair; that always made me feel better. I returned to my seat and snuggled up close to him. Soon, I was fast asleep. When I awoke we were landing in London and the sun was just coming up.

"Wake up, sleepy head," said Bill. "This is the first day of the rest of our lives."

Chapter Twenty-six

The Honeymoon of a Lifetime

Every day of our honeymoon just got better. Bill and I were like kids again. It took about a month for us to settle into a normal routine. We had both been so busy all of our lives that it took that long to learn how to relax, and relax we did. Some days we did nothing but eat and sleep and lay in the sun. We saved our energy for the nights. Lovemaking became a normal thing between us, almost part of our routine. We felt so fortunate to have such freedom.

Our trip took us from London to Paris and on to Rome. Finally, we were to spend a whole month on the isle of Capri. We blew off the normal tourist hotel and, instead, rented a little villa with a view of the Mediterranean. We filled our days with long walks and long talks. I was surprised when one day Bill asked me, "Cynthia, are you happy, truly happy?"

"Yes," I said. "As long as I am with you."

"Cynthia, I don't want to bring up unhappy memories, but you have never mentioned why you thought you saw Dan and your father and your mother in the hotel bar after the reception."

"Well," I said as I held his hand softly. "I guess it was all the excitement, and all the champagne. In a way I guess to me they represent one and the same thing, a challenge to my happiness." I surprised myself by saying this. "But I did see him at the church."

"Yes, the lousy bastard was there," he said. "It was a real low-class thing for him to do. But I assure you that is the last that you will see of him ever.

You couldn't possibly have seen him after that. My brothers took him away. Don't you remember that?"

"Yes, but what do you mean when you say that they took him away?" I asked.

"We just made arrangements for him to disappear," he said.

"You didn't kill him did you?" I said with a little laugh.

"Cynthia, I am a doctor. I cure people. I don't kill them," he replied. "But please, can you just trust me on this? You will never have to worry about him again. He is far away. Will you not question me more on this?"

"Just one," I said. "Is he still alive?"

"Yes, of course," he said. "He is still alive, but where my family sent him, he will never find his way back to you. You are safe wherever you go. Will you trust me, my dearest, my darling?" He held me tightly and kissed me softly on the lips.

"Yes, I will trust you. I will never question you on this again," I said. I knew that I would not have a choice in this matter. I didn't want to ruin the remainder of our honeymoon or the remainder of our lives. I wanted desperately to feel safe. And I still wanted to be a good little girl and please my husband in whatever way he asked me to do so. And I did.

That night I had a dream. I saw Dan floating through the air in a dirty tuxedo. He was bleeding through his eyes, his ears, his nose and his mouth. He had been torn to pieces by something. Then my father appeared in the dirty linens of the prison hospital. They floated together for a while, side by side. Then Father blew a cold icy breath over him, and suddenly Dan faded away while he spiraled downwards. My father smiled kindly at me and he too disappeared as he floated upwards. I awoke feeling very calm and remembering every detail of the dream. I knew that I was safe. I couldn't explain exactly why, but I knew Bill was correct. I was safe. My love for Bill grew and grew throughout the remainder of our honeymoon. We both sort of changed a little. But I knew that we were safe and that we would be together for many years.

Together we saw most of the world during those six months. It was a growing time for both of us, together and separately. It gave us time to plan our life together as well as that can be done. I decided that I wanted to become a writer and to champion the rights of women. He decided that he wanted to stay in medicine, but he also wanted to do research and to teach. He didn't want me to lead the unsteady and lonely life of a usual doctor's wife, a stay at home rich woman, bored and boring, with too much time for shopping. He had too many colleagues that were already in that predicament. He was glad that I wanted to be a real contributor to the world. I didn't tell him then, but I was sure that I was going to organize these women into some sort of worthwhile achievements. These women were already rich and had the best connections. We could start a charity to raise money to benefit all sorts of different things, maybe battered women with shelters for them to go as safe places. That could be our start. Where we would go from there I didn't know.

The last leg of our honeymoon brought us to the romantic islands of Hawaii. I was glad to be back in the United States. It had been five months since I had seen my family. I was lonely for them. A six-month honeymoon is a long time. I asked Bill a favor.

"Bill, would you mind terribly much if we turned the last leg of our honeymoon into a family reunion? I love you dearly, but I miss my family," I said.

"To tell you the truth, I miss my family too," he said. "Let's telephone them and just see how many of them can spend the last two weeks with us here on the Island of Oahu. They can see all the islands from here by just a short plane ride."

Half his family made the trip. It was just after school and hot in Chicago and New York. Carolyn brought Janie and Marie and Jonathan. They were out of school for the remainder of the summer anyway. During those two weeks our two families merged and really became one. It was some of the best times of our lives.

Chapter Twenty-seven
Another Death

The next spring, Mother died. We had not seen her since she had been released from prison. Her doctor called me in Chicago and asked me to come. He told me that she was very ill and he didn't know how much longer she would live. I called Jonathan. He and Janie met me in the Atlanta Airport. Carolyn stayed with Marie.

"Hey, sis," said Jonathan. "You look great."

"My gracious, Janie," I said. "I do believe that you have grown another inch."

"I most certainly am not getting any taller," she said defensively. She was almost as tall as father had once been, almost six feet tall.

"I wasn't talking about the height, silly," I replied.

"Oh, well, the right brassiere helps, you know," she said.

"I know. I know." We all laughed and were glad to be together again. We were having fun, not knowing exactly what we would find at the home with Mother.

We arrived early the next morning. The nurse ushered us in. "She's been moaning and moaning, but I don't think that she is in any real pain. It is just part of the dementia. She's on a lot of pain medication. She's in an out of consciousness. She's never made any sense to me, but this last month she has gone down a lot. Last week she stopped laughing and started singing hymns, little verses that she knew. Three days ago she stopped taking any food. So far today, she has taken not a drop of water or any fluid. The doctor will be in soon. You all have to decide if you want to insert a feeding tube pretty soon—now."

The doctor did come in shortly thereafter. He told us that she was dying. There was nothing that we really could do. We could hospitalize her and try keeping her alive, but he advised against it. "She's really gone," he said. It was a cold thing to say, but it was the truth.

The three of us went to the little chapel and sat there for a while. I tried to pray. I never asked Janie or Jonathan what they did. I know that they were there with me. We went back to Mother's room and the doctor was there. "I don't think she has much time left," he said. "Moving her now would not be advisable. She had been awake a little, and she had been talking aloud to someone, saying, 'Mama, Mama?' I will leave you with her for a while. If you need me I will be just outside."

We all gathered around her bed and just stood and stared at her. After a while she opened her eyes and looked at each one of us. She reached up and touched Jonathan's hand. "Papa, can I go with you?"

"Yes," Jonathan said. "You can go with me. We'll go together. You will be safe, now."

"Saved?" she asked. "Saved?"

"Yes, dear, saved," he replied.

She looked over at Janie and said, "You were always prettier than me. All the boys liked you best." We had no idea about whom she was talking. Then she looked over at me and said, "Will you be all right, if I go. Who will take care of you?" Her voice was broken and her breathing was heavy. You could smell death all around us. I wanted to hate her so much. I suddenly realized that I hadn't really hated her in a long time. It had been too heavy, too much of a burden to drag around with me. I must have been letting some of it go a little at a time, but all of it rushed out of me now. I could only feel sympathy for her.

"Yes, Mama, I will be okay. You can go on and go. You go on and go with Papa," I said in the same broken kind of English that she was using. I didn't know where it was coming from. She had always been so proper in her speech. She lingered through the night. We were all exhausted the next morning.

Just as the sun was coming up she opened her eyes and held out her hands. She had the clearest look on her face. The three of us each held on to one of her hands.

"Tell me it's not my fault, not my fault," she said to no one in particular. The three of us looked at each other in despair.

"Mama, it's me, Cynthia," I said. "Can you hear me?" I asked. I was practically lying across her.

She looked directly at me and nodded yes with her head. Her mouth just hung open with no words.

"Mama," I cried. "Cynthia says that it's not your fault. Mama, it's not your fault." She nodded her head yes. Her hands went limp and her eyes closed. She breathed slowly and faintly for a little while. We called the nurse. She came in and listened to her heart.

"It's just going to be a few more minutes," she said solemnly.

Her breathing just stopped. The nurse listened to her heart. "Her heart has stopped and she is not breathing," she said. "I'll have to pronounce that the time of death was 6:03 A.M., this date. Do you have any funeral arrangements made yet?"

To us she sounded a little cold. We resented it.

"No," I said.

"Our administrator will be in at 9:00 A.M. He can help you make the arrangements through the local funeral home. There is only the one so that will have to be it," she replied. She pulled the sheet over mother's face, and ushered us out of the room. "I can go ahead an call the funeral home if you want me to."

"Yes, of course, whatever you suggest," I said.

"Come along. I'll show you to our lounge," she said. The three of us talked there for a short time.

"How do you feel?" I asked each of them.

Janie said, "I feel a little sad. I knew that it wasn't ever going to be any different for a long time, especially since we came to Carolyn's. But I have always wished that Mother had had a better life."

Jonathan said, "I don't really know. I'm just glad that it is over and we can put that part of our life behind us forever. I hope. Cynthia, how do you feel?" he asked.

"Relieved," I said. "Relieved that we have no more duty to either one of them." I could only hope that they understood my feelings as I tried to understand theirs. We didn't say much of anything else.

Mother's funeral was a short one with only the three of us there. I felt a little sorry for her. She was buried in a little black dress that was part of the funeral package. The funeral director was also a preacher. He simply said a short prayer and it was over. He shook hands with all of us and offered us his condolences. Mother also was cremated. He thought it would be the best thing. The funeral home arranged for the disposal of her ashes. The director promised that it would all be done with the greatest of respect. "In cases like these, we usually dispose of them by dropping them into the ocean from a helicopter," he said. We all agreed. We had no idea of any other way to handle it.

It occurred to me on the plane ride home that Mother had never been up in a helicopter. I was determined not to laugh. But the more I thought about it, the funnier the idea became. Before long I started to giggle. Jonathan and Janie insisted that I tell them about what I was giggling. When

I told them, they were both quiet for a moment, then they, too, started to laugh. Before long all three of were laughing hysterically with tears running down our faces. The more we tried to stop, the more we laughed. The more we laughed, the more we cried. Pretty soon we were just crying and holding each other again. We had nothing to say to each other. We had all been her children. We all had lived through the horror of that. We were each lost in our own thoughts of her and father and our lives as children. I was sure that in our hearts, we prayed that we would be better parents.

I returned to St. Alban's with them. It was time to tell Marie. She was doing well in school and making many friends. She seemed to be well adjusted. She was growing up so fast. She looked very adult. Soon, she would be working at Graham's. She was so looking forward to that. Jonathan and Janie and she would be there at the same time. I was glad for that.

When we entered the foyer of the big house, she was just sitting on the stairs, alone. Carolyn was at the store. I surmised that Carolyn had already told her.

"Hi, everyone," she said solemnly. "Did everything go all right?" We ushered her into the living room and sat down around her.

"Yes, dear, then you know?" I asked.

"Yes, they are both gone now," she said. "Do you think that they are together in heaven and that they are finally happy?"

Jonathan and Janie and I looked at each other. I know that I felt so ashamed. I had never thought of it that way.

Janie spoke up first and said, "I am sure of it. They were happy once, a long time ago, and now they are happy again."

"They must have been in love, too, at least at one time," she said. "Does having children always make you do mean things and become a sad person?"

We all assured her that that was not the case. Our family was one of millions of families on earth, and we had just had a bad break. But thanks to Carolyn, we had always had a home and been together.

I called her therapist. She would have to increase her sessions to twice a week for a while. "There is just no positive way that I can explain things to her," I said. "I am hoping that you can help her grieve through this and not blame herself."

"Naturally, I will do all that I can," she said. "We won't dwell on it though. It would be a good thing for her if she could get involved in another school project very quickly."

The next day I talked to Marie's principal and drama teacher. A spring play was planned. They thought that would help. "Marie is such a good actress already," said her teacher. "We'll see to it that she has a good part."

"You'll have to give her the lead," I said. "She has never been satisfied with anything less." I made a sizeable contribution to the drama department. "You will let me know the dates," I said.

They all assured me that they would take excellent care of her and that I wasn't to worry about a thing. Jonathan and Janie would make sure of that too, after all she was Marie Graham, adopted daughter of Carolyn Graham. Jonathan brought that to my attention. It had made a great difference in their lives since Jonathan and the girls had come to live with Carolyn and she had adopted Janie and Marie, and they carried the Graham name. I asked him if he still wanted Carolyn to adopt him and change his name also. "Yes, I think that I do, but it sounds so silly. I'll be graduating this year. I am practically grown. But, yes, I think that I want it. I think that we should erase the name of Thomas from our lives."

Even that pained me a little, but I agreed. Carolyn was ecstatic when she heard the news. "Now, I will surely have someone who will carry on the Graham name, its traditions and all for which it stands."

It occurred to me that she wanted it for herself and not so much for the children, but I knew she loved them and I did not fault her for this. Within two months and before his graduation from St. Alban's, my brother's name was Jonathan Graham. I had no idea how much difference that would make in his life, or the difference in the lives of Janie and Marie for also being named Graham.

Chapter Twenty-eight

Bill Wants a Child

Upon my return to Chicago and Bill, I tried to put all thoughts of father and mother behind me. I didn't want to remember much about any of it, especially my childhood. I didn't want to think about their imprisonment or their deaths. It made me feel like I had never had parents at all, but my therapist kept reminding me that although I had made great strides in overcoming some of the injustice, that I still could mold the future. She reminded me I was married to a loving husband and was now a published author and a career woman. My young life as it was could not be rewritten up to now. But I could mold the future. She reminded me that I had always had that as a goal and was actually living it. I had made such progress against all odds. She encouraged me to get involved just as I had done for Marie.

"Don't let this set you back," she said. "Stay busy. Stay positive. Love with all your heart. Care about a cause," she advised. "You have so much at your disposal, so many connections, and there is so much good in the world that has to be done."

She liked my idea about championing the cause of women. I continued to write little articles for different newspapers, periodicals, and magazines. I helped Julie start the day care center for children at Paul Packard Consulting. Once again, my name was in the news and now on television. I didn't want to be in the public eye. I just wanted to be in the background making things happen. I didn't want the credit. Julie insisted that I stay busy along with Bill. When I was idle, I was lost and so unhappy.

I started to think about all the other women who may have gone through some of the same things as I had, and had done some of the same things. I wanted women to know that they had choices to be whoever they wanted to be. This was fairly difficult and easy at the same time. It was a real dichotomy for me. Women were ready for it, but glamour was one thing from which we could never escape. We could burn our bras, but I didn't know a single woman who would leave her home without makeup. I thought that this said a lot about us as women.

I started a high-level discussion group with some ten prominent women in Chicago. After about six weeks we had outlined a continuing discussion on women's issues. This group of ten women each started their own group of ten, and they started theirs and so on and so on. Soon thousands of women all over the country were taking part in these discussions. Mothers were pulling in their daughters for these discussions. Sisters were flying coast to coast starting other discussion groups about women. Finally, women were starting to take time out for themselves and talk about issues that were important to them. We were establishing a new order for women, or so we thought. It was still a man's world.

There was that old-boy network. If you were a man, you simply expected women to look, to talk, to walk, and to act in a certain manner. Men were still prone to promote their male colleagues over women and to pay them more. The women were trying to network for themselves, but I don't think there ever really became the same kind of network.

The discussions became another book for me. It was another bestseller. I appeared everywhere to promote the issues, but some women thought that I was just participating in the old-boy network and only trying to promote the book so it would sell more to make more money. I was praised on one hand, but martyred on the other. Many women disagreed with me and confused the issues. Many thought that I wanted women to become more like men. I never wanted them to lose their femininity. I just wanted women to speak up for themselves and to have equality in the work place, the same respect and the same privileges.

Surprisingly enough, I almost always had the support of gays and lesbians. I received thousands of letters from them saying that they understood my cause, my reasoning, because they were facing discrimination because of their lifestyle which also involved their sex. Most of them lived in fear and behind closet doors always having to pretend to be part of the straight world. I knew that my life must be easier than theirs. I was only living one life not two.

I seemed to have more and more in common with Junior and Michael, because they understood the issues and they understood me. We would spend long hours talking about people's rights. But something was happening in the gay community. More and more gays were getting a sickness and dying very quickly. It was a very scary time for me and Junior and Michael.

Some of my very first supporters who were straight strayed away from me and formed their own groups. They simply didn't understand that so many different and diverse groups suffered from the same oppression.

As the decade of the seventies rolled on, the issues just got more confused and complicated. People were burning the American flag all around the world and even in the United States. The disco craze offered an escape, and more and more women would dress in their shorter skirts, almost just a slip of a dress, and go out every night with their painted faces to dance and drink and do drugs and to bring home a different sex partner. And the men went looking for them. It was no different in the gay scene. Life was changing so quickly that it was hard to keep up with the real issues, which I thought really stayed the same, but sexual liberation was now a general discussion, and it meant so much more that I had ever realized.

Fundraisers became a part of my life. I say my life, because Bill could not or would not always participate. He would always make a large contribution, but I wanted him to work with me side by side. This caused a separation between us. I felt him slipping away. I desperately wanted us to share the same ideas. His ideas about research and teaching soon disappeared as he realized that seeing more patients meant a higher income. He worked endlessly with health insurance agencies and trained his staff in how to accomplish this goal. He and other doctors started referring patients more often to each other so that more and more insurance claims could be made. He insisted that the more doctors know about their patients and specialized in a certain area the healthier the nation would be. But they all shared in the profits. Insurance premiums went sky high by the end of the 1970s and would never come down again. More and more people were becoming uninsured; they just couldn't afford the private premiums. Even this changed as more and more large corporations offered umbrella policies for their employees. It was called part of their benefit package. It seemed to me that Bill and I were growing further and further apart, but he insisted that we were closer than ever because we talked more than other couples even though we almost always disagreed.

One thing that we both agreed on and that was that we wanted a child. We tried desperately to have children. We finally went to every specialist in New York and Chicago, St. Louis, and finally to Canada. No matter what we tried, I never got pregnant. We talked about adoption, but we really wanted at least one biological child of our own. I think that was one of the biggest disappointments and mistakes for both of us. Our careers became our children.

Even as my own therapy continued, new issues arose. My sessions were becoming more like arguments, but I was realizing even more so the things that were important in life and some of these sessions helped me in those regards. I finally started a program for battered women. I never gave one speech about how I personally had been abused and beaten by my father and how that had almost continued and repeated a pattern with my association with Dan Callahan. For not sharing my own experiences I felt guilty, but I read and educated myself about that sort of syndrome. My therapist worked with me on this project. This was my poorest fundraiser ever. No one wanted to talk about it, not many women, and especially not men. It was our toughest issue yet. I still had a little core group of women who wanted to work with me. It was our private talks that kept the ball rolling. Everyone finally admitted that they knew or had heard about someone who had been beaten regularly by men, or had been beaten and or raped by their fathers. It was a taboo topic then, but we continued.

One by one the action committee picked up steam and more and more women started to participate, but fundraising was always a part of it. It took money to keep things going and men who seemed to be our targets always owned the biggest companies. Those are the ones who could have made the largest monetary contribution, but didn't.

Once again, Junior and Michael came to my rescue. They formed their own discussion groups with their lesbian friends. Both gay men and lesbian women were admitting that they had suffered at the hands of others, some by their own fathers, mothers, uncles, and aunts, beaten and/or abused in one way or another. I still would not tell my own story. I knew that there were others like me that were just too ashamed to tell and to let the world know that their perfect and pretty world was partly just an illusion. I always wanted to listen and to talk about other women's problems. I would not talk in public about my past.

We finally raised enough money to open a small private clinic in a poor part of Chicago. Bill and I worked very closely on this. I still wasn't getting pregnant and that worried both of us. He even got some of his colleagues to work there a few hours a week for free. Soon, we had women coming in for treatment, but they were always hesitant to implicate their husbands or boyfriends, or whoever had beaten then. They were always afraid. They just wanted their lips sewn up, or their torn eyelids fixed. They were afraid to go to a regular hospital, or to report anything to the authorities. The cops always labeled the situation "a domestic dispute." The term "domestic violence" wouldn't come on the scene for some time yet.

These were the kinds of important issues into which I threw myself. The war in Vietnam had ended earlier in the decade. Jonathan has missed it. I was glad that he had not had to go. We had put a man on the moon in the late sixties; the struggle for space exploration seemed to have slowed. The things that had so held the nations interest seemed to change. I believe that the nation started to look inward at some of its own problems and to recognize some of its own illnesses. The hippies of the sixties turned out to be some of the best-informed, active, and relevant people of the seventies and made some of the best action people.

In 1979 I buried two of my dearest friends from the mysterious gay death. Both Junior and Michael died within four months of each other. It seemed that things were just getting worse instead of better. It would still be years before the gay death would be identified as AIDS, Acquired Immune Deficiency Syndrome. In the early eighties my group held another large fundraiser for this cause. Chicago needed a hospice house and a free clinic. Many gays were afraid to even mention the subject to their own doctors. This fundraiser was to be a gala event featuring celebrity attendance and talent.

Most of the front money to produce such an event came from my own savings account and Bill's. We solicited donations and raised some money. To my surprise, my closest supporters contributed smaller amounts than they did to our other causes. I think that they were afraid to learn more of the truth about this disease. Everyone knew from the beginning that although this was being called a gay disease, that it affected every person in the world, regardless of race, religion, national origin, or sexual orientation. They were just afraid to admit it. Any disease, especially AIDS, took away a lot of your freedom.

I still wasn't pregnant. All my doctors advised me to slow down and spend more time at home. Bill agreed. One night I came home to a candlelight dinner. Bill was home early and had arranged this surprise for me.

"Bill," I said with glee in my voice. "What on earth are you doing?"

"I've given cook the night off and wanted to be alone with you. I thought this was the best way," he said. He showed me to our bathroom. He had filled it with scented candles and filled the bath with rose pedals. All my favorite flowers decorated the room.

"I want you to take a nice long soak," he said. "It is just the two of us tonight and I have something special to ask you. Now, go relax, while I finish in the kitchen. Madam may enter at her own leisure. By the way, there is a little box on the bed for you." He led me to the bedroom and closed the door.

I loved the bath and the flowers, so I just took my time. He had surprised me. I would make him wait just a little longer. I lingered. When I was all but shriveled like an aging peach, I stepped from the tub and dried myself. I brushed and brushed my hair furiously and tied it up with a little white ribbon, one that I had saved from my wedding dress. I couldn't help myself. I was feeling romantic. To my delight the box on the bed held a pair of baby blue silk pajamas and slippers to match. With our busy schedules, it had been a long time since we had given each other such surprises. It was a luxury we didn't allow ourselves very often.

During dinner we had our first heart to heart talk in a long time.

He said, "Cynthia, you know that I love you. I have never lied to you. I have always tried to show you the truth and have supported all your causes. Sure, we have disagreed on many subjects, but, in the end, we have agreed to disagree on many. We never fought about it. I have always enjoyed your keen sense and approach to things. Your sense of humor always makes me laugh and I know that it adds years to my life. You show me aspects of myself that I never even knew existed. I have wanted to ask you something for the longest time, but I was afraid that maybe your causes were becoming more important to you than our marriage."

"Oh, Bill, I think that we have been married to long for you to have that doubt now," I said.

"But marriages have to be worked on every day, especially when you are a doctor and are away from home so often. The life of a doctor's wife is a hard one, and you have been the most successful. Your causes have been so worthwhile. I haven't told you often enough how much I really admire you, along with loving you."

"Well, that is such a sweet thing to say, Bill, but what is it that you want to ask me?" I said.

"Take a year off and just be my wife. Let's plan a long vacation together," he said. "My practice and your causes have put a lot of distance between us. I love you, Cynthia. I do believe that we have gotten off the track of marriage a little. Even though our careers and your causes have flourished, I know that our marriage, as good as it is, can be better. Maybe, with more rest here at home, you will get pregnant. I can take on fewer patients and spend more time with you, just you and me together. I promise. Can you? I love and adore you and I want us to have a family, even if it is just one child. I will never ask you this again."

It had been a long time since he had opened his heart to me in such a manner, and I knew that I only had only one choice in this matter. "Yes, Bill. We will do it together," I said. "But you know that I am in the middle of my first AIDS fundraiser. What am I supposed to do?" I asked. "I can't drop out now."

"Start learning how to delegate responsibilities. You can't do everything," he said. I agreed. That night we had the best lovemaking that we had in a long time.

I remember one thing that Bill whispered to me during the heat of our passion, "Cynthia, you absolutely intoxicate me." I climaxed at that exact moment.

I can't tell you how hard we tried to get pregnant during the next six months. Bill and I had taken a little vacation. We both tried to relax. We spent more time together. I tried to delegate, but the fundraiser was getting bogged down. I had to get more involved. He didn't seem to mind. He said that he understood. At the end of six more months I still wasn't pregnant. We started adoption proceedings. We were approved almost immediately. It was to be a private adoption through my doctor. It seemed that it was a long time before the baby would be born, about another six months.

My doctor was arranging a private adoption. It would cost us some money. It was not a new approach to adoption. My doctor wanted us to have the best and healthiest baby. He even matched skin color, eye color, and hair color. He tried to present us with a baby that matched our own family history, at least, the one that we presented to him. He even interviewed Bill's parents. He had several girls that he was treating. They were pregnant, not married, wanted careers and were willing to give up their baby to achieve their goals, and so that their baby would have the best parents possible. Bill and I would have to pay for the cost of everything. We agreed wholeheartedly.

It did occur to me that it had been my educational and career opportunities that had saved my young life. The young woman who was having our baby must have wanted the same thing. She was willing to give up her baby so that she could pursue her education and a career. I had sought an education and a career to escape a bad childhood. I had also wanted to be married and to be a good parent. I wanted to break the cycle of my parents. I knew that I was well on my way to achieving that goal. I would have to plan on how I could have a career, a happy marriage and children.

Within six months, we were parents of the most beautiful baby girl ever born; at least, we thought so. I guess all parents must think that. Julie gave me a baby shower after the fact. We had let only a few people know in case anything changed. I almost felt like a bride again, and Bill must have been the proudest father ever. We named her Angelique. We just knew that she was an angel sent to us from God. She was three days old when we brought her home from the hospital. We would never meet the mother.

My efforts at my AIDS fundraiser had continued. During the very middle of arranging this event, to my surprise I skipped my period. This alarmed me, as I was always as regular as clockwork in this manner. To my surprise, my doctor was happy to announce that I was indeed pregnant, but that I would need almost constant bed rest. Julie came to my rescue and continued all the preparations as the chairperson. To some degree, having Julie in the forefront now may have even helped the event. People were beginning to tire of me as the champion of another cause, and Julie was able to tap into her own resources along with Paul's. She and Paul had shared so much over the years with Bill and I. They had had more children. I envied her for this and was once again ashamed of my feelings.

I was so glad when the event had to be postponed one year. I would have more time to spend at home with my new baby and Bill. He was so delighted, but alarmed that I was practically bedridden. He was glad for my pregnancy. It was very seldom that he allowed me to get up in the middle of the night with the new baby. I was home every day with her and he hired a nanny to help me. I knew from the beginning that she was meant to be there. The new baby and I spent the next nine months in bed together.

Bill found us a bigger apartment. I was sad that I was unable to help him look. I felt a little left out. It was lovely, but it didn't have the lake view. It needed a woman's touch. Bill insisted that I be moved by ambulance. I was so embarrassed, but somehow we moved in. Naturally,

Carolyn flew in to help. Every time I saw her in action, I was inspired. I absolutely adored her.

By the time I was due to deliver, Angelique was already pulling up and trying to walk. She was a fast learner. I was so disappointed when my doctor told me that I was to deliver my caesarean. It would all be over in a matter of a few minutes. I was to be spared the pain of a normal delivery. I would also have to spend at least another six weeks in bed. Bill took his vacation time during this period and stayed with me. To our joy the new baby was a boy. He was named William after his father. The new baby, Bill, Angelique, and I bonded happily during this time. I can't help but believe that starting my own family affected everyone and everything around me.

Julie had changed a lot of my planning of the AIDS fundraiser and the event had grown. Top talent of the nation wanted to be involved. A song was to be written especially for the event by the top twelve recording artist of the time. Her planning and organization far surpassed my own. The event started to take on a life of its own. Many talented people in the arts and entertainment community were dying. You heard about more and more people every week. We knew that it had become an epidemic, even before the government would admit it.

Even though Julie was chairing this event, as I recovered from having the baby I became more and more involved with it. But to my surprise and amazement, I soon was bedridden again. I was pregnant for the second time.

My doctor said, "Well, once you start, it is sometimes hard to stop. Something has happened in your life and your babies are just coming at this time." I didn't know what this meant; I just decided to go along with it. After this baby, Bill and I would have to practice birth control.

That was a hard time for me. Bill and I wanted another healthy baby so much. We had not planned for it and certainly didn't expect it so soon. Soon we were to have three children. I was afraid that I was a better career woman than wife and mother.

I stayed in bed constantly. Having been so active, I became bored and restless. I wasn't always pleasant to everyone. I could have been kinder to Bill Jr. and Angelique. I could have never made it through this period successfully had it not been for our nanny and Carolyn. Bill always acted so understanding, but some nights I could hear him and Carolyn talking. She understood me so well, and she understood our situation. It was something that she had always wanted for herself. She wasn't about to let us fail. It meant her success, also. I didn't want to repeat my parents' resentment for having children. I wanted to love them and had always planned that I would be the perfect parent. I resumed therapy and was sorry that I had ever stopped.

Bill spent all his free time with us. And even arranged little dinner parties in my room with friends. Jonathan, Janie, and Marie visited me often. They had no children of their own and were glad to be aunts and an uncle.

Little Marie was now big Marie. She had developed a weight problem, even though she continued her drama studies and appeared in several off broadway productions. She was receiving good reviews. None of my siblings were dating steadily; they just didn't seem interested in having a permanent partner. I never heard of any of them dating. Marie was always making baby clothes and mailing them to me. She was becoming quiet a seamstress.

Jonathan had his law degree and had stayed in St. Alban's. He had tried the big city of New York and decided that he liked the small town life better. He was a confirmed bachelor. He lived with Carolyn. Janie had also succeeded to a degree. Her MBA didn't help her break through the glass ceiling of the corporate world. After several years of working in advertising in Chicago, she too returned to St. Alban's and took over the managing of Grahams. Carolyn was glad to have her and soon retired. They were my constant inspirations. They always championed any and all of my causes.

The planning of the fundraiser continued. Julie and I talked on the phone constantly. What she had thought would take one year, was now going on two years. Secretly, I was glad. I would be up and around and able to help with the final arrangements after the second baby was born. I was glad when the time came. During the surgery, I had my tubes tied as it was commonly referred to. I was tired of being pregnant and helpless. I wanted our normal sex lives to begin again. I didn't want to practice artificial birth control. Angelique would soon be two years old. Bill would almost be one year old.

We had another boy. We named him Andrew. I knew that God must have a plan in all of this. We had a girl and two boys, all under the age of three. It was a miracle time for all of us. It was hard to believe that we didn't want any more children. We had tried for such a long time. Suddenly we had three. It was all so overwhelming. Naturally, I had postpartum depression. I would have never thought of doing it, but during my confinement to bed, Carolyn had insisted that I read everything that was ever written about having children, raising children, and making a place for them in a better world. She even bought me a book on how to pray.

My therapist helped me during this period. I have always been glad for not being afraid of seeing a therapist. It seems that for some reason, all the bad things that happened to me in my younger years were being healed in my later years. I learned to pray and to believe in the power of it.

It was to my own amazement that all the help and guidance I needed in a world that had all but gone crazy were surrounding me. The world was becoming a more dangerous place. We knew it. We just didn't realize it.

Chapter Twenty-nine

The Last Fundraiser

Finally, the night of the AIDS benefit arrived. My whole family was there. I was grateful to have them around me. Bill's whole family came. I was also glad that Julie had been in charge of most of it. She seemed to be everywhere at once. I know that I could not have made this event such a success. I was so proud of her. All of Chicago was in a buzz about this event. It had received media attention due to all the celebrities and talent coming into the city at the same time. People were flying in from coast to coast to attend. Public Broadcasting was filming most of it, especially the celebrities and the talent for broadcasting later.

"Cynthia," Julie had said. "By getting this event on television, we will be able to reach millions and millions of people all across America and maybe, eventually, even Europe. More people need to know about this disease. There needs to be more education in the schools, more research. I can't think of enough to say about it," she said with excitement. Of course, I had heard these thoughts many times from her before tonight. She had collected several doctors and research teams from across the nation to start the evening's proceedings. She had expanded it beyond my wildest imaginations.

With her ideas my little dinner dance had been turned into a media event. Thousands of tickets had been purchased in advance. More were sold at the door. In my way of doing things we could have controlled who attended. That would have diminished the impact of the event. I couldn't even remember why I had wanted it to be by invitation only. I guess that I thought exclusiveness would make it more special. But Julie had expanded it to include the whole country. Anybody could attend, anybody who could afford the fifty-dollar ticket. That was a high-priced ticket then.

The parade of people there included people of all ages, races, colors and sexual orientations. There were men in tuxedos and women in expensive evening gowns. There were some women in tuxedos, and some men in drag. The gays were doing their part to support this effort and they were coming out in number. Some people dressed up and some people dressed down. There were people of all types mingling together. All seemed to be having a wonderful time. I wished that the whole world could exist like this every day. The event was about to begin.

"Bill, excuse me," I said. "I am going to see if Julie needs any last minute help. If I am not back in thirty minutes, come looking for me," I said with a little laugh over my shoulder as I walked away.

I ducked into the ladies' room at the last minute. When I walked out just about everyone had been seated. There was one lone man in a tuxedo standing in the lobby. His back was turned to me.

"You better take your seat," I called out to him. He turned to face me and I was horrified. It was Dan Callahan.

"Hello, Cyn," he said with a menacing smile. "Have you been missing me?"

I turned to re-enter the auditorium, but he crossed the lobby in three long strides. He grabbed me by the arm. He was drunk. I shrank away from him. He had my back up against the wall.

"What's the matter, Cyn, don't you have anything to say to me?" he said with insolence.

"No," I said. I cast my eyes to the floor.

"Well, I have a lot to say to you," he whispered in my ear. "You are going to hear and feel all of it, and the time is now."

I was trying to maintain my dignity. I wasn't about to let him ruin this evening, but a few latecomers were just buying their tickets and I started to scream for them.

"Oh, I wouldn't do that if I were you," he said. "Now, you are going to walk out these doors with me as if everything is all right, and climb into that limousine that I have waiting. I've spent every last penny that I ever had on tonight. I want it to be special."

"Take your hands off me, you fool. You're a drunk and a lowdown coward of a fool for coming here," I said. "I can't believe that you have the nerve to face me." I was talking madly, trying to think of anything to say to make him let me go.

"I do believe that fact has already been established, my dear," he said.

"Your little event can be a success or it can be marred," he continued. "I could let you go. And I can also walk in there and tell the whole world about you, about how you really are. I could tell them all about our old sex parties and how you loved them. Oh, I'll probably be charged with battery or something like that. I'm not afraid. You see I have spent some time in jail. I sort of enjoyed it. But you can be sure, Cyn, that all the cameras will be turned on us. Go ahead. Scream. I dare you."

"Well, what do you want?" I asked.

"Oh, just to talk over old times and sort of catch up, if you know what I mean," he said.

About that time, someone came into the lobby from the auditorium. The door almost hit me in the back. "Oh, pardon me," the woman said. I looked up, and to my relief it was Carolyn. Dan was startled and I gave him a little push backwards. It was all the time we needed. She grabbed me and ushered us to the front of the auditorium. Dan came rushing towards us.

The program had just started with Julie standing at center stage thanking everyone for coming. She was announcing all the talent we had for that night. Her speech was to last only ten minutes. We had just about made it half way down the aisle, when I noticed both Bill and Paul coming towards us. All our friends were sitting around us and they were staring. Dan grabbed my arm, again, and said as loud as he could, "Cynthia Thomas, can't you even say hello to your long lost lover?" I was so embarrassed and afraid and humiliated.

Bill and Paul pulled him out into the lobby. Carolyn and I followed. The security men finally knew something was wrong and came running.

"Okay. Okay," he said. "I get the picture. I'm just not wanted here. Don't worry. I'm leaving. But, I just want to ask Cynthia one question. Did you ever care about me, even a little?"

"No," was all I said.

The look of surprise and bewilderment on his face will haunt me forever. He was so disappointed. I guess that his only hope, especially while he was in prison, had suddenly become such a huge disillusionment to him that he was silent. I could tell that he was hurt.

Bill and Paul summoned the security officers who were about to escort him out of the lobby when a few of Dan's old buddies that had also come for the event came stumbling into the lobby from the auditorium. Dan turned and said to them, "She said that she never cared for me. I can't believe it." He grabbed his heart as if to pretend to faint or have a heart attack.

"Get him out of here, and all of you better go with him," Bill said to Dan's cronies. As they stepped from the lobby onto the sidewalk, the cold night air must have hit him in the face, because Dan did grab his chest. He had a heart attack right there in the middle of the sidewalk, half way rolling into the gutter. He died instantly. By the time the paramedics arrived. there was nothing they could do.

Neither Bill, Paul, nor Carolyn said anything to his buddies. As soon as I assured all of them that I was okay, just a little shook up, she pulled me aside.

"Cynthia, are you okay?" she asked.

"No, not really. I am so rattled. I am sure that I am going to have a nervous breakdown any minute," I said.

"You are most certainly not," said Carolyn. She quickly scribbled a little note and gave it to Paul.

"Here. Take this to Julie on stage," she said. "Tell Julie to keep talking. Cynthia is about to make a little speech and also thank everyone for coming." I protested, but Carolyn insisted.

She took me to the little ladies' room in the lobby. Bill waited for us. She re-did my makeup and fixed my hair. She said, "You have to do it, Cynthia, or you will never be able to hold your head up in this town again. It could be a scandal. You have Bill and your family to think about. I promise, just do as I say, and the whole incident will be forgotten by intermission. You have to trust me. Here, take one of my little green pills."

I did as I was told. She led me back to my seat. I was so glad that she was sitting beside me. Bill was on the other side of me. I calmed a bit. Julie was just running out of things to say and introduced me.

As my name was called, there was thunderous applause all around us. It helped.

"Just remember to smile and be joyous," Carolyn said as she gave me a little kiss on the ear. I stood and walked to the stage. Bill helped me out of my seat and gave me a big hug and a kiss.

"I know you can do it," he said.

Julie helped me on stage and introduced me as co-chairperson even though my name was not on the program. I said my lines perfectly just as Carolyn had instructed me.

"Well, I didn't mean to start the show early," I said with a laugh and a big smile. That brought the house down with laughter and applause. "You know Chicago is known as the Windy City, maybe it should be known as the friendly city, too," I said with another laugh. Carolyn's little green pill was kicking in and Julie put her arm around my waist.

"Thank you all for being here. Your presence here means that you care and caring is always the beginning of healing," I said sincerely. There was more applause.

"Thank you, Cynthia," said Julie as Bill came to help me to my seat.

Julie continued for a few minutes catching on to my train of thought and the evening's entertainment began. The event was an overwhelming success.

Within six weeks, the city had donated an abandoned building and the renovation process for the hospice house and the free clinic began.

Chapter Thirty

The End and the Beginning

Julie was very much in demand for fundraising after this time. I was glad to slide back into the shadows once again. I was always happy when she asked me to help and I did. She seemed to flourish in that environment. I saw a part of this time as an ending of one time and the beginning of another. The eighties were a turbulent time one day and a jubilant time another day. My father was dead. My mother was dead. Dan Callahan was dead. All the people that had truly hurt me were gone. After Dan's death, I really began to feel relieved. I was relieved of his presence in my life. I knew that he could never hurt me again. I eventually tapered off on my therapy sessions to once a month. I was happy being a young mother and the best wife that I could to Bill and my children. I wanted to be there for them every minute that I could. I was lucky. My life had been raised and saved. It had been a struggle, but I had survived. I always wanted to be there everyday when my children came home from school and when my husband came home, even though he was always tired and didn't always have a lot to say. He knew that I was there for him. He and our children helped my life feel whole.

I still continued to write, especially about women's issues, but I turned more so to issues concerning the rights of society and the individual that seem to be eroding. There will always be a champion for that cause.

In 1990 Carolyn had a stroke. It was Bill that decided that we should move to St. Alban's. I was spending almost all my time there seeing to her every need. He sold his practice and opened his own clinic there. I felt like I was home again. Carolyn eventually improved and with one year she was well again. She would always need our care, but she also knew that everyone needed his or her own space. She had her vast acreage divided into individual plots for each of us. She wanted Bill and I to live in the house with her and gave that to us along with five acres of land surrounding it. Jonathan, Janie, and Marie got the remaining property, equally divided. She helped them build smaller estates on each property so that it would always compliment "the big house" as she called it. All of us agreed. We were glad that we were together. My own children started to call her Granny. They were all in grade school by now. We were all moving forward in our own lives, but still taking care of each other. She was very happy about that. This was a happy time for us. She died in 1999 after a brief but not debilitating illness. I have always felt blessed that my children were able to know her while she was alive. They speak of her often, and I believe that they will always remember her and never forget her.

Her will left most of her wealth to Jonathan, Janie, and Marie. Their names were Graham, and, after all, they were her adopted children. Smaller portions were left to my three children. It was still in the millions of dollars. I received a substantial amount of her holdings, but nothing compared to the others. My name was not Graham; I had kept the Thomas name. Still, I knew that she loved me, and it didn't matter to me.

Her will only had a few stipulations, one of which was that Paul and I would be the executors until each heir reached the age of thirty-five years old and had gained their own financial independence. It would be up to each of us to work together to see that that happened. A large part of Janie's inheritance was to continue to manage Grahams for as long as she liked.

At the reading of her will, her lawyer had a letter from her to me. It read, "Dear Cynthia, you know that you have always meant the most to me. You let me dedicate my whole second half of my life to you and what was always really yours, your siblings. Thank you for letting me be a part of it. I have always tried to do what I think was best for all concerned. You have always been an inspiration to the children. I would have been lost without you. You are truly my child. I know that you and Paul will manage to keep all the estates and properties together as long as you are all alive. I believe that you loved my place so much that it just naturally became home to all of you. I didn't want it to go to strangers. Please, always try to keep it in the family. It means so much to me."

It continued, "You are a very precious and wonderful woman. I want to think that I had, at least, a little something to do with that. I can see it in how you are raising your own children. You are a loving woman, and you have made such large contributions to the world already. Never underestimate the role of wife and mother, sister, and friend. Where would the world be today if it were not for people like you? Let kindness, understanding, and patience, and most of all forgiveness, guide you all the days of your life, as I have often seen you do. Believe in the power of prayer and pass that on to your siblings and to your children. You have within you the power of more peace and happiness than you know, already. Never let anybody rob you of them."

Her letter stopped as if she had been interrupted, or maybe she had fallen asleep. I have always believed that she continued the next part at a later time, maybe the next day. It read, "Cynthia, you have always been such an energetic person with a going body. I hope that you realize that what really energizes you is your inner spirit. Always nurture it as well as your body, maybe even more so, for without believing in the power of your spirit, the body is just flesh and blood. Pass that on."

Her letter stopped there, but I believe that she had more to say to me. I never tried to imagine what that might have been. She had said it all already. I visit her everyday. I still feel her presence around me, especially in times of stress or inspiration. I talk to her. She is buried on a high and dry acre surrounded by a grove of evergreens some distance from our house on our property. There is a rose garden on one side and a garden of calla lilies on the other. She had carried her first wedding bouquet full of these, and I will never let her be without them.

THE END

A Note from Jonathan

I believe that Cynthia has presented the facts here as truthfully as possible. I congratulate her for finally being able to tell her story, which is really our story, the story of our family. I have always admired her.

I do remember the terrible beatings that Dad used to give her. I and Janie and Marie received our share, but nothing to compare to those of Cynthia. Ours were more like spankings, but with the added and dreaded emotional emptiness. Our house was always full of fear. Being the only boy, he treated me differently, with less severity, but not with more love, just with the lack of it. I cannot ever remember him showing one ounce of affection to Mother. I hated him more for that than anything. I tried desperately to love her. There were those times that she did try with me, but failed miserably. Their life together was only a sad existence. I am surprised that they kept it together for as long as they did.

It is true that you do what you have to do to survive. And we did. Cynthia took the worst of it for all of us. I knew that I would have to take over when she went away to college. When she did, our house almost became calm, not happy, just not as violent. Even that helped. I and Janie and Marie lived for those moments when we would hear something from her. A phone call from her to my friend's house was like a magic uplifting. It gave me the courage to just keep going on a little longer. My graduation day was our release from prison, but I tried to never hate anyone. I was glad to leave that house. I felt like such a failure for not being able to rescue Mother. In a way I guess that

I always loved her and wanted her love. When I left that house, I felt like I was abandoning her, but I was so desperate. Being just a kid myself, I did the only thing I could. I hope that you don't think of me as a coward for that. I left those two miserable souls to themselves and their imprisonment that followed.

After we were safe with Carolyn and Cynthia, I was always glad that Janie and Marie got the therapy that they surely needed. Since I was practically a grown man, therapy wasn't considered for me. I played the game of the grown man so keenly, that no one ever considered that I might have been scarred also. I think that I was, and from time to time I have had some sessions of my own, but I have never continued them. Carolyn always expected me to be such a man, that I just naturally played the role for her. Without her help I probably would be dead today. Having me work at the store gave me confidence. She trusted me. She always knew my true potential and I lived up to it. I became a lawyer just for her.

I have the success that I do today because of her and Cynthia. I owe them both so much that I could never hope to repay such a debt of gratitude.

I never dated much. I never had the time. When I did have the time and the money, I just wasn't very good at it. I never really made any close friends, and still don't have any today. Oh, I play racquetball, handball, tennis, and golf with my law associates and clients, but I never cross that line leading to friendship. I am a loner. They know that, and they allow me that distance between them and me. I am just a confirmed bachelor, and I am sure that I will always be.

I continue to surround myself with my family. I do pray. I thank God everyday for Cynthia and her husband, Bill, and my nieces and nephews and for Janie and Marie. I never let a day go by that I don't talk to my sisters. I love them so.

One of my most cherished possessions is a framed picture of Carolyn taken about the time that she came into my life. I keep it on my bedside table. She is the first thing that I see in the morning and the last thing that I see at night.

A Note from Janie

I don't know that I could ever love anyone more than my brother and my sisters. How could you have anything less for an older sister that took all those beatings and saved the rest of us? Our house was always full of fear. Father never beat me like he beat Cynthia. He was always overly strict with me and I had my spankings that hurt like hell, and afterwards he would never let anyone comfort us, not even each other. Once Mother tried to show me a little kindness after father had given me a little spanking; for what, I can't even remember. He screamed and threatened her into submission. The look on her face was so sad that I cried more for her than for me.

I always knew that I wasn't wanted, at least, not as a girl. One of my earliest memories is hearing him say, "I wish Janie had been another boy. Boys are just easier to raise. She better not be another Cynthia." I couldn't have been more than four or five years old and I was already fearful. That's when I tried to start taking better care of Marie. I helped her take her first steps; otherwise she may have been left in her playpen forever. If I wasn't wanted because I was a girl, then I knew that Marie was wanted even less.

I always knew that father had greater hopes for Jonathan than for Janie and me. He treated him differently because he was a boy, but he spanked him also. He would never let him cry. "Real men don't cry," he would always say. "Don't be a sissy, Jonathan. Go to your room and stay there and don't anyone talk to him." It was like being in prison, first torture, then the isolation.

I was terrified when Cynthia went away to college. She tried to explain that she would come back for us. It was hard to believe her, especially since I was always getting her old hand-me-down clothes, and we looked so much alike. I just knew that father was going to start the heavy beating on me now that Cynthia was gone. My own fear increased. It was Jonathan who intervened first. He was always such a great actor, and he never knew it. He was always taking chances with father for me. He was the only one that father ever really talked to, but that was so seldom that it hardly even mattered. Just as Jonathan was starting to try and trust him, he would get another beating or berating. Father often talked to me through Jonathan. Unless I was getting a whipping, he usually just ignored me; except for those hard looks he would throw my way from time to time. I knew not to say anything to him unless he spoke to me first.

My hopes that Cynthia would save us increased every time Jonathan secretly told us that he had heard from her. She came just in time. I was barely hanging on to sanity, and I knew that Marie was already slipping away into a fantasy world of her own. I even started reading the daily paper to her, not that she really understood what was going on in the world. I tried to keep her interested in the things that were happening in the world, but I don't believe that helped very much.

Naturally, I have a great deal of love for Carolyn. She gave me opportunities that I otherwise would never have had. She really wanted to be a mother to me, but I already had a mother for whom I felt sorry. Carolyn and I decided to be best friends. She knew that she wasn't my mother and never would be. That helped. She talked with me and not to me. We always had long conversations about what I thought and what she thought, and somehow we always reached a compromise. She never forced anything on me. After that I didn't mind having my name changed to Graham. I was proud to be her adopted daughter. She always showed me great kindnesses. She has always been a source of deep inspiration in my life. I am happy that she lived long enough for us to be real grown women together. I will always miss her terribly. Her death is a great loss to me. Of course, living here in my little estate always keeps her memory alive in my mind. And, in the course of managing and owning Grahams Department Store, I am always wondering if I am doing things the way that Carolyn would have wanted me to do. I hope so. Before she died, I tried to leave St. Alban's and went to Chicago just as Cynthia had done. My degree in marketing from St. Alban's just wasn't enough. It was a hard lesson that it was a man's world. I don't know what made me think that I could break that glass ceiling of the corporate world. Carolyn happily welcomed me home and within one year I was the manager of Grahams.

I guess being called Ms. Graham is a little spooky. I am not Carolyn, but it offers a little continuity here in this small town. I am satisfied with that. I have never been involved in a personal relationship with a man. In high school and college I was the one who always organized little groups to go out together. Hardly any one I knew dated as a single couple. That was enough for me then. Now I fill my days with the managing of the store and organizing charity events. Naturally these events are not on the grand scale that Cynthia accomplished in Chicago, but I am satisfied that I am doing some good here in St. Alban's. I will probably end up an old maid as they say. That does not sadden me. In a way it may even empower me.

I am trying for the first time to be a mentor. I spend four afternoons a week with a five-year-old boy in our local orphanage. I started a year ago. There is nothing wrong with him except that he was left there on the steps when he was just a baby. He is bright and funny and very good in school. He is also very handsome. He just suffers from having no family. At this time there is not a large demand to adopt African-American children. I may not have broken the glass ceiling of the corporate world, but I sure have enough power to break the color barrier that still separates our country. I want to adopt him, but only if he wants me to.

I am always happy that Cynthia married successfully. She loves her husband and she is a good mother to her children. I try to be a good aunt to them. I give little parties for them, and they like to spend the night over here with me on weekends. They love camping out in the living room. I am sure that I spoil them. Cynthia and Bill spend a great deal of time together. They are involved in many of the same charity benefits. I am so happy for Cynthia that she has broken the circle of violence in our family and that she has finally had the courage to tell her story.

I find peace in living on the same grounds that were once Carolyn's home, and that she arranged for Cynthia and her family, Jonathan, Marie, and I to stay so close together. She knew that would be important. Every morning I have my first cup of coffee on my front porch, and I find a feeling of safety in being able to see each of our houses all nestled privately together behind the big iron gates that still carries the initial "G."

I am thankful for the respect that I share from all the people I know. I can't love everyone and everyone can't love me, but we can all have respect for each other and share kindnesses that may eventually bring peace to the whole world as it has to our family.

I truly believe that a random act of kindness is more powerful than all the world political summits can ever achieve.

A Note from Marie

I am the baby of the family and therefore the youngest. I can't imagine what Cynthia was thinking when she asked me to add a note to this book. I am not a writer. I was never very good in school. I did manage to graduate from college, but only with the help of all my sisters and my brother and tutors. After I decided to major in drama, it got a lot easier. I am called the "drama queen" of my family, but I know that it is all in good humor. And sometimes it snaps me back into reality from which I stray daily. They all watch me very carefully, which sometimes makes me want to rebel. But I will never really be a rebel, because I am too afraid. I am too afraid of not being loved, especially by them. I would never do anything to hurt them, or embarrass them, or threaten the love that I know that we share.

The story that Cynthia has told here must be true. I don't remember all of it, just the feel of it. I remember a beautiful dress of Cynthia's. I pretended that she was a fairy godmother and would someday rescue me from my fear and loneliness. One day she did. I remember our house. It was full of fear. I never drink ice water, although I don't know why. I remember something about ice water and blood. It makes me sick to my stomach. I don't take baths either, but I do take a quick shower everyday. I shampoo my own hair. I don't care to be touched.

I too left St. Alban's after college. I went to New York City. I wanted to be a great actress on the stage, on Broadway. I know that my family worried terribly about this. Carolyn insisted that I stay with friends of hers who had a large penthouse in the heart of the theatre district. They had no children of their own, but they treated me as an adult. For this I was grateful. Everyone let me try until I decided to come home. They gave me time. I only managed small parts in off-Broadway plays. Finally, the fear of rejection drove me home. I just didn't have the right look. I gained weight that I now have under control. I continue therapy.

I have managed some supporting roles in romantic comedies in the film industry, for which I have gotten good reviews. There is even talk of an Academy Award nomination for best supporting actress in the current film that I am in. But then, there is always talk. It is good for the picture, but not always good for me. I am determined to stay involved in the film industry. One day I will direct. You must think that after all this talk about myself that I am introverted, which I am. I admit it. I have been lost in my dreams since I was just a young child. They were and still remain my safety net. I feel that I have to claw my way out of bed every day just to keep going.

I will never marry. I never date. I will never trust anyone with myself to that extent. I have such a huge fear of not being loved and of not having the capacity to return that love that may be shown to me. I save that only for my family. My marriage is to the world of art and literature from which so much story telling comes and the capturing of that on film or offering myself in that capacity on stage. I may be a film actress now, but I will always long to be a stage actress.

Of course, these dreams of mine could never have been possible without the help of my family, that is, Cynthia, Jonathan, Janie, and, of course, Carolyn. They love me. I love them. They have always protected me. I guess that they always will.

A Note from Cynthia

I have always strived to be more that just the role of female in which the fate of society had cast me by birth. By that I mean that I never believed that just because I was born a female that I was less than a male, or that I should be treated less than a male, or that I should have fewer choices in the world than a male, or that I should settle or accept less, and, especially, that I should never be paid less for the same work done by a male. I have always been struggling to be treated as an equal for myself as should all women. I don't know where that came from. Maybe it came from having to fight my father at an early age. Maybe it came from the enjoyment of knowing Eddie. Maybe it came from being under the spell of Dan Callahan and the fight to overcome him.

But believe me, I never wanted to be anything other than a woman and I have always fought to preserve my femininity, that is, femininity with equality. I think that Carolyn may have helped me find my true femininity.

I am not proud of all the things that I have done in my life. I hope that you, the readers, have not been offended by my being so candid. I didn't want to lie. Some of the things that I did were risky. Some were just plain dumb. I believe myself to be a guided person. Some people call this luck. I truly believe that I have been guided. The actual people about whom you have read here have guided me, but I believe that I have also been guided by a higher power. In most of my successes I have put the power to do so in the hands of that higher power and simply asked to be led. When I followed, I succeeded. When I didn't, I failed.

When I was at my lowest I always called on my spirit within me to keep me going. I know now that I should never wait until I am at my lowest to call upon my sprit. I desperately try to nurture it and commune with it daily. I try to put it first and foremost. When I do so, it never lets me down. When I don't, it still lifts me up, and then I remember to thank it and reward it in some way.

I don't hate my father and mother anymore. Once I stopped hating them, I knew the true meaning of the word forgiveness. This act of forgiveness is so powerful that I can't even start to describe what it means to me, but I know that I use it every day. It helps me to love.

I also believe in the power of kindness. An act of random kindness can reap more rewards that all the world political conferences ever can. Try it. You will be rewarded in ways that you never dreamed possible. Once you have put that act of kindness into motion, it never stops. It just keeps going and going.

Patience is a virtue with which I struggle everyday in myself and with others. I do believe in it and try to practice it everyday. It is my way of saying thanks to all the people who have ever been nice to me and to the whole universe and the power that it took to create me and keep me alive and growing spiritually, and for the many bounties that I have been given. It is my way of appreciating the fact that I have been so fortunate, even more so than others.

Appreciate your brothers and sisters. You can never replace them. They are a part of you, and that you can never escape. It has been easy for me to do so. I know that for others it is a hard and sometimes almost impossible act to achieve. They were born to be with us our whole life. Husbands and wives can come and go, but no one can alter the fact that they have a brother or a sister. Sometimes, they do try, but in reality once you have a sibling, it can't be taken back. Always try to nurture that relationship. Sometimes they won't let you, but you can always let them know that you are there for them. Perhaps at some future time they will come to you. Always be ready. There is no way to break the bond of blood.

I could go on and on, but I will stop for now. I don't believe in preaching. I do believe in sharing as I have tried to do here. If you are a woman and have read my story, I hope that in doing so you have found something by which you can benefit. If you are a man and have read my story, I hope that you have learned something from it. In any event, never be afraid to change. Do not try to be me. You will never find me. Pursue your own dreams with a belief in your spirit. A better tomorrow is always within you.

Cynthia Thomas Thompson